Anne Baker trained as a nurse at Birk̲... but after her marriage went to live first in Libya and then in Nigeria. She eventually returned to her native Birkenhead where she worked as a Health Visitor for over ten years before taking up writing. Anne Baker's previous Merseyside sagas are all available from Headline and have been highly praised:

'A fast-moving and entertaining novel with a fascinating location and warm, friendly characters' *Bradford Telegraph and Argus*

'A wartime Merseyside saga so full of Scouse wit and warmth that it is bound to melt the hardest heart' *Northern Echo*

'A gentle tale with all the right ingredients for a heartwarming novel' *Huddersfield Daily Examiner*

'A well-written enjoyable book that legions of saga fans will love' *Historical Novels Review*

'Truly compelling . . . rich in language and descriptive prose' *Newcastle Upon Tyne Evening Chronicle*

'With characters who are strong, warm and sincere, this is a joy to read' *Coventry Evening Telegraph*

To find out more about Anne Baker's novels visit www.annebaker.co.uk

By Anne Baker and available from Headline

Anne Baker

WARTIME GIRLS

headline

First published in 2014
by HEADLINE PUBLISHING GROUP

First published in paperback in 2015
by HEADLINE PUBLISHING GROUP

1

Cataloguing in Publication Data is available from the British Library

ISBN 978 1 4722 1226 9

Typeset in Baskerville by Avon DataSet Ltd, Bidford-on-Avon, Warwickshire

Printed and bound in Great Britain by Clays Ltd, St Ives plc

MIX
Paper from
responsible sources
FSC® C104740

Headline's policy is to use papers that are natural, renewable and recyclable
products and made from wood grown in sustainable forests. The logging and manufacturing processes are expected to conform to the
environmental regulations of the country of origin.

WARTIME GIRLS

CHAPTER ONE

24 March 1933

AT BREAKFAST SUSIE INGRAM said, 'Mum, isn't it marvellous that we've both got this afternoon off? I want you to come shopping with me. I haven't any shoes to go with my wedding dress, and it's only two weeks away.'

It was Friday and Grand National Day. Half the population of Liverpool either went to the races or stayed at home glued to their wireless sets. Traditionally, it was a day given over to pleasure and celebration, and as a result many employers were closing their factories and offices for the afternoon. There was even talk of changing the hallowed day to Saturday, in order to stem the loss of production.

'All right,' Louise said, 'the big shops won't be crowded today.' As they both worked, finding time to go shopping wasn't easy. 'I'd like to get myself a new hat. My navy straw isn't too bad, but it is your wedding. I'll meet you straight from the office at half twelve.'

Later that afternoon, in Lewis's shoe department, Susie tried on three pairs of satin slippers and several more in white leather, until at last she found a pair of smart silver sandals that pleased her. She took a few steps wearing them. 'Mum, aren't they gorgeous?' The little heels suited her long, slender legs, not that her legs would be seen when she was wearing her wedding gown. 'I love them.'

Louise bit back the thought that being silver her daughter wouldn't get much wear from them. 'They're really quite expensive,' she said.

'Mum!' Susie giggled. 'They're to complete my wedding outfit, and that isn't going to cost the earth!' Her eldest sister, Martha, was a dressmaker. As a gift, she'd bought a length of ivory silk and made Susie's wedding dress.

'Go on then,' Louise laughed. 'Anyway, I've drawn a good horse in the sweepstake at work, perhaps it'll win.'

'The Grand National's great fun, isn't it? I've drawn Windrush, there was a lot about him in this morning's paper.' Susie's big almond-shaped eyes sparkled up at her mother. They were a soft golden brown and at times like this, when she was excited, they were as bright as the morning sun. 'Wouldn't it be marvellous if one of us won some money?'

At just seventeen, Susie had blossomed into a beauty. Her hair was blond, an attractive shade of ripening wheat. She had a lovely wide smile, a clear peaches-and-cream complexion and seemed to glow with health. She took after her father's side of the family.

Up in the hat department, Louise picked out a stylish confection of feathers and tried it on. She stared at her reflection, altered the angle of the hat, but it didn't help. She'd never had her daughter's neat, even features and dramatic colouring, and now, at forty-two, her brown hair was fading and here and there had a silver thread in it. Still, she had kept her figure.

'Try this, Mum. It's the same shade of blue as the two-piece outfit you're going to wear. I think it'll suit you.'

Louise put the hat on and smiled at her reflection. 'It does. It really does. How did you know?'

Susie laughed. Louise could see she was sparkling with anticipation, very much in love and looking forward to her marriage to Danny Curtis.

'If we catch a bus now, we could be home in time for the big race,' Susie suggested. 'Martha said we must go to her place to listen to the commentary on her wireless.'

Louise had been saving up to buy a wireless of her own, but that had had to go on the back burner until after Susie's wedding.

'Come on, let's get back.' Susie took her mother's arm and hurried her to the bus stop talking non-stop. She was excited at being on the brink of marriage. Everything was happening for her now.

On the bus, the conductor was discussing the merits of one horse over another with several vocal passengers, and Susie listened with avid interest.

Louise looked out of the window, musing that of her three daughters, Susie, the youngest, had had a charmed life; everything had gone well for her. Unlike her older sisters, when she was growing up Susie had had no idea how she wanted to earn her living. Her best friend at school had been Fiona Curtis, Danny's sister, who on leaving at the age of fourteen had been entered for a two-year course in the best secretarial school in the city. Susie had told her mother that Fiona wanted her to go too, but there was no way Louise could afford the fees.

Louise had played an important part in the life of St Biddolphe's, the church where her husband Harold had been curate and where Susie was to be married. She did not know how it came about, but she was as pleased as her daughter when the vicar told her that Susie's secretarial school fees could be paid from the church fund built up to help poorer families in the congregation. Susie was now working as a shorthand typist in the offices of Bibby's soap company, a job found for her by the school when she had passed their final exams.

As she'd grown older, Susie had also helped with fundraising and was popular with the church members. Since her early teens she'd regularly attended the church youth club, where Danny Curtis, her fiancé, was a fellow member, and the vicar had recently asked Susie to take over teaching a class in the Sunday school.

Louise knew the Curtis family well: Danny was the third eldest of six children, and his sister, Fiona, the fifth in birth order. Their mother Victoria sat on some of the church committees with Louise, and did even more work for the church.

Louise approved of Danny; she'd watched him grow up. He was a jolly lad, tall and handsome, with a mop of copper-coloured curly hair. Red hair ran in his family, his father and two of his siblings blessed with varying shades from sandy to ginger. He was hard working and employed by one of the largest ship repairing businesses in the port of Liverpool. Everybody said Danny would soon follow in his father's footsteps and rise up the ladder to senior management.

Since Harold's death, Louise had been troubled by feelings of guilt and self-doubt. She was accepting unlimited help from St Biddolphe's, but would Harold think she was doing enough?

4

She'd tried to be both mother and father to her three daughters, and she'd seen it as both her duty and her role in life to bring them up to be caring citizens and take part in the life of St Biddolphe's. Harold would have wanted them to have his firm religious faith, but she wasn't sure whether she could impart that. What she wanted was to give them as happy a life as she could.

These days, much of what she did was for Susie's sake, and to tell the truth, there had been times when she'd felt a prickle of jealousy towards Danny because Susie was spending so much time with him. She'd had to tell herself not to be silly; Susie had grown into a beautiful young lady and what she wanted her to have now was a happy marriage. Louise was delighted to see her so excited at the prospect, and felt a quiet contentment that she was achieving what she'd set out to do.

'Mum,' Susie was tugging at her arm, 'you're daydreaming. You'd go past our stop if I didn't watch you. Come on, don't you want to know which horse wins?'

Of course she did. Louise gathered her parcels and they both got off at the bottom of Milner Street. There were meaner, smaller houses at the bottom of the street where many families were in the grip of real poverty, and it was quite a steep climb up to their house, but Susie's feet seemed to have wings. She leapt up the two steps and knocked on the front door of number 24. Martha had it open almost before Louise reached the step. 'Come on in, they're calling the jockeys to line up for the start. I was afraid you were going to miss it.'

Martha was twenty-four now but looked older. She'd had rheumatic fever as a child and had had a lot of pain in her joints since. Already her shoulders were slightly bent and her finger joints were beginning to knot. Her eyes seemed enormous in her small face, her other features petite and even, and she would have been pretty if she'd not looked downright ill.

She'd been married for six years and seemed very happy, but poor health and bad luck had dogged her. She was pale and frail, and had repeated bouts of ill health. Her much longed for third pregnancy barely showed. Twice she'd miscarried within the first three months; she was only two months now, but they were all hopeful she would carry this baby to term.

Bert had taken the tenancy on the house next door to Louise, so she would be on call if Martha needed her.

'Bert has gone to Aintree,' Martha said, 'but he thought it would be too much for me.' Beside her, Susie with her energy and rosy cheeks seemed to glow with good health. Susie regularly did shopping for her and ran to tell the doctor when she wanted him to call, and Louise had been known to step in to cook them a hot meal.

'Bert drew a horse called Windrush in the sweepstake being run by the local pub and he's given the ticket to me.' Martha was all smiles. 'He said I can treat myself to something if it wins.'

Susie chortled, 'I drew Windrush in the office sweepstake this morning. I do hope we win.'

Fortunately, they still had a few minutes to sit down before the race started. 'What's the name of the horse you drew, Mum?' Susie asked.

'I can't remember.' She was turning out her handbag. 'I've got it here. Yes, it's Kellsboro' Jack.'

Then the horses were off and took all their attention. Three commentators were spread round the course describing what they saw, and their voices were rising octave on octave until they were almost screeching. Susie was letting out little squeals of excitement every time she heard the name Windrush mentioned, while Martha had a huge smile on her face. Their horse was going well. He was up near the front of the pack.

Louise couldn't help feeling the thrill of the race. She knew Kellsboro' Jack had made a good start, and she didn't think his name had been mentioned amongst the horses that had fallen, but as she'd heard nothing of him since the horses had completed the first circuit of the course, she had no idea where he was.

Susie wailed her disappointment when they heard that Windrush had fallen at Becher's Brook the second time round, and Martha groaned and tore up her ticket.

Then the commentator was screaming that Kellsboro' Jack was in the lead and Louise was suddenly bursting with hope and pleasure. For a long moment, hooves thundered past, obliterating the voice from the airwaves, but she caught the name again – her horse was still there.

'It's pulling away, increasing its lead,' Susie shouted, 'it's going to win.'

'Yes!' Louise was on her feet, but the commentator was screaming with excitement and in the end none of them heard his final worlds because there was a huge roar from the Aintree crowd that ended in an outburst of cheering. Louise held her breath, her hands clenched.

'What? What?' Susie was asking. They were looking askance at each other, until they heard the name of the horse repeated.

'Mum, Kellsboro' Jack has won,' Susie yelled, 'you've won!'

Louise could hardly believe her luck. The horse she'd drawn in the sweepstake at work had won the Grand National!

'Marvellous, blooming marvellous luck!' Susie was laughing with the joy of the moment. 'Well if Martha and I can't win, I'm glad you did.'

'How much will you get?' Martha wanted to know.

'I haven't the slightest idea.' The sweepstake had been set up by her colleagues in the office; Louise had only bought a ticket because it was expected of her and it was part of the fun.

'Was the sweep for the whole factory or just the office?'

Louise shook her head; she hadn't asked.

CHAPTER TWO

SUSIE OPENED UP THEIR packages to show Martha the wedding finery they'd bought, and changed into her new silver sandals to help break them in.

'I love your hat, Mum,' Martha picked it up, 'it's very smart.'

'Try it on,' Louise said. 'Yes, it looks good on you too.'

Martha smiled at them. 'You must be in need of a cup of tea,' she said, and led the way into her kitchen to light the gas under the kettle. Susie and Louise helped to get out the cups and saucers while Martha put out the custard cream biscuits she'd bought that morning. They were all fizzing with excitement after the race and Mum's win, and it was quite a jolly occasion. It took them the best part of an hour to quieten down.

Susie thought her mum looked tired, and would have stayed talking, but she wanted to get a move on as Danny had said he'd come round between six and half past to take her to the pictures.

Back at home, while her mother warmed up the pan of scouse she'd made for their evening meal last night, Susie put a match to the fire she'd laid that morning and set the table.

'What are you going to spend your winnings on?' she asked as they sat down to eat, though they'd already talked at length about this next door. 'A wireless would be just the thing.'

9

'It would, but I probably won't win enough for that.'

'I'd love to have a wireless of our own.'

'Susie, love, I can't decide on anything until I know how much I have won, and there's going to be a lot of extra expense with your wedding.'

Mum tended to be rather staid and set in her ways. She couldn't let herself enjoy her windfall in case they really needed the money later. She was too much of a sober-sides, always worrying about something – if it wasn't the family, it would be church matters or the need for more thrifty housekeeping – but Susie loved and admired the way she coped with everything. She knew her mother would give her the world if she could.

Mum had agreed that Danny should move in and live with them when they returned from their week's honeymoon in the Lake District. She'd even offered to buy them a double bed as a wedding present and had taken them to choose it before she'd ordered it. The very thought of having the new bed in her own bedroom and sharing it with Danny, thrilled Susie to bits. Though he thought Louise lived in gentile poverty, he was more than happy to live with her and Susie because his parents had strong ideas about what their children should be allowed to do and tried to exert control over them.

Susie didn't see much of his father, but Mrs Curtis was a powerful lady who liked to think the Mother's Union and the frequent church fetes wouldn't function if she didn't manage them. She was inclined to order the other helpers about and many were in awe of her.

Susie knew that Danny came from a more prosperous family than hers. She had been visiting the Curtis home for most of her childhood and thought it rather grand. It was a large, detached and very comfortable house, and with six children fairly close together in age, there was always something interesting going on there. They had a family room which the adults rarely entered; table tennis was set up almost permanently on the table, and they often rolled the carpet back to dance to their gramophone. She felt she'd grown up with Danny and his big family and knew them through and through.

Danny was just twenty-one and his parents thought he was too young to marry, that he and Susie should be sensible and save up until they could afford a home of their own. Jack, the eldest Curtis brother, was twenty-five and doing just that. Danny had tried, but then he'd used what he'd saved as a down payment on a motorbike, and now he had weekly payments to make on that for the next six months.

'Once I've paid for it,' he said, 'I'll have a side car put on to make it more comfortable for you. Anyway,' he went on, 'why wait for marriage when we know we love each other and it's what we both want?'

Susie took her new shoes upstairs so Danny wouldn't see them before the wedding, and started to wash and change ready to go out.

Louise was looking forward to a restful evening and had settled down by the fire with her knitting, but her eyes were drawn to the photograph on the mantelpiece. She'd had it taken professionally in the spring of 1916, especially to send to Harold. A carefree image of herself smiled out at her; she'd been twenty-five at the time. She was wearing a new dress she'd bought especially for church functions, and had dressed their three beautiful girls in pale sprigged muslin. Martha had been seven years old, Rebecca had been six, just fourteen months younger, and little Susie a baby of eight months.

Even as a child Louise had wanted babies; they were revered in her family. She was an only child but knew her mother had longed for more. She'd had three miscarriages and a baby boy who had died in infancy, and Louise had watched her mother cuddle the babies of her friends and peep into every pram they saw; together they'd taken delight in baby smiles. Above everything else Louise had wanted to be a mother, and she felt blessed to have three pretty daughters.

When the Great War broke out in 1914, Harold had been the curate of St Biddolphe's Church on the edge of Liverpool's dockland for eight years. Everybody thought the war would be over by Christmas; optimism was widespread, men were volunteering in droves, and Harold had seen it as his duty to volunteer with them. He'd been sent to France as an Army chaplain and he'd also helped the injured in the heat of battle.

He'd told Louise he wouldn't be in as much danger as the fighting troops, but in a battle on the Somme, the first-aid post where he'd been offering comfort to the injured had been shelled and totally destroyed. Harold had lost his life, as had two stretcher bearers, a doctor and several patients.

The news came as a profound shock to Louise; Harold hadn't told her he was so close to the front line. She felt paralysed with grief and the responsibility of bringing up their three daughters on her own.

Her mother, who lived nearby and who had been widowed when young, said, 'I'll give you all the help I can. You know I love to spend time with my granddaughters, but it isn't going to be easy.' Louise knew she could rely on her for support.

The members of the congregation were sympathetic and offered help too, but the house she was living in belonged to St Biddolphe's. Now Harold would not be returning to his post as curate, the vicar, Mr Roger Saunders, told her she would have to find somewhere else to live.

She was heartbroken at having to leave the home she'd shared with Harold, but amongst the church members there was an estate agent. He and Mrs Saunders had helped her sort through the local houses available for rent, and had taken her to see a few. Mrs Saunders had gone with her to see 26 Milner Street for a second time. Louise had decided it would suit her, and they were living there still.

It was a Victorian terraced house where the front door opened directly on to a long street winding down to the docks that bordered the Mersey. It was double-fronted with a bay window on one side of the front door and a flat one on the other. Behind it was a yard that provided a wash house and the only lavatory.

Mrs Saunders had shaken her head at that. 'With young children, especially Martha, an outside lavatory might prove difficult.' Martha often felt poorly. 'If you're sure about this house, we could negotiate to have a bathroom fitted in the smallest of the four bedrooms before you move in, and have electricity installed as well.'

All the remaining rooms upstairs and down were of good size. It was in a respectable district, not too far from the church, and she considered it one of the better houses in Liverpool.

Louise had known that she'd have to support herself and her children from then on. She'd trained and worked as a book-keeper before she'd been married, and now she applied for similar jobs, but Britain was in the throes of war, and though war work was easy enough to find, a permanent job as a book keeper proved more difficult.

After morning service one Sunday, Mr Ralph Randall, another devout member of St Biddolphe's congregation, said, 'I hear you are thinking of returning to work?' He was the manager of Peverill's Preserves, a large factory on the Dock Road, making jams and other spreads.

'Yes, I need to find a job,' she said. She had Susie in one arm, Martha hanging onto her other hand, and with such a young family, some of the lady members of the congregation had told her she'd find it impossible to work for a few years. 'Come and see me in my office,' he said, 'and we'll discuss it.'

Louise went dressed in her best. She was nervous because it was eight years since she'd worked outside her home, and for all she knew Mr Randall might want his books kept in a different manner to the one she'd used. He was plump and genial and his eyes twinkled up at her from deep pockets of flesh. He took her around the part of the factory where strawberry jam was being made, and told her a little about the business.

Peverill's Premium Preserves was founded in 1886 and made several varieties of jam, two types of marmalade and also lemon curd and other spreads. It had expanded quickly in its early years and now had several small factories in northern towns. The firm took a paternalistic attitude towards its employees, providing a canteen that served hot lunches at reasonable prices, and there was always a Christmas party, a summer outing and a week's paid holiday for everyone. The girls working on the factory floor were provided with white overalls that were laundered for them, and as they were required to cover their hair at all times, turbans in pastel colours were provided too. It employed mostly women and girls; many had worked there for years.

Mr Randall then took her back to the office and introduced her to the accountant, and also to the girl she would be taking over from who was leaving to be married. Louise thought the salary she was offered was generous, but was afraid he was only giving her the job out of the goodness of his heart, and not because she was the best applicant. That took away some of her confidence, but she knew she was lucky to be given this chance.

Louise had gone straight round to see her mother and asked her to come and live with her and help her care for the children. Her father had died many years before so her mother was living alone.

'I'm pleased to be asked,' she'd said, 'and I want to help you and be near the children, but you know I've got a dickey heart and I'm getting older.' She'd married late in life and had been nearing forty when Louise was born. 'I'm afraid I might end up more of a liability to you than an asset.'

'Mum, I really need you now and I know you'll be a huge asset. I wouldn't be able to work full time without you. You'll be there for the children when they come home from school, and if Martha isn't well enough to go, I won't have to take time off. We'll face any future problems when they come.'

They'd all settled into their new home. Louise took care of the cleaning and the washing while her mother did the shopping and prepared most of the meals. Her older daughters attended the church school, and her mother and other ladies of the church looked after Susie until she was three, when she was considered old enough to join the nursery class at the school.

On Sundays, the whole family went to morning service in the church, and in the afternoon the older children went to Sunday school. Louise enrolled them in the Brownie pack held in the church hall, and when they were older there would be the Girl Guides. She arranged for them to be occupied in one activity or another until she returned from work, so that her mother would not be over-burdened. She took her annual leave during the school holidays, but the children were off for much longer and the church ladies rallied round arranging other activities and outings.

In return, Louise acted as the unpaid treasurer of the church's accounts, she was an organising member of the Mother's Union, and helped unstintingly with all fundraising. She cleaned the church, arranged flowers, baked cakes and helped at church fetes and Sunday school outings. It was a relief to know she could cope, and the years began to pass.

When in 1919 the flu pandemic spread round the country, Martha, whose health had always been poor, caught it and they were all very worried about her. Louise had been hearing of deaths in the houses nearby; it seemed a worse carnage than that in the trenches in wartime France. The other two caught it one after the other, but fortunately they all recovered quite quickly. Louise had relied on her mother to look after the girls while they were ill and felt very guilty when she said she hadn't been feeling well for a day or two, but had kept going so Louise could go to work.

When Louise came home one afternoon and suddenly realised how ill her mother was, she sent her straight up to her bed. She scribbled a note to the doctor, asking him to call, and gave it to a neighbour's boy playing in the street, together with a penny, and sent him to put it through the doctor's front door.

They had all come to know and trust Dr Raymond Grant, their GP, who was very young and fortunately another member of St Biddolphe's congregation. He came that evening but shook his head when he examined her mother. Forty-eight hours later she was dead.

Louise felt bereft all over again. She missed her mother's calming presence about the house and so did the girls. Her mother had fitted into the household very well and was always thinking of some little treat for the girls. She had been teaching them to cook and they loved making cakes. Harold had already been away from home for nearly two years when he'd been killed, but her mother had been very much part of their life; Louise had come to rely on her and felt all her responsibilities more keenly now she had no one to share them with.

And it seemed there was one problem after another. Her family was barely over the loss of Grandma when Martha fell ill again, and this time she was so ill she was admitted to hospital. It took a worrying fortnight before she was diagnosed as having rheumatic fever, a very serious complaint which put her on bed rest for several weeks. She came home more fragile than ever and still in need of rest.

It had been the start of the summer holidays and Louise could see no way round this problem except to give up work. When she spoke to Mr Randall about it, he said, 'Take a month of paid holiday instead of your annual week. You work hard here, you deserve it.'

'You're very kind,' Louise had gulped, feeling tears of gratitude start to her eyes. She knew jobs were getting ever harder to find, and if she'd had to give it up, she doubted she'd get another that suited her as well and was so near to her home.

'I know how hard it is because my elderly mother has been an invalid for years,' he sighed. 'I'm often juggling jobs, trying to find time to fit everything in,' he gave her a wan smile, 'but we get by.'

By the end of the month Martha was allowed out of bed, but she had by no means recovered. Louise felt she had to go back to work.

'Is your eldest daughter better?' Mr Randall asked her.

'She's made a turn for the better, but she's not fully recovered yet,' she said, and told him how she was managing.

Once again her neighbours and the lady members of St Biddolphe's congregation had rallied round to help. Louise had got to know Nurse O'Brien better since she'd first come to visit Martha in her professional capacity as district nurse. There was an aura of serenity and calm about her that soothed Louise's anxieties. She was friendly and full of empathy too, so Louise came to rely on her when Martha had a bout of ill health. If she had time, she would prolong her visit and have a cup of tea.

The school holidays were not yet over, so Miss Maddocks, a school mistress, came for several hours each day until the two younger girls went back to their classes in the church school. Her fiancé had been killed within three weeks of being sent to fight in France, and she'd told Louise of her disappointment at not being able to marry and have children of her own. She was very caring towards the children she taught and Louise knew she could not have coped without help from her and Nurse O'Brien and was very grateful.

Mr Randall said, 'I'm afraid the work is stacking up on your desk, but if it would help to come in an hour or so later in the mornings and leave a little early, do feel free to do so.'

'Thank you. I shall try to work normal hours. How is your mother? Better, I hope.'

'I'm afraid it's not the sort of illness from which she's likely to get better,' he said.

Louise worked hard to catch up with her work, even taking some home in the evening, and she eventually managed it.

She was sorry to see Mr Saunders, the vicar, retire in 1920 and take his wife to live with their daughter in the Lake District. She'd counted Mrs Saunders as a friend and did not feel quite the same about the new vicar and his wife, the Reverend Mr and Mrs Thomas Coyne, but she felt she'd been well supported by St Biddolphe's throughout the years. She and her daughters had been part of the community and that had provided them with a social life and with friends. She knew almost everybody in the district and felt able to manage her little family.

CHAPTER THREE

HER MOTHER HAD DRAWN the living-room curtains and was sitting by the fire knitting. Susie sat down on the other side of the sofa and said, 'I've been waiting for Danny to come. He said he'd be here about half six. Is that clock right?'

'Yes.'

Another half hour crept by and Susie began to feel edgy. 'Danny's not usually late, this isn't like him. Perhaps I should walk up to his place to see what's holding him up. We're going to be late for the second house at this rate.'

A moment later there was a ratatat on the door. 'That'll be him,' her mother said, as Susie leapt to her feet, snatched up her coat and opened the door.

'Oh! Hello, Jack.' She pulled up short when she found it was the eldest Curtis brother on the doorstep. 'I was expecting Danny, is something holding him up?'

Jack looked serious, as though he had the troubles of the world on his shoulders. 'Can I come in, Susie?'

'Of course.' She stood back and opened the door wider. 'Has something happened?'

'Yes . . .'

'Come to the fire, it's cold out there,' her mother called.

20

Susie felt anchored to the spot with fear. 'What's happened?' she asked urgently. 'Tell me.'

Jack put his hand on her arm as though to calm her and led her into the living room. 'Danny has had an accident,' he said slowly. 'He's been knocked off his motorbike in town. There was heavy traffic when the races finished.'

Susie gasped. 'Is he hurt?'

'Yes, I'm afraid so. He's been taken to the Royal.'

'Oh goodness! He hasn't broken a leg or anything?'

'I don't really know, but I think it's his head.'

'His head?' she echoed and held onto a chair for support. 'That's awful, is it serious?' She hoped this wouldn't mean they'd have to delay their wedding.

'My parents have gone to the hospital to find out more. Dad asked me to come to let you know.'

'Poor Danny. I want to go to the hospital,' she said.

'You want to go now?'

'Yes, of course,' she wailed, 'take me there, please. I want to see him, I must know how badly he's hurt.'

She felt her mother throw her arms round her in a hug. 'Do you want me to come with you?'

'No . . . Yes. Yes, Mum, please do.' Susie put her head on Louise's shoulder and wept.

It was a cold, wet evening for the time of the year and they had to wait at the bus stop. Susie had a sinking feeling in her stomach and couldn't stop shivering. She hung onto her mother's arm on one side and Jack's on the other. None of them had anything to say. To Susie, it was a nightmare – worse than a nightmare.

A mantra was going round in her head like a train: don't let

Danny be hurt too badly; don't let Danny be hurt too badly.

They got off outside the hospital. 'I think the Casualty department is this way,' Jack said, guiding them towards it, 'Danny will have been taken there.' As they entered, the strong smell of disinfectant made her feel sick. By then she was frightened but burning with anxiety and impatience to know more. If he'd broken a leg and they weren't able to get married in April, she didn't know what she'd do.

Her mother squeezed her arm. 'We don't know yet how badly he's hurt,' she murmured. 'Perhaps the wedding can still go ahead.'

Susie forced herself to look round. She was in a large hall, a busy and frightening place. A row of chairs extended down its length, many occupied by patients waiting for the white-coated doctor to examine their injuries and fill out an orange treatment card. Then, clutching their cards, they waited again until one of the nurses brought a treatment trolley and attended to them. She could see no sign of Danny. Nobody here seemed badly hurt, but a row of small rooms opened off the back and there were lots of people bustling round them.

'There they are. There's Mum and Dad.' Jack waved his hand towards the back of the hall and headed towards them.

Susie's heart missed a beat. They looked as sombre and scared as she felt. 'How is Danny?' she gasped. 'Have you seen him?'

Mr Curtis answered, 'He's in there,' he indicated one of the small rooms with a closed door, 'the doctors are examining him now, doing what they can. We were told one of them would come and speak to us when they have news.'

Susie gulped and sank down on a chair. This was even

worse than she'd expected; it didn't bode well for Danny. Her mother sat next to her and took her hand between both of hers. Danny's mother sniffed, looking close to tears.

They didn't have long to wait until the door opened and several staff came out. A doctor came towards them. 'Mr and Mrs Curtis?' he asked, then looked at Susie. 'The Curtis family?' She saw compassion in his eyes.

'Yes,' they all agreed and struggled to their feet.

'No, don't get up,' he said, and his words sent Susie's hopes plummeting. 'I'm very sorry to have to tell you that your son didn't regain consciousness. We did everything we could, but he had severe head injuries. He'd lost a lot of blood before he came in.'

Mrs Curtis let out a wail of distress and collapsed against her husband in noisy sobs. Susie gasped with shock and felt the tears burning her eyes. He was saying Danny was dead! She couldn't believe it. Surely he couldn't have gone so quickly?

'Can we see him?' his father asked.

'Yes of course.'

They were ushered into the room. In the middle was a treatment couch with a still body lying on it covered with a white sheet. Pushed into a corner was a metal stand holding aloft a half-used bottle of saline, its needle and rubber tube tossed back over it. All around the room were other items of equipment and trolleys holding the detritus of treatments that had failed.

Susie closed her eyes as the doctor folded back the sheet so they could see just the face. 'I'm so sorry we couldn't do more for him. You can stay with him for as long as you want to.'

Susie had to force herself to look, but she'd never seen

Danny asleep and the still, cold figure seemed somehow unfamiliar. She shook off her mother's arm and rushed for the door. Everybody else followed, and while Danny's mother wept noisily and the others mopped at their faces with their handkerchiefs, Susie remained dry-eyed. Danny was gone, and so was the golden future she'd so been looking forward to. She couldn't believe it.

Feeling searing pity, Louise put an arm round her daughter's shoulders and pulled her close. She could feel her shaking. Wasn't this what had happened to her? She understood only too well what Susie was feeling, the overwhelming sense of loss. Harold's death had drawn her closer to their children, tightening the bond between them. She'd made it her first aim to give them as happy an upbringing as she could. She'd been especially drawn to their baby; it had made Susie the most important person in her life,

'I need to get my wife home,' Danny's father sounded agonised. 'Please excuse us.'

Jack Curtis said awkwardly, 'Is there anything I can do, Mrs Ingram? Call a taxi for you?'

'No, no thank you, Jack,' Louise said. 'We'll go back on the bus.'

Once home, Susie seemed to be made of stone. She sat by the fire, staring silently into it. All the colour had drained from her face, leaving it like parchment, but her eyes remained dry and hard. She refused food, and though Louise warmed a mug of milk for her she drank less than half of it. She had to be persuaded to go to bed.

During the night Louise heard her tossing and turning and went in to comfort her. She was crying then and her eyes were puffy and red. 'Mum, what am I going to do?' she implored.

It broke Louise's heart to see her daughter so distressed. She sat down beside her and gathered her into her arms, 'There's nothing you can do but accept what has happened, and it's very hard to do that, as I know. It must seem that Danny has been snatched away with savage speed.'

'It does. This afternoon I had everything to live for, and by bedtime . . .' She let out a cry of agony. 'Why did this have to happen to Danny?'

Louise held her until her sobs quietened and then said, 'Go and bathe your eyes with cold water while I make us a cup of tea. It's two o'clock, and we both need to get some sleep.'

When she came back with the tea, she said, 'I do understand, love. When I got the telegram telling me your father had been killed on the Somme, I felt so alone it was like the end of the world. You were just a baby and at first I saw you as a huge responsibility, but I found my greatest comfort in you. I know I can't take Danny's place, but I want to help you all I can, as you helped me. It will get easier in time.'

'It won't,' Susie was vehement. 'It won't.' And she had another storm of tears. When that died down, Louise tucked the blankets round her daughter, put out her light and went back to her own bed.

Yet Louise still couldn't sleep. It seemed both Susie and Martha were going to have hard and difficult lives.

It had gone nine o'clock the next morning when they woke up, and Louise hoped Susie would feel a little better, but she said, 'I'm not going to church. God should not have let this happen.'

That reminded Louise of Rebecca, her middle daughter,

who'd said much the same thing at the start of her rebellion, and Louise had insisted she came with them and keep to the family routine. That had not worked out with Rebecca, so she said nothing and went to church alone. Prayers were said for Danny, his family and his fiancée. The congregation offered sympathy, their compassion plain to see, but Susie wasn't there to take comfort from that. She spent most of the day in tears. On Monday morning, she didn't want to get up and go to work.

'I have to go,' Louise said. 'We need my wages to pay the rent, and yours helps to put food on our table.' Knowing Susie had spent most of yesterday in tears, she thought she'd be better off going to work instead of staying at home by herself. Eventually, she persuaded Susie to go to work too.

When Louise reached her desk she found her fellow workers in a jolly mood and still discussing the highlights of the Grand National. They'd expected her to be excited because her horse, Kellsboro' Jack, had won and she'd scooped the largest slice of the company sweep. The sum turned out to be twenty-six pounds, more than she'd dared hope. At lunchtime she went out to the furniture shop to try and cancel her wedding present of the double bed. The assistant was sympathetic and said he'd have to discuss it with his manager, but if she returned later in the week, he'd probably be able to give her the money back. Before returning to the office she bought cream cakes for her colleagues to enjoy at their teatime break, because that was what the winner had done in previous years.

Susie came home with red and puffy eyes but said everybody had been kind and sympathetic. Louise told her how much she'd won and said, 'I think we'll be able to buy that wireless.' She hoped it might help to take her mind off Danny's accident.

Susie sniffed and nodded, as though she no longer cared one way or the other.

The vicar came to see them that evening and told them that Danny's funeral would be on Thursday morning. He asked Susie if she'd like to read one of the lessons.

She shook her head.

'Or say a prayer?'

Again she shook her head.

'Or choose a hymn?'

She straightened her lips in a firm line and again shook her head.

'Did Danny not have a favourite hymn?' he persisted.

Susie couldn't look him in the face. 'It would be better to ask his mother,' she said, 'she'll know more about that.' She was stony faced again and taking little interest in what the vicar said. Louise could see the effort she was making to hold her tears back.

At the door, when she was showing him out, Louise whispered, 'I'm afraid Susie is very upset.'

'Yes, I would have married them in two more weeks. It's very hard for her, poor girl.'

Louise had hardly returned to the living room when Fiona Curtis, Danny's sister and Susie's friend from childhood, came round. 'I've brought you some books you gave to Danny, and Mum thought you might like to have his signet ring and watch.'

Fiona, or Fee as her friends called her, was a pretty girl with a strong family resemblance to Danny, though she had dark hair and dark eyes rather than her family's typical red colouring. She tried to comfort Susie by telling her how her family were

27

getting on, but it was as if she was turned to stone again. Susie couldn't relax and Fee didn't stay long.

Louise was starting to think about the funeral. 'I'll have to ask my boss if I can take Thursday off, and you must do the same.'

'Yes,' Susie said, as though she couldn't care less.

'We should send some flowers or a wreath.'

'His family will provide all the flowers Danny needs.'

'But you should send some too. It will be expected of you.'

Susie sniffed.

'Tomorrow after work, we'll meet at the bus stop and call in at the florist's on the way home.' Louise knew the couple who ran the local florist's shop because she had served on the committee that regularly bought flowers for the church.

The couple offered condolences and were very kind to Susie. 'We could make you a small posy of cut flowers,' they suggested, 'and surround the posy with a white doily. It will stand out because the Curtis family have ordered exactly the opposite, big ornate wreaths.'

Susie shrugged.

'Yes please,' Louise said quickly, relieved that it didn't sound expensive.

As they walked the short distance home, she asked, 'What are you going to wear to Danny's funeral?'

'I don't care.'

Poor Susie seemed to be in denial that anything had happened to Danny, but the congregation would expect her to wear mourning. Louise owned a black hat and coat, but black would be very sombre for a young girl like Susie, and perhaps it would add to the depression she was obviously feeling.

Louise said as cheerfully as she could, 'Fortunately you have a smart new suit in silver grey.' She held her breath, expecting Susie to object, because she'd chosen that to wear when she went away on her honeymoon.

But she said nothing so it seemed she'd agreed. Susie wasn't fond of hats and hadn't bought a new one. Instead she'd decided to wear the straw boater she'd worn on every church occasion for the last two summers. To make it last a third year she'd smartened it up by sewing artificial spring flowers round the crown. It looked a little too bright for a funeral, but there was no time to do anything about that.

The Curtis family was a large one, and they provided a lavish funeral for Danny. His coffin, with Susie's little nosegay of flowers on the front and copious heavy wreaths covering the rest of it, was carried in an open carriage drawn by four black horses.

Susie received a lot of attention from the vicar during the service, and the Curtis family and the congregation could not have been more sympathetic. She kept her head up and her tears under control, although all around her the Curtis family and friends were in darkest mourning and weeping openly.

It was a bright, sunny morning and Susie could not have looked smarter and her outfit more spring-like. Yet her face was full of despair under her pretty hat and she seemed to be avoiding her friends. Refreshments were provided in the church hall afterwards, but Susie stood apart and hardly answered, even when people spoke directly to her. Louise took her home as soon as she reasonably could.

They spent a quiet afternoon and Louise hoped that now

the funeral was over, her daughter could slowly recover from her loss and their life would return to normal. She was relieved that she'd been able to stop the double bed being delivered, and had been given her money back, but the days were passing slowly.

The fifteenth was the day that had been set for Susie's wedding. She went to work without remarking on it, but her mouth was set in a hard, straight line and when she came home she was red eyed and dejected.

'At least it's all behind her now,' Louise said to Martha. 'Poor Susie, she needs a quiet routine to recover, but it'll take time.'

CHAPTER FOUR

I N BED THAT NIGHT, Louise wept for Susie. She'd been the
daughter who had given her the least worry as she'd grown
up. She'd believed her to be the daughter who would be
happiest and have a good life.

Martha's health had always been a major worry. Louise
had wept to see her suffering with rheumatic fever as a child,
but there was worse to come; it left her with a weakened heart
and painful arthritis from which she'd never since been free. At
one point Louise had given up hope of Martha ever being
really well and was afraid she'd have the restricted life of an
invalid.

Martha had big blue eyes set wide apart, often with shadows
beneath them. They gave her a look of childlike innocence that
made people want to protect her. She had been a sweet girl,
kind and considerate, doing her share of the household chores
without having to be reminded, and she seemed content to
accept her limitations and do what she could.

Before Martha had reached the age of fourteen and was due
to leave school, she'd known exactly how she wanted to earn
her living. She loved embroidery and needlework of every sort.
'I want to be a dressmaker,' she said, so Louise asked around
her fellow members in St Biddolphe's congregation about the

31

best training available to her. Martha spent two years helping a local dressmaker and loved it, then started making clothes for herself and her sisters.

At sixteen she was apprenticed to a top tailor in Bold Street and said she was delighted to learn her trade in such depth. Martha was such an undemanding girl in every other way that they didn't seem to mind her taking time off when she was ill. If she went in on one of her bad days they would send her home and tell her to rest.

She was even happier when she took up with Albert Dolland, known as Bert. He was their local butcher and throughout her childhood Martha had taken her turn to go to his shop to buy the family meat. If anyone asked her how long she'd known Bert, she would laugh and say, 'I've always known him.'

Louise had not been pleased, though she knew Bert's interest in Martha had only started two years after his wife died. She thought Martha was too young to be involved with a widower of thirty-one. He was a man of the world, too handsome, and had too flirty a manner with his younger lady customers. It was not until Martha had another bad turn, and she saw Bert fussing round her and rushing to get the doctor, that she could believe he really loved her.

Yet although Louise had worried endlessly about Martha's health, it was Rebecca who had given her real nightmares.

Martha and Susie would do as they were told – they were sensible, sweet-natured and biddable, would fall in with any plans that were made for them – but Becky was strong-willed and made plans of her own. She could be confrontational if pressed to do something she didn't want to, and had always been the most difficult to handle.

At eighteen, Martha still had the body of a skinny child, whereas Becky had started developing into a woman at thirteen. By fourteen, she had an hourglass figure, with a flat tummy, full hips and generous bosom, and she was not shy about showing any of it off. Susie also developed early, but she kept herself modestly clothed.

Becky was much darker in colouring than the rest of the family. She had dark hair and light olive skin, with rosy cheeks and dimples and laughing brown eyes, and she had a totally different personality to the other girls. Her manner was bold and confrontational to those in authority, both at school and at home. She was quick to criticise others and made no secret about being out to have as much fun as she could.

'I'm sick of church,' she'd complained to Louise one Sunday morning, 'you ram it down our throats. We have to do this or that for St Biddolphe's, and we never go anywhere else. I've had enough to last me a lifetime.'

When Louise tried to persuade her, she said, 'You go, Mum, and say a prayer for me. God won't listen to me.' After that, whenever the family was going to church, Becky would stay at home alone or go out with her friends.

'I need to know where you're going and who you're going with,' Louise always told her, but though what Becky told her sounded harmless enough, she suspected it wasn't always the truth. 'You must be in by nine o'clock when you go out alone at night,' she told her, and when she failed to keep the deadline, Louise stopped her going out for a few nights. It only made her more rebellious.

Becky was a honey pot to the young lads in the district, which frightened Louise. 'Becky, love, you must be careful with boys. You must not allow them to take liberties with you.'

'No, Mum.' She was po-faced.

'I've explained how you could have a baby, haven't I? And if you do that it would be a disaster at your age.'

'Yes, Mum.'

Louise felt her warning was not getting through. 'Becky, love,' she put a hand on her arm. 'You may have a boyfriend who has no self-control, and if you let him do what nature intends to prevent the human race dying out, then you could have a baby.'

'I'll be careful, Mum, don't you worry.'

'I do worry about you, Becky. You put having a good time above everything else in life.'

'What's wrong with me enjoying myself?'

'Nothing, I hope you do. Just be aware of what could happen. Keep your wits about you. Look after yourself.'

'I will, Mum, honest.' She kissed her mother's cheek. 'It's just that I'm a bit weak on duty and work and church, that sort of thing.'

Becky continued to go to the youth club and to dances in the church hall throughout her fourteenth year. Occasionally, she went to one of the church functions if she thought it might be fun, but she was making friends who had no connection with St Biddolphe's and bringing them to their dances. They were said to be an ill behaved and rowdy lot.

Dancing lessons were what Becky craved, and she found a Saturday job in a local fish and chip shop to earn the money for them. The year she left school, she found herself a job in a family-run boarding house in Childwall that needed a girl to live in and help generally with cleaning and cooking. Within a week she told Louise, 'I hate it, this isn't my idea of fun. I've got to find a better job than this.'

Louise had to smile when Becky said she wanted to earn her living on the stage. She asked the ladies of St Biddolphe's for advice on how to go about it, but they didn't approve of careers in the theatre and knew less than she did.

In truth, Becky was a bit of a show off. She loved dancing, and she had a strong singing voice, not particularly sweet but slightly husky and just what was needed to croon the popular songs of the moment.

Becky had taken part in a few amateur shows organised by various dance schools, and when she heard there were going to be auditions at the Liverpool Empire Theatre for dancers to appear in Cinderella, the Christmas pantomime, she was determined to try.

She took Martha into her confidence, swearing her to secrecy. 'I'm not going to tell Mum,' she said. 'She'll say I'm too young and forbid me to go near the place. I'm not having that, this could be my chance.'

Becky was thrilled when she found she'd succeeded and was taken on for the duration of the show, which would probably last ten weeks. She went home to confront Louise with the news. 'You thought I'd never get a job on the stage, didn't you, Mum?' She was exultant. 'Wait till you see my name up in lights outside a theatre.' She was gripped with ambition from that moment.

'What about the job in Childwall? That poor woman will be relying on you. You must explain . . .'

'Not yet, she'd kick me out straight away. I need to work for another three weeks until they start rehearsals. For the money, I mean.'

'And then?'

'I'll be ready to go. Who in their senses would choose to clean and look after those awful kids when they could be on the stage?'

'You aren't planning to walk out at a moment's notice?'

'Yes. Why not?'

'Becky! Have you no thought for other people?'

Almost as soon as she started at the theatre, Becky said, 'You're going to have to give me a key to the front door. We're going to do two shows each night and the last one doesn't finish until eleven.'

'What? You can't do that, the buses will have stopped running by then.'

'Don't worry, Mum,' she said. 'There are fifteen of us girls taken on locally and we share a couple of taxis to get home. The theatre pays for them, it's part of the deal.'

Louise was afraid for her and at the same time felt guilty. Becky was only fifteen, though she'd pass for eighteen when she got dressed up, and had probably told them she was. She would have liked to stop her taking the job, but past experience had led her to believe it would be impossible. To have a fight with Becky and lose would make matters worse.

It was 1925 and these were dangerous times for young girls. The newspapers were full of the exploits of flappers. It surprised Louise that Martha had stayed close to her sister. 'Becky knows how to do the Charleston and the Black Bottom,' she said, 'and she's trying to teach me.' Later she smiled ruefully and said, 'I've got two left feet,' but the truth was that Martha lacked the energy and did not have Becky's lithe body and ease of movement. She would never be much of a dancer.

Louise had never seen Becky so happy as when she was dancing in Cinderella. Not that they saw very much of her. As requested, Louise had given her a front door key so she could get in without getting everyone out of bed, and it reassured her to hear the taxi stopping outside, although at a very much later hour than eleven. Becky said that was because she had to stay with the other girls, and most were dropped off before her.

Then she was asked to understudy the Fairy Godmother's part, which delighted her. She was given several short dance routines and a song about Prince Charming to learn. One Sunday morning when her mother was getting ready to take her sisters to church, Becky said, 'Please, all of you pray that the Fairy Godmother will be indisposed.'

Louise was horrified. 'Becky, that's really naughty, asking us to pray for harm to befall another person!'

'I don't mean real harm, of course,' she said quickly, 'just enough to make her feel unwell so that I get a chance to play her part.'

The Fairy Godmother did indeed have a bad bilious attack and missed going on stage for two days. Becky played the part in four evening shows and one matinee. The producer told her she was great. Susie and Martha begged to go and see her, but by the time Louise bought tickets Becky was in the chorus line again. They all agreed she looked very professional.

'She's marvellous,' Susie was enthusiastic. 'Will she be a star one day and act in films in Hollywood?'

'Everybody has to start somewhere, but I don't think so, love.'

'You didn't think she could get this far,' Martha said, 'that's why she didn't tell you she was going to audition for it.'

February came and Becky understood the show would soon close, but was then told it was selling enough seats to stay open until the end of the month.

'What will you do then?' Louise wanted to know.

'I've been offered a dancing part in the summer show in Scarborough,' she said triumphantly.

Louise had not expected her stage career to be extended beyond Cinderella. 'On the end of the pier?' she asked.

'Yes, it'll open at Easter and rehearsals start the last week in April.'

'So you'll be out of work for a few weeks?'

'I'll still be able to pay you the pound a week for my keep,' she said. 'I've saved a bit, and I've seen an advert in a newspaper about a family in Scarborough needing a live-in mother's help starting in March. I've applied for the job; if I get that I'd be in the right town.'

'But you'll need a reference.'

'The producer said he'd give me one.'

'But that would be about your dancing ability.'

'A character reference, he said.'

A few days later, while Becky was out, a letter arrived for her with a Scarborough stamp. Louise turned it over several times while she considered what she should do. She needed to know if Becky was telling her the absolute truth. 'I'm going to open it,' she said to Susie. 'She's only fifteen and I need to know what she's really up to.'

But it was a reasonable, business-like response to the letter Becky said she'd written. A Mr Walter Dennison confirmed that he was seeking a mother's help to stay with his wife in Scarborough, who was awaiting the birth of her third child, and who had two other children to look after.

I am working in Liverpool Monday to Friday, though I return home most weekends. Please come to the Adelphi Hotel next Monday at seven in the evening for an interview, and bring your references. Ask at reception for me and I will come and meet you in the lounge. If this is not convenient for you, please phone for an alternative time. Two telephone numbers followed.

It was as Becky had told her and went some way to quieten Louise's suspicions.

'You opened my letter,' Becky flared when she got home that night.

'I felt I should,' Louise said. 'You're only fifteen. I'll come with you for that interview.'

'Mother, you will not! I don't need help. I'm not one of the lame ducks from St Biddolphe's.'

'Becky, he seems to want a mother's help for the foreseeable future, and I'm afraid you only intend to stay for a few weeks until you start rehearsals.'

'Yes,' Becky agreed.

'You aren't going to tell him?'

'Mum, I'm not daft. That's why I don't want you to come with me.'

'That is dishonest, Becky.'

'It's looking after myself.'

Louise shook her head. 'You should give some thought to the needs of other people. It seems St Biddolphe's and I have taught you nothing.'

'Let's go to bed, Mum. I don't want you to start on St Biddolphe's again now, I couldn't stand it.'

'I don't think I should let you do this. You're too young to go off to the other side of the country on your own.'

'Don't try and stop me, otherwise I'll leave home and never come back.' She raced for the stairs and Louise heard her bedroom door slam.

Two weeks later, a defiant Becky told her family that she'd been given the job.

'She's pleased,' Martha said, 'everything's going her way.'

'I hope it always does,' Louise said.

Before Becky was due to leave for Scarborough, she bought Martha a gramophone and half a dozen records to play on it. Louise heard 'Yes! We Have No Bananas' played over and over until she was heartily sick of it.

'Marvellous,' Susie breathed, and thereafter she and Martha saved up their pocket money to buy more records.

Louise had a heavy heart when she saw Becky leaving with her suitcase one Friday evening. She was to meet Mr Dennison at the Adelphi again, and he would drive her to his home.

'You mustn't worry about Becky, Mum,' Martha said, 'this way it couldn't be easier or safer for her, could it?'

Louise couldn't agree. She sighed and sank down on the sofa. Susie and Martha were gentle and kind, but Becky was bold and confident; she meant to enjoy life and do it her way. Louise felt she had good reason to worry. She was afraid that sooner or later Becky would land herself in trouble.

Both her sisters and Louise wrote to Becky as soon as she'd left for Scarborough, but she didn't like writing letters. Once in a while she wrote to Martha, who passed it round the family. They read that Becky and her troupe of dancers were working again, and that their show had opened on the pier. She had two songs to sing and was having a marvellous time.

'Please, Mum,' Susie begged over and over, 'can we visit Scarborough to see Becky in her show?' But Louise couldn't afford to do that; Susie needed new shoes and a winter coat.

That September, Becky wrote that the show would soon close, and that she meant to go straight down to London with the other girls in the troupe to try her luck there.

That worried Louise more, and though she wrote to Becky regularly over the following years, asking for her news, as did her sisters, they received little in return but the occasional postcard or Christmas card. Louise was afraid they were losing touch with her and pleaded with Susie and Martha to keep writing. Then at last she began sending an occasional newsy letter to Martha.

Susie said, 'It looks as though Becky is having a great time.' She was back in Scarborough, sharing a flat with another girl and taking driving lessons and talking about buying a small car. Louise breathed a sigh of relief at least she knew where she was and something of what was happening to her.

CHAPTER FIVE

O NE SUNDAY EVENING IN 1928, when young Susie had
been invited to Hillbark, the Curtis home, Martha
made up the living room fire after supper, pushed her mother's
armchair nearer and said, 'You relax, Mum. I will clear away
and wash up.'

Louise was more than happy to oblige and was enjoying a
rare moment of leisure, retrimming the black felt hat she'd
worn to church for the last three years with new petersham
ribbon and grey feathers, when Martha's boyfriend Bert
Dolland rang their doorbell and she heard them laughing
together in the kitchen.

Louise tried on her hat, standing up to see the effect in the
mirror over the fireplace. The feathers were sticking up at the
wrong angle and she began unpicking her stitches to try and
right them when Martha came in, pulling Bert behind her.
'Mum, can we have a word?'

'Of course, love. Hello, Bert.'

'Good evening, Mrs Ingram.' The formality of his reply
made her look at him twice. He looked nervous and was
wearing his best grey lounge suit. Mostly he wore slacks and
pullovers when he came to see Martha.

'Is something the matter?' she asked.

'No, Mum.'

Martha nudged Bert, who seemed to be searching for the right words, but then they all came out in a rush. 'Mrs Ingram, I want to marry Martha, and she is . . . Well, we want to get married, and I have to ask if you'll give your permission. I mean, Martha is only nineteen and . . . Would you be willing to let her get married?'

'Oh!' Louise had been half expecting it. Bert had become a regular visitor to her house and Martha had been wearing his ring for the last six months. She felt a little wary of Bert because his family was of German origin, and she hadn't fully recovered from the war in which Harold had lost his life. She had other reservations about Bert too, but tried not to show it. It bothered her that he said he was a Methodist but never seemed to go to church or chapel. 'You mean you want to get married soon?'

'We don't want to wait. We know what we want and we'd like to go ahead in the spring.'

'You said you were married at seventeen,' Martha said, trying to be helpful.

'I was, and I never regretted it. I believe in early marriage. I'd have had a marvellous life if only Harold hadn't been killed on the Somme.'

When Martha had become engaged, one of the well-meaning ladies who did a lot of work for the church had said, 'The poor girl is never well. Is it wise for her to think of marriage when she has such poor health? If she's able to bear children, she won't have the strength to bring them up.'

That had made Louise think twice, but Martha had had so little in her life and she'd always said she wanted babies of her own. 'It's what she wants,' she'd said. 'And I want her to be happy.'

Now she smiled at the couple. 'I'm not against you getting married if you're both quite sure.'

'We're absolutely certain,' Bert assured her, and both had huge smiles on their faces.

'Then I'll happily give my permission,' Louise said. Martha gave her a hug and the couple were effusive in their thanks. Martha laughed; it was easy to see she was sparkling with anticipation, very much in love and looking forward to marriage to Albert Dolland.

Bert was easily the most handsome man in the street. Susie said his glossy brown hair, dark eyes and narrow pencil moustache gave him film star good looks. He stood very straight, was tall, slim and broad shouldered, which he said he owed to always eating plenty of meat.

Martha had told them quite a lot about Bert. His family had been in England for many years before he was born. They all spoke good English, without any trace of a German accent; if anything, their accent was Liverpudlian. But though they maintained publicly that they wanted to be thoroughly English, at home they still celebrated the old German traditions.

At Christmas, Bert talked about the feast of St Nicholas, and their big celebration was held on Christmas Eve. He had never stepped foot in Germany, but Louise saw him as a very Continental personality. Being wary of him, she'd asked him a lot of questions about his background and Bert had told her that his grandparents had left Munich in the 1880s, hoping to find an easier life in Liverpool for their family of three sons. His grandfather, Ludwig Darmstadt, had been a butcher by trade and soon found work in a butcher's shop owned by another émigré from Germany.

The family settled down and his grandfather achieved his ambition of opening a shop of his own, specialising in German preserved meats and sausages. His grandmother had worked in the kitchen behind the shop making the sausages, and preserving and cooking the meats. Their three sons entered the business as soon as they left school, one of whom, Walter, was Bert's father. They all worked hard and the business prospered. Their sons grew up and married and had families of their own. Bert's mother was English by birth, but she'd also worked in the kitchen behind the shop. She'd given her sons the names of Albert and Edward, which were popular in English families.

During the Great War there had been a lot of ill feeling against the Germans. Butchers' shops in Liverpool were attacked and vandalised, so Bert's father had changed their name to Dolland by deed poll, and although he went on making the same white and smoked German sausages, bratwursts, knockwursts and frankfurters that he always had, he gave them English names. He also began making the sort of sausages familiar to Liverpool housewives, and boiled hams and roasted pork and beef to sell in slices as well.

When the Royal family also changed their German name to that of Windsor, Bert knew his father had done the right thing.

Martha seemed to perk up the moment the date for her wedding, 24 June 1928, was set. She gained a little weight and lost the pinched, greyish look from her face, and she seemed to have more energy. But Bert Dolland was not the husband

Louise would have chosen for Martha, and she was afraid he'd tire of a sickly wife.

Bert's first wife Carlotta had died in 1926 of TB after a long illness, and they'd had no children. One thing in his favour was that he was running a very profitable butcher's shop with Edward, his younger brother, which they owned between them. They had been brought up in the flat over the shop premises, but Bert had moved out to a nearby rented house when he'd married Carlotta, leaving the flat to his mother and his Aunt Gertrude, who both worked in the business. His brother had done the same when he married. Bert had said he was envious of Edward's growing family of three boys.

When Carlotta had become too ill to manage the house, Bert had moved her back into the flat, and the family had helped him look after her. He'd stayed there until he was about to marry again. At that time, the house next door to Louise's, number 24, became empty, because the man who had spent most of his life there had grown frail and had gone to live with his daughter.

'Would you like me and Martha as neighbours?' Bert asked Louise. 'I think she wants to stay close to you.'

'An excellent idea.' Louise was pleased both by his thoughtfulness and Martha's wish to stay close. 'We'll be able to give her a hand when she has a bad day.'

'Mum likes to have someone to look after,' Susie said.

'I can't wait to move into my own house!' Martha's face was full of happy anticipation. Louise had never seen her look so well.

Bert had a bathroom installed and the house redecorated and improved generally. Martha was thrilled and went round the big Liverpool shops choosing furnishings and colour schemes. The house was ready, looking smart and fresh, a week before their wedding, and Martha showed it off with pride to anyone who was interested. She had made her own white satin wedding gown, and also a blue taffeta dress for Susie who was to be her bridesmaid.

Martha had always been close to Becky and wrote to invite her to her wedding, and the family was thrilled to hear that she intended to come home for the occasion.

The marriage was to take place on a Wednesday afternoon, early closing day for shops, so that Bert's family could come. It was, of course, held at St Biddolphe's church, which would be decorated with flowers by the ladies of the parish, and most planned to turn out to witness one of their own take her vows. In the absence of a male relative, Martha had asked Dr Grant if he would give her away.

The bridal couple had agreed that the reception was to be held in their new home and combined with a house-warming party. Bert's family would produce most of the food, though Louise and Martha planned to make cakes and trifles. 'We don't need a lot of guests,' Bert had said, 'we'll keep it mostly to our families,' though Martha felt she had to ask Miss Maddocks and Nurse O'Brien because they had spent so much time looking after her as she'd grown up.

Becky arrived by taxi just in time to wave the bride off to the church with Susie and Dr Grant. In her bridal finery, Martha's face shone with happiness. When they'd gone, Becky threw her arms round Louise and said, 'Sorry, Mum, I've been a real pig to you in the past, but I'm more sensible now I've grown up. Will you give me a second chance?'

Louise almost wept for joy; she couldn't believe the difference those lost years had made. Becky was wearing a lot of make-up, but she looked really beautiful. Not only was her appearance elegant and polished, but she had become more socially adept. She seemed at ease and bubbling with well-being and pleasure to be in church with her family, witnessing Martha's wedding.

When Bert saw her at the reception, he said, 'Wow, Becky! You've changed since you used to pop into the shop for three-quarters of mince. You're quite a fashion plate now. Did Martha say you're back in London now? It must agree with you.'

'London does, but I'm back in Scarborough for the summer.' Her eyes were dancing. 'You and Martha should try getting about more.'

'I can't,' Bert said, pulling a face, 'I'm pegged down in Liverpool by my business.'

'You get holidays don't you? You could come and see me, Martha would love it.'

'I'm taking my holiday now.'

'But this will be your honeymoon.'

The celebrations went on until late in the afternoon, and afterwards Bert took Martha away for a week's honeymoon in the Lake District. For almost the first time in her life she looked radiant and healthy.

After they'd cleared away what was left of the food and helped the Dollands tidy up the house next door, Louise and Susie went home to a quiet house. Louise straightened the photograph of her three little girls in sprigged muslin dresses. Martha was settled, and Rebecca had seemed a reformed character, almost a different person, with her elegant clothes and professional hairdo. To know they were all happy and doing well lifted her spirits.

'You needn't have worried about Becky,' Susie said. 'She seems to be managing better than any of us.'

Louise prepared a hot meal to welcome Martha and Bert back from their honeymoon, and in the following days Martha sang as she took up housekeeping in her new home. She'd given up her job just before her wedding, as Bert didn't want her to work outside the home.

Louise was delighted to hear that Martha was going to be the first Dolland wife not to work in the shop. Bert thought she wasn't strong enough to be on her feet all day and tried to protect her from over-work. In any case, she had her own trade and preferred to carry on with that. Martha put a notice in the local tobacconist's shop window offering a dressmaking service, and soon she began to get the work she enjoyed that way.

Bert smiled indulgently and said, 'It will give her a little pin money to spend on herself.'

Within a few months they came round to her house in a flurry of excitement and announced that Martha was expecting. 'I'm absolutely delighted,' Bert said. 'I really want a family, and if possible boys to follow me into the business. It's what my family does.'

Martha bought towelling and flannelette by the yard and began sewing baby gowns and napkins. They were thinking about buying a cot when suddenly, in her tenth week, Martha was rushed to hospital and miscarried. When Bert brought her home afterwards, her hopes dashed, she clung to him. Louise could see how disappointed she was and Bert was distressed too, and full of compassion for her. 'It's early days,' he told her, 'we can try again. You'll be all right next time.'

But she wasn't. With her next pregnancy she miscarried in the twelfth week, and this time their grief was terrible to see. Martha's energy was sapped and her healthy glow faded; it took her much longer to get back on her feet.

One good thing was that Becky was writing letters to Martha to try to cheer her up. They were all delighted when at the beginning of March they heard that Becky wanted to come and see them. She now had a new Austin Seven of her own and had learned to drive.

She drove over and stayed for the best part of a week with Martha and Bert. Louise and Susie had asked to have a couple of days from their annual week's holiday so they could spend time with her. On a sunny morning she'd taken them to Crosby beach, but there had been a bitter wind off the Irish Sea and after a brisk walk they'd been glad to get back into her car. She'd treated them to hot soup in a nearby café and afterwards had driven on to Southport where they'd gone round the shops and had afternoon tea in a very smart hotel.

Louise counted it a very good week and hoped Becky would remain in contact with them from now on. It seemed she would because she came as soon as she heard about Danny's accident, and spent a long time talking to Susie, commiserating with her over her loss, though it failed to lift her spirits.

CHAPTER SIX

USIE WAS HAVING SLEEPLESS nights. It had started as a vague worry, which she made a big effort to ignore. Forget it and it'll go away. Wasn't it enough that Danny's death had turned her life completely around? She'd lost everything she was looking forward to – the wedding, the honeymoon in the Lake District, and there was no Danny to turn to for support.

But as the days passed into weeks, she became increasingly scared and could no longer deny this was happening to her. She was having a baby. Her mother would be horrified, and so would Danny's family, not to mention the whole congregation of St Biddolphe's, and she didn't know what to do about it.

The more she thought about it, the more frightened she became, until she had to tell somebody. But who?

Certainly not her mother – she expected better things of her. Martha perhaps, but she was pregnant herself and in seventh heaven about it, always talking about the joys of motherhood and the delight of having a child. But then she was married, had had two miscarriages, and was desperate for a baby; she would not see Susie's position as the disaster it was.

Fiona would understand. That Tuesday, Susie thought about it all day at work, and in the evening walked up to

Hillbark with the intention of telling her if she had half an opportunity.

Hillbark was a handsome Georgian house and had been the home of Mrs Curtis's family for three generations. She had been brought up there and considered herself to be of county stock, though her family had not prospered in the twentieth century. Once Hillbark had had land and a home farm, but all that had gone as the Port of Liverpool grew and industry spread. The house had had three mortgages on it by the time Victoria had inherited it.

Victoria considered she'd married beneath her, but she was decidedly grateful for William Curtis's earning ability. He was in trade and successfully building up the cake-making firm he'd started. When they married he'd redeemed the mortgages on Hillbark for her and brought the old house up to date.

The Curtis parents always withdrew to the drawing room after dinner, while the children went to the family room. When Susie arrived, all five were there with cups of coffee, but she hadn't seen that much of them since Danny's death and felt shy and subdued. They'd always been friendly and made an effort to jolly her up, speaking readily of Danny.

Jack and Rory the two eldest, were both working in their father's business, and were said to be his favourites, having each received a car on their twenty-first birthdays. Danny had come next in age, then Jamie, Fiona and Julia. Jack was setting off to visit his fiancé, taking Julia, already in her Girl Guide uniform, to be dropped at the church hall. Rory left too, to meet his girlfriend at a nearby cinema.

To be back in the familiar playroom with books and games spread everywhere took Susie back to more carefree days.

Jamie collected the cups. 'I'm going to make more coffee, you'll have a cup, Susie?'

'Yes please,' she said, and he went to the kitchen. 'Fee,' she said urgently, knowing they might not be alone for long, 'I've got to talk to you. I feel desperate. You've got to help me.'

Fiona showed concern. 'Of course, what is it?'

Susie blurted it out. 'I think I'm having a baby.'

'What? Oh my God! Danny's baby?'

'Yes, I'm scared stiff. My monthlies have stopped.'

'But does that always mean . . . ? Are you sure? Have you been to see Dr Grant?'

Jamie came back saying, 'Peggy hasn't gone home yet, she's still washing up. She'll make us more coffee. What's the matter, Susie? Aren't you well?'

That put her into a dither. 'Yes, I'm fine,' but she could feel tears scalding her eyes, and soon they were rolling down her cheeks. 'No, I'm not.' Jamie pushed a handkerchief into her hand.

Fee gave her a hug. 'Can I tell him?'

'I didn't want anybody to know but you,' Susie sobbed, her face buried in Fee's cardigan, 'but I just had to talk to somebody about it or I'd go mad. I'm in terrible trouble, Jamie. I think I'm having a baby.'

She saw his jaw drop. 'Susie! Fate couldn't be so cruel!'

'I'm afraid it can.'

'What's your mother going to say?' Fee asked.

'She'll be horrified. I've let her down, let everybody down.'

'Then there's our mum,' Jamie said, 'and the good ladies of St Biddolphe's. Oh my goodness, they'll have a field day.'

'I know. What am I going to do? I wish I could get rid of it, but I don't know how.' Susie saw the blank horror on their faces. She should have known they'd know no more about it than she did.

'Don't try for goodness sake,' Jamie said, 'it's dangerous.'

'This is Danny's fault,' Fee said.

Susie blew her nose. 'It takes two, and if he was here it wouldn't matter, we'd be married. Everybody would be congratulating us.'

There was a tap on the door and they stopped talking. Susie turned her face away as the maid brought in another tray of coffee. 'I've put some biscuits on,' she said. 'I hope it isn't too soon after dinner.'

Fee said, 'Thank you,' and waited until the door closed again. 'Susie, Dad would be more understanding. He'd know the best thing to do.'

Susie shook her head. She knew the Curtises were not the large happy family that Victoria Curtis tried to portray. Danny had said they were a family divided, and they all found their father easier to turn to with their problems.

'No, I've been trying to screw myself up to tell my mother for ages. I ought to do that.' Susie mopped at her eyes. 'She'd be hurt if she thought your father knew first.'

Fee took both her hands in her own. 'Sooner or later everybody is going to know, but you're right, you need to tell your mother first.'

'Or see Dr Grant, so he can confirm it one way or the other,' Jamie told her.

'I don't think there's much doubt.'

'I'm sorry,' Fee said, 'we don't seem to have been much help.'

But in a way they had. Susie felt she was no longer facing

this alone, though the thought of telling her mother was still paralysing. She'd be upset, worried and disappointed in her.

'Let's have this coffee,' Jamie said.

Louise had been on edge since she knew Martha was pregnant again. Bert was telling her to take things easy, and had had a telephone installed in the house so she could let him know if she didn't feel well. He spoke to her several times each day, asking if she was all right, and hardly allowed her to lift a finger until she had passed the fourth month.

Martha was doing her best to cheer Susie up. Her third pregnancy seemed to be going well, and she was really looking forward to the birth. 'This time I'm going to do it,' she laughed. 'I can't wait to hold my baby in my arms.' Bert too seemed very keen, but their enthusiasm did not rub off on Susie.

May came and the days were growing warmer and more spring-like, and still Susie didn't pick up. Louise took her shopping one Saturday afternoon to choose a wireless, but when it was delivered and the aerial erected, she didn't seem all that interested in listening to the programmes. Louise had expected Susie to grieve, but not remain listless like this.

One Sunday morning after the service at church, Fee invited Susie to come round that afternoon. Her mother said, 'Jack has marked out the tennis court again, come and have a game with Fiona. You used to be in and out of our house all the time, we miss you.'

'Thank you,' she said, 'but I've got a bit of a headache. Could I leave it to another time?'

Fee said, 'The days are getting longer, come round one evening, say Tuesday. Is that all right?'

'Yes, thank you,' Susie said, but walking home she told her mother she didn't want to go.

'You should,' Louise said, 'they're trying to be kind.' But on Tuesday morning it was Louise who rang Mrs Curtis from work to say Susie wasn't well and didn't feel like playing tennis.

'It would do her good,' Victoria said in her rather overbearing manner. 'You should encourage her to get out and take exercise.'

Louise sighed; she was doing her best to do exactly that.

Saturday afternoon was a damp, grey day for a change. Fee came round and Louise sent her up to Susie's room where she was 'resting' on her bed.

Fee left the door ajar and Louise heard her say, 'Jamie and I are going to the pictures this evening, would you like to come with us? It's Clark Gable and Jean Harlow in *Red Dust* at the Lyceum. Mother has forbidden us to go to the pictures because we're in mourning for Danny, but he'd be all for it. It's a good film and I don't want to miss it.'

Yet even that didn't tempt Susie, and Fee clattered downstairs and left.

Louise was worried about her. It seemed nothing would cheer her up. She didn't look at all well, her face was grey and she'd been listless for weeks. Louise remembered feeling paralysed with grief when Harold was killed, but she'd had her three girls to look after and she'd had to get on and make decisions for the future. Susie seemed to be opting out of everything.

'There's only two weeks until the Spring Fair,' she said one morning. 'I've told Nurse O'Brien we'd make some cakes. You'll do the scones and the fairy cakes like you did last time?

We need to make a list of the ingredients we'll need to buy.'

Susie groaned, 'Are these church fetes coming round more often?'

'We haven't had one since Christmas, love, and it's one of the best ways of raising money.'

Susie was vehement. 'But it'll be all go from now on. We can look forward to the Summer Fete, the Sunday school outing and the Harvest Festival.'

'Nurse O'Brien has put you down to help in the refreshment tent this time. It's what you said you wanted.'

Susie wailed, 'I don't feel like it.'

'It's still two weeks off, perhaps you'll feel better by then,' Louise said with all the patience she could muster. 'You usually enjoy helping out. Perhaps you should see Dr Grant,' she said. 'I don't think you're well.'

It surprised her when Susie didn't answer. She didn't like going to the doctor's and always protested it wasn't necessary. Fortunately it rarely was.

'Anyway, it would do no harm. A tonic might help.'

'I'll help with the refreshments and I'll finish the tea cosy for the handicrafts stall.' Susie sounded as though she'd given up, which only made Louise decide she must see Dr Grant as soon as possible, which would be Monday evening. No appointment was necessary; it was just a question of waiting one's turn.

'I'll walk down with you,' Louise said, sensing that Susie might not go unless she took her.

For Louise, that Monday was a busy day at work. A firm of auditors had sent in three men as it did every year to check the company accounts. Christopher was in and out to see how they were getting on, though they dealt mostly with

Gordon Wilson, the accountant, Louise's immediate boss.

Their presence in the office raised the general tension because everybody knew they were there to search out errors, and Louise knew the accountant's figures were based on those in the daily ledgers which were her responsibility. They had open in front of them the books Louise had kept for last year. Occasionally they asked her to explain how she'd arrived at such and such a figure. She found it nerve wracking.

She was late leaving that afternoon, which meant there were several other patients waiting to see Dr Grant ahead of them. Louise thought of going back home to start cooking their evening meal, but she was tired and sat back, glad of the chance to rest. Susie had indicated that she'd prefer to see the doctor on her own, and it seemed she'd be his last patient for the evening. She was restless and clearly on edge until her turn came.

Louise could hear the sound of their voices but not what they were saying. It was a soft drone in the background that went on for a long time. She began to feel drowsy and didn't hear the surgery door open until the doctor said, 'Mrs Ingram?'

'Yes,' she was jolted back to wakefulness.

She'd known Dr Grant since he was a young, newly qualified GP, though now he was stout and bald. For years he'd supported her through Martha's frequent bouts of ill health, and now he looked serious. 'Would you come in please?' He stood back to allow her to pass. 'Take a seat.'

The shock of seeing Susie slumped in a chair, hanging her head, the picture of despair, rooted her to the spot. Louise felt a stab of alarm. She could see it was going to be bad news. 'What's the matter?'

'I have to tell you that your daughter is pregnant.'

'What?' Louise felt fuzzy, the light reflecting off his rimless glasses dazzling her. 'What?'

'Pregnant,' he repeated, 'about sixteen weeks. It's a normal healthy pregnancy and I've worked out her dates. She'll be delivered about the twelfth of October. Do you want me to book the local midwife, or would you prefer the hospital?'

Louise wasn't taking it in; she felt the room begin to swing round her, everything was going black, and she knew the doctor stepped forward to prevent her falling.

The next thing she heard was Susie's sobs and Louise found she was lying on the examination couch. She tried to lift her head. 'Lie flat for a moment, Mrs Ingram. It's just a simple faint.'

'I'm sorry, Mum,' Susie sobbed, 'I'm so sorry.'

'It came as a shock to you,' the doctor said. 'You'll feel all right in a few minutes.'

'I'm all right now,' Louise sat up, 'it's lack of food.' Dr Grant seemed upset and ill at ease too. This would affect his opinion of her and her family. 'I've had only a sandwich since breakfast.'

'Right, well, if you feel you can walk home . . .'

'Yes.' Louise was aghast, she felt sick. At the same time it bothered her that she hadn't guessed. There was now logic to Susie's recent behaviour.

She was on her feet; what she wanted to do now was to talk to Susie. 'Thank you, doctor, we'll be all right now.'

'Wait a moment, Susie, you should take iron tablets now.' He wrote a prescription. 'Take one a day and come back and see me in a month. We can make arrangements then for your delivery.'

Once outside Louise took her arm. 'I'm sorry,' Susie said again. She looked really ill and her face was blotchy from crying.

'You should have told me,' Louise said, 'you must have been worrying about this all along. It must have been awful to face it on your own. Have you had morning sickness?'

Susie nodded. 'I was ashamed. It's such a disgrace, not just for me but for the family. I was afraid you'd throw me out.'

'I'd never do that to you!'

'I tried to tell you, I really did, but I was scared in case . . . There was a girl at secretarial school – Mary, her name was. Her parents threw her out as soon as they knew. Her friend Lily took her home, but her parents didn't want anything to do with her.'

'How could you think I'd do that to you? I wouldn't! But Susie, this will complicate everything. You can't keep hidden for ever – in fact, not for much longer.'

'What am I going to do, Mum?' she implored. 'Please help me.'

CHAPTER SEVEN

L OUISE NEEDED TIME TO think. She had a little weep after she'd seen Susie into bed, afraid that this was going to ruin her life. She felt Susie had been very unlucky, because if her baby had been born after seven months of marriage, it would have been welcomed and greeted with joy.

The more curmudgeonly ladies of the church might have counted up the months and shaken their heads, but nobody would have accused Susie of sinning. But now, with no husband, it made her a woman to be shunned. It had been hard enough for her to lose Danny almost on the eve of their wedding, but to have this as well was terrible.

Louise could also see that being a close member of St Biddolphe's church would provide an added complication. She'd thought it right that her family should be regular churchgoers. It had given them a secure and stable life, but St Biddolphe's did not expect members of their congregation to have babies out of wedlock. For Susie that was a sin of the first order.

St Biddolphe's helped to support a home for 'fallen girls'. It provided living accommodation for six weeks prior to the birth and for six weeks after – a safe place for them to have their babies. The girls were also helped to have them adopted.

Louise had knitted shawls and bonnets and stitched tiny flannelette nightgowns for the babies, but she decided there and then that Susie would not be going. The last thing she wanted was for her grandchild to be given up for adoption.

Over breakfast the next morning she tried to impart all this to Susie. 'We need to plan what we are going to do, and I think we should start by telling Danny's parents. They'll help to support you through this. I'll ring them from work tomorrow morning and ask if we can go round and talk to them.'

Susie looked appalled at the idea. 'No, Mum, not yet. Let's keep it to ourselves. Just you and me – and Dr Grant.'

'They need to know, love, it's only right. You're making me a grandmother, but you are making them grandparents too. I'll arrange it and we'll go together.'

'No, Mum!'

'Yes, better to get it over. You'll worry until it's done.'

Susie went to work the next morning feeling terrible. Why had she not told her mum that she'd already confided in Fee and Jamie? Well, she knew why, because Mum would feel hurt that she'd confided in her friends and been unable to tell her. It seemed there was no end to the embarrassment this was causing. Mum had taken it more lightly than she'd expected, she'd been great, but now there was no stopping her.

Susie didn't want anybody to know, and the longer it was kept from the Curtis parents the better. Her mum didn't know them as well as she did. Fiona had been her friend since nursery days and she'd spent a lot of time at their home. She'd seen how the family functioned, and though Mrs Curtis tried to give the impression that it was a serene, God-fearing, happy family,

Susie had felt the undercurrents of unrest. More recently, Danny had explained the problems he had had with his parents.

William Curtis had been nicknamed Rufus as a boy on account of his red hair. Susie knew he took a great interest in his children and was a hands-on father, though his wife had employed a nanny and a nursery maid when the children were young. He'd included Susie in many of the expeditions and parties he'd arranged for them, and welcomed her to the house as Fiona's friend.

But he was a controlling father, determined to teach all his children how to run the family firm, and make more money from baking those delicious cakes. According to Danny, he'd told them many times that they'd all inherit a share of the business. It was his gift to them and would ease their path through life. He meant well, Susie knew, but Danny didn't want anything to do with cakes. He was more interested in ships and wanted to be independent and make his own way in the world.

They'd all been encouraged to grow up and think for themselves, but when they'd achieved that, they were still governed by what their parents wanted them to do. Jack had started as an apprentice in the business as soon as he'd left school, and his father held him up as an example to the rest of them. Rory had taken his law exams last year and had been working in the business since, as expected.

There were rules laid down for them all to follow. 'Sensible and practical rules,' Mr Curtis had said. 'Following them through life will stand you in good stead.'

On Sundays, they must go to morning service at St Biddolphe's as a family, and help their mother regularly with her good works. They must learn how to run the family business, which would give them time to plan their future and save up to buy a house. There must be no hasty marriage, not before twenty-seven or twenty-eight. Their parents gave generous gifts for compliance.

Danny had been the first to rebel. When the time came for him to leave school, Bunney's department store, one of the largest in central Liverpool, was advertising for staff, and Danny had applied. He was offered a job as a junior member of the buying team, but his father had had a word with Mr Bunney and asked him to withdraw his offer.

Danny was furious and refused point blank to enter the family business. There had been a stand-off, until eventually it was agreed that Danny could work for another firm for a year or two to gain general experience, and his father found him a job in ship building. But Danny had earned their wrath again by making arrangements to marry Susie as soon as he'd turned twenty-one.

As punishment, he did not receive a car for his twenty-first, so instead he bought a motorbike using a saved deposit and hire purchase. Danny thought he would escape by coming to live with her. His family did not understand how trapped he felt.

When Louise rang Mrs Curtis from her office the next morning, she and Susie were invited round to afternoon tea on Sunday.

At church that morning, Mrs Curtis smiled at them and said, 'We look forward to seeing you both at four this afternoon.'

Susie's eyes were wide with apprehension all day and she was restless and growing more so as the time drew closer. They set out to walk up to Hillbark and met Rory and Julia taking their dogs, two brown and white cocker spaniels, for a walk. They were a handsome pair of teenagers, tall and well set up, with brown hair that curled rather more than they wanted it to. They turned round and walked back with Susie and Louise, chatting about tennis and urging Susie to have a game with them. 'Fee will want to play too. We'll have a doubles match.'

Louise needed Susie to stay with her, and she didn't want the Curtis children to be present at the meeting with their parents. That would be totally embarrassing for Susie. It made her feel awkward as they were led into a large, over-furnished formal drawing room because she didn't know how to broach the subject. Near the hearth was an enormous mahogany tea trolley set with a delicate china tea service and several plates of tiny sandwiches and the cakes that were so popular in the shops.

Mrs Curtis was pouring boiling water from an ornate kettle on a spirit stand into an equally ornate silver teapot. She came forward to greet them, a tall, thin and bony lady with dark hair drawn back severely into a bun. She held her head high and had an aquiline nose and a severe expression. She was a commanding presence.

Louise was relieved to find she understood the situation. 'You two will have to amuse yourselves for a little while,' she waved her children away, 'Susie and her mother have come to have a chat with me.'

'Can't we have tea?' Julia asked in surprise.

'Of course you can, dear, I'll give you a call shortly and you can come in to finish off the cakes. Do sit down, Mrs Ingram,' she said, indicating a large armchair. 'I'm afraid my husband has been called out to deal with some business problem and can't be with us. How are you, Susie?'

Louise could see that simple question had thrown Susie off balance, and she gasped before sinking silently into a neighbouring armchair. Victoria Curtis wheeled the trolley closer, and in between remarking on the lovely weather they were having, she asked if they took sugar and milk.

Louise took a deep breath; the time had come to say her piece, though she could find no easy way to put it. 'Susie and I have something to tell you,' she began.

'Oh yes?' Mrs Curtis was bringing a cup of tea to the small table beside Louise's chair.

She managed to blurt out, 'Susie is expecting a baby.' It sounded painfully blunt. 'It will be born in October.' The cup lurched in their hostess's hand and a wave of tea splashed into the saucer, but it was put down safely.

'I beg your pardon?' Indignant dark eyes were probing into Louise's.

Until now Louise had prided herself on being able to stand up to Victoria Curtis on the church committees. She made herself go on, 'The doctor says everything is going along normally and Susie is keeping well.'

Mrs Curtis looked shocked, her bony bosom puffed out as she pulled herself up to her considerable height. 'You mean . . . ?' She rounded on Susie. 'What have you been up to?'

Susie's gaze was fixed on the carpet. She was sinking lower in her chair.

This was not going the way Louise had expected, and she was struggling to stay calm. 'We thought we should let you know, after all this will be your grandchild, your first grandchild.'

Mrs Curtis's face was turning crimson. 'It will not! How dare you infer it has anything to do with us?'

Louise gulped. This was terrible. 'Susie and Danny were about to get married, he is the father.'

'He is not! No son of mine would get a girl into this sort of trouble.'

Louise held her nerve. 'But he has.'

'You can't accuse Danny of such a thing when he can't defend himself. I know it can't be him. We brought him up to have high moral principles. Susie must have boyfriends you don't know about. You've always gone out to work, so she's never had the supervision young girls need. I'm shocked and surprised at you, Susie. I didn't think you'd go off the rails like this, and I think naming Danny is extremely underhand.'

Susie leapt to her feet, her hangdog look gone. 'Mrs Curtis, I have not gone off the rails. Danny and I were in love, we've been inseparable since I was fourteen. I've never looked at anyone else, never needed to. Everybody knows that.'

'I don't believe you. Danny wouldn't do such a thing. You're trying to saddle him with your illegitimate baby. You're hoping we'll help support it. Hoping the church will help support it, as it has always supported you and your mother.'

Susie was angry but cold and calm. 'I knew you'd never accept that he was the father. It comes as something of a stain on your family's reputation, doesn't it? You would no longer be the perfect family. It might ruin your hopes of being the most important family in the parish.'

Mrs Curtis looked as though she was about to explode; she was too incensed to get any words out.

'Mum thinks you do your best to help everybody, but I've

seen a side of you that she has not. You think you are a cut above the rest of us and you want to be a power in St Biddolphe's hierarchy, but what you do is for your personal gratification, it expands your ego. You are a snob and a self-satisfied hypocrite. Come on, Mum, we're wasting our breath here.'

Louise felt weak as Susie towed her out of the room. 'Goodbye,' she said lamely, before Susie slammed the door behind them.

CHAPTER EIGHT

OUT IN THE FRESH air, Susie stormed ahead. 'I told you Mrs Curtis wouldn't want to know. Now she'll spread the news through the church and everybody will turn against me.'

'No they won't,' Louise was trying to keep up with her. 'They'll want to help you. They've always helped you, haven't they? It's what St Biddolphe's does. They have committees to decide where their help is most needed.'

'Didn't you hear what she said? You didn't bring me up properly. You went out to work instead, as if you had any choice! And I'm trying to blame Danny in the hope St Biddolphe's will continue to help us both, as it always has. She's an unholy bitch.'

'They have always helped us, Susie.'

'Because Dad was a curate there, you were part of the organisation, so they had to help you. But it's scratch my back and I'll scratch yours. You're always working like a beaver for them.'

'You mustn't be ungrateful, love, they paid your fees at the secretarial college.'

'I'm very grateful for that, and for everything else they've done for me. The problem is they've helped to bring me up as a respectable young lady, haven't they? I've been through their full training course, and now I'm expected to be an exemplary member of St Biddolphe's. Instead I've sinned. I'm going to produce an illegitimate baby. They won't want to help me now. I'm one of the "fallen women".'

When Louise unlocked their front door, Susie shot into the living room and threw herself on the sofa in another storm of tears. She sat down beside her daughter and felt for her hand.

Susie wailed, 'What are we going to do now?'

'We'll manage, we always have.'

'I wish I wasn't having this baby. It's the last thing I want. I won't be able to work for months. I'll not be able to contribute anything towards the rent and the housekeeping. I'm pushing all responsibility for that on to you.'

'Susie, I'm happy to look after you, I always will.'

'You've spent most of your life doing that, but now I'm grown up I should be doing my share and making things easier for you.'

'You mustn't worry about that.'

'I'll have the baby adopted. I'll get back to work as soon as I can.'

'No, Susie, don't make up your mind about that now. You might feel differently when it's here in your arms.'

'I won't, I don't want it. It would be different if Danny were here, if I was married, but it's all gone wrong. I've brought shame and disgrace on both of us. I'm sorry, Mum. What are we going to do?'

'For the time being, what can we do but carry on normally?'

That evening, Louise watched the coals glowing in the grate for a long time, musing that the early death of her husband meant she'd gone down in the world, and Susie having an illegitimate baby was going to drive them lower.

Poor Susie, it was bad enough losing Danny, but now this. For her sake, she'd have to stay as strong as she could. Until now she'd thought Susie was going to escape major trouble in her life, but it seemed none of her daughters was to have an easy time.

On Monday evening, Susie was walking up Milner Street on her way home from work when she saw Martha walking slowly ahead of her looking hunched and unwell. Susie caught up with her and Martha turned with a smile.

'Susie,' she said, 'I was just thinking of you. I've got a new customer wanting a wedding dress in a hurry. Her fiancé has landed a job overseas and they've brought the date forward. Do you want to sell the wedding dress I made for you? She's just about your measurements and she's picked out the same style from my pattern book. I told her about your dress. I could make it fit her without much trouble.'

Susie felt a pang at the thought of parting with it, but she couldn't wear it now and she was going to need money when she could no longer work. 'Yes please, I'd be grateful if you would. I'll bring it round, shall I?'

'Yes, after tea. Bert's going out tonight so I'll be on my own.'

'Mum is going out too, there's a meeting up in the church about the Spring Fair.'

As soon as she'd washed up after their meal, Susie slid her wedding gown off its hanger and took it next door. Martha tossed it expertly inside out to examine the sewing. 'Yes, there are big darts here that I can let out. This girl isn't quite as slim as you are. The material is beautiful, very good quality. She'll be pleased with it. I think we could ask five pounds for it.'

'That'll come in very handy,' Susie told her, 'it's two weeks' pay.' She earned £2.10 shillings a week. She'd wanted to confide in Martha for days, and now blurted out, 'I'm going to need it. I'm expecting a baby too.'

'What?' Martha was aghast. 'Oh my goodness! You're pregnant with Danny's baby? And now he's been killed! How awful for you. Oh, Susie!' She threw her arms round her in a hug. 'Does Mum know? Is she all right with it?'

Susie nodded; it was taking all her strength not to break down in tears again. 'Danny's mother says she doesn't believe it can be his. She says I must have other boyfriends. She was quite nasty to me and Mum, and she'll turn the ladies of the church against us.'

'Take no notice of them, Susie.'

Susie went on to confide every detail of what had happened and found it helped to unload her pain and grief.

Martha always seemed happy, although her swollen arthritic fingers were beginning to make it hard for her to do embroidery or fine hand-sewing. As usual, her living-room table was covered with cloth and paper patterns and she had a treadle sewing machine under the window where it got all the daylight possible. Often Susie helped her with tacking or other simple tasks while they chatted. Martha was everybody's friend.

At nine o'clock Martha suggested a cup of cocoa and they went into the kitchen to make it. While the kettle was boiling she decided they must each have a sandwich too. The Dollands always had what the Ingrams considered to be exotic sliced sausages and cured hams in their larder. Susie helped to butter the bread and watched while Martha covered it liberally with the preserved meats.

'What is that one called?'

'It's known as Bristol sausage in the shop, but it's really a black German sausage called Schwarzwurst.'

'It's delicious.'

The following Sunday morning, Susie was mutinous. 'I don't want to go to church,' she said, and once again Louise was reminded of Becky, but she persuaded Susie to stick to their normal routine.

'Just be yourself, forget what has happened. Act as you always have and everybody will do the same.'

They arrived just as the Curtis family were getting out of their car. 'Hello, Fee.' Susie was trying to pretend nothing had changed and said, 'How was the youth club dance last night? Did you and Jamie go?'

Her mother hustled her along before she could answer, and said frostily, 'They did not. We are all in mourning for Daniel, and dancing is not an appropriate activity.'

That riled Susie. 'But tennis is?'

'Only in private, on our own court,' and ignoring Louise, she swept past into the church porch.

Only then did Louise remember she'd seen her name on the rota to help Mrs Curtis arrange the flowers later that week, and she'd meant to have a word with her about what was needed.

During the service, the vicar asked for special prayers for those with troubled minds. Louise hoped she was mistaken and she hadn't seen him look at her as he'd said that.

Afterwards, the congregation usually stood about chatting

outside for a few minutes. Louise approached Mrs Curtis. 'About the church flowers, I see there's a wedding on Friday morning, do you want me to order extra flowers for—'

'No, you don't need to do anything,' she said briskly. 'The bride's family will decorate the church, and the flowers should last until Sunday. I'll pop in beforehand and remove any that are fading.'

'That's kind,' Louise said, 'thank you.'

Susie hurried her mother away. 'Mum, she's trying to tell you she doesn't want any more of your help. Mrs Pole and old Mrs Mathews have cut us dead, but worse than that, the Curtises are too. Even Fee! I told you they would. This is all my fault.'

Louise spent the afternoon trying to persuade Susie that she was reading more into what had happened than was intended, but she couldn't agree. 'It *was* intended, Mum.'

Later that day, Louise answered a knock on the front door to find Fiona Curtis on the step. 'Come in,' she said, glad to see her and to know Susie's friend wasn't going to desert her. Susie had been lying on the sofa but she pulled herself up to sitting position as they went into the living room.

'I've come round to say how sorry I am about what has happened,' Fee said. 'Whatever Mum says, it's exactly the sort of thing Danny would do. He had no patience and could never wait for anything. I know you and he were always close, and none of us, even Jack or Jamie, doubt that he's the father. But my mother has ordered me and, well, all the family really, to have nothing more to do with you.' She sat down beside Susie and gave her a hug. 'You've been my best friend for years. I am sorry.'

Louise could see tears welling up in her daughter's eyes, but Susie said, 'Don't apologise. We were very close until we left secretarial school, but it was more than we could hope for that they would find us jobs in the same office. You could say we've not been so close since then.'

'Don't say that!'

'Fee, it's true. It was seeing Danny so often that kept me in touch with you, but now he's gone . . .'

'I feel terrible about what our family has done to you. Danny being killed gave us a bad knock, but to be left having a baby . . . It must be hell, even without Mum turning half the ladies of the congregation against you. I am sorry. Life can be awful, can't it?'

On Wednesday evening, Susie and her mother were washing up after supper when the doorbell rang. Susie ran to answer it and was taken aback to find the Reverend Mr Thomas Coyne on the step. Susie saw him often at church functions and he visited when they were ill, but not otherwise.

He was balding now, in late middle age, and his dark eyes regarded her sympathetically. 'My child,' he said, 'I hear you are in difficulty. May I come in?'

Susie was quaking, but habit made her reply politely, 'Of course, Vicar, please do.'

'I was afraid you'd be troubled. I'll pray for you and give you all the help I can.'

Louise came to greet him. 'That's kind of you,' she said. 'Susie's upset, and of course she's worried about the future. To be honest, so am I, we really don't know which way to turn.'

Susie was heading for the stairs, wanting to escape, but

Mr Coyne said, 'Susie, my dear, please stay and talk to me. I want to help you through this.' Reluctantly she returned to perch on the edge of the sofa and was glad when her mother sat down beside her and held her hand.

'Please sit down, Vicar,' Louise said. 'What is the best thing for Susie to do? We'll both be glad of your advice.'

To Susie, the atmosphere seemed suddenly stiff and formal and she was afraid she was going to get a lecture from him.

'Well, my dear,' the vicar's manner was ponderous, 'you will have less time to worry if you fill your day. The Spring Fair is almost on us, so the preparations for that will keep us all busy this week. What are you doing to help it along this year?'

'I'm knitting this tea cosy for the handicraft stall.' Susie pulled it out from under a cushion to show him. 'I've almost finished.'

'Ideal,' he smiled, 'a traditional family tea cosy.'

Her mother said, 'We'll both be busy baking on Friday evening and Susie will help in the refreshment tent on Saturday.'

'Excellent,' he smiled at her. 'I do hope we'll have a fine day for it. It makes such a difference, doesn't it? I'm sure we'll all enjoy ourselves.'

'Yes, Mr Coyne,' Susie said.

'Mrs Bird tells me you have agreed to start taking a Sunday school class. We both think that's a good idea and we'll all be very grateful if you would. The Sunday school is thriving under Mrs Bird, isn't it? Perhaps you could see her and arrange to start next Sunday?'

Susie couldn't see how doing all these things would help her – quite the reverse in fact. 'No,' she said, 'I've changed my mind about doing that. I have a full-time job and I have to help

Mum about the house, because she's at work all day too. I'm not looking for more to fill my day. In fact I could do with less. Surely I'll need to rest more now?'

'Well, perhaps yes, but not immediately,' Mr Coyne conceded. 'Of course, you must look after your health, but I really believe you should keep yourself busy and not cut yourself off from our social activities. I know the ladies of the congregation will bear your problem in mind and support you in every way they can.'

Susie was still smarting from her clash with Danny's mother. 'I doubt that. Mrs Curtis has told me in no uncertain terms that she doesn't believe Danny is the father. She thinks I've gone off the rails with other boyfriends because Mum has been out at work earning a living for us. She's turning all the other ladies against us. I'm not expecting much help from them, Vicar.'

'Oh dear, dear! That can't be right about her turning the ladies against you.'

'It is. She says she doesn't believe Danny is the father.'

'That is a little strong, yes. Susie, dear, you must forgive Mrs Curtis. She has two young daughters of her own and may fear that the same thing could happen to them.'

'Forgive her? She disgusts me. She knew Danny and I were in love. How could I be carrying another man's child?'

'She is upset too. Danny's death was a tragedy for us all. And now you have this to cope with too. We must all pray for guidance and help. Please continue to do as much for us as you always have, Susie. You've enjoyed what you've done, haven't you?'

'Not always. To be honest there are other things I'd prefer to do in my spare time. All my life I've had church functions pressed on me as my duty and I'm sick of it.'

'Oh dear, you are angry. I'm sure when you've had time to think about it you'll change your mind. If you pray for help to feel remorse and show it, I'm sure everybody will give you all the help they can. I can promise you that.'

'Remorse? What is that? I feel I've let you and everybody else down and I'm ashamed of that. But I'm almost over-whelmed with guilt because St Biddolphe's paid for me to go to secretarial school so I could earn a reasonable living, and because Mum will have to keep me while I can't work. What I've done is turning people against Mum and they're showing it, and I'm changing her life when she was content with what she had.'

The tears were rolling down Susie's face. 'I can hardly believe . . . In fact I don't really understand why this baby is changing so much for us. If only Danny had not been killed, people would be congratulating me, they'd be pleased for me, and the baby would be welcomed. It makes his death ten times worse. I'm torn apart by it.'

It was her mother's arm she felt go round her shoulders. 'That's remorse, love, and it's also heartfelt grief.'

Mr Coyne cleared his throat. 'I think I could get you into St Biddolphe's House a little earlier than is usual, so you can leave your normal social scene before your trouble becomes too noticeable. Would you like that?'

'No!' Susie burst out. 'I don't want to go to that home for fallen women.'

'It will solve your practical problems. You will find peace there.'

She felt her mother squeeze her hand. 'No, Vicar, thank

you,' she confirmed. 'Susie has a home here with me and I want her to stay. Dr Grant will arrange for the midwife to attend her.'

'Oh!' Mr Coyne seemed at a loss. 'Well, we'll do our best to ease and hasten the adoption process. Make it as speedy—'

'No, Vicar, please,' her mother held up her hand. 'I want Susie to take her time over an important decision like that.'

'You mean you want her to keep the child? Bring it up?'

Susie was squirming inside. 'I want it adopted, Mum, I told you.'

Both her mother's hands were now squeezing her one. 'When the time comes, we'll see about that, love.' Louise turned to the vicar. 'Since I lost Harold, bringing Susie up has been my life. I've needed her.'

'But your circumstances were different, you were married. For Susie, having this baby adopted would allow you both to return to your normal way of life. Isn't that what you want?'

'Having a baby is a life-changing event and Susie will never be able to forget it. If she agrees to adoption, I'm afraid she might regret it when it's too late. I want her to have time to think about it before she makes up her mind.'

Mr Coyne stood up and moved towards the door. 'You could be right, Mrs Ingram. You know your own mind, but please do encourage Susie to keep on playing her part at St Biddolphe's.'

When her mother had the front door open, he said, 'I'll see you both at the Spring Fair on Saturday. Good day to you.'

Susie collapsed in a tirade of tears. 'He's a sanctimonious prig, I hate him.'

'Susie, love, he means well. Don't upset yourself.'

CHAPTER NINE

Susie woke on the morning of St Biddolphe's Spring Fair to find the sun peeping through her curtains. They had had a week of glorious weather, unseasonably warm for mid-May, but it was forecast to end. The church held its fete days on Saturdays, and her mother always arranged to take the morning off as part of her annual holiday entitlement so that she could help get everything ready.

Today Susie struggled to get out of bed. She needed to be up half an hour earlier than usual so she could help carry the cakes up to the church hall before going to work. Mum would come home again for an hour or so to make a start on the week's washing, but it meant when she walked back to the church to help set up the stalls, she could carry up the last of the cakes. It saved her one return journey and a lot of energy. She thought Mum tried to do far too much.

When she got downstairs her mother was already setting out their breakfast as she listened to the wireless. 'Listen for a moment,' she said as Susie started to speak, 'it's the latest weather forecast.'

'Temperatures will peak this afternoon at up to eighty-two degrees Fahrenheit. The present spell of warm weather is coming to an end and there are likely to be thunderstorms in some areas this evening.'

She switched the set off. 'Let's hope it stays fine for the Spring Fair,' she said.

They were both yawning because they'd been baking until after eleven the night before. Every surface in the small kitchen was filled with trays of scones, gingerbread men and fairy cakes for the refreshment tent, and they'd made large Victoria sponge cakes for the cake stall. The delicious scent had spread all over the house. Still eating, her mother started packing them carefully into six large, flat baskets and covering them with clean tea cloths.

It was a beautiful, fresh and sunny morning as they walked to the church hall, though Mum had insisted Susie take her mackintosh. 'You might need it by this afternoon,' she said. Mum believed in being prepared for everything life could throw at her. Susie caught the bus to work from the church and was glad not to have to spend the morning as well as the afternoon helping out there.

By lunchtime the sky was cloudy and grey and the air hot and heavy. Susie went straight to the field where the fete was to be held, knowing her mother would bring sandwiches for her to share. The field was next to the church and belonged to the Carrington Temple family, relatives of Victoria Curtis.

Sir Cyril Carrington Temple had been knighted for his services to commerce in Victorian times, when he'd founded and built up a large ship repairing business. He'd given the land and part of his fortune to St Biddolphe's to erect the church. He'd also built a substantial family home nearby, surrounded by gardens of ten acres. But the business had been losing money since the end of the Great War.

Sir Cyril had made the mistake of building his home too close to his business and the docks in general. Even while Queen Victoria was on the throne, he'd had to sell off some of his land to survive, and that had allowed the streets of red terraced houses to creep closer and surround it. As times had grown even harder, a further acre and a half had been fenced off and had become the field now rented out for social functions. The house was in a state of disrepair now and far too large for the Dowager Lady Carrington Temple, its sole occupant. She was the childless widow of Sir Cyril's grandson, in her mid-eighties and confined to a wheelchair.

The heir to the baronetcy, a distant cousin by the name of Randolph Bennett, who was said to be managing what was left of the Dowager's fortune, was seeking a buyer for the field. This was causing consternation amongst the members of St Biddolphe's fundraising committees. This might be the last year they could hold their fetes there.

Susie arrived to find the refreshment marquee, the stalls and their awnings all erected, and the stall-holders busy setting out their wares. Her mother, who on this occasion was in charge of the handicraft stall, was laying out the aprons, antimacassars, duchess sets and tray cloths to best effect. The tea cosy Susie had knitted was there, looking a bit misshapen because she'd been running out of wool and had had to cast off too soon with a row of knitting that was too tight. She pulled it into a better shape and hoped that wouldn't be noticed.

'I'm glad you're here,' her mother said. 'I'm hungry and could do with a sit down. Let's go and eat our sandwiches.'

As she led the way to the refreshment tent, there was a vivid flash of lightning followed by a distant growl of thunder.

Susie studied the sky and, ever hopeful, said, 'It might still pass over.' The dry grass crackled under their feet. The hot spell had baked it after a recent mowing.

'There's a lovely smell of hay in here,' Susie said as they went into the refreshment tent and sat at one of the small tables set out near the entrance.

'Gosh,' Louise said, 'it's hot. Would these tables be better outside?'

'Not if we're going to get a storm.'

Cakes of all kinds were set out on the long counter. Many of the ladies baked for the event, and their offerings were labelled home-made. There was a more exotic display of cakes donated from the Curtis factory and these were labelled 'professionally made' rather than 'shop bought'.

The marquee was bustling with activity. Nurse O'Brien had the big brown enamel teapot filled with tea and was handing out steaming cups to the ladies who had been working there for some hours. Miss Maddocks was fiddling with the oil stove behind the counter, trying to bring the huge kettles to the boil again. Miss Thornley was unpacking the cups and saucers and setting them out in readiness, and others were arranging the cakes for sale on the counter. Mrs Curtis was in charge and making sure that everything was done to her satisfaction.

Previously, Susie had been greeted cheerily by the ladies of the congregation, but today they mostly ignored her. Louise sank wearily onto a chair and took their packed lunch from her bag. 'A couple of sandwiches each,' she said.

Susie opened the packet. 'Goody, you've brought the couple

of scones and fairy cakes that got a bit burned.' She was hungry too and began tucking in.

Nurse O'Brien, the rather jolly district nurse, came over with her teapot and said, 'Louise, I've seen a pretty duchess set on your stall, the one with the silver thread embroidery. I want to buy it. Will you put it on one side until I can get there? You'll have a cup of tea with your lunch, won't you?'

Susie got to her feet to fetch two cups and saucers to their table and Nurse O'Brien was filling them when suddenly Mrs Curtis's voice thundered out, 'Susie! You're not eating the sandwiches we've spent all morning making? You must remember they were meant to swell the church funds. I do hope you mean to pay for them.' She stood with her hands on her hips, her face hostile. The clatter of cups and buzz of conversation ceased abruptly. All the ladies turned to watch and listen.

'Here, here,' seconded Mrs Allsop, the rather prim and proper postmistress. 'We need all the money we can raise. The Missionary Fund is very low.'

Louise replied quietly and without heat, 'I made these sandwiches at home especially for Susie and I to share for our lunch, they're cheese and lettuce.'

Mrs Curtis was somewhat discomforted. 'Oh! But Mrs Ingram, you have scones and fairy cakes there, you can't deny that. You must pay for those.'

'No,' Susie said defiantly, 'I don't think we need to. Mum and I were up until eleven o'clock last night baking these. What we're about to eat are a couple that got burned. I was getting tired and left one batch in the oven too long. Mum buttered them at home and I can guarantee the plum jam is our own too.'

Victoria Curtis drew herself up to her full height, threw out her thin chest and said, 'Susie, you're being cheeky! I'm sure your mother will have drawn on church funds to pay for the ingredients, she always does. So they are not entirely yours.'

'Yes, she'll have done that,' Susie admitted. 'The only thing we can afford to give is our labour. But I'm sure you'll have donated all the tea and we are going to drink two cups of that.' She felt for her handbag. 'You charge tuppence a cup, don't you? Let me put the money in now.'

The gasps of horror were hastily subdued and the listening ladies returned to their tasks. Mrs Curtis ignored the proffered coins and turned her back on them to start unpacking the glasses for the lemonade.

Louise dropped her head in her hands.

A small crowd was gathering for the fete, but there were more flashes of lightning and the thunder sounded closer. At two o'clock prompt, the band of the Boys' Brigade struck up a somewhat discordant rendering of Handel's 'Trumpet Voluntary'. An elderly retainer pushed the Dowager Lady Carrington Temple across the uneven grass in her wheelchair, to a small hillock which they'd traditionally used as a dais. She was known locally as Lady Maude, and as this promoted her socially to the peerage, she and Mrs Curtis fully approved.

The vicar introduced her through a loudspeaker. 'I am delighted to tell you that Lady Maude has agreed once again to open our Spring Fair.'

Her voice was weak, and with its geriatric creak was barely audible, but the crowd listened politely and clapped when she finished. The sky was growing darker and the wind was getting up and buffeting at the awnings over the stalls. There was the occasional crack as canvas flapped. Louise hammered the tent pegs on the handicraft stall further in before going behind the counter.

The Boys' Brigade then struck up 'The Skye Boat Song'. The vicar accompanied Lady Maude and her butler on a round of the stalls, where the men tried their luck on the coconut shy and Lady Maude bought a jar of rhubarb jam and a large chocolate cake.

Susie felt uneasy about returning to the refreshment tent, but helping there was the job that had been allotted to her. There were few customers to start with and she stood around with the other helpers, trying to keep out of Mrs Curtis's way. She attended to Lady Maude's group and stood chatting to them when they came in. Susie saw her choose one of the cupcakes she'd made to eat with her tea.

Mrs Allsop pinned Susie down behind the counter. 'I was shocked and dismayed to hear such evil things about you. You were one of us and you've strayed. You must repent, my dear, and ask forgiveness.'

Miss Thornley, a secretary, looked on pityingly. 'I'm sorry for your poor mother. After all she's done for you. You shame her with your conduct. You've let the devil tempt you away from us.'

'And your attitude is so wrong. Answering Mrs Curtis back like that makes it look as though you don't care.'

It was all Susie could do to stop herself shouting that they were a lot of vicious cats and she didn't care what they thought.

'Perhaps it is just as well your father isn't alive to see this. It would grieve him.'

Susie was glad when people had had time to look round the

stalls and began to drift in. Serving the customers gave her and the ladies more to do. She told herself to put what they had said out of her mind.

The sound of thunder was growing ominous and nobody doubted now that a storm was coming. Some left early for home. Midway through the afternoon heavy raindrops began to patter on the canvas roof, then suddenly the heavens opened and rain was dancing down. This caused a stampede into the tea tent because there was nowhere else to shelter and the demand for tea peaked. Susie and the others who were serving were run off their feet. Mrs Curtis was wringing her hands because they were running out of clean cups and saucers and water to refill the kettles.

'Susie,' Mrs Curtis said, 'could you run up to the church hall, take up this tray of dirty cups and saucers and bring down some more water?'

The church hall was next to the church itself and some fifty or sixty yards away. Like everybody else, Susie had left her mackintosh there, and as the rain was now cascading down, nobody wanted to leave the shelter. But Susie felt she had to do as she was bid and she picked up the tray and jogged as fast as the rattling crockery allowed.

The church hall was deserted and, although already damp, she paused just long enough to don her mackintosh and sou'wester before returning with two heavy drums that had been filled with water for this purpose.

She said to Mrs Curtis, 'Somebody needs to be up there to do the washing up.'

'You do it,' she retorted, 'and be as quick as you can. There's a queue building up for tea.' Susie felt Mrs Curtis was picking on her for being cheeky and for naming Danny as the father of her coming child.

Nurse O'Brien said, 'I've loaded the dirty crockery into the flat baskets. It'll be easier for you and there'll be less danger of breakage.'

Susie found she could carry twice the weight of crockery and run faster across the field, but once inside the church hall she had to take off her mac before she could set to work. There was a geyser for hot water over the sink, but after three attempts to light it she gave up and filled the sink with cold water. Then, with all the speed she could muster, she washed up, refilled the baskets and made the return journey to cheers from the waiting queue.

'More water,' Mrs Curtis told her, giving her one empty drum while another basket of dirty crockery was waiting. By now Susie was thoroughly soggy and jogging back and forth couldn't make things much worse. By the time she'd washed up, the kitchen floor in the church hall was covered with muddy foot marks, had pools of water on it and every tea cloth was wet enough to wring out.

As she put on her dripping mac again, it occurred to Susie to put Nurse O'Brien's mac over her arm before picking up the baskets. The nurse was grateful, and was prepared to return with her to do more washing up. 'No,' Mrs Curtis ordered, 'not yet, we need you here to serve.'

So Susie made another trip on her own. By now the rain-swept field with its drenched canvas looked anything but inviting. She could see her mother had some cover under the open-sided tent that protected her stall, and like many of the other stall-holders she was packing up her unsold wares.

The wind was roaring across the field as Susie made the return trip. Suddenly, above the screaming gale she heard several loud cracking noises and saw the awning over the plant and flower stall collapse and bowl down the field, dragging its poles, leaving Mrs Gibson the lady in charge screaming and waving her arms in panic. Flowers were swirling everywhere and plants in small pots were hurtling round powered by the gale. One hit Susie painfully on the leg.

Her mother's handicraft stall was next to the flower stall, but that awning was still pegged firmly to the ground. Louise, wearing her fawn mackintosh, had gone to help Mrs Gibson. Susie knew she was calling to her but her words were snatched by the gale and she waved to her to come. She put down her load and tried to obey but found she could barely move against the force of the driving rain. As she drew nearer she could see fifteen-year-old Julia Curtis in a blue flowered dress lying on the ground.

Louise was bending over her, and when she looked up her face was agonised. 'She must have been hit by a tent pole or something,' she said. There was blood in Julia's hair and it was trickling down her face. Louise was trying to stem it with the tablecloth that had covered the counter.

'Oh my goodness!' Susie said. 'Is there anything I can do?'

'Get help. Have you seen Dr Grant?'

'No, no, I don't think so.'

'He was here earlier. Run to the vicarage and get them to phone for an ambulance.'

'The vicar's in the tea tent. So is his wife.'

'Ask the maid. If she's not there just use the phone yourself.'

Julia was horribly still; she looked dead. Susie felt gripped with a terrible urgency and did as she was told. At the vicarage, she skidded in the gravel at the front door, rang the bell and rattled the letterbox. The place seemed deserted, so without waiting she ran round to the back door, which opened to her touch. She paused. 'Hello? Is there anybody here? Hello?'

An elderly maid in a frilly cap and apron came slowly from the hall looking outraged. 'Whatever is the matter? You can't come in here like this!'

'Please ring for an ambulance,' Susie was puffed. 'There's been an accident on the fete field.'

She followed the maid up the hall to the telephone, but she hesitated for so long that Susie snatched the receiver up. 'Number please,' the operator's voice asked.

'I want an ambulance urgently.'

'Yes,' there was a slight pause, then, 'I'm putting you through to the ambulance station at Mill Road Infirmary. That seems to be the nearest to you.'

Susie got all tied up as she tried to explain where she was and what had happened to Julia, and all the time she could feel cold water trickling down her neck.

She ran back to her mother. 'It's on the way,' she told her. 'Thank goodness for that.'

There were several other people trying to help Julia now. The rain was beginning to ease and others were heading for home.

'How is she?'

'Susie,' Louise said, 'can you go and let Mrs Curtis know what has happened?'

She was reluctant. Mrs Curtis had taken a dislike to her and people were known to blame the messenger for bad news, but she did as she was asked and ran down to the tea tent.

Mrs Curtis was standing at the entrance. 'Whatever has been going on out here?' she demanded. 'All these flowers blowing about! What a waste, and what is that coming into the field? No cars are allowed in here.'

Susie turned to see an ambulance rocking over the rough ground. Someone in the group round Julia was waving it forward. 'I'm afraid there's been an accident.'

'What sort of an accident? There'll be another with that large vehicle sliding on the wet grass, churning up the mud.'

The vicar had come up behind her. 'Can I be of any help?'

'It's Julia,' Susie said. 'She's had a bump on the head. I've phoned for the ambulance from your house, Vicar.'

Mrs Curtis paled. 'What? Oh my goodness! Dear God, please don't take her away from me too.'

She set off towards the ambulance at a brisk pace, and others from the refreshment tent were fanning out in her wake. Louise came towards them still carrying the tablecloth now stained with blood. There were smears of blood on her hands as well as on her cheek and her mackintosh.

Victoria Curtis demanded imperiously, 'What have you done to Julia?'

That made Susie cross. 'Mum has been doing her best to help her.'

Louise said quietly, 'She's in safe hands now. They're going to take her to Mill Road Infirmary.'

'But I don't understand. What's happened to my daughter? What's the matter with her?' Mrs Curtis's face had turned paper white, raindrops were running down her cheeks and her new permanent wave was a frizzing wet mat against her scalp.

Louise took her arm. 'Julia was hit on the head when the canopy over the flower stall blew down. The doctors will explain what her injuries are. Don't you want to go in the ambulance with her?'

Victoria Curtis was visibly sagging at the knees, and it was Louise who caught her considerable weight and lowered her to the wet grass.

'Oh my goodness!' The vicar was wringing his hands in distress. 'What a shock for her. She's fainted.'

Louise said, 'Susie, please ask the ambulance driver to come down here and pick her up.'

CHAPTER TEN

WITH THE AMBULANCE MAKING its way back to the gate, Susie said, 'Mum, you did well. You kept your head when the rest of us were falling apart.'

'Yes indeed,' agreed the vicar, 'your mother always knows what to do in an emergency, such a sensible woman.'

Nurse O'Brien said, 'Louise, you're wet through, come into the tent and have a cup of hot tea.'

'I could do with one,' she said wearily.

Susie sat down with her. 'We both need to get home and change our clothes,' she said. 'I'm cold, and Mum, you must be too.'

Louise shivered. 'Yes, I'm shattered.'

'Yes,' agreed the vicar, 'very wise. You two get off home as soon as you've finished your tea. You'll be able to come back this evening, Mrs Ingram, won't you? Just to count the takings and make up the accounts. Say eight o'clock at the vicarage?'

Susie took hold of Louise's hand and said firmly, 'No! I think Mum has done more than her share towards your Spring Fair, and what's more, so have I. Couldn't somebody else help you count the takings for once? They can't be very great after this. It's been a disaster, a complete washout.'

'Oh my dear! Indeed it has, and a very great pity. We are

93

very grateful to your mother. She does so much for us that we've come to rely on her. But she is the church treasurer.'

'There is a limit to human strength,' Susie said quietly. 'She will not be coming back tonight. Come on, Mum,' she pulled her to her feet, 'I want to get you home before you catch cold. We'll have to stop at the church hall so you can wash that blood off your face before you walk through the streets, or people will think you've murdered someone.'

Louise pulled herself together. 'Some of the unsold stock on the handicraft stall was damp when I packed it. Could somebody make sure it's all dry before it's stored for the Summer Fete? Otherwise it may spoil.'

'I'll see to that,' Nurse O'Brien said, 'don't you worry about it.'

Susie pulled a face. She'd recognised some of the antimacassars that had remained unsold through several of St Biddolphe's events. 'Goodbye.'

'Thank you both very much for your help today,' Mr Coyne said.

When they reached home the house was cold and the back yard full of the wet washing Louise had done that morning. 'Go upstairs and put on dry clothes,' Susie said. She put a match to the fire Louise had laid ready and followed her upstairs to do the same.

The next morning Louise was up early to go to church, but noticed all was quiet in Susie's room. She put her head round the door. Susie was still snuggled under her eiderdown. 'It's Sunday, love. We'll be late if—'

Susie turned on her back and opened her eyes. 'Mum, I've had enough. I keep saying I don't want any more to do with St

Biddolphe's but you keep persuading me to carry on. But after yesterday, enough is enough. I'm not going to church. Not this morning or any other morning. Why should I go there to be insulted? Why should you?'

'But we always go to morning service, we always have. It's a family tradition.'

'Family routine, you mean, and from now on I'm changing it, church is off. I'm having no more of it, and,' Susie said, 'if I was you, I wouldn't put up with it either.'

Louise was at a loss. 'Your father was the curate at St Biddolphe's. It's hard to turn my back on all those years. It's just that some of the ladies have turned against me.'

'It's me they've turned against really, but it makes it worse that they're including you in this too.'

'It's not all of them,' Louise said, 'it's just an inner clique that feels so holy that they think nothing like this could ever happen to them.'

'I wish it would.'

'Susie, don't take it so to heart. What would your father say?'

'He'd say those women are an insufferable lot of old cats, and as for the Reverend Mr Thomas Coyne, he's a pompous ass.'

'He means well, Susie.'

'He's putting on you, Mum, but you must make up your own mind as to what you do. You work harder for St Biddolphe's than anyone else, and you have a full-time job.'

'But St Biddolphe's has done more for us than it's done for other families; more for you, Susie.'

'And I'm very grateful, particularly for my secretarial school fees. I know you're grateful too, but yesterday Mrs Curtis was trying to put you down and Mrs Allsop was backing her up. They must want to get rid of me or why would they be so nasty? For the last seventeen years, you have done all you can to repay St Biddolphe's for the support they've given you, but that counts for nothing now I've transgressed. Now we both have to be punished.'

'It'll blow over, this sort of thing always does. I'll go to church on my own then.'

But Louise didn't like being alone. First Rebecca had refused to come and now Susie; it made her feel she'd been a failure as a mother. Martha was still going to church of course, but Bert liked to have a lie-in on Sunday mornings, so she went to the evening service and took him with her.

Louise really missed having her daughters beside her in church because the atmosphere was not as friendly as it had once been. Mrs Curtis cut her dead, which she'd expected, but so did several of the others. Only Miss Maddocks and Nurse O'Brien wished her a cheery good morning and paused to pass the time of day.

Louise hardly heard the sermon; she was musing about the ladies who made up the larger part of the congregation. For the most part, they were her generation, spinsters and widows, made so by the Great War. They'd all benefited from the modern practice of training girls for employment outside the home so they could support themselves. On the whole, she thought the spinsters tended to have advanced further in their chosen careers. They had not had a break in employment for marriage and motherhood, and they had not been left with dependent children. So they were managing rather better than the widows, but they had all suffered one way or another.

When the vicar came to the notices, he spoke of the disastrous events of the spring fete and asked for prayers to be said for the Curtis family and young Julia Curtis who had received a head injury needing ten stitches that would keep her in hospital for another day or two.

When the service ended, Louise was ignored again by the ladies who used to speak to her. Susie was right, it was hurtful.

The following Sunday, Louise made up her mind to go to St Mark's instead. It wasn't much further to walk and the church itself was quite handsome, but she didn't know anybody. Nobody spoke to her at all except the vicar as he stood at the door to shake the hands of his congregation as they were leaving.

'Welcome to our church. I haven't seen you here before, have I?' His handshake was firm. 'Have you just moved into the neighbourhood?' Louise felt she had to say no to that. 'I hope we see you again,' he said with a pleasant smile.

Louise returned to St Biddolphe's the following Sunday. She'd decided she was too set in her ways to change now, and anyway, Miss Maddocks was organising the Summer Fete and had asked her to help. She couldn't refuse Miss Maddocks, because she'd done so much for her when the girls were young.

CHAPTER ELEVEN

As MAY TURNED INTO June, Louise was encouraging Susie to spend more time next door with Martha, because she was very much looking forward to the birth of her baby. Susie, on the other hand, was not looking forward to motherhood. The weeks were dragging in one sense but speeding by in another. She wanted to get this maternity business behind her, but she didn't like to see her abdomen getting larger and her condition more obvious. She did her best to hide it, because she had to go on working for as long as possible. According to her mother, she was keeping her figure longer than most, but it was summer and she couldn't wear heavy jumpers that might have disguised it.

Martha gave her the most help. 'The secret,' she said, 'is not to wear maternity smocks, they draw attention to your bump. You need summer dresses with full skirts and the waistline in the normal place, but made several inches wider than normal. Then, as your baby grows past your waist, it can be accommodated, and though you may look as though you're putting on weight, it's the sort of weight you'd gain if you ate too much. I'll make you two new summer dresses, and next year we can take them in at the waist so you can wear them again.'

Louise did most of the sewing for Susie because Martha just

didn't have the time or energy to do much now, and she found Martha's designs did help a lot.

Louise was delighted to hear that Martha and Becky were continuing to stay in contact. She was hearing more about her middle daughter than she had for years. Since she had spent that week with them in March, Martha and Becky had seemed closer.

Martha had been off colour in early July, and was getting better when she came round excitedly waving a letter. 'It's from Becky,' she said. 'She's written to say that the girl who shares her flat has landed a job in repertory theatre in Leeds, and at the moment she has the flat to herself. She's invited me and Bert to spend a week with her and have a holiday.'

Louise was pleased for her. 'It'll do you good to have a change of air. Is Bert able to go with you?'

'Yes, I've just phoned him, he says his brother Edward will stand in for him. I'm thrilled, I've always wanted to go to Scarborough. Becky is doing shows on the pier again all this summer. She loves it there.'

'Will you be all right to travel?'

'Of course, Mum. My baby won't be born until October.'

Becky came in her car to collect them while Louise and Susie were at work. 'It is really too far for her to drive there and back in one day,' Louise worried. 'We could have put her up for one night and it would have been nice to see her again.'

They had a postcard from Martha during the week saying they were having a fine time, though the weather wasn't all that good, but Becky brought them back the following week looking suntanned and healthy. 'It was marvellous,' Martha said. 'I thoroughly enjoyed it and I've never felt better.'

Bert told them that apart from his honeymoon in the Lake District it was the best holiday he'd ever had, and he thought the bracing sea air had done Martha good.

A few weeks later when they had a hot spell, Liverpool felt airless and sticky, and Louise wrote to Becky telling her that Martha no longer looked as well as she had when she'd returned from her holiday. Becky answered immediately, saying she was writing to Martha inviting her to come and stay for the rest of the summer and have a complete rest. She asked her to persuade Bert to let Martha come.

'It won't be much fun being left on my own,' he said, but he was persuaded because he thought it would be good for his wife. To make the journey as easy and comfortable as possible for her sister, Becky came to collect her again. The arrangement was that Martha would come back to spend the last three weeks of her pregnancy at home.

Martha sent postcards and said she was living the life of a lady, that Becky wouldn't let her lift a finger. Bert usually had his meals at the shop with his family, and said he was missing Martha and counting the days until she came back. On most Sundays he drove his van over to Scarborough and returned on Monday. 'It's worth this long separation,' he said, 'because Martha is feeling really fit.'

But two days before Becky was due to bring her back, a frantic Bert came knocking on their door at eight o'clock one night to say Becky had just rung him with the news that Martha had gone into labour three weeks early. She'd taken her to the local maternity hospital where Martha had had a baby boy with the very healthy birth weight of seven and a half pounds.

Bert drove to Scarborough to see them the next day, and returned to report that they would have to stay in hospital for the usual two weeks, and that they had decided to call him Jonathon Joseph, to be known as Jonjo.

When they were discharged, Becky drove them home and Louise and Susie rushed out into the street to see them moments after the car drew up outside. Bert rushed out too and Louise saw tears of joy in his eyes as he greeted his wife and new son. He thanked Becky profusely for looking after them so well.

Louise thought it a miracle that Martha had finally given birth to such a strong, healthy baby because she still looked pale and fragile.

CHAPTER TWLEVE

SUSIE REACHED THE EIGHTH month of her pregnancy before her boss invited her to his office with another woman as a chaperone and asked her outright if she was pregnant. He said her work hadn't been noticeably affected but that he had to give her a week's notice. No woman should be working full time in her condition.

Susie asked if she might return after she'd had the baby, but he gave no firm commitment. 'You can apply if you want to but it will depend on the needs of the business.'

'You've done very well,' Louise told her when she got home. 'It had to happen sooner or later. You'll only have three weeks to go when you stop work and you'll need to rest more by then.' Inevitably, she spent more time next door with Martha and Jonjo.

Louise could see that Martha was clearly delighted with her new baby, and she and Jonjo continued to thrive. It seemed that Martha was settled and content and would provide Susie with the best possible company during her last few weeks.

When Louise received a letter from Becky, she felt a flurry of excitement and handed the letter to Susie. Becky wrote: *I would like to introduce you to somebody really special to me. Can I bring him to meet you and the family one Sunday? Max has a car and will drive us over.*

'She wants to marry him,' Susie said immediately. 'If he was just another boyfriend she wouldn't bother bringing him here. I can't wait to see what he looks like. I bet he's rich.'

Louise invited them both to come to Sunday lunch the following weekend, but she was a little concerned. 'Becky calls him a man friend and he has a car – something tells me he's much older than she is.'

She ordered a generous joint of beef from Bert, and on the day had it in the oven with a Yorkshire pudding and roast potatoes in good time, with an apple pie to follow. She and Susie were dressed in their best, Martha and Bert had come round to help, and they had the table set for lunch for six when the car drew up in front of the house. It was a big luxury car and Louise found she was right, Max Goodwin looked twice Becky's age. He was a figure of authority and had the veneer of self-confidence that only comes with power and status.

He presented her with a large bunch of hothouse flowers which sent Susie scurrying round both their house and Martha's looking for large vases. Becky gave her mother chocolates and a bottle of sherry, and Martha had to hunt through the kitchen cupboards for their rarely used sherry glasses.

'You look different,' Louise told Becky.

In her heather-coloured wool suit and high heels, she could have graced the cover of a fashion magazine.

'Absolutely glamorous,' Susie said.

In Louise's experience no young girl could afford such expensive clothes, and she certainly looked as though she'd spent a lot of time and money in beauty parlours. She felt shocked and reduced to a bag of nerves. All her fears for Becky rushed back to her. Was she living with this man? The very thought upset her. If so, she could easily end up in the same condition as Susie. Whatever was happening to her family?

Max appeared relaxed and carried the conversation. He told them he had a new job managing an engineering business, making parts for motor cars, and that he lived on the Wirral. Bert was telling him about his shop and they seemed to be getting on well together.

So how had Max met Becky if she was living in Scarborough? Louise knew she was not being her usual hospitable self, but it didn't seem to matter as her daughters had taken over, pouring the sherry into ill-matched glasses. Later, Bert carved the joint while Martha and Susie put the meal on the table. Everything was beautifully cooked and Max congratulated her on the apple pie and custard, saying how much he enjoyed it. He seemed to be trying to charm her.

Afterwards, Max and Becky kept Louise in the living room while the others cleared away. Bert and Martha went home and took Susie with them, leaving Louise with the feeling it had been arranged to happen like this, and that filled her with trepidation. Becky made them a cup of tea and opened the box of chocolates. 'Mum,' she said, 'Max and I would like to be married.'

Louise's mouth fell open in shock and she couldn't stop the words coming out. 'But you hardly know him!'

'I do, Mum, we've known each other a long time.'

She had to ask, 'You're not in the same position as Susie? You're not pregnant?'

Becky laughed. 'No, no, nothing like that, of course not. Mum, you're embarrassing Max. Martha has been married for five years, isn't it my turn now?'

'It doesn't work like that. If there's no hurry, I really feel you should wait a little and get to know—'

'This is probably my fault,' Max said in soothing tones. 'I'm sorry if you think I'm rushing Becky into marriage. We met in London three years ago, but I've not had a settled life since. The company I work for has moved me about, to Middlesbrough and then Leeds and I've spent all this summer in Australia helping to set up another small factory.'

'Max and I have been kept apart by our work,' Becky said. 'I've never had a job that's lasted more than a few months so I'm always on the move. We both want a more settled existence.'

'I asked for a permanent position,' Max said, 'and I've been give charge of this factory near Chester. I have a home on the Wirral. I know I'm a lot older than Becky, but I'm established and can now give her a comfortable life.'

'How old are you? I'm sorry, that sounds a little rude, but this has come as a shock.'

'Not rude. These are things you need to know. I'm forty-four and I don't want to wait any longer before settling down. Becky and I suit each other, really we do, and we've talked it through half a dozen times.'

'But Becky, I thought you were keen on a stage career? You won't be carrying on with that?'

'No, Mum, I had to give it up. I wasn't making much progress.'

'I thought it had really taken off. But the age difference . . .'

She turned to Max, 'Becky will want to be out and about, while you're talking of settling down.'

'I know she's giving up her youth for me, but she says it's what she wants to do. I'll take great care of her, Mrs Ingram. Please give us your blessing.'

Louise sighed; she knew there was no way she could make them wait for marriage. How could she say she didn't trust her daughter to make long term decisions and get them right? Or that she felt very wary of this man whom she'd just met? 'It feels rushed,' she faltered, 'though I know it isn't about how I feel. Marriage is such an important step.'

'It is,' Becky said with a touch of resentment, 'and I'm ready for it. It's my life and it's what I want to do, Mum. It's what we both want to do.'

Louise looked from one to the other. Becky's lips were straightening into a hard line. 'You might just as well say you're happy about it because we're going to do it anyway. We've been living together off and on for the past three years, Mum, and getting married is Max's way of putting things on a formal basis to please you and the world in general. Don't you agree it is to my advantage?'

Max gasped, and seemed almost overcome with embarrassment.

'You've been living together? After all I've tried to teach you?'

'I love Becky. It was love at first sight.'

Louise knew Harold would be shocked and so would the congregation of St Biddolphe's. She felt somehow she was to blame, she hadn't been a dutiful mother to Becky. She said with a touch of irritation, 'You've always wanted your own way with everything, and you know exactly how to get it.'

Max's dark eyes beseeched her as he said gently, 'I'd feel happier if you'd give us your blessing.'

Louise was not far from tears. 'Do you care? Well, if you've already been living together, I am happy that you're getting married.' She didn't trust Becky and it hurt that she'd thrust her wedding arrangements on her in this way. But it shouldn't surprise her; Becky had been going her own way since she'd been fourteen.

The wedding came a fortnight later and, under the circumstances, Louise welcomed it. This time, she, her family and St Biddolphe's had nothing to do with it; Becky and her husband-to-be made all the arrangements.

On the day, Louise, Bert and her two daughters went on the bus down to the Pier Head to catch the ferry. Max Goodwin sent a hire car to meet them at Woodside in Birkenhead, and it took them to the Chester Register Office where the ceremony was to be held.

Louise wanted to meet Max's family in order to get to know him better, but there were only six guests waiting with the bridal couple in the register office when they arrived. Becky looked beautiful in a pale cream dress of mid-calf length with flowers plaited into her hair. All the men wore dark lounge suits and looked very smart indeed. Max introduced them just as they were being summoned to another room where the ceremony would take place, so Louise took in very little about the guests.

Martha smiled happily and clung to Bert's arm. He had taken her out and bought her a smart new winter coat and dress for the occasion, now that Jonjo had been born and her figure had returned to normal.

'I feel like a bloated whale,' Susie whispered, 'and a country cousin in this gathering.' She was wearing her best coat and really looked very nice, but she had to keep it open as it wouldn't quite meet across her swollen abdomen. Louise was ill at ease and thought Susie was too. She'd bought herself a new hat, but it wasn't in the same class as those worn by Max's friends.

To Louise it didn't seem like a real wedding, and it was over very quickly. A few photographs were taken on the steps outside and then they were driven to Max's home, where he told her he'd lived for the last twenty years. That was another shock – it was a near mansion, ringed with tall trees for privacy. None of her family had ever lived in such a grand house as this; Louise had never been inside a finer one. They were received by two maids dressed in black with frilly aprons and caps, one of whom held a tray and offered a glass of sherry. Louise was shocked again to find two of the guests were his sons from a previous marriage, which Becky hadn't even mentioned to her. 'John and Alan,' she was told.

'What happened to their mother,' Louise asked Becky.

'Divorced,' she whispered, which didn't make Louise feel any more optimistic about this marriage.

There was a splendid buffet lunch set out in the dining room, of lobster and prawns, cold chicken and ham, with several sorts of salads and other delicacies Louise didn't recognise. There was also a grand three-tier wedding cake and champagne.

'We're motoring down to Torquay tomorrow to start our two-week honeymoon,' Max told them. 'We shall tour along the south coast and spend the last few days in London. We'll have a good time, won't we, Becky?'

Louise thought he loved Becky, his eyes full of affection, following her round the room, but she wasn't so sure about Becky's feelings for him. She spent a lot of time laughing with his sons who were nearer her own age, but it seemed neither now lived at home.

When Becky showed them round the house, Martha and Susie gasped at the size of the rooms and the splendour of the furnishings. 'It's a gorgeous house, Becky, you are lucky to be living here.'

When they were leaving, Becky kissed her mother and sisters and said, 'You see, you needn't worry about me. I'm not likely to want for anything.'

'I wish you every happiness,' Louise said, as Max shook her hand.

In the hire car going back to the ferry, Bert said, 'Your Becky has got herself a good meal ticket there. Lucky girl, she's done all right.'

Louise had thought Martha had done very well for herself by marrying Bert, who earned enough to provide comfort, but what Becky had now was luxury.

CHAPTER THIRTEEN

October 1933

LOUISE WAS CONCERNED THAT Susie's pregnancy was now at term and she'd still not made any effort to put a layette together for her baby. When she'd suggested they go to the shops to start buying napkins and baby clothes, Susie had said, 'I'm going to have it adopted, so there's no point.'

'You're going to give birth here, Susie, in your own bedroom. The baby will immediately need napkins and vests and nightgowns, and somewhere to sleep.'

She shrugged. 'Martha's got loads of stuff next door. She'll lend us what we need, won't she?'

'How can she when she needs it for Jonjo?'

Martha was taking more interest in the coming child than its mother, and couldn't understand Susie not wanting to keep it. She said to Louise, 'Jonjo's growing so fast, some of his first size things are already too small. I've washed and aired them so they'll be ready for the new arrival. Just say the word and I'll bring round what I no longer need.'

'Susie's not looking forward to the birth.'

'Mum, she's still grieving for Danny. Every day I have to make her come round at lunchtime or she wouldn't bother to eat. She's spending too much time alone, she seems depressed.'

Susie was getting up late, but she always cleaned the house, reset the fire and brought in the coals. Then she did any washing that was needed and prepared a meal for when her mother came home from work. Since she could no longer earn her living, she felt it was the least she could do, and she knew her mother appreciated it. Once Susie had finished her chores, she lay on the sofa in the living room, reading or listening to the wireless.

She hated being pregnant, felt lethargic, ungainly and ugly. Mum kept giving her shopping lists, Martha repeatedly invited her to take trips to the local park or the shops with her and Jonjo, but she was ashamed of meeting people she knew now her pregnant state was so obvious.

The ladies of the church and the girls she knew from school or work eyed her abdomen with horror and revulsion. Susie knew she was the subject of scandalised gossip in the neighbourhood and was considered a fallen woman who had brought disgrace on her family. She wanted this whole awful business over and done with, so she could get on with her life. She was dreading the birth itself, but was frustrated and restless when she went three days over her dates. 'Don't worry,' the midwife told her, 'the baby will come when it's ready.'

Before she went off to work one morning, her mother brought her a cup of tea in bed and told her to rest. Susie enjoyed the luxury of an extra hour in bed, but today she'd woken early and had backache. As she pulled herself up to drink her tea she felt her first contraction. 'Mum,' she called, but she heard the front door click shut behind her. She'd gone to work.

Susie's heart was thudding and she lay back, scared now it seemed the waiting time was over. She drank her tea and heard Bert drive off to the shop. It was such a long time before she had another pain that she wondered if she'd been mistaken, but when it came it left her shaking. Thank goodness Martha was only next door. She pulled on the clothes she'd worn yesterday, pushed her feet into her slippers and ran to hammer on Martha's door.

'Come in,' she said, 'I'm just dressing Jonjo.'

'This is it! I'm in labour. I've had two terrible pains.'

'If you've only had two, there's plenty of time. Come and have some breakfast with me.'

Susie doubled up as another pain came. 'I couldn't eat a thing,' she gasped. 'I want you to ring for the midwife.'

'Thank goodness Bert had the phone put in,' Martha said as she went to do just that.

Susie was persuaded to have tea and toast, though she was growing scared and impatient. Every minute seemed like five as she watched Martha feeding Jonjo. The midwife came and seemed thoroughly relaxed and jolly, wasting more time playing with Jonjo and talking about the weather. It seemed an age before she said, 'Come on, let's get you home to your own bedroom and I'll take a look at you.' Martha and Jonjo followed her in.

After she examined Susie, the midwife said, 'Not for a few hours yet. I've got two new babies I need to check on, so I'll do that this morning and come back later. I'll give you something to help with the pain now and your sister will stay with you, won't she?'

'Yes, oh yes,' Martha said, 'I'll leave Jonjo here with you

while I go next door to fetch a few baby clothes.'

'Can you clear some of these things off the dressing table,' the midwife asked. 'I'll need somewhere to put my stuff out, and I want you to see there's plenty of hot water on hand.'

'Yes, I know what to do,' Martha assured her. The midwife helped her spread a rubber sheet over Susie's mattress and some old newspapers on top of that, before making up the bed again.

'Right, so everything is organised. I wouldn't go to bed straight away, Susie, you'd be better pottering around downstairs for another hour or two. I'll be back in plenty of time.'

For Susie, it was the longest, most uncomfortable morning she'd ever lived through. She was afraid the baby might be born before the midwife returned and could sense Martha's anxiety about that too. Jonjo, who usually was no trouble at all, seemed to sense that all was not normal, and was irritable and demanding of Martha's attention.

'The pains are getting worse,' Susie said, bending double each time. 'How much longer can this go on, it's terrible?'

'I'll do boiled eggs and soldiers for lunch,' Martha said, 'is that all right with you?'

'I don't care. I'm not hungry.' But she managed to eat when Martha set it out on the table.

'I think I'll go to bed when I've finished this tea,' Susie said, but before that, both were relieved to see the midwife propping her bike up on the kerb outside the front door.

'I'll take Jonjo home to put him down for his rest,' Martha said when she let her in, 'and I need to make preparations for our evening meal.'

The midwife wanted to examine her again so Susie pulled

herself upstairs to her bed. 'You've made good progress,' she was told.

'But how much longer will it go on?' Susie gasped. 'This is awful.' She was sweating now.

'Not all that much, later on this afternoon I should think. I'll unpack the gas and air machine, that should help you.' For Susie the afternoon passed in a blur of pains that grew steadily worse.

'It isn't called labour for nothing,' the midwife smiled at her. 'Everything's going well, it's all perfectly normal.'

Martha returned, having left Jonjo with a neighbour so she could help the midwife. It had gone four o'clock before the baby was born. Susie heard the mewl of the newborn baby and lifted her head to see it, but failed to focus on anything.

'It's a girl,' the midwife told her, 'a good size, not too big and not too small, I'll weigh her in a minute. She looks healthy. Yes, a perfect little girl.'

Susie lay back against the pillows feeling exhausted, but thanking the powers that be that it was at last over. A towel-wrapped bundle was pushed into her arms.

'Say hello to your mother.' Susie shrank from it but it continued to lie against her. 'What are you going to call her?'

'I don't know.' Susie could feel the baby moving and used one finger to edge the towel back so she could see her face.

'It was going to be Daniel if it was a boy, wasn't it?' Martha craned forward to look. 'You could call her Danielle if you don't think it sounds too French. Gosh, she's got red hair like her father!'

'She's pretty,' Susie said with wonder in her voice.

'A very pretty baby,' the midwife agreed. 'Let's have her back.' Susie's arms tightened round the bundle. 'Just to weigh her, you want to know her birth weight, don't you? Let's see now, yes, I think that's seven pounds two ounces. Come and check it, Martha, it's not easy to read this spring balance.'

'Yes, seven pounds two ounces.'

'Excellent. I expect the new mother could do with a cup of tea, what about making one for us all?'

'I could certainly do with one,' Martha said, and went to put the kettle on.

Susie lay back looking at her newborn daughter in wonder. 'She's just like Danny,' she said, and her arms tightened round her in a joyful hug.

Louise came home from work to find the midwife packing her equipment onto her bike and about to leave. Martha was seeing her out. 'It's all over, Mum,' Martha's smile was radiant. 'Susie's had a little girl, seven pounds two ounces and she's thrilled with her.'

'Both are well,' the midwife told her, 'no problems. Susie's tired but happy.'

'The baby's got Danny's red hair,' Martha chortled. 'Go up and see her. I've made enough stew for us all, so don't worry about dinner. I want to fetch Jonjo home before I put the potatoes on.'

Louise was delighted and her step was light as she ran upstairs. Her daughter was propped up on extra pillows. 'Susie, I hear all went well. I bet you're glad that's behind you. I must have a look at the new arrival. Martha says she's got Danny's red hair.' The midwife had emptied a drawer of Susie's underwear, put it on the floor and made up a cot with bedding

Martha had brought round. Louise went to look at the sleeping baby. 'She's lovely.'

She smiled at Susie and saw that her lip was quivering. 'Oh, Mum, what a fool I've been.' Louise sat on her bed and put her arms round her in a hug. Tears streamed down Susie's face. 'Thank you. You stopped me giving her away.'

'Most mothers bond with their babies, love, and I was sure you would. It's human nature.'

'She's like Danny – how could I give his daughter away?'

'She's certainly got the Curtis red hair,' Louise smiled. 'One in the eye for Mrs Curtis.'

'Oh, I'm really going to love showing her round the congregation.'

Over the next few weeks, Susie felt totally wrapped up in her baby. Fiona Curtis called round and brought her brother Jamie to see the new arrival. 'The spitting image of Danny,' they laughed, 'that won't please Mum. What are you going to call her?'

'I can't decide between Rosanna and Rosina, which do you think is the prettier?'

'Does it matter?' Jamie asked. 'You'll probably call her Rosie anyway. Or plain Rose.'

'I like Rosanna,' Fiona decided, and Susie thought that perhaps she did too. 'We've brought her a present.'

'Thank you.' Susie took off the gift wrapping. It was an expensive-looking dress and was far too big.

'Gosh, it won't fit her for months,' Jamie said.

'It's lovely and she'll grow into it.'

'We thought pink would be safe for a baby girl, but we never thought about her hair being red,' Fiona said. 'Do you want me to change it for a different colour? They had white and yellow.'

'No,' Susie shook her head. 'It will look well on her. I like it.'

CHAPTER FOURTEEN

ONCE SUSIE WAS ALLOWED out of bed, she found her day filled with baby care, and was very glad Martha was next door offering help and advice. In addition, she was knitting matinee jackets and bootees as fast as she could. Louise was crocheting a shawl for her, and Martha was giving her vests and nightgowns, some of which were blue and a little masculine, but Susie didn't think that mattered – it provided a wardrobe for Rosanna and meant she could have clean clothes when she needed them.

Susie felt guilty that she'd not welcomed the baby and made preparations for her. She had to borrow Jonjo's pram to take the baby out until Bert bought her a second-hand one from one of his customers.

Soon, she began to feel guilty about what she was accepting from her family. Without her wage, money was short and the country was in a depression. She felt she ought to return to work. When she asked Martha if she'd look after Rosanna while she did so, she said, 'Of course I will. You know I'd love to, and with Jonjo I'll feel I have a proper family.'

Susie applied to the company she'd previously worked for but not with any great hope. Her bosses had reacted with shock and condemnation to find her working so late in a hidden pregnancy. She received a brusque note in return saying they had no vacancies at present. The number of unemployed in the city was growing, and work was no longer easy to get. Susie was disappointed that her plan was not working out, and it rankled that when she occasionally met one of the ladies of the congregation, they would not acknowledge a polite greeting.

On a Saturday early in December St Biddolphe's held its Christmas Fete with an Advent Service in the church the following day.

Susie said she wasn't going to help but on Friday night she was up baking with her mother until late. Louise had taken the Saturday morning off and gone to the church hall early in the morning. She took a sandwich with her for lunch, leaving Susie to do the weekend shopping. She was taking pleasure now in bathing and dressing Rosanna to look her best before pushing her out in the pram, though she was reluctant to put a bonnet over Rosanna's red hair. She took her shopping bags and had completed the list her mother had left her and turned for home before she met Fee, Jamie and Julia, who still had a slight scar on her forehead.

'We've been sent to help in the church hall,' Jamie said, 'is that where you're going?'

'No, my face doesn't fit any more. Not since they heard about Rosie.'

'No, she's caused a bit of a rumpus, hasn't she?' Jamie peered into the pram; he'd not seen her until now. 'My goodness,' he laughed, 'you're right, there's no mistaking she's a Curtis. She's got red hair.'

'Like Danny,' Susie said.

'I knew you'd call her Rosie,' Jamie smiled.

'But Rosanna is nicer for formal occasions. She's not asleep, is she?' Fiona always made a fuss of the baby. 'Can I lift her out?'

Nothing pleased Susie more; Rosie was a good-tempered baby and she enjoyed showing her off.

'How d'you like being a mother?' Fiona asked. 'I bet it's a full-time job.'

'I love every minute of caring for her, but I'm looking for another job. I need the money.' She filled them in with all the details.

'I bet you miss Danny. He would have taken care of you both.'

'Perhaps Dad could give you a job?' Jamie said. 'He has no trouble finding jobs for us. Perhaps you should ask him?'

'He said he'll be bringing some stuff down to the church hall. I say, wouldn't it be great to take Rosie to the church hall now and show her off to the ladies? They'll all be there.'

'Our mother won't, she'll come later on when the work is finished,' Jamie said, 'then she'll rearrange the display of toys and put the two dolls she's dressed in the front of the stall.'

'Nobody could believe she isn't Danny's baby, not with this hair,' Fee said. 'They've been saying quite nasty things about you. You'd get your own back on the old fogies. Make them eat their words, so to speak. Why not?'

That felt like balm to Susie. She giggled with them. To have fun with her friends took her back to her carefree years. 'Come on,' Fiona urged, 'let's do it.' She put Rosie back in her pram and took over the pushing of it. Jamie took Susie's arm.

As a noisy, laughing group, they had reached the gates of St Biddolphe's when Susie saw the Curtis family car pull in ahead of them. Their father and older brother Jack got out and opened up the boot, where she saw a stack of three commercial trays of fancy cakes.

'Hello, Susie, how are you?' William Curtis asked.

'Dad,' Fiona said, 'could you find a job for Susie?'

His kindly gaze met Susie's. 'Surely with a new baby you won't have time to work?'

'I don't want to be a burden on my mother,' she said.

'Well, perhaps . . . You all seemed to be having fun, what was the joke?'

Jamie spoke up. 'The ladies of the church aren't being fair to Susie. They're spreading malicious scandal. They're saying they don't believe Danny is the father of her baby, that she's had other boyfriends. Dad, just take a look at the baby and see what you think.'

Susie lifted her out of the pram, and as Rosie gurgled and smiled up at them, she watched Mr Curtis's expression as he stared at the child. His face was stern and his mouth opened in surprise, bewilderment and concern. His children were not laughing any more.

Fiona said, 'One glance will tell them they're wrong. That Mum is wrong.'

Jamie said, 'They're wrong, aren't they?'

It took William Curtis a few moments to recover. He took a deep breath. 'Susie, I don't doubt that you and Danny have given me my first grandchild. It's not just her colouring, she's very like Fiona was as a baby. She's a Curtis through and through.' That was balm to Susie's feelings. 'But,' he went on, 'there will be no gain to you or your child by facing the ladies and making them admit they're wrong.'

'It would give me satisfaction,' she said grimly.

'I know, but they'll like you even less. You'll start up a whole new wave of gossip about yourself, the baby and your mother. It would be wiser to carry on as you have been doing. Stay away from them and find your interests elsewhere.'

Susie was reluctant to give up. 'I just want to prove—'

'No, Susie, you'll make matters worse. Here, Fiona, carry in this Christmas cake for me. Come on, Jamie, help me carry in these trays of fancies. Jack, you can see Susie and her baby home, and make sure she gets into no trouble.'

As Susie slid Rosie back in her pram, she heard Jamie say, 'We thought it would be a joke, a bit of a laugh,' and watched him and Fiona being herded through the gates of St Biddolphe's.

Jack laughed and got the pram moving in the right direction. 'Dad seems to think Jamie has a childish sense of humour and I'm more reliable. Fiona is your friend and wants to stay loyal. They feel sorry for you and Danny, we all do. Life has played a devilish trick on you.'

'It has.'

'Nobody likes to be proved wrong, and after Danny's tragic death, it would make the church ladies feel foolish and spiteful for repeating gossip like that about you.'

Susie took a deep breath, 'It looks as though he doesn't want to give me a job.'

'Susie, he didn't say that, he said "perhaps". Don't turn against us.'

'Sorry, I'm not. You're the only friends I have now.'

'We'd all give anything to have Danny back and things as they were. But Dad is usually right about things like this; it would only get people's backs up.'

*

Over the following weeks, Susie scanned the newspapers for jobs for which she'd be thought suitable, and found there were very few close to her home. There were a few in the centre of the city and she applied for all those, even though it meant she'd have further to travel and more to pay in bus fares. She did manage to get two interviews but no job.

'The problem is,' Louise told her, 'that it's hard for anybody to get a job. You can see the men out of work hanging about gossiping on street corners. They all desperately need work.'

Susie remembered Danny's father saying that perhaps he could find a job for her, and came to the conclusion that he was her best chance of finding work.

She told Martha of her plan. 'I could ring his secretary and say I'd like to speak to him, and ask if a time could be arranged for me to go to his office. I wouldn't take Rosie. I need to look as business-like as possible.'

'I'll look after her,' Martha said. 'You say he's friendly, so it can't do any harm.'

Susie made the call straight away on Martha's phone, and as she had to leave a number where she could be contacted, she sat drinking tea with her. Within the hour, the secretary rang back to say, 'Come at three o'clock this afternoon.'

'Marvellous!' she crowed, in high spirits. 'It's not what you know these days, but who you know.'

'Hang on,' Martha said, 'he hasn't given you a job yet.'

Susie went home to look out her smartest outfit, and decided it must be the silver grey suit she'd bought for her honeymoon. She'd also worn it for Danny's funeral, but she had nothing else that was half as smart, and beggars couldn't be choosers.

She wouldn't wear a hat, her blond hair was thick and did not suit hats, and anyway she couldn't wear a straw boater in December.

Feeling full of optimism, she made sure she arrived five minutes early for her appointment. She didn't feel as nervous as she had going to the previous interviews because William Curtis had always been kind to her, and hadn't Jamie recommended that she ask him for a job? Besides, he understood her situation; he'd seen Rosie and accepted that Danny had fathered her.

William Curtis and Sons Ltd, bakers and confectioners, had their premises down in the dock area. It was a series of buildings and yards, having been extended several times. Their products were considered the best on the market and they supplied many of the high-class shops, cafés and hotels in North West England with bread and cakes of every description. It seemed their business was surviving the downturn in trade very well, and their fleet of cream vans with pictures of colourful cakes on both sides were often to be seen about the city. Susie had regularly enjoyed their cakes and knew they were bought up quickly at St Biddolphe's fetes. She could see that the Curtis family earned a generous living from the business.

As soon as she got off the bus, Susie could smell the delicious scents of baking. One of their buildings was giving off steam and it seemed to scent the whole district. The main door was quite grand and the offices provided the sort of background she associated with Mr Curtis. She hadn't been there before, and had to ask her way to his office.

His secretary was middle aged and smartly dressed, and Susie was ushered straight into a large office with far-reaching views of the Mersey from the window behind the desk. Mr Curtis stood up and came forward. 'Hello, Susie, come in and sit down.'

'It's kind of you to let me take up your time, Mr Curtis. The thing is, I need a job, and you said that perhaps you could find one for me.'

'I did.' His red hair was losing its brightness now it was peppered with grey, and he was putting on a little weight in late middle age. 'With hindsight I think it was wrong of me to do so.' That sent Susie's hopes sinking like a stone. 'It's not that I couldn't find a job for you, Susie, but that I'm afraid it would not be politic for me to do so. We both know that the birth of baby Rosanna has caused a storm of gossip and condemnation amongst the good ladies of St Biddolphe's. As I said the other day when we met outside the church gates, the wisest course for us all is to do nothing and let it die down. If I were to employ you here, it would start their tongues wagging again, and arguments to flare up.' Below the level of his desk, Susie was twisting her fingers in agony. 'Anyway, I can't see how you can possibly work and look after a young baby. She must take up a lot of your time?'

'Yes, but my sister Martha lives next door to us and has offered to take care of her. She really loves babies and can't get enough of them. The thing is, Mr Curtis, I need to work. My mother is more than willing to support me and the baby, but she doesn't earn enough. You know what she's like; she's willing to do anything for anybody, but I feel I'm sponging off her. I can't play around at home with Rosie while she has to earn our living. I really do have to work.'

He was looking at her intently. 'Forgive me, Susie. I wasn't looking at it from that angle. Perhaps I could help you find a job somewhere else. You worked for Bibby's as a shorthand typist, is that right? Did you receive any promotion?'

Susie shook her head. 'I worked in the typing pool, but I have filled in for several secretaries when they went on holiday. I can do it.'

'Yes, and you've had what – a year's experience?'

'That's about it, yes.'

'Would they not take you back?'

'No, you see I hid my pregnancy from them, so I could work for as long as possible.'

'Oh! And how long was that?'

'Until three weeks before.'

'Oh my goodness! Quite a feat.' He smiled. 'I don't know, Susie. Leave it with me and I'll see what I can do. I feel I should help you.'

'Thank you, Mr Curtis.'

'I'll write to you when I have news. Leave your address with my secretary.'

Susie left with her head in a whirl, half disappointed because she'd expected a job in his company. Hadn't Fee been saying he wanted her to work in the business? Certainly she'd heard that from Danny and Jamie, but he wasn't denying that he could fit her in. She hoped he was going to find a job for her somewhere else, but she had nothing definite to hang her hopes on and found it hard to stay optimistic.

CHAPTER FIFTEEN

LOUISE HAD ALWAYS HAD to work to support her family, and did not feel that Rosie need keep Susie at home. She could see Susie was trying hard to find a job, and she'd heard what Mr Curtis had said to her. She felt that in the long run, Susie would be better going to work and meeting people. That at eighteen, she was too young to be isolated within the family. Louise felt sorry for her as the weeks went on and she had no success.

Louise had been working for Peverill's Premium Preserves for seventeen years and had always been very happy there. She began to feel she should ask if a job for Susie could be found at Peverill's. Ralph Randall, the manager who'd taken her on, had retired in 1932. The staff approved of his successor, Christopher Berry, because he'd been his second in command for the last six years and they all knew him. Louise knew him rather better than most because he'd been the organist at St Biddolphe's for even longer. He'd run the business efficiently in a kind and benign manner, and had the reputation of being fair to everyone. Many of the staff had worked there for a long time, though the accountant, Gordon Wilson, Louise's immediate boss, was the third she'd worked for. She had known him slightly before he started, because he too was a member of St Biddolphe's. She got on well with them all.

Peverill's was thought to be a good employer – there had never been a strike during the years she'd worked there – but now there were other larger firms making jam who were taking over the trade, and the smaller factories were earning less in the economic downturn.

Chris Berry was a rather tall and lanky man in his mid-forties with a slow smile and a kind and gentle manner. Louise also knew his wife Mabel. She had played the organ for Sunday services too when she was well enough, but she'd always been something of an invalid and had not joined in the fundraising and other work that Louise had been involved in. Chris had found a young man of nineteen, Claude Vane, a student at the music school, to join his other volunteers and play on some Sundays, so that he could spend more time at home with Mabel. But he was still the church organist, and if one of the other volunteers was unable to play, he filled in.

Louise had liked him and found him friendly, and in the spirit of St Biddolphe's had offered her help. While he played the organ for the Sunday evening service, she'd sat with Mabel on several occasions because he no longer liked leaving her alone. But she was reluctant to ask Chris to take Susie on, because she was afraid he'd feel compelled to return the help she'd given him. However, it was beginning to look as though that would be Susie's only chance of getting another job. He asked after her and the baby from time to time, and the next time he did so, she screwed up her courage to ask if she could be employed in the office.

He frowned as he gave it some thought. 'Possibly, yes, in the new year. Miss Stanhope is retiring. Let me see, when will that be?' He went to his filing cabinet while Louise felt a shaft of hope. 'Yes, the end of January.'

'But she is your secretary. Susie is not that experienced.'

'I've already decided to promote Miss Rawlings, but that leaves a vacancy in the general office. Would that suit Susie?'

'Yes, perfectly.'

'Then ask her to come in and see me. Miss Stanhope will fix a convenient time and date.'

'I don't know how to thank you. '

'We have to help each other.' He smiled gently as his dark eyes met hers.

'Susie's a good worker, I'm sure she'll fit in.'

'If she's anything like her mother, she will.'

Susie was delighted to be summoned to see Christopher Berry and know she'd be offered work. She'd become quite downcast since she'd spoken to Mr Curtis, and very disappointed that he didn't seem to be doing what he'd promised.

Christmas was coming and the preparations were beginning to fill Susie's mind. Becky wrote that Max had booked them into a luxury hotel in Chester for a short holiday over Christmas, so would Louise bring the family to lunch on the last Sunday before Christmas so they could meet up? Bert reluctantly said he couldn't make it, as it was the busiest time of the year for him, with the poultry being ordered and the extra sausages and cooked meats to prepare. So Louise wrote back to thank Becky and say she'd bring her sisters and their babies.

A week after Susie had accepted the job in Peverill's Preserves, she heard a letter drop through the door one morning just before her mother set out to work. She found it was for her and ripped the envelope open.

'Mum, it's from Mr Curtis, the letter that he promised! Gosh, it's handwritten.'

Dear Susie,

I've been thinking how best I can help you. Your bearing and behaviour impressed me the other day, because you didn't ask for money, only for a job so that you could earn some.

But I still feel that over the first few years, a baby's greatest need is to have her mother close by, so instead of helping you get a job I have set up a small Trust Fund for Rosanna, the income of which will be paid to you until she reaches the age of twenty-one. I have aimed to provide an income commensurate with the amount you would be likely to earn at the present time, and ask you now to open a bank account in your name, and let me know where, so that the money can be paid to you regularly.

Danny would want me to help you in this way and I willingly take over his responsibility. I would ask you to be discreet and not talk about it except to your immediate family. I'm sure I can trust you to do that.

With every good wish for the future,
William Curtis.

'I can't believe he's been so generous.' Susie felt quite emotional and had to blink back the tears that rushed to her eyes.

'Many would say he can afford it,' Louise said, 'but it shows he really cares about you and Danny. You'd better open that bank account today, so you can write and thank him, and do be careful that you tell nobody else about this. You must respect his wishes.'

'Not even Martha?'

'Well, if you do, swear her to secrecy. You mustn't let it go any further. I'm very glad, though, as it'll take the worry out of providing for Rosie. He's a real gentleman. He's done the right thing.'

'I'm really thrilled and I will tell Martha. Mum, you're going to miss your bus if you don't get going.'

Susie gave a lot of thought to staying at home with her baby, but decided she would prefer to carry on with her plan and take the job Mr Berry had offered her. Both Danny and Fee said their father expected to dictate how his children lived their lives, and she hoped he wouldn't mind that she was disregarding his wishes. She was quite looking forward to starting work in the third week of January and going in every morning with her mother.

Later that day, having opened a bank account, Susie sat down to answer the letter.

Dear Mr Curtis,

I can't thank you enough for settling so much money on Rosanna. It has taken away my main worry, which was how I and my family could support her while she was growing up. I am truly grateful to you.

After considerable thought, she went on. *You strongly advised me to stay at home to care for her, and I do understand that you have given me this money to enable me to do that. But in the month since I saw you, I have accepted a job with Peverill's Preserves where my mother works. I think Mr Berry took pity on me too. I feel I have made adequate provision for Rosanna to be cared for by my sister, and that I shall quite enjoy my job.*

*I hope you will forgive me for going against your wishes, but it
is my family's way to work for their living. I will always be grateful
to you.*
    Yours sincerely,
    Susie Ingram.

To Louise, it seemed Christmas had begun as she took her
daughters and grandchildren over to meet Becky for her
celebration lunch. She'd said she'd meet them as they got off
the ferry, but they couldn't see her Austin Seven at first. Then
they saw her running down to kiss them, all smiles and wearing
an elegant fur coat. 'Max thought the brakes unsafe on my old
car and replaced it with a Morris Twelve. It's larger and more
comfortable,' she laughed.

'You are lucky,' Martha told her.

Max and Becky's house was decorated with holly and
flowers and was beautifully warm. Louise thought it sparkled
and decided she wouldn't want to spend Christmas anywhere
else if she had a house like this.

Becky made a great fuss of the babies, exclaiming at how
heavy Jonjo had become. She played with them both, but Jonjo
was sleepy. Rosie was more responsive, reaching up to pull
at her dark hair, but neither took much notice of the toys
she'd bought for them.

The dining table was beautifully set. Max led them in and
opened a bottle of wine and filled their glasses. When the
maid brought in the turkey with all the trimmings, he carved
them generous helpings. It was Becky who served the Christmas
pudding and later poured the coffee in the sitting room.

'You're a good cook,' Louise told her daughter. 'Who taught

you? You left home when you were so young. I know it couldn't have been me.'

Max laughed. 'We have a cook who has provided this lunch, but Becky has started a course on *haute cuisine* cookery. You know, more elaborate dinner party stuff.'

'I'm enjoying it,' she said.

'I have to do a bit of entertaining,' Max said, 'it comes with the job, so I'm delighted to show off what Rebecca can do. I'm enjoying eating it as well, but I'm going to have to watch my weight.'

Louise could see from their polished performance that they did quite a lot of entertaining. They had tea and cake before they left and each of them was presented with a gift-wrapped package; Martha was even given one for Bert. When Becky was about to take them out to her car, Max joined them.

'We're leaving the day after tomorrow for our little holiday, so we'll not have time to finish off all the turkey. Perhaps you'll be good enough to take it,' he said. He followed them out to the car carrying a large cardboard box. 'I've put in a few other bits and pieces that might otherwise go to waste. Have a good Christmas.'

Louise tried to tell Becky how generous she thought they'd both been, and how much they'd enjoyed the festive lunch and appreciated what she'd done. It was already dark when they boarded the ferry and they headed straight for the saloon. Once seated, Susie and Martha eased the lid off the box to see what it contained.

'Oh goodness, he's given us the whole carcass and there's loads of turkey left. And there's a whole iced Christmas cake!' Susie was pleased. 'Oh, and mince pies too, and a cheese.'

Martha was trying to see what else there was. 'It looks like boiled ham and there's a box of fancy biscuits and another of chocolates. They've been very generous. What a good job I made Becky some cushion covers and a tea cosy.'

'I feel guilty,' Louise said. 'All I gave her was a pair of silk stockings.'

'I did the same,' Susie said, 'we thought she'd like them. But I gave Max that prize I won in the church Summer Fete. You know – that fancy gadget.'

Martha began to laugh. 'We none of us knew what it was until Bert worked it out.'

Susie was in tucks. 'It turned out to be a special clip-on cork to keep the bubbles in champagne once the bottle had been opened. And by the look of the box, it had been doing duty on St Biddolphe's prize table on many occasions.'

'You couldn't have given it to anyone better.' Martha couldn't stop laughing. 'Max will know what it's for and may even use it.'

'If he hasn't already got one,' Susie giggled.

By the time they got off at Pier Head to catch the bus home, they had quietened down. 'What a life of luxury Becky has,' Martha said, with wonder in her voice. 'She has a cook and a maid, not to mention a beautiful house and a car.'

'And a husband who thinks she's gorgeous,' Susie added. 'How did she manage to find him? We don't know any men who can provide like that.'

Louise thought that perhaps Becky had tried to show off her new lifestyle, but she was truly amazed at how improved her financial circumstances were. She was ready to acknowledge she'd been wrong about Max, just as she'd been wrong about

Bert. They appeared to be good husbands and her daughters seemed happy with them. She'd worried about the age difference between Becky and Max, and she'd worried about Martha's health, but they were both happy so she need not have done.

She'd liked Danny Curtis and had thought Susie had the best chance of happiness of the three, but now Susie was unmarried with Danny's child to bring up alone, and even with her unexpected extra income, she was in a much less favourable position. At times like this she ached for Susie.

Louise had thought the Dolland family's German ways rather odd to start with, but at Christmas she welcomed the way they celebrated with their main feast on Christmas Eve. This meant Martha and Bert could enjoy that with his mother and aunt.

Louise went alone to St Biddolphe's for the midnight service and got up in time to roast the goose Bert had given her and put a full Christmas lunch on the table by one o'clock, to which she had invited Martha and her family.

She loved Christmas – the build-up of making little gifts for her family, and the two-day holiday giving her extra time to spend with them made it a real celebration. On Christmas evening Bert and Martha held open house for their friends and relatives, with a cold supper and carol singing round the piano. All Bert's family excelled at playing the piano.

In the New Year, Louise was shocked when Martha brought Bert and Jonjo in to tell her they were expecting another baby.

'So soon?' Jonjo wasn't quite five months. 'I thought Bert believed in giving you plenty of time to recover?'

'Not very much this time, but there's no need to worry,

Mum, I've done it once, I can do it again. I was fine when I was having Jonjo.'

'Not all the time,' Louise pointed out, 'you had a few bad days.'

'Perhaps she'll be better this time,' Bert said. 'Martha's heart has always been set on having more than one.'

Susie seemed filled with doubts. 'Will you be able to manage Rosie too? I mean, that will give you three babies to look after. It's going to be hard work for you.'

'No, looking after babies doesn't seem like work to me. I love it. Of course I'll be able to manage Rosie.'

CHAPTER SIXTEEN

L OUISE WENT BACK TO work later that week, and on Saturday Chris Berry asked her if she would sit with his wife while he played the organ in church for the Sunday evening service. 'Mrs Pollard's name is on the rota to do it,' he said, 'but she was taken to hospital with appendicitis on Boxing Day.'

'Of course,' she said; he'd been so kind to her that she couldn't refuse.

Christopher Berry employed a maid who worked nine to six on weekdays, and for the last six months he'd employed a nurse to work the same hours to look after Mabel. She'd been a semi-invalid for years but she was getting weaker and was now bedridden. Nurse O'Brien and Miss Maddocks took turns to sit with her on Sundays, but both had gone to stay with relatives for Christmas.

'It's very good of you to come like this,' he told Louise as he let her in on Sunday evening. 'She's not been at all well today, so I'm glad I asked you to come. I used to leave her and she'd be all right for a couple of hours, but she was in so much pain earlier that I had to give her more painkillers and since then she's been a bit restless. I haven't been able to get her to eat or drink much over the last day or so. This is her feeding cup, will you see if you can get her to take some of this milk?'

'Yes, I'll do my best.' She'd spent so much time nursing Martha that Louise felt confident about caring for ill people. Christopher led the way up to the sick room. There was a small fire in the grate and the hot, fetid atmosphere seemed familiar, as did the many medicines ranged round the room.

'I've been reading to her,' he said, indicating the newspaper lying on the bed, 'she likes to know what's going on in the world. I'm halfway down page three.'

Mabel was propped up into near sitting position, but her eyes were closed and her skin was waxy and sweating. She looked very much worse than when Louise had seen her last.

Chris bent over the bed to speak to his wife, 'I'm going to church now,' he said, and her eyes flickered open. 'Louise has kindly come to keep you company until I get back.'

Mabel hung onto his arm. 'Don't be long.' Her voice was almost a whisper and he had to peel her hands away to free himself.

'I won't, dear. Try and drink something for Louise.'

Louise sat down on the chair placed close to the bed. 'Hello, Mabel, shall I carry on reading to you?'

She did, but Mabel gave little sign that she'd heard her. A cinder dropped in the grate and Louise noticed it was getting low. She poked it up and put more coal on. 'Would you like some milk now, Mabel?'

Louise held the feeding cup in position and obediently she took a few sips. 'Cloying,' she gasped, pushing it away.

'Would you prefer water?'

Louise only just caught her reply, 'Lemonade.'

A jug of home-made lemonade stood ready with a gauze

cover over it, but there was no other feeding cup. Louise went to the bathroom and emptied the milk into a tumbler she found there and rinsed it out. Mabel had a good drink of lemonade and afterwards Louise returned to the newspaper and continued to read until there was little left but the sports pages. She looked round for a book. Her patient had appeared to be dozing but suddenly she was throwing herself round the bed.

'What's the matter, Mabel? Aren't you comfy? Shall I shake up your pillows?'

Louise didn't catch her reply and had to ask her to repeat it. 'Commode, need commode.'

Mabel hadn't the strength but was trying to throw the bedclothes off and get out of bed. Louise had helped her use the commode on an earlier visit; she removed the cushion, lifted the seat, and dragged it nearer the bed. Mabel seemed to have no strength at all, and Louise feared she would not be able to lift her, but it seemed she still expected to get out to use it.

Louise put an arm round her waist and told herself she need not have worried, Mabel was just skin and bone, poor thing, and weighed little, but once she had her feet on the floor she was swaying and difficult to keep upright. Louise managed to turn her round so she could back her onto the commode, but suddenly, with a little gurgle, she went limp and all her weight collapsed against Louise's shoulder, almost knocking her off her feet.

'Mabel?' As Louise steadied herself against a chest of drawers she felt a shaft of fear. Something had happened and she didn't know what. 'Mabel, are you all right?' She could no longer see her face and she could barely support her full weight. Louise managed the couple of steps back to the bed and with superhuman effort slid Mabel back on to it. It left her panting for breath. 'Mabel?'

Louise gave a little yelp of surprise, she hadn't been expecting this. Mabel looked . . . 'Oh my God!'

She pulled the pillows away so Mabel could lie flat and a wave of panic washed over her. What should she do? For a moment she couldn't move a muscle. Then she shot downstairs to the telephone in the hall. She knew Dr Grant was Mabel's doctor, but what was his number? She was shaking all over, but when the operator answered she was able to give her Dr Grant's name and address and ask to be connected. While she waited, she worried that he could be in church this evening. His wife answered and after she'd spoken to her, she heard Dr Grant's voice.

She could hardly choke out the words to tell him she was with Mabel Berry. 'She collapsed against me,' she said, 'she looks awful. I'm afraid she could be dead.'

'Is she breathing?'

'I . . . I don't know.'

'I'll come straight over,' he said in matter of fact tones.

She had to make herself go back to look at Mabel. Her knees felt like jelly and she had to pull herself up on the banister as she climbed the stairs. Mabel's mouth had sagged open but she hadn't moved. The house was silent and still and Louise sank down on the chair to wait, but she was up on her feet again in moments; she couldn't sit still.

Was Mabel breathing? She remembered reading somewhere that a mirror held over a patient's lips would mist over if she was breathing. Her handbag was on the floor beside her chair, she felt for her small mirror and held it over Mabel's mouth, but at that moment the front door bell rang through the house, startling her.

Louise ran downstairs. 'Thank goodness,' she gasped when she saw Dr Grant's bulk on the step. Swinging his bag, he bounded upstairs ahead of her. It didn't take him long to say, 'I'm afraid you're right, she is dead. What happened?'

Louise was still shaking. 'Mabel said she wanted to use the commode. I got her up and she collapsed against me.'

'Possibly she had a heart attack. An urge to pass water isn't uncommon prior to that.'

'It was all so sudden.' Tears were rolling down her face. 'I didn't know what to do for the best.'

'You did the right thing, you called me. It'll have given you a nasty shock.'

'It has.'

'Sit down. When will Christopher be back?'

'He's at evening service.'

'Playing the organ?'

'Yes.' Louise felt guilt ridden. 'Oh my goodness! What will he say?' At that moment she heard the front door opening and footsteps coming into the hall.

'That will be him. I'll go down and break the news. You sit here and rest.'

But Louise couldn't sit and look at Mabel now. She followed him out onto the landing and hung over the banisters at the top of the stairs while Dr Grant took Chris into the sitting room below. It seemed only moments before they were both coming back. Chris looked drawn and his face was chalk-white.

The tears were streaming down Louise's cheeks. 'I'm so sorry, I feel so guilty. I let Mabel die.'

'It wasn't your fault,' Dr Grant said. 'If she's had a heart attack, there was nothing you could have done.'

'You mustn't feel guilty.' Chris was blinking back his tears too.

'It's such a shock when it comes as suddenly as this,' Louise gulped.

'And very upsetting for us all,' Dr Grant murmured.

Chris's head was sinking lower. 'It wasn't sudden. Poor Mabel, she's had seven long years of pain and had given up hope of ever being well again. She told me she'd be glad to die.'

'Chris!' Louise felt a rush of compassion and threw her arms round him in a comforting hug.

His head went down on her shoulder. 'She asked me to help her die,' he whispered, 'but I couldn't.'

'Of course you couldn't,' the doctor told him, lifting him away from Louise. 'You've had a hard time. Come along both of you, I'll drop you off at home,' he told Louise, 'and you Christopher must come home with me. This is not a time for being alone. We'll think about what needs to be done later.'

Louise was grateful for the lift home but still felt shaky. She unburdened all her tensions on Susie, who made her comforting cocoa, but she couldn't sleep when she went to bed. She couldn't rid herself of the cold fear she'd felt when Mabel had slumped against her, nor of her sympathy for Chris at the sight of his tears.

The next day at the office, she looked out for him. He didn't come in, but the news that his wife had died did. She thought he must have spoken to Miss Stanhope and asked her to let everybody know. On Wednesday morning, Louise was climbing the front steps on her way in when she heard him call her name. She paused and he caught her up. She thought he looked white and drawn, and asked, 'Are you all right?'

'As right as I'm likely to be. I knew Mabel couldn't last much longer but it was still a shock,' he said. 'Come to my office with me.' Half a dozen people stopped to sympathise as they walked in. As soon as he'd closed his office door behind them, he said, 'I feel I have to apologise for putting you in a difficult position on Sunday evening.'

'You didn't know what was going to happen.'

'If I had I'd have stayed with her. That I wasn't there at her end upsets me.'

'I felt I should not have let her die when you'd trusted me to look after her. I felt I'd let you down.'

He looked up and his sad eyes met her gaze for the first time. 'Louise, what could you have done to prevent it? Thank you for the help you gave her. I'm very grateful.'

'If there's anything else I can do, I'll be glad to.'

He shook his head. 'Thank you, there isn't.'

The funeral was on Saturday morning, and it was not well attended. Louise took time off to go, and saw a few of St Biddolphe's parishioners there: those who looked after the ill and infirm, and those who played the organ. Mabel had been confined to her home for some time and everybody said she would see it as a release.

It took Louise some time to get over the shock, and naturally it took Chris longer. His colleagues in the office were full of sympathy and rallied round with offers of help, but over the following weeks, he seemed sad and a little depressed, and he was making mistakes he'd never made before. Louise found her fellow workers silently correcting his errors, covering for him, and doing everything they could to keep the factory working at full tilt.

Louise felt that being with Mabel when she'd died had drawn them closer. They'd shared a few deeply emotional moments. She would have liked to show him more support, but didn't know how to when he was running the business and she was just a cog in the accounts department.

He'd never been an outgoing personality, but now he seemed almost withdrawn. She had reason occasionally to go to his office, and she made an effort to chat to him when she did, but it seemed he'd lost his friendliness and preferred to be left in peace.

CHAPTER SEVENTEEN

In the third week of January, Susie started her new job and their new way of life began. Louise felt she'd enjoyed a time of comfort having Susie at home doing the housework and getting a hot meal ready by the time she came back, but now Susie was at work too and Rosanna would have to be fed, bathed and put to bed when they returned home, she was afraid it would seem as though there weren't enough hours in the day.

Bert was in the habit of bringing meat home when he came for his lunch, so that Martha would have time to prepare it for their evening meal, and he began doing the same for Louise and refusing to take payment. 'You and Susie make cakes and scones and share them with us,' he told her.

Martha remained fit and well as her pregnancy advanced, caring for the two babies, and she often peeled potatoes and prepared vegetables for them too, to lighten their load.

The inner circle of ladies in St Biddolphe's congregation had not softened towards Susie. She complained that if she met them in the street or the shops they ignored her. Mrs Curtis had not relented and Susie no longer went to the youth club or the tennis courts, cutting herself off from the places where she used to meet her friends.

Louise knew Susie yearned for a husband and was embarrassed at being an unmarried mother and being frowned upon generally. The typing pool was made up of girls of about her own age, and there were young men there too, working in other departments. Louise hoped Susie would enjoy her job in the factory and make new friends there.

On her first day, Susie was glad to be taken into the office by her mother and introduced to her supervisor, Miss Glegg, who controlled the work and distributed it amongst the girls of the typing pool.

'I'll start you on some copy typing,' she said to Susie, handing her some pages. 'Three copies please. This will be your desk and your typewriter, and this is Hilda Jones,' she waved her hand towards the girl at the next desk. 'Hilda will take you under her wing for a few days, and show you where things are kept. Ask if there's anything you want to know.'

'Hello.' Hilda came over and opened the drawers of her desk, checking on the things she'd need to do the job, and then showed her the cupboards from which supplies could be obtained. She was friendly and had fluffy, white-blond hair and looked about Susie's age.

'How long have you been here?' Susie asked.

'Three years, straight from secretarial school. It's all right when you get used to it.'

The typing pool was at one end of a large open office, with the rest of the space being taken up with junior staff working in other departments. Over the next few days Susie became aware that some of the men were eyeing her up and down. Some were friendly and tried to chat her up, and one she thought rather flashy began fetching cups of tea for her from the trolley when it was pushed in at mid-morning and mid-afternoon. He said his name was Tom, and he was growing a small moustache.

Being new, she was glad to talk to anybody, and was rather surprised when Hilda came to perch on the corner of her desk to say, 'I'd be careful of Tom, if I was you. He tries to get off with all the good-looking girls, but there's only one thing he wants.'

Susie was even more surprised when Tom came over in the afternoon and invited her to go to the pictures with him that evening. 'Sorry,' she smiled, 'but I can't. I have a baby to look after.'

'Well, I had heard that, but I wasn't sure whether to believe it or not.'

'It's true,' Susie winced as she realised she'd already been the subject of gossip.

'You look too young to have a baby, but surely your mother would babysit for once? She works here, you could ask her now.'

'No, thank you, I prefer to look after Rosanna myself.' Susie watched him weave his way between the desks to his own, and was afraid that having a baby gave her the reputation of being a fast woman.

A few weeks later, Susie had been advised by both her mother and Martha that she should start weaning Rosie, and she was trying her on a little of the mashed potato loosened with juices from the stew they had eaten for their evening meal, when she heard the front door bell. Her mother put down her teacup and went to see who it was. Moments later she was bringing Fiona and Jamie into their living room.

'Susie, your friends have come to see if you'd like to go to the pictures with them tonight,' she said.

Susie jerked up in surprise and let gravy run down Rosie's chin and onto her bib. This visit was so unexpected, especially as she'd spurned their earlier attempts to invite her to the pictures. She'd been pregnant then and feeling awful about losing Danny. Now she'd love to go, but . . .

'Do come,' Jamie urged.

'It's Noel Coward's *Cavalcade*,' Fee told her with her wide smile, 'it was a huge success as a West End play.' She hadn't changed a bit.

'At the Lyceum in the village,' Jamie added.

'I can't, I have Rosie to look after now.' Her voice was agonised.

'I'll see to her tonight,' her mother offered. 'You go. It'll do you good to go out.'

'Are you sure?' Susie asked.

'Of course I'm sure.' Louise lifted the baby off Susie's knee. 'You go and get ready.'

'Thanks, Mum, I won't be long, Fee,' and she shot up the stairs while Rosie let out a wail at having her supper interrupted.

Louise turned round to smile at the visitors. 'Thank you for thinking of Susie. She can't get out very much now she has a job and a baby. I'm afraid she's missing out on the fun she used to have.'

'Let me hold her,' Fiona said, 'I'd love to, she's lovely,' but the infant was waving her fists about and getting angry now. 'Rosie, I'm your auntie!' She clicked her tongue and rocked the baby but it got her nowhere. 'I can't stop her crying; she doesn't seem to like me.'

'Usually she loves people making a fuss of her, but she's hungry and wants her supper,' Louise said. 'Here, pop a spoonful of this potato in her mouth. There we are then, all sunshine again.'

'How do you manage when you both go to work?' Jamie asked.

'Martha lives next door and says it's no trouble to look after her while we're away. She already has Jonjo to look after, you see.'

'Is she well?'

'Yes, she's very well at the moment. She's having another baby. Martha loves babies. She says they keep her going.'

'I bet you all have to work very hard,' Fiona said sympathetically.

When Susie had gone out with her friends, Louise finished feeding Rosanna with her solids and gave her a bottle of milk. Her eyes were closing and she was ready to go down for the night, but Louise continued to nurse her, musing on the changes the child had brought to Susie's life.

This trip to the cinema was the first time she'd been out with friends of her own age since Rosanna had been born. No, longer than that, ever since her pregnancy had become known locally. Louise herself was used to it, but Susie had lost her social life and had had to give up many things that had brought her pleasure. At eighteen, that had to be hard.

Louise tried to talk to Susie about it at breakfast the next morning. 'Did you enjoy going out with your friends?' she asked.

'Yes, it was a good film.'

'They haven't deserted you. You should do it more often.'

Susie cracked open her boiled egg. 'Fee talks of nothing but boyfriends, clothes and dancing, and having a good time, she makes me feel old. I've left all that behind.'

'And Jamie?'

'He just tags along. Fee is trying to sort him out with a girlfriend.'

'Oh, but it's good for you to get out once in a while.'

'Mum, don't worry about me. I don't for one minute regret having Rosie. She's all I have left of Danny. She's magic to me, the best thing in my life. I love her to bits.'

But Louise knew her life was now filled with work, domestic chores and baby care. This was not the life she'd have chosen for fun-loving Susie, though they all loved Rosanna and would not want to be without her now.

Jamie Curtis could feel the tension building as his family sat waiting for their soup plates to be removed at dinner that evening. Nobody spoke as the maid set out the vegetable tureens, the gravy and the mint sauce on the table. She laid the dish in front of his father and whipped off the silver cover to reveal lamb chops, before leaving the room and closing the door quietly.

His father began serving them out. 'Fiona,' he said, 'I do not want to hear any more argument about this. I want you to give in your notice on Monday and come and work in the family firm.'

As the silence lengthened, Jamie could see his mother bristling as she accepted her plate with two chops. 'You must understand, Fiona, that this is your inheritance,' she added, as she reached for the dish of potatoes. 'I don't know what's the matter with you children, you don't seem to realise what a huge advantage your father is giving to you.'

'Rory does,' Jamie pulled a face at his older brother, who had recently qualified as a solicitor and had joined the legal department of Curtis Cakes. 'He's happy to do what you want.'

'Don't be cheeky, Jamie,' his mother said.

Fiona was bristling. 'Dad, I'm very happy in the job I've got, I don't want to leave it.'

'I know, but one year's experience in that solicitor's office is quite enough to fit you for our office. I want you to learn our ways, so you can eventually run the office.'

Jamie knew very well why Fiona wanted to stay where she was. He'd met Leonard Ross, an articled clerk in the same firm. He knew she'd been out with him a few times and was beginning to think of him as her boyfriend. The last thing his sister wanted was to leave her job and therefore see less of him, but they all knew that would not be sufficient reason for Dad to change his plans.

And worse, one word about Len and Mum would set about checking him and his family out, and would decide whether he was suitable as a friend and partner for her daughter. Jamie understood how embarrassing that could be before things were properly settled between them, and he doubted that a solicitor in training would get his mother's approval.

'But what harm would it do if I spent more time there?' Fiona persisted. 'Six months say, or another year?'

'I don't want any more argument, Fiona, just do as I say.' Dad was glowering round the table at them all.

Jamie had had similar arguments with him. He'd been persuaded to start working in the family firm two years ago, straight from school at the age of eighteen, but it had not been his choice. He'd wanted to join the Royal Air Force and train to be a pilot, but his parents had laughed at that and called it pie in the sky. Dad had overruled him, but had suggested legal training first if he didn't feel ready.

'As a solicitor, you would be of real use to the firm,' he'd said, 'and that would further your own interests at the same time.' Jamie had said no to that, but had regretted his decision. At least it would have put off his entry into the firm.

He missed Danny, though he had frequently led him into trouble. He, Danny and Fee had made up a close trio; they'd been friends as well as the siblings nearest in age. They'd been a small army of dissidents fighting Dad's rod of iron regime.

Jamie longed to rebel too, but it had turned out such a disaster for Danny that he'd been too scared. It looked as though it was Fee's turn to decide between compliance and rebellion now.

Susie had begun to feel settled in her new job. It wasn't exciting, but it kept her busy and stopped her yearning for what she'd lost. But from the middle of March onwards, there was no way she could avoid the thought that Grand National Day was coming round again. It was the first anniversary of Danny's death and she didn't want that to fill her mind, but everybody was talking about it and she couldn't stop the memories flooding back.

Grand National Day put her colleagues in high good humour. People who normally didn't read newspapers folded them to the racing pages and kept consulting them to confirm opinions. The senior foremen in the factory organised the sweepstake, and the young men speculated about form and tried to sell as many tickets as they could. Susie bought one because refusing to do so might draw her into explanations she didn't want to give.

They all had an unofficial afternoon off, and the day before Fiona rang her up at work to commiserate about Danny. 'Everybody else loves horses and racing,' she said, 'but since Danny's death I can't bear to think of it. Not that it had anything to do with what happened. It was just the day of his accident, pure fate.'

Susie hadn't seen her recently and gathered she was going out with her new boyfriend. 'Len is taking Jamie and me out to get away from the horse racing fuss. Would you like to make up a four and come with us? We thought of a trip to New Brighton if it's sunny tomorrow afternoon, and in the evening going to see Clark Gable and Jean Harlow in *Red Dust*.'

'Yes, I would,' Susie said, and she arranged to meet them straight from the office and have a bite of lunch with them first.

Not much work was done in the jam factory on the morning of Grand National Day; everybody was in a fever of anticipation. The draw for the horses took place and Susie was considered lucky when her ticket drew Miss Muffet. 'A good horse,' she was told, 'you're in with a chance.'

She had arranged to meet Fiona and Jamie straight from the office, but was surprised to find Jamie standing outside on his own. He looked rather downcast, in stark contrast to her fellow workers. 'Fee sends her apologies,' he said, 'you're stuck with me, I'm afraid.'

'I don't see that as a hardship,' she smiled, 'what's happened?'

'She had a flaming row with Dad last night. Mum is backing him up, and they're insisting she joins the firm. Fee wants to be alone with her boyfriend to plot her next step. She says she's going to refuse to do what they want.'

'Oh dear! That's what Danny did, isn't it?'

'Yes. Mum and Dad ruled that he was too young to be married to you, and he needed to grow up first. Danny blew his top when they ruled that you and he should be engaged for at least five years and save up for a house of your own. He had the guts to tell them he was going to get married as soon as he'd turned twenty-one.'

'Well, he knew he was safe to do that because my mother said he could move in with us after we were married.'

'I know, and our parents were not at all happy about that. In fact my mother has never forgiven yours for offering to take Danny in. But for that he wouldn't have been able to marry you last April. Did you know?'

'Yes, Danny and I talked it through. We decided not to tell my mum that your parents wanted us to put it off for five years. Danny was twenty-one and we wanted to get married. We couldn't see any point in waiting, but it turned out a disaster, didn't it?'

'It did, but safe or not, I wish I had the guts to go my own way,' Jamie admitted. 'I'm not happy working in the business, I don't fit in with Dad and Jack. He's top of the popularity pole and can do no wrong. He has waited the obligatory five years and they're planning a big wedding for him now. Rory's on course too; he hasn't decided who he wants to marry, but he's articled to Dad's choice of a firm of accountants. When the parents aren't holding them up as role models, they're having another row with me or Fee.'

'But you aren't dying to marry your childhood sweetheart, and you've no idea what you want to do.'

'Yes I have, I want to get right away from the family. I'd like to join the Air Force but Dad thinks that's a crazy idea. For two pins I'd walk out and do it.'

'No, Jamie, you're just in a black mood.'

'I am, and so is Fee. Look, it's a rotten day, chilly and overcast, let's scrub the trip to New Brighton and go to the pictures this afternoon.'

He took her to Cooper's Café where they had tomato soup and ham sandwiches, and he ordered a cake for her to have with the coffee.

'Don't you want one?' she asked, as she bit into a delicious fresh cream sponge.

'No, those are Curtis cakes, and I've had enough of those to last me a lifetime.'

They went to the matinee at the Odeon, but somehow the outing wasn't a success. Jamie was miserable about the trouble he had at home and though the film was good, Susie's mind was on Danny. They talked, recalling little anecdotes about him, the good times and the bad, until both were near to tears.

When they came out into the grey afternoon to join the merry crowds thronging the streets, they learned within minutes that Golden Miller had won the big race. The name was on everyone's lips and the jollity and high spirits grated with their present mood.

'Do you want to go to a café for a cup of tea, or shall we go straight to the pub?' Jamie asked.

'No to both, thank you. They'll all be rowdy in the pub, drunk before six o'clock.'

'Most of them sound drunk now.'

'I think I'd rather go home,' Susie said sadly.

They caught a bus and he walked up Milner Street with her. 'Can I come in to see Rosie?' he asked.

'Of course, she's much more fun now she's nearly five months. She can sit up and she jabbers away at us.' She led the way and found the child dozing, hemmed in with cushions in the corner of the sofa. Her mother came to the kitchen door. 'I'm cooking,' she said, 'dinner is just about ready.'

Jamie was staring down at the child. He put out his hand to ruffle the thin covering of red curls on her head. 'She's beautiful,' he choked. 'Poor Danny.'

'Would you like to stay and eat with us, Jamie? I think it will stretch for three.'

'No thank you, Mrs Ingram.' He looked at Susie and she could see tears welling in his eyes. 'I have to go.' She followed him to the front door. 'Poor Danny,' he repeated, 'and poor you too.'

Susie went back to her baby, blinking back her own tears.

'I listened for the name Miss Muffet in the racing commentary,' her mother said. 'I think it fell at the first fence, so no luck on the horses this year.'

CHAPTER EIGHTEEN

Now susie could be contacted by phone at her desk, Fee rang her from time to time, so she knew she had capitulated and given in her notice. 'I'm starting in Dad's office next week,' she said. 'Len thought it better if I didn't upset him.'

Susie thought he was probably right. 'How's Jamie?' she asked.

'He's still with us. I'm trying to fix him up with a girlfriend to cheer him up.'

But Susie heard nothing from him and didn't know whether to be pleased or otherwise at that.

Within a few weeks, Louise came home from church to say the banns were being called for Jack Curtis's wedding. She was able to tell Susie that it would take place at the end of April and according to church gossip, it was going to be an extravagant wedding and the honeymoon would be spent in Paris.

A day or two before the wedding, Martha was taken ill again. She was five and a half months pregnant and kept busy looking after Jonjo and Rosie. Dr Grant prescribed a few days' bed rest, and Bert's Aunt Gertrude immediately came to look after her and the children, but it was an anxious time for them all. That Saturday lunchtime, Louise and Susie rushed home from work to relieve Gertrude because it was a busy day at the shop and she was needed there.

The weekend shopping had not been done, and as it was a warm and sunny afternoon, Susie strapped Jonjo to sit at the bottom of Rosanna's pram, and set off with two shopping bags to do it. She'd forgotten it was Jack Curtis's wedding day until she was passing St Biddolphe's. A small crowd had gathered outside to see the bride come out of church, and as the doors were being thrown open at that moment and the organ could be heard, Susie paused to watch the bridal couple come out.

Jack Curtis in full morning dress had never looked smarter, and Kathleen, his bride, looked gorgeous in white lace with a fluttering veil and a magnificent trailing bouquet. She was a few years older than Susie, but they knew each other quite well; they'd seen each other often enough at Hillbark and at St Biddolphe's. There were six bridesmaids dressed in matching eau de nil silk taffeta, one of whom was Fiona.

The crowd gasped at the magnificence of it all, and watched as they and their guests posed for photographs. The bridesmaids were being grouped round the bride against the backdrop of the church when Susie noticed someone trying to attract her attention.

'Hello, Susie.' It was Jamie Curtis in top hat and morning dress.

'Hello.' Susie was embarrassed at being caught watching in this way. 'Jack and Kathleen are having a very smart wedding.'

'I've been an usher, hence the get-up. It's only what you and Danny would have had if he hadn't gone and had that accident on his motorbike.'

Rosie started to whimper so Susie lifted her up, and once in her arms she smiled round at everybody. Aunt Gertrude had dressed the child in her best, on the principle that she'd grow out of her clothes long before she could wear them out. At six months her limbs were firmly rounded and her back was straight. She was growing ever prettier and her eye-catching red hair had grown into a curly cap.

Jamie made a fuss of the baby. He had the Curtis curls but not the red hair; his was conker brown. 'With this red mop you look a real Curtis.' He smiled at Susie. 'Nobody could doubt she was Danny's work now. Who is the other child?'

'He's Martha's, his name's Jonjo. She's ill again so I'm looking after him.'

'Poor Martha, give her our best wishes. Susie, why don't you come and join us? You were always up at our place at one time.'

'I couldn't!' The photographer was now posing the bridal pair with their parents, and Fiona came to join them. 'How are you, Susie? How's the baby?'

'Fine. Fee, you look lovely.'

'Come and join us, why not?' Jamie demanded. 'It's ages since we've seen you. I'd like us to get together so we can catch up with things. Mum is calling it the wedding breakfast, but it's just a party, you'd enjoy it, wouldn't she, Fee?'

But Susie could see their mother looking daggers at her and Rosie. 'I'd love to catch up, Jamie, but I can't now, I've got to do the weekend shopping or we'll all go hungry. Congratulate the bride and groom for me, and say I wish them every happiness.'

Hurriedly, she put Rosie back in her pram and rushed on along the road with tears stinging her eyes. She couldn't possibly join the wedding party when she hadn't been invited, though she would have loved to. Victoria Curtis would put a dagger in her back if she did, especially with Rosie's obvious resemblance to her family. People were remarking on it, and it made her look silly for saying she didn't believe Danny would ever father a child until he was married.

When Martha went down with another recurrence of her illness in June, they were all concerned for her and afraid that caring for two toddlers was proving too much for her. Once again, Bert brought his Aunt Gertrude in to look after her and take care of Jonjo and Rosie while Susie was at work. She was a plump and placid lady, who said her ambition had been to be a photographer, but that it had been her lot to be the help in the butcher's shop and she was pleased to have a change from that.

She had a Box Brownie and took very good pictures with it, and when she photographed Rosie she had an extra copy made for Susie. She bought a frame for the one she liked best, Rosie sitting in her pram and peering up with the sun on her face, and it was now set up on the mantelpiece. This time Martha was back on her feet in four days, and announced that she was fit and well.

They were not seeing so much of Rebecca this year, but the following month she did come to stay for a few days to look after the children while Bert took Martha to the Lake District for a rest. Martha's second baby was due in August, and both Louise and Susie had saved their week's holiday to tide them over the child care they'd need for that. They planned to take separate weeks to double the time they'd be able to cover.

'Don't book definite dates for your holiday,' Chris told Louise, 'wait until the baby arrives and take it from there. You'll find it easier that way.'

The colour was coming back into Christopher's cheeks now that he was recovering from the loss of his wife, and he began playing the organ regularly for church services again. Soon he was doing it on three Sundays out of four. Louise knew he had help at home on weekdays but was alone on Sundays, and would have liked to ask him to have lunch with her and Susie, but she was his bookkeeper and wondered if he'd think her forward if she did.

Louise still felt a cooler atmosphere at church, except from those she counted as friends. She made a point of having a few words with Chris after the service, even if she had to wait for him to finish playing. One Sunday she noticed Mrs Curtis leading him off towards their family car and guessed he was going to her house for lunch.

On Saturday the following week, she found the courage to invite him to her home for Sunday lunch. His dark eyes smiled at her. 'That's very kind of you,' he said, 'I'd like to come, thank you.'

Susie never did go to church these days. She stayed at home with Rosie, and said it was no trouble to cook for one more. She produced roast beef with Yorkshire pudding and apple pie to follow. Soon Chris was having lunch with them more often than not on Sundays. Occasionally, Louise asked Martha to bring Bert and Jonjo to eat with them too.

To repay them, he began inviting Louise and Susie to his house on a weeknight, when Mrs Coogan, his cook and housekeeper, was there to cook a meal for them. Playing the organ was his hobby and he had one in his home, and sometimes he'd play for them before driving them home.

One day in the office Chris asked Louise if she would like to go to a concert at St George's Hall. 'It's to be mostly Rachmaninov's music.'

'Yes, I'd like that very much,' she said. She was pleased at the way he was opening up opportunities for her to do different things. She enjoyed going out with him. St George's Hall was one of Liverpool's largest historic buildings and was used for many civic purposes. There were two assize courts and the Liverpool Philharmonic Orchestra had been giving performances in the concert hall since the Philharmonic Hall burned down in 1933.

On Saturday night Chris picked her up in his car. 'I'm looking forward to seeing inside the building,' Louise said. 'Harold took me once but it's so long ago I've forgotten what it's like.'

They arrived early, so Chris said, 'Come and see the Great Hall first. This is what St George's is famous for.'

Louise gasped at its enormous size and magnificence.

'It seats two thousand five hundred persons and is used for public meetings and special occasions.

'But not for the concert tonight?'

'No. The organ here is one of the largest in the world. It has a hundred and eight stops and thousands of pipes. I have played it. They used to give recitals here on Saturdays and I took my turn but I had to give up when Mabel became ill.'

He smiled. 'The Liverpool Philharmonic Orchestra are going to give a special concert to raise funds to rebuild their own hall. Bach's *Organ Concerto* is on their programme and I have been asked to be their organist for the night. It's quite an honour.

'Come on,' he said, taking her arm, 'we'd better take our seats for tonight's performance.' He took her to the smaller concert hall in the same building.

The members of the orchestra were taking their seats as they arrived. Chris pointed out the second violinist to her. 'Do you recognise him?'

'Yes, from St Biddolphe's, Mr Worth. His wife is very proud that he plays with a famous orchestra like this.'

'He's done me a great favour. Leonard Worth put my name forward and that's how I came to be invited to play at their special concert.' His face shone with enthusiasm, and it was the first time Louise had seen him so full of joy since his wife had died.

'I'd have loved to make my career in music,' he told her. 'When I was young I was very keen. That was my intention.'

'You gave it up to work in industry, to manage a jam factory? What made you change your mind?'

He was thoughtful. 'I suppose it was the influence of my parents. They were members of St Biddolphe's and I was brought up to take heed of what they thought would be best for me. My father had managed to make a good living in industry and thought it would stand me in good stead, which it has. He pointed out that the time would come when I'd want to support a wife and family, and once I married, it would be my duty to do so.'

Louise knew it was what she would have advised. She thought of the Curtis children with even greater reason to accept their parents' wishes, but they had rebelled. So had Becky.

'We all have to earn a living, Louise, and it's not as easy in music, especially when the organ is my real passion. Orchestras like this have varied programmes and rarely play organ music, so they only need a part-time organist. Someone they can call on when needed.'

'Wouldn't you have liked to do that?'

'I'd have loved it, but they chose Claude Vane. You've heard him play in church?'

'Yes, but he's so young! Weren't you disappointed?'

'As I said, I'd have jumped at the chance, but they tend to choose a music student who might yet go far.'

'Will Claude go far?'

'He's a gifted organist, I believe he might. I always come to hear him if I can. He was studying music at the university here but he won a scholarship to the Royal College of Music in London, and has gone.' Chris smiled. 'I'm thrilled to get the chance to play with the Liverpool Phil now.'

'When will it be? I mustn't miss that. I might get Susie to come with me.'

Louise was swept away by Rachmaninov's music and she knew he was too. Afterwards he suggested going to The Supper Club. 'To finish off the evening,' he said, 'and by way of being a celebration too.'

Louise had never heard of it and it was another new experience. The Supper Club was a sophisticated restaurant catering for an after-theatre clientele of mostly middle-aged couples. The lights were dim and soft, tinkling piano music was playing. Louise relaxed, Chris ordered wine and she thought he was relaxed too.

'I used to bring Mabel here after we'd been to a concert,' he said. It was the first time he'd mentioned his wife since her death.

Louise said, 'I remember her playing the organ in church on Sundays.'

'We shared a love of music; she was a talented organist and pianist. Mabel was beautiful as a girl, full of energy, always good humoured and taking an interest in something new; it cheered me up to come home and be near her. We were happy, very happy. I believed we'd grow old together.'

'Ill health can be heartbreaking, it changes everything.'

'Yes, you probably saw what it did to little Martha,' he said. 'When Raymond Grant first started to talk about Mabel's heart problem, I didn't believe it would change what we had; she would just have to take things easier. He sent us to specialists, but inevitably over the years she lost her energy and her joy in life. It was a cruel illness and her death has left a cavernous black hole in my life.'

His devotion to Mabel and obvious grief touched Louise and made her own eyes sting with tears. 'I wish there was more I could have done to help.'

'Louise, you helped me enormously, nobody could have done more.'

She could see tears glistening in his eyes. 'I thought I was over all this,' he said, taking out his handkerchief and dabbing surreptitiously at his face. 'I can't stop thinking about her.'

'It takes more than a few months to recover.' His hand was on the table and she covered it with hers.

'I blame Rachmaninov too. His music is so emotional and my feelings are still raw and easily churned up.'

'Time will help, but it takes years. I lost my husband and even now I think about him and long for his help through life's bumps and knocks.'

A week later Chris offered Louise two tickets to hear him play the organ in St George's Hall, but by then Rosie wasn't well and Susie had decided she'd rather stay with her.

'Then I'll invite Gordon Wilson and his wife too, they've been very kind to me,' Chris said. He gave Louise her ticket and told her she'd find them in the next seats.

Louise counted it a red letter evening. The Wilsons were friendly and good company, and when Chris began to play, she couldn't believe the difference between the organ in the Great Hall and the one at St Biddolphe's. The deep throatiness of the crashing chords moved her more than she'd expected.

Afterwards, Chris took them back to his house where he'd laid out a cold supper on the dining-room table. His dark eyes shone with excitement and triumph as they congratulated him. He opened a bottle of champagne. He seemed a very different person to the man who had taken her to The Supper Club two weeks earlier.

One evening towards the end of July, Susie came home from work alone because Louise was working on something she needed to finish, and she was shocked to see the midwife's bicycle propped up outside the Dolland house. Martha's baby wasn't due for several more weeks, and she knew it could not be a routine visit at this time of day. She then saw Mrs Powell, Martha's neighbour on her other side, signalling to her from her window.

Mrs Powell was an elderly widow who spent much of her

time watching what went on in the street. She opened her door, wiping her hands on her pinafore. 'Bert came home about twelve and took the babies across to Mrs Smith's.' Lena Smith lived opposite and was friendly with Martha. 'The midwife has been there since one o'clock,' she went on, 'and if Martha is still in labour she must be having a hard time.'

At that moment, the midwife came out and started strapping her bag and equipment onto her bike. 'Is all well?' Susie wanted to know.

'Yes, Martha has had a little girl.'

'But she wasn't due for another three weeks. Doesn't that make it premature?'

'A little early, but babies aren't like trains running to a timetable. They're both well.'

Susie was heading for Martha's front door. 'Let her rest for a few hours before you go in,' the midwife advised, 'she's very tired and her husband is with her.'

'Martha hasn't got that much strength,' Mrs Powell said softly, 'it doesn't sound as though it went all that well for them.'

'At least it's all over,' Susie said, and crossed the road to Lena Smith's front door to collect the children. As soon as it opened Rosie came crawling up the hall. 'Mama,' she said. Susie lifted her onto her shoulder and began telling Lena the news.

Seconds later little Jonjo threw his arms round one of her legs. 'Oozy,' he said. That was the nearest he could get to saying Susie.

He was a sturdy child with a mischievous smile, plump rounded limbs and a mop of dark hair. He could crawl at twice the pace Rosie could, was never still and went round opening cupboards and handling ornaments, Susie was always leaping to her feet to protect her mother's belongings.

She took them home and let herself in to start preparing a meal. When Louise arrived half an hour later and heard the news, she shot straight out again to see Martha.

An anxious Bert opened the door. 'She's very tired,' he said, 'but happy.'

Louise thought she looked grey and absolutely exhausted. 'She'll be better tomorrow when she's had a night's sleep,' she said.

'We've decided to call her Wendy,' he said, putting the baby in her arms. She was tiny and seemed as light as a feather.

Louise was shocked. 'I didn't ask what she weighed?'

'Just a smidgeon under five pounds.'

Louise stared down at her. 'I expected her to be more like Jonjo, a large, strapping baby. I hope taking care of Rosie as well hasn't been too much for Martha.'

'She said not. The midwife said the baby was all right; she's light because she's been born a few weeks early.'

'But Jonjo was born a few weeks early too,' she said.

'Well, yes,' he was frowning.

'It could be because this new baby has come so quickly after Jonjo. Would you like us to look after him this evening so you can concentrate on Martha and the new one?'

'That would be a great help.' Bert was grateful. 'After Martha's tried to give the baby some milk, I'm going to settle her down for a good sleep tonight.'

Susie went to work the following day, but Louise started her holiday so she could take care of Martha and the children.

Susie didn't get to see Wendy until that evening. As soon as she got home, she swung Rosie up in her arms for a hug. Jonjo was clamouring for a hug too, so Louise picked him up. 'You must be dying to see Wendy,' she said, and the whole family trooped up to Martha's room.

As she climbed the stairs, Susie could hear the new baby mewling like a kitten. Martha was sitting up in bed nursing her, 'I think she's got colic, poor darling,' she said, but she seemed absolutely besotted with her new daughter.

'Can I hold her?' Louise asked. She put Jonjo down on his feet and he immediately tried to climb up to his mother. 'Hello pet,' she said as he threw his little arms round her neck.

Louise rocked Wendy and tried to soothe her with comforting sounds. She was equally enamoured with the new baby and parted the shawls to show her to Susie. 'Would you like to give her a cuddle?'

Susie was shocked to see that Wendy was as skinny as a plucked chicken. 'You're better with babies than I am,' she said. She couldn't see why everybody drooled over a baby like that, not when Rosie and Jonjo were so much more attractive and responsive.

She'd already heard that several heads along Milner Street had nodded over little Wendy. 'A puny little thing, I don't give her much of a chance. Martha will be lucky if she manages to bring that one up.'

'Is she hungry?' Louise asked, and Martha put Jonjo from her to undo the front of her nightdress to put her to her breast.

Jonjo screamed. Susie moved Rosie to her other shoulder and picked him up too. 'Do you want us to keep Jonjo for another night?' she asked.

He shouted, 'Want Mummy. Want Mummy.'

'Better leave him with me for now,' Martha said.

'Your Mummy needs to rest, darling,' Louise said, fondling his head. But they could hear Bert coming upstairs after spending some time at work, so Susie took her mother and her daughter home.

Later that evening, almost an hour after they'd put Rosie down for the night, Bert brought a rather sleepy Jonjo to their house. 'Will you have him for the night?' he asked, and carried him up to Rosie's bedroom where last night's makeshift bed, the mattress from his cot and some of his bedding was still in one corner.

'He's being quite difficult,' Bert said when they came down again. 'He tried to hit the new baby. Martha had to get up to see to him. Wash him and put him in his pyjamas. He wouldn't let me do it.'

'He's jealous,' Susie said, 'poor Jonjo.'

'Martha shouldn't let him see her making a fuss of the new baby,' Louise sighed.

When Louise's holiday finished, Susie started hers. Every afternoon she pushed Wendy out at one end of the pram with Rosie at the other so that Jonjo could have some time alone with Martha.

'He's all right,' Susie told Bert, 'he's not naughty when he's with us. Boisterous perhaps, and never still, I daren't take my eyes off either of them.'

'He hasn't taken to Wendy,' Bert said.

Susie could see why, and she couldn't understand why both Bert and Martha rated Wendy so much higher than Jonjo.

She found him much more fun. Sympathy was what she felt for poor, puny Wendy.

At the end of a fortnight, Wendy was putting on a little weight and Martha was up and gaining strength, but Dr Grant thought she wasn't fit enough to take charge of a newborn baby and the two little ones.

Jonjo was now nearly a year old, walking into everything, a real ball of mischief. At ten months, Rosie was as pretty as a picture with her red hair and big round eyes. She was up on her feet, feeling her way round the furniture, but able to move like quicksilver on all fours.

When Christopher came for his Sunday lunch and saw the position, he told Louise to take another week off to look after her family.

CHAPTER NINETEEN

DURING HER UNEXPECTED WEEK off work to look after Martha and the children, Louise finally got round to visiting Mr Coyne at the vicarage and asking him directly to find somebody else to take over the job of treasurer. 'I've done it for almost twenty years but now I'm finding it too much,' she said. 'I want somebody else to take it over. I'll show them how I keep the books and help over the first month or so, but I can't go on.'

She had been saying this to the vicar since Easter, and telling him she was having difficulty finding time to work on the church accounts. 'Of course, I do understand you have a lot to do,' Mr Coyne said sympathetically. 'I'll see what I can do.'

Louise let a month go by and then as he shook her hand at the church door after morning service one Sunday, she said, 'Can I ask if you've found a replacement for me yet? I have quite a pile of bills waiting to be entered.'

'I'm so sorry, my dear,' he said, 'not yet, but I'm doing my best. Give me a little more time, if you would.'

She asked him again a month later and Mr Coyne wrung his hands and said, 'Nobody feels they can do it as well as you, my dear. Do you realise how valuable your work is to the church? We all very much appreciate what you do, so please think again about continuing to do this little job for us.'

When she told Susie, she said, 'There's no reason why Mrs Coyne can't do the accounts, or he can do them himself. They just don't want to be bothered.'

By three months of age Wendy was quite lively, smiling up at anybody who hung over her pram. Martha was finding the new baby and two toddlers very hard work. Bert's Aunt Gertrude came one day a week to help clean the house, and his mother came regularly to take both the toddlers to the local park so Martha could rest.

One Saturday lunchtime, Louise bought two fresh herrings on the way home from work to fry for lunch. She let herself in and flopped down in the living room to change into her slippers. Susie had the table set and the fire burning up nicely.

'Susie,' she called upstairs as she took the fish into the kitchen, 'I'm home.'

The fish was frying gently and Susie was cutting bread when they heard a frantic knocking on the front door and ringing of the bell. Louise was alarmed; she knew Bert was home for his dinner because she'd seen his van parked outside.

Susie rushed to open the door. Martha let out a wail of anguish and came flying inside to hurl herself into her mother's arms. 'Mum! Mum! Help me!'

'What is it? What's the matter?'

'It's Wendy . . .' She was trying to tell them what had happened, but in her panic couldn't get the words out.

'Is she not well?' Louise led her out. 'Let's go and see. Susie, turn the light out under the fish.' Once inside the next door house they went straight upstairs. A harassed Bert was holding

Wendy in a bundle of shawls in one arm and trying to put the other round Jonjo, who, having heard his mother's cries, was screaming too.

Martha snatched the baby from him. 'I can't wake her.'

Bert's face was screwing with agony. 'I'm afraid she's dead,' he said.

Louise's mouth went dry with fear. 'Surely not!'

'Please take this one. We really can't cope with him now.' Bert dumped Jonjo in Susie's arms where he clung to her in terror. At that moment an ambulance screamed to a halt outside. Martha was weeping and hugging the bundle of shawls to her. Bert tried to take it from her but she wouldn't let go. He hurried them both out to the street and the others followed. The front door of number 24 slammed behind them. A small crowd of neighbours was already gathering in the street.

Within moments, Martha, the baby and Bert were inside, and the ambulance was racing away towards the hospital. Louise found she was shaking and her knees felt quite weak. Tears were streaming down both Susie's and Jonjo's cheeks. 'Mummy,' he wailed, struggling to free himself from her arms.

The neighbours were coming into the street to ask, 'Was it the baby? What's happened?'

Louise could only shake her head, 'We don't know.' She turned to go back into number 24, because she could see Jonjo had wet himself and needed clean pants.

'Are you locked out?' the neighbours asked.

'It doesn't matter, the back door will be open and we can reach it easily through our backyard.'

'You take him,' Susie said, 'while I see if I can find dry pants for him next door.'

174

Louise took him up to their bathroom. She wanted to cuddle him but he was fighting her off in frustrated rage. 'Want Mummy,' he kept sobbing, and couldn't be quietened by being told Martha would be back soon. Tears were streaming down Louise's face too by the time Susie returned from next door with clean clothes for Jonjo.

'Poor Martha,' Susie said, 'she's tried so hard to have babies. She wanted them so much. Now they've lost Wendy.'

'We don't know that yet,' Louise was determined not to give up hope. 'Perhaps they'll be able to bring her round. Let's wait and see.'

Louise was watching when Martha and Bert returned in a taxi later that afternoon. She didn't need to ask if the news was good or bad. Bert had his arm round Martha's waist and she was sagging against him. His shoulders were bent and both held their heads low, despair in every line of their bodies.

'We'll go round and ask,' Louise decided. 'Perhaps they'll want to talk about it, and anyway, they'll think it strange if we don't.'

'They'll want Jonjo now, won't they? Surely he'll be a comfort to them,' Susie said. The child had finally fallen asleep in her arms and she'd put him down to sleep on the sofa.

Louise thought for a moment. 'We'll bring him back if they prefer him to stay with us.'

Bert was on the phone in the hallway, telling his family the awful news, and he signalled to them to go through to the living room. Martha was alone, staring into space with black despair in her eyes.

'Yes, Mum,' Louise could hear Bert saying. 'I can't come

back today. I can't leave Martha, she's very upset. Are you very busy? Yes, I know Saturdays are always busy. A cot death, they said. It was nobody's fault, just one of those things. Yes, of course I'm upset too.' The phone went down and he came in to sit next to Martha on the sofa.

Jonjo was bouncing up and down, chortling with joy to see his mother again. Susie put him down on the floor and he walked over to her and tried to climb up on her knee. She ignored him. It was Bert who picked him up, but Bert's knee was not what Jonjo wanted. He fought to escape his arms and finally Martha realised what was happening and pulled him onto her knee, where he settled down quietly.

'This is a hundred times worse than a miscarriage,' she said. 'I was made up with Wendy. We both were. I don't know what I'm going to do, I'll be lost without her.'

'You still have Jonjo,' Susie said.

Martha screamed and jumped to her feet, letting Jonjo slide to the floor. 'I want a baby that is mine and Bert's! I want Wendy. Why did this have to happen to her? What have we done to deserve this?' Bert pulled her down on the sofa again and slid an arm round her quaking shoulders.

Louise scooped Jonjo up and hugged him, but she couldn't quieten his crying. Her heart went out to Martha, she could see how badly she was taking this. 'We've all known and loved Wendy,' she said, 'and this will leave a huge hole in our lives, but I know how much worse it is for you and Bert. We'll go home. Do you want us to take Jonjo with us and keep him overnight?'

'Yes please,' Bert said. 'Martha needs to rest now and I want her to get a good sleep tonight.'

Louise stood with Jonjo in her arms by the front door while Susie went upstairs to bring down his bedding and some of his toys and clothes. She pondered, not for the first time, why Martha didn't clasp Jonjo to her for comfort. Bert had said he wanted sons to follow him in the shop, yet Jonjo, a fine, fit, healthy baby was being pushed over to her while they grieved for poor Wendy.

She'd half suspected from the day Martha had brought him home from Scarborough that Jonjo was Becky's baby and not hers; that Martha's long visit to Becky's flat had been a well-planned manoeuvre to hide that fact. He was said to have been born at thirty-seven weeks too, yet he'd weighed in at over seven pounds, while Wendy had been less than five.

And just now, when Susie had tried to comfort Martha by reminding her she still had Jonjo, she'd said, 'I want a baby that is mine and Bert's.' That seemed to confirm her worst suspicions, as did the fact that they didn't want Jonjo near them tonight. Louise shivered. Martha had been obsessed about having a baby and Bert had been encouraging her. Had she hidden a third miscarriage and agreed to take over Becky's unwanted child? Those two had always been close; they could have arranged it so, but what of Bert? It hardly seemed possible that such a switch could have been hidden from him.

Becky had married Max soon after Jonjo was born, and seemed happy with him, but if Max was Jonjo's father, why give him to Martha? It didn't make sense. None of it made any sense, but she felt something very wrong might have been done to poor little Jonjo.

Christmas was coming and Louise continued to worry. If Susie could end up with a fatherless child, it was something she couldn't rule out for Becky. An illegitimate baby would have ruined her reputation, and with a baby to care for she could hardly have carried on with her stage career and gone out every night. But she'd given that up shortly afterwards to marry Max anyway.

But Louise had to put her family worries out of her mind for a while and concentrate on Christmas. Susie said it passed enjoyably, very much as it had done in previous years.

When the New Year began, Louise stayed up until midnight one night bringing St Biddolphe's accounts up to date, and the next day she telephoned the vicar to ask if she might call and see him at five thirty that afternoon on the way home from work. When she rang his doorbell, she had with her the St Biddolphe's ledgers and a file of correspondence.

'Do come in, Mrs Ingram.' It was the vicar's wife who opened the door to her and led her up the hall towards his study. 'Poor Tom has been desperately busy today sorting out parishioners' problems. It's all go for him, I'm afraid.'

'We're all very busy, aren't we?' Louise suspected Mrs Coyne had guessed the reason for her visit and was trying to pave the way for her husband to decline to take over the job. His study door was ajar and Louise saw him whisk the newspaper he was reading into a drawer as his wife ushered her in saying, 'Tom, Mrs Ingram has arrived.'

He stood up. 'Do come in, my dear, you're well I hope? Take a seat, do. Would you like a cup of tea?'

'Thank you no, I need to get home to cook our dinner.' Louise sat down.

'Then what can I do for you?'

Louise took the ledgers from her bag and put them on his desk. 'You may remember, Mr Coyne, that all last year I was telling you I wanted to give up my post as St Biddolphe's treasurer?'

'Yes of course, but I thought I'd persuaded you to carry on for a little longer? We have nobody else so well qualified to take on the job.'

'It doesn't need any qualifications. It's simple, straight-forward double entry book keeping, just adding together the weekly church collections and the money made by fundraising and setting the expenses and donations against it. I'm sure a man of your education would find it easy.'

'I am so pressed for time, my dear, that I feel I cannot take on any more work.'

'I've had to struggle to find the time for it for years, and now Susie has a child to take care of as well as a full-time job, she can't help as much with the housework, so I need to be relieved of the burden of keeping your accounts.'

'Oh dear!'

'I'd like you to sign this. It's a receipt for these two ledgers, the file of correspondence, and this purse containing two pounds four shillings and four pence, which is the sum currently in the petty cash account.'

'Petty cash? What do we use that for?'

Louise sighed. 'Cleaning materials for the church, tea and biscuits for the Mother's Union, laundry, that sort of thing.'

'I see.'

'And this is the bank statement showing the current balance of church funds. I paid money in this morning to tidy things up.'

'But I don't know . . .'

'Here is the statement, you can read the figures, and if you're concerned we'll count the petty cash.'

'That won't be necessary.' He picked up his fountain pen and signed. 'Do you know of anybody who would be able to take on this job?'

'Well, Mrs Curtis is always ready to help, isn't she? She might like to be appointed treasurer.'

'I did mention it to Mrs Curtis, but she has a large family that keeps her busy.'

'Then what about your wife? I'm sure she'd find it easy enough, and as I've said I'd be willing to give any guidance she needs to get started.'

'Oh dear! Dora has so much to do that she never seems to stop. No, I don't think . . .'

'No, well, perhaps one of the other ladies will. They're all very willing to help St Biddolphe's, as I'm sure you've found out.' Louise tucked the receipt in her handbag and stood up. 'Goodnight, Vicar, do let me know if my help is needed.'

She walked home feeling sorry that she'd had to be so heavy-handed with Mr Coyne, but knowing she would have had the job of treasurer permanently if she hadn't.

CHAPTER TWENTY

SUSIE WAS GETTING USED to her life as a working mother and finding her pleasure in Rosie and her family. She was doing her best to help Martha over the loss of Wendy. 'Time will help,' she told her. Martha had replied with a sniff of disbelief. 'It has helped me,' she went on. 'Now Danny's death is further away, I don't think about him so much. It does get easier.'

Grand National Day was coming round again and Susie wasn't looking forward to it. She'd been seeing much less of Fee and Jamie, but Jamie rang her up in the office as the day grew nearer. 'Are you being given the usual afternoon off? Shall we have something to eat and then go to a matinee like we did last year?'

'I'd like to, but Martha is a bit down at the moment, so her husband is taking her to Aintree to cheer her up. I told her I'd rush home from work to look after the toddlers. It seems the least I can do when she has them all the time.'

'Wouldn't your mum be willing to do that for you?'

'Probably she would, Jamie, but she does so much for me, not to mention doing things for everybody else, that I don't want to ask her. Grand National Day doesn't stir up the bad memories for me like it used to. How are things with you?'

'I suppose I'm over it too.'

'We'll go out some other time then?'

'I hope so, we need to catch up again, don't we?'

'We do. How are things at home?'

'No better. All is not well. Dad and Mum used to lay down the law with Draconian force to us, but now they spat at each other too.'

It seemed that Jamie was no happier.

Martha was excited at the thought of actually going to Aintree and seeing the Grand National. She had never been before, though Bert had gone to the course every year since she'd known him. She had either been pregnant or ill, and it was thought the crowds and the standing about would be too much for her.

She suggested to Bert that they take his Aunt Gertrude too, to repay her for her kindness in coming to help with the children whenever they had a crisis. Gertrude was delighted to be asked. Martha discussed with her what they should wear. 'I've made myself a new dress,' she told her.

'You'll need a coat to cover it, the weather forecast isn't that good,' Gertrude replied, 'and wear flat shoes, we'll be walking on grass.'

'In the newspaper photos the ladies look dressed to the nines and all seem to wear high heels.'

'The ladies they photograph are the wives and mothers of the trainers and owners. They sit behind glass in the private bars and enclosures sipping champagne, not fighting the crowds in the public places. Doesn't Bert come home exhausted?'

'Well, yes, he's usually tired.'

'It's not as glamorous as it looks in the photographs, Martha. Not for us ordinary folk. Dress for warmth and comfort, I'm going to, and let's hope it doesn't rain.'

That night Martha reported to Bert what Gertrude had said. 'Oh dear, what am I thinking of?' he asked. 'I usually just pay to get through the gates, but you two won't be able to walk round all afternoon and push your way onto the rail to see what's going on. I'll book seats for us in the grandstand where we can sit down and get a good view of the course.'

Previously, Bert had gone there by bus, 'But I'm shattered when it's over and there are always long queues to get a bus home. I'll take the van, that'll get us home more easily, though it only has two seats.'

'I'll go in the back,' Martha said.

'We'll put plenty of cushions in,' he said, 'it'll be less tiring for you both.'

Martha was really looking forward to it. On the day of the race, Bert worked in the shop during the morning and brought his aunt home to have lunch with them before setting off. Martha prepared a fancier meal than they usually had. The morning papers carried a build-up to the big race, and Bert studied the list of runners and the published opinions on racing form until he was word perfect; Martha tried to do the same.

Gertrude brought her camera. 'I've put in a new roll of film,' she told them. 'I'll take a few pictures of you and try to capture your high spirits when you find you've backed a winner.' They set off as soon as Susie returned home.

A row of flags was fluttering in a stiff breeze outside the main entrance and a military band was playing a stirring march. The crowd was brimming with eager anticipation as it poured through the turnstiles on to the course, and Martha felt herself being swept along with it. It was cold, but the thin sunshine was bright and the excitement of the crowd was infectious.

Bert got racing cards for them, but the horses were already lining up for the two o'clock race and they had to rush to take their seats to see it. Martha knew nothing about the horses in this race, but the thundering hooves and the screams and shouts of encouragement from the crowd whipped up a general feeling of excitement.

'We need to get some bets on before the next race,' Bert said, leading them out of the grandstand and towards the row of bookies. 'Have you decided which horse you want to back?'

Gertrude had her camera out and said, 'I've got a good one of you, Martha, waving your race card and looking as though you're having the time of your life. Hang on, I'll take another of you, Bert.'

Martha was fascinated by the elegant and fashionable outfits some of the ladies were wearing, and was studying them, wondering if she could make clothes of such striking designs. A woman in an eye-catching yellow dress worn with a fur tippet and a huge hat caught her eye; she was partnered by one of the gentlemen wearing a top hat. Martha laughed aloud because she'd not immediately recognised him. 'Look, there's Mr Curtis waiting to put a bet on,' she said. Gertrude turned and inadvertently took a photo of him instead of Bert, and ended up having a fit of giggles.

'Who is that with him?' Bert wanted to know. Martha turned for a second look; the very attractive young woman was smiling up at him. 'I've no idea,' she said slowly, 'I've never seen her before.'

'I thought you knew the Curtis family?'

'I do, but Susie knows them better. She'd probably know.'

They returned to their seats for the two-thirty race, and had an excellent view of the finish, but they won nothing. Bert was a good host and took them to see the horses and put on more bets. After the three o'clock he decided it was time to go to the café for tea and cakes. They had to wait to get a table, but they had Curtis cakes which Martha and Gertrude considered a great treat. 'Though it's twice the price for tea and cakes here than it would be down the road,' Gertrude said to Bert. 'I fancy a second cake, but it's daylight robbery at these prices.'

'Go on,' Bert said indulgently, 'we don't come often.'

As a result they glimpsed the horses racing in the three-thirty from the café window, and Gertrude learned from the loudspeakers that she had a small win. They threaded their way through the crowd and waited in line while she collected her winnings, and while they were there they put on their bets for the big race. Gertrude was still full of energy, taking photographs of them and the horses.

Back upstairs they went to their seats in the stand. The horses ran in the four o'clock race, but by now everybody was waiting for the big race, the Grand National. Bert insisted they go down again so they could see the competing horses' parade before the race. These were the horses they'd read about in the papers. Bert had picked out Reynoldstown as his choice to win, and Martha and Gertrude decided to put a little bet on him too. Gertrude took a photograph of the horse and rider.

As the time for the big race drew close, Martha could feel the mounting tension. She was enthralled. The horses lined up and the crowd fell silent. Then they were off and thundering down the course, and she soon lost sight of the horse they'd backed. The steeplechase was over four miles and thirty fences that were higher than on any other course. There was no place from which the racing horses could be seen throughout the race, but there was a commentary broadcast over the loud-speakers to help them follow it, except that the cheering and shouting of the spectators drowned it out at times.

The race was twice round the course, and as the horses came thundering into view again, the crowd in the grandstand leapt to their feet, waving their race cards, cheering and screaming with excitement. Nobody was louder or more excited than Bert.

There were fewer horses in the race now, but Martha knew Reynoldstown was up amongst the leaders and she could no longer sit still. Bert grabbed for her hand, his eyes alight with anticipation. She thought she caught a glimpse of their horse but then lost him again. The crowd exploded in a crescendo of shouts, cheers and screams as the first horses shot past the winning post. Martha was holding her breath and straining her ears, and the announcement that Reynoldstown had won left her tingling.

Bert had hold of Martha on one side and Gertrude on the other as he rushed them down to the queue to collect their winnings. 'We've all won! It'll be more than enough to cover all our outgoings,' Bert crowed. 'Isn't that marvellous?'

'I shall buy a new outfit with mine,' Gertrude said.

'It's been a fabulous day,' Martha smiled happily.

For Louise, time began to pass more quickly, filled to bursting point with work and the minutiae of everyday events. She derived contentment from it and from her family, but she was still afraid Susie was missing her carefree youth.

'We're settled now,' she told her, 'and this will be our life from now on. Not everything is how we'd like it, but we have to accept things as they are. At least we have a roof over our heads, plenty to eat, and we have our family round us.'

Not that they saw very much of Becky. Two or three times a year she invited them over to her home, where her extravagant lifestyle showed them what they were missing. Louise always invited them back, but somehow she never felt close to her middle daughter.

Becky was generous, and Louise received many expensive gifts from her, as did her sisters. She showered Rosie and Jonjo with toys and clothes, and handed on a lot of her own expensive clothes to Susie and Martha who were delighted with them.

Martha continued to have bouts of illness. In the summer of 1938 she'd felt stiff and full of pain, and Louise had had to call on Miss Maddocks for help looking after the children for a couple of hours each day.

As Martha recovered, Dr Grant advised her to swim regularly. She had never learned to swim but Bert arranged for her to have lessons at the local baths, so she went every morning as soon as Miss Maddocks arrived and said it made her feel much better. As soon as she learned to swim she started taking the children with her, and both were very quick to learn. Once they could do a length of the baths it became an enjoyable way to pass a wet afternoon, and Martha felt her swimming continued to improve with practice.

Louise watched her grandchildren growing up and was

delighted to see how attached to each other they had become. 'They seem more like brother and sister than cousins,' she said to Susie.

'Or twins,' she smiled. 'Only a month separates them in age, though Jonjo is a couple of inches taller.' He was a healthy, sturdily built lad, who wanted to kick balls about and play games. There was little family resemblance, though. Rosie was a pretty, dainty child with a mop of glorious red curls. He was boisterous while she was quieter, enjoyed stories and nursery rhymes and soon had a wide vocabulary. Louise acquired lots of picture books and nursery toys and games from St Biddolphe's fundraising sales in order to help Martha keep them occupied.

The term before they were to start at the church school, Martha went down with another flare-up of her illness. Miss Maddocks, who taught the nursery class, suggested Louise bring the children to school for the morning so Martha could rest. Bert collected them at lunchtime and Martha managed to look after them in the afternoon. This went on for a month, and they all hoped that when they both started full-time school that September they would take to it like ducks to water.

Martha found life much easier once the children were at school during the morning and continued to swim regularly. In the school holidays, when she had the children to look after all day, she took them with her and soon Jonjo was doing so well she entered him in a swimming club so that he was able to compete in races against children of his own age.

Susie took her annual week's holiday at the beginning of the school holidays and took over the childcare completely in order to give Martha a rest. 'It's a novelty for me,' she told her, 'and I enjoy it.'

She was hoping for fine weather, but on the first Monday it was raining heavily. Jonjo was keen to go swimming, so Susie agreed to take the children. She had never learned to swim and asked Martha if she could borrow her swimsuit.

'I have several,' she smiled, 'come and see.' Susie followed her upstairs to her bedroom with both children trailing behind.

Martha pulled out a drawer. 'I have these two that are made of wool. Traditionally it was considered the best material for swimsuits because it clings to you, but when it's heavy with water the weight makes it droop. Wool is fine if you just want to parade on the beach, but it looks terrible after a swim.'

'This red one is quite smart,' Susie said, spreading it out on the double bed.

'You can have it if you want, but you want to get it wet, don't you?'

'Of course.'

'Then look at this one that I've made.' It was green with a small floral print and made of dress-weight cotton. 'It's now possible to buy elastic thread I can use on my sewing machine, shirr elastic it's called. I cut a pattern from that red suit, hemmed it, and joined the front to the back down one side. Then I stitched rows of shirr elastic on it half an inch apart and joined it up on the other side. It was very easy and it's marvellous to swim in because it's light and clings to your body. I've made trunks for Jonjo and a little swimsuit for Rosie. Here, Rosie, what d'you think of this?'

She squealed with delight, holding the pink confection against her. 'It's lovely! I want to put it on now.'

'No, it's too cold,' Martha said.

'Just to try it on,' she wheedled. 'I need to do that, don't I?

Auntie Martha, we always try on what you make for us.'

'I know it will fit you. That's another good thing about shirr elastic, it expands to fit several sizes. That will fit you for years, Rosie.'

Jonjo had been quietly turning over the contents of Martha's drawer, and was spreading photographs along her dressing table. 'There aren't any of me and Rosie in this lot,' he complained.

'No, they're what Auntie Gertrude took when we went to the races,' Martha said.

'Let me see,' Rosie pushed forward.

'Susie,' Martha said, 'why don't you borrow my new swimsuit and if you like it, I'll make one for you. It takes very little cloth.'

'Doesn't it squash the boobs a bit?' Susie stretched the top part out.

Martha laughed. 'You're right, but I've been thinking how I could solve that. I can shape the rows of elastic to circle round underneath. Perhaps draw the lines with French chalk on the wrong side first, to make sure I get them even and in the right place.'

Susie sighed. 'I wish I could sew like you.'

'You learned to type instead.'

Susie turned to collect together the photographs Jonjo had spread out. 'These of you at Aintree are good.'

'Bert kept saying he was going to buy a frame for that one, but he never got around to it.'

'To remind you how smart you could be if you made more effort,' Susie said. 'You've got one here of Mr Curtis.'

'Yes, I've shown them to you before, haven't I? We only saw

him once and I think Gertrude wanted to get the atmosphere of the crowd. Who is he with, do you know?'

Susie studied the picture and was reminded that several times Jamie had said over recent years that his parents were no longer on good terms. Could it be that Mr Curtis had another girlfriend?

'No,' she said, 'I don't know who she is, but she's very glamorous.' If he had another woman, it was none of her business. 'I don't know all his friends and relatives.' He'd been very good to her and Rosie, and with Mrs Curtis being the sort she was . . . Well, she wouldn't blame him.

Chapter Twenty-One

THE RAIN HAD EASED a little by the time Susie set off to the swimming baths with the children, but it was a damp, unpleasant morning. It was a new experience for her. Jonjo said he was old enough to use the men's changing room, and Rosie aired her superior knowledge by taking her to the women's changing room and showing her where their clothes must go to be safe.

Martha had been right about the swimsuit: it fitted her like a glove. Jonjo was already swimming up the pool when she went out, but at first glance Susie found so much green water a little intimidating.

'There's a shallow end if you can't swim,' Rosie led the way. There were not many people in the pool and most of them were children.

'What about your swimming ring?' Susie began to blow it up.

'I don't need that any more. Auntie Martha must have meant it for you.' She jumped into the pool with a splash.

Jonjo came swimming back, rivulets of water running down his face. 'I can swim underwater,' he told her, 'and I want to try a dive.'

'You're like a fish in the water,' she told him.

'Rosie can't swim as well as me. Mum thinks she needs her swimming ring to be safe.' Rosie was doing a laborious breast stroke but she'd crossed to the other side of the pool.

'I can do a width,' she shouted, 'watch me, Mum, I'm coming back.'

'Yes, you can swim,' Susie told her, lowering herself gingerly into the water. It seemed very cold.

'I'll teach you to swim,' Jonjo said, brimming with confidence. 'You've got to come deeper than that. I'll hold your chin up and you must move your arms and legs like Rosie's doing.'

Susie was afraid Jonjo wouldn't be much help to her. He was blowing up the blue and red swimming ring. 'You need this,' he said, 'go on, try it.'

Wearing it, Susie managed three strokes before she felt she was going under and put her foot down. 'It's no good being scared of the water,' Jonjo said. 'Put your head under a few times so you get used to it.'

'No,' she said, 'no.'

One of the other mothers took pity on her and took over. 'Come and hold onto the rail here,' she said, 'and work on getting your leg movements right first.'

Susie followed her advice. She'd noticed the woman when she'd first come in. She had a trim figure and was wearing a stunning bathing costume in scarlet, but it was of traditional wool. She'd been teaching a young boy how to dive, but seemed to be looking after several children.

'It's a question of getting your arms and legs moving together,' she told her. 'Slow down, and you need to keep your body level in the water.' Susie felt she had to keep her head high so she could breathe. 'That pushes your feet down. Turn on your back and try to float, then you will be level in the water. Come on, I won't let you drown.'

Susie did as she was told and the girl supported her with a hand under her back. 'Now kick with your feet and you'll swim.' Susie felt she was making progress.

'Mummy, come and teach me to dive,' a small boy yelled.

'Have a try on your own,' the girl said to Susie. 'I need to keep an eye on my children.'

'I need to be in shallower water,' Susie said, moving away, 'so I can stand up when I need to.' She tried but knew she hadn't got it quite right.

Suddenly, she was aware of frantic splashing a few feet from her, and standing up she lifted a gulping child free of the water. 'Mummy,' the little girl wailed. 'Mummy!' She was about Rosie's age.

The same woman came rushing back to take the child from Susie's arms. 'You're all right, Caroline, don't cry,' her mother gave her a cuddle. 'Thank you,' she said to Susie. 'What happened then, pet?' The child was wearing a rubber swimming ring but it had no air in it.

'Her swimming ring has let her down,' Susie pointed out.

'Yes, I wonder why? It's a new one. Oh my goodness!' Another child, even younger, was wailing for her attention. Expertly, she scooped him up with her other arm and lifted both out to sit on the side. 'You're doing well, Bobby, I'm proud of you. You've made good progress this morning.'

She lifted herself easily on her arms to sit between the children and turned to smile at Susie. 'It's not easy looking after three when only two can swim. Let's have a look at that ring, Caro.' She lifted it over her head. 'Gosh, there's quite a big tear just where it blows up. No, it's come unstuck, no wonder it went down suddenly.'

Caroline, the older child, had stopped crying and was looking at Susie. She patted her knee. 'So much water is scary until you can swim, isn't it?' she said.

'You're lucky both of yours can,' the mother said.

Susie giggled. 'Having Jonjo as my teacher made me feel a bit of a fool.'

'Your son is telling you the right way to go about it,' she laughed. 'He's a good swimmer for his age.'

'He's my nephew,' Susie said, and asked the little girl, 'Would you like to borrow Rosie's ring? It held me up so it won't let you down.'

'No,' she said, 'I don't want to swim any more.'

'Oh dear,' her mother said. 'That would be a pity because if you give up, Bobby will soon be a better swimmer than you are, and you wouldn't like that when he's two years younger. Put on this blue and red ring and I will stand one side and this kind lady will stand on the other, so you'll be as safe as houses.' The child was persuaded back into the pool.

'Better this way,' she mouthed at Susie. 'That frightened Caro.'

Five minutes later and with a lot of splashing, Caroline was moving away from them, her fright forgotten, and her mother went back to sit on the side next to her son. 'It's easy to keep an eye on them from here,' she said as Susie pulled herself up alongside. Jonjo had joined a group of small boys, and Rosie was happily ploughing back and forth across the width of the pool.

'I'm Lily Milman, by the way,' the girl said. 'You all have

lovely bathing suits, I've not seen anything like them before. Could I ask where you got them?'

'My sister Martha, Jonjo's mother, is a dressmaker and she made them. This one belongs to her, but she's going to make one for me. I've told her she needs to do something to accommodate the bust. It's flattening me.'

'Is it comfortable? I hate the way this sort is dragged down by the weight of the water. If I don't keep hitching it up it would be round my knees.'

Susie laughed. 'It is comfortable and stays put, but yours is a very smart swimsuit.'

'It is when it's dry, but the water pulls it out of shape. Would your sister make swimsuits for me and my children?'

'I expect she would, though she doesn't do all that much any more, except for family and friends. She has poor health.'

'Will you ask her if she would? I do a bit of high diving in competitions,' she said, 'and I've never been able to get a swimsuit that stays in place.'

'High diving? That sounds exciting. Do you teach people to swim too?'

'I used to – once it was my bread and butter – but I'm not having much success with Caroline.'

'I'll ask Martha, although perhaps you've already met her? She regularly brings the children here to swim. I've brought them this morning to give her a rest while I'm on holiday, but she'll be bringing them next week because I have to go back to work.'

'No, I've not been here before, we usually go to the Prescott Baths but they're closed temporarily for a refit. Will you be coming again tomorrow?'

'I thought perhaps I'd take them to the museum if it was wet. I could give you Martha's phone number and you could ask her yourself.'

'Excellent. I'll do that. When I'm dressed I'll write it down.'

She did, and afterwards Susie noticed Lily Milman ask the staff to call a taxi to take her and her three children home.

'Those children don't go to our school,' Rosie said. The rain was still drumming down when they went out. They started to walk but a bus came along when they were near a stop, so Susie hustled them on to it.

'We should have kept our wet bathing suits on,' Jonjo said, 'then the rain wouldn't have mattered, we wouldn't be able to get any wetter.'

Susie heard from Martha that Lily Milman had rung her and that both had arranged to take their children swimming on Thursday morning so they could meet. Martha was going to take her tape measure and find out exactly what Lily wanted. Susie was glad to have a morning to herself and went shopping in town.

When she went home for her lunch, Martha said, 'Lily is friendly and very nice. She wants a black bathing suit with white trimmings. I had the feeling I'd done a small sewing job for her before, but I didn't recognise her name and she says she lives in Gatacre and doesn't often come this way. D'you remember that photo Aunt Gertrude took at Aintree? She reminds me of the girl we saw with Mr Curtis, what do you think?'

'I vaguely remember. She was good-looking.' Jonjo was sent upstairs to fetch the whole packet down so Susie could see it again.

She pondered over it. 'It's hard to say. I remember her in her bathing suit with wet hair, not dressed in her best like this.'

'But you said you saw her dressed before you left.'

'Yes, in her mackintosh. I suppose it could be.' Susie wasn't sure and would prefer to think Lily Milman had nothing to do with Mr Curtis.

'Well, before I start making the swimsuit for her, I want you to try on the one I've made for you, so I can see whether I've got the couple of rows of stitching round the bust in the right place. I finished it as soon as I came home and I've left it on my bed.'

Susie went upstairs and was surprised and delighted. Martha had told her it would take very little material, and had offered her a choice from her collection of off-cuts. She'd chosen a swirling pattern of blue and white, and the extra elastic round her breasts made a huge difference, showing off her figure brilliantly. She rushed downstairs to show her sister.

'Great,' Martha said. 'I'll do the same for Lily.'

'I'll have to carry on going to the baths now I have this,' Susie chortled, but though she took the children there again, she didn't see Lily Milman.

At the end of the week, she said, 'Weather wise, I didn't pick a good week for my holiday, did I? I hope Mum does better, but it's been a great change from the office.'

She'd been back at her desk for several days when Martha told her Lily Milman had come with her children to pick up the swimsuits she'd made for them and that she was very pleased.

Turning the office calendar to August, Susie was reminded that Fiona would soon be having her twenty-second birthday.

She hadn't heard from her for some time, so during her tea break she tried to ring her at work, but the operator said, 'Miss Curtis is not in the office this morning.'

'Jamie Curtis then, is he there?'

'Yes, hold the line please, I'll put you through.'

'Susie?' he said in a guarded voice. 'I tried to ring you last week but you weren't at work. I can't speak here, I'll meet you tonight straight from work.'

'Sorry, Jamie, I can't do that, Martha's going out. What about tomorrow?'

'No, this is my last day here. What about lunchtime?'

'Yes, all right. I've brought a sandwich.'

'Outside the jam factory gates then, it's one to two you have?'

'Yes, see you at one.'

Susie put the phone down and wondered what had been happening to the Curtises. It seemed Jamie had made up his mind to leave at last.

As she ran out at lunchtime she could see him looking forlorn and miserable as he waited at the gates, but as soon as he saw her approaching, a broad smile lit up his face.

'I'm glad to see you're happy,' she told him, 'I was afraid something bad was happening to your family.'

His smile slipped. 'It is, you're right there, but it's changed everything. Shall we walk to the Pier Head and eat our sandwiches there?'

'Yes, where's Fee gone?'

'She's done a runner, eloped with Leonard Ross.'

'What?' Susie stopped walking. 'Gone off with him just like that?'

'Yes. The parents have been doing their usual thing. They wouldn't give their approval for her to marry Len, and of course they hoped that with time she'd change her mind. Well, I don't have to explain it to you. Mother doesn't like him. She thinks he isn't good enough for her daughter.'

'So Fee got fed up with waiting?'

'It wasn't just that. We've had a proper family dust-up. Real trouble. Mother found out that Dad had another girlfriend. Well, not just a girlfriend but another family. It seems we have three half siblings we didn't know about, all much younger than us, of course.'

'Goodness!' Susie immediately thought of Lily Milman. Had Martha been right about her?

'Well, the parents have been holding our family as a cut above every other. Dad is determined to provide us all with a good living and Mother has brought us up strictly to believe in St Biddolphe's principles. We are morally bound to follow the good examples they have set us and respect them and their wishes at all times. Fee started packing the night the news broke. "I'm getting out of here," she told them. "I'm going to follow your example Dad."

'It was the opening of the floodgates. I'm getting out too. I've joined the Air Force, volunteered in fact.'

'I thought National Service had already started, that you'd be called up soon anyway?'

'It has started, and that was a big comfort, that I'd be called up and there was nothing I or they could do to stop it. But the government is calling men up in batches by birth date, and mine hasn't come round yet. So I thought I'd volunteer and jump the gun, so to speak. Volunteers have the advantage of choosing which service they go in and what they do.'

They hung over the railings at Pier Head to eat their sandwiches, as the wall where it was possible to sit was in full use. 'We'll have a cup of coffee in that café when we've eaten,' Jamie said.

'Great.' Susie had decided she would never say anything about Mr Curtis's secret to his children, but as the news had already exploded within his family, there seemed to be no further point in hiding it. 'Jamie,' she said, 'does the name Lily Milman mean anything to you?' She could see by the instant horror that came to his face that it did.

'How do you know her name? Surely the story isn't round the Parish already?'

'No. She's a passing acquaintance of mine. Martha is doing some sewing for her.'

His hand was covering his mouth. 'You mean she's told you?'

'No, a few years ago, Martha caught a glimpse of her with your father at Aintree, that's all.'

'Heavens! Oh goodness! Does Dad know?'

'No, how could I tell him? She doesn't know I have any connection to him. It was just so obviously their secret that I felt I had to keep my mouth shut – until you mentioned it.'

He took her arm and laughed. 'Come on, let's have that cup of coffee. I need it.' A corner table was just being vacated and they sat down. 'You know, Susie, I feel as though I've known you all my life. You were always around our house, first as Fee's friend and then as Danny's fiancée. You seemed to fit in more at Hillbark than I ever did.'

'I don't know about that. Your mother wouldn't agree.'

'Danny's death and the aftermath has split my family in two. There's Mother and Julia on one side and Dad with Jack and Rory on the other. Fee and I have upset both of them. We're out on our own now.'

'Time will quieten things down, and you're leaving tomorrow anyway.'

'Yes, I've had my medical and been told to present myself at Harden Aerodrome by midday tomorrow.'

'I'll miss you. Is there any way I can get in touch with Fee? I'd like to wish her well.'

'She charged out in high dudgeon when she found out about Dad's additional family, saying, "I don't know how you have the nerve to lay the law down to me. This is a case of do as I say, not do as I do." She didn't leave a forwarding address, but Fee is old enough and sensible enough to look after herself. She'll marry Len; it's what they both want.'

'And you'll get what you want too.'

'Yes.' He hesitated, and she knew he felt emotionally drained. It was a big step into a very different way of life. 'Will you write to me?' he asked.

'Of course, do keep in touch. I have to go. I'm going to be late back as it is. I'm going to miss you. Bye, Jamie.'

She felt quite sad to be losing him. She'd always enjoyed his company. Jamie meant a lot to her.

CHAPTER TWENTY-TWO

JAMIE DIDN'T SLEEP WELL that night. He told himself it was because he'd finally rejected his parents' plans and taken the steps to leave home, but that wasn't entirely it. He'd let Danny show him how it should be done, and it was only after Fee had followed suit that he'd screwed himself up to get out too. He'd been hopelessly slow to make up his mind, and after seeing Susie yesterday he wasn't sure he'd done the right thing.

There was something about Susie that touched a chord with him, and always had done. She was truly beautiful, and yesterday her big golden brown eyes had been full of friendship and understanding. How had he been so slow to make up his mind about her? He could have taken up with her at any time over the last few years, but he hadn't, and now he was going away, he wished he had.

He'd been too ready to accept the girlfriends Fee had pushed in front of him. He'd taken Sybil Watts out for the best part of a year. He'd liked her, and thought they were getting on well, but when he'd invited her home to play tennis on their court, she'd shown a preference for Rory. That hadn't lasted more than a few months either.

Fee had invited other girls to play tennis with them; there had been a real procession of them until he'd taken a fancy to

203

Hannah Mortimer, though she'd never given him much hope and he'd suffered from unrequited love for her for a couple of years. Fee kept introducing him to the girls she worked with and had even brought Angie Ross, a cousin of her boyfriend, home. Angie was fun, but the spark had not been there.

Had he been a complete fool over Susie? He remembered coming out of St Biddolphe's on Jack's wedding day to find her outside. He'd felt then that she could be very special to him, and that had not been the only time.

But Susie had said she'd write to him. He could write back and tell her how his feelings for her had changed, that he wanted more than friendship.

As time went on, rumours of a coming war began to circulate, and Susie knew nothing could have frightened her mother more. She'd lost so much in the Great War, and to her it didn't seem all that long ago. Bert and his family were also very troubled at the thought of another war with Germany. He'd never visited that country but had relatives living there who corresponded with his mother and aunt. 'It's going to tear our family apart, half on one side and half on the other,' he said.

The whole family lived in dread of war and felt powerless to do anything about it.

Susie received her first letter from Jamie telling her that Fee and Len had gone down to London where both had found jobs. They had married in the register office just as soon as they could arrange it and had settled into a flat of their own. He gave her their address.

He'd also written, *I took too long making up my mind and left it too late. By the time I volunteered for the Air Force, war was on the horizon and conscription had started. When I told the recruiting officers that I wanted to be trained as a pilot they smiled benignly at me and said, 'All you volunteers want to be pilots but what we need is navigators. Let's see, yes, you've got your Higher School Cert in maths, you can be trained as a navigator,' and that's what I'm doing. It seems I've swapped parental rules for Air Force discipline, but I've had a couple of flights in a trainer plane and I'm going to love flying. It beats selling cakes into a cocked hat.*

Susie read it through twice and wrote back telling him of the minutiae of her life and that she hoped he'd be happy in the Air Force. Fee also wrote to her before she'd got round to writing herself, asking her to keep in touch and saying that marriage was heaven. Now Susie was reduced to writing letters to her two best friends, she realised how much she missed them.

Louise continued to go to the Sunday morning service at St Biddolphe's. It had become her habit to wait for Christopher Berry, who had to finish playing the organ, and to take him home for lunch afterwards. He was very reserved and rarely told her anything of his history or his background, though she spoke often of her own family affairs. He played with Rosie when he came to their house and often brought her a little gift. Over the meal he would tease Susie, treating her as a fond uncle would. He told them he regretted not having a family of his own.

She knew Mabel's death had left him feeling low for several years, but over time he'd become more relaxed in her company, and in the office he came to her desk for a chat most days. At one time he used to invite Louise and Susie to a meal at his house during the week, and occasionally he invited other guests too, but that was when they could push Rosie there in her pram.

As Rosie grew older, Susie preferred to put her to bed at home and stay with her. Christopher was, after all, her mother's friend, not hers.

He'd referred to this as repaying them for their hospitality, but when Susie dropped out he said to Louise, 'I'm afraid I might tarnish your reputation with the St Biddolphe's ladies by inviting you to come to my house on your own. Would you allow me to take you to a restaurant instead?'

Louise smiled and said, 'Thank you, I'd like that.'

Susie laughed when she told her, and said he had some very old-fashioned ideas. 'So he invited me as a chaperone for you?'

He frequently invited Louise to the concerts, and quite often took her to the theatre or the cinema. Nowadays on these evenings out, he came to collect her from home and brought her back afterwards. She made a point of being ready and waiting at the appointed time. Often she watched from the window and when she saw his car draw up outside, she went out to greet him.

Susie laughed and said there was a lot of gossip in Milner Street about her 'posh gentleman friend', and that she'd heard the girls in the office referring to Louise as the 'boss's lady friend'. 'They're all asking when he's going to make it official.'

Louise was a little embarrassed by this and afraid Christopher would hear of it and not like it.

Last week he'd spoken of getting tickets for *Chu Chin Chow* at the Royal Court Theatre, a show that was being talked about in the office as being all the rage. For Louise, who could count the number of times she'd been to a theatre or a restaurant on one hand, it seemed she was living the high life.

As they drove up Milner Street, he said, 'I hope you won't

be disappointed, but I haven't booked the show. I'd like us to talk and we can't do that in a theatre. I've booked a table at the Stork Hotel for dinner.'

'It's a great treat for me to be taken to dinner at the Stork,' she told him. They had a drink in the bar first. Louise enjoyed the celery soup, the roast lamb, and the confection of fruit and ice cream, but was beginning to wonder what he wanted to talk about. He'd been restless and said little all evening and she could feel the tension building. She thought it might be about her job and felt he didn't know how to begin. When they had their coffee in front of them she prompted him by asking, 'What was it you wanted to talk to me about?'

He started to stir his drink noisily. 'You've been a good friend to me, a companion when I had nobody else,' he said. 'I know you took pity on me being on my own, but it's over four years now since Mabel died, and this has become our routine.'

His attention was suddenly riveted on her. The intensity of his gaze told her how important this was to him. 'I'd like more from you. Much more. Would you be willing to marry me?'

Louise gasped in astonishment. Recently he'd pecked her cheek with a social kiss when she was saying goodbye, but he'd never once mentioned feeling anything more than friendship for her. They'd never spoken of their feelings for each other. Her hand was resting on the table and he covered it with his own. 'I can see this has come as something of a shock to you.'

'I certainly wasn't expecting it,' she smiled uneasily, 'not quite like this.'

'I know you offered your support and friendship at a time when I was in need of it. That's the tradition of St Biddolphe's, isn't it? But it has gone on for five years. I'm sure we know each other well enough. I'm fifty-five now and set in my ways. I'm lonely at home. I look forward to Wednesdays and Sundays because you'll be with me.'

'But Chris, we see each other at work every day.'

'Yes, but there I have to concentrate on my job.'

Louise felt at a loss; here they were, one each side of a table, discussing marriage as they'd discussed jam across his desk.

'I'll quite understand,' he went on, 'if you say you don't love me. We're both well on in life now, and we've experienced love, but it isn't necessarily the only basis for marriage.'

That shocked Louise again. He wasn't saying he loved her, wasn't asking how she felt about him. She knew he was a shy and rather self-effacing man, but she needed to know how he felt about her and he wasn't telling her.

She took a deep breath. 'You're offering a sort of platonic marriage?'

'I suppose you could call it that. I'm a habit-bound old man. Marriage, yes, of any sort you want to have. What I'm trying to say, Lou, is that you don't have to share my bed if you don't want to.'

She couldn't stop another gasp at that. 'I don't know what to say.'

'You don't have to say yes or no now. You can think about it, take your time and let me know what you decide.'

It sounded more like a business arrangement than a proposal, but was that really how he'd meant it to sound? She'd have sworn this wasn't how he'd thought of Mabel. When he'd spoken of her in the past, he'd come over as a real romantic, and certainly shown his deep love for her. Louise was afraid he was thinking of her as second best, a companion to stem his loneliness.

She'd felt close to him and thought she'd seen him look at her with real affection. If only he'd said, 'I love you,' or even, 'I'm growing fond of you,' she'd have felt happier about it. She was more than fond of him. How could she not be when they'd shared so much and spent so much time together?

She knew he was waiting for her to say something, and finally managed, 'I was seventeen when I married Harold and eight years later he was killed. I've almost forgotten what marriage is like.' But she remembered the love they'd shared and the fizz it had brought to her life. 'Since then I've battled on alone to bring up my three daughters to be decent citizens.'

'But they've grown up now, Louise. Don't you want to think of yourself for a change, please yourself?' His gaze was honest and she knew he was speaking from his heart. 'I'd like you to move into my house and take charge of it, smarten it up if you can. As my wife, you wouldn't have to come to work unless you wanted to. I can provide you with every comfort. I'll look after you, care for you. I'll have a good pension when I retire.'

Louise felt she had to stop him. 'Chris, the girls still need me. You understand how it is with Susie? She relies on me and Martha to take care of Rosie, and it's only because we stick together and support each other that it's possible for her to work. She couldn't manage without me.'

'You'd not be far away, you could still help her.'

'Not in the way I do now.'

He stood up, his manner suddenly stiff, as though he wanted to bring this to an end. As he drove her home he said, with his eyes on the road, 'Think about it, won't you? And please,

please, whatever you decide, don't push me away. I want our friendship to carry on. I'd be lost without you.'

When he drew up outside her house he pecked her cheek as usual. She went indoors to find the table set for breakfast. She peeped in on Rosie, who was fast asleep with her clothes laid out for morning. Susie was reading in bed. Louise said goodnight and went to her own room with her head in a turmoil.

She'd thought about Chris a good deal over recent years. He'd given her so much that lifted her life above work, duty and endless thrift. She'd told everybody that she liked him, but deep down she knew it was more than that.

But why did he have to propose over a restaurant table with waiters hovering and the buzz of conversation from other customers all round them? He could have driven her to some pleasant viewpoint and proposed in the privacy of his car. If only he'd shown more affection for her – if only he'd said he loved her in a place where she could have thrown her arms round him. Louise found the thought of marriage without love rather off-putting, and was afraid she wanted more from him than he was offering. He'd acted as though he didn't have a romantic bone in his body, though she knew he had.

Susie was setting off to work with her mother the next morning when the postman handed her the letter he was just about to push through the letterbox. She was pleased to see it was from Jamie and pushed it into her handbag. In her family, letters were usually handed round for others to read, and instinctively she knew she didn't want to share Jamie's with anyone else. Once she reached her desk she tore the envelope open.

Dear Susie,

I have five days' leave, and intend to come home to make my peace with my parents. Fee has apparently already managed to do that and Dad has written saying our well-being was his only aim.

Fee has always reckoned I need a girlfriend and then I'll be content with my lot, and goodness knows she introduced me to dozens, but I couldn't help measuring them all against you. You came out top as the prettiest and most fun, even though I thought of you as almost my sister-in-law.

Would you be willing to come out with me on Wednesday evening? That will be the day I arrive home, but please keep the other evenings free for me too. I'm giving you plenty of notice as I know you are at work all day and will need to organise babysitting.

I'm glad you didn't take against us Curtises after Danny left you to cope alone with his baby and our mother refused to believe it was so.

Please say you'll come. All the news when we meet.

As ever,

Jamie.

Susie sat back in her chair, unable to start work immediately because her mind was too full of Jamie. She'd been thinking about him a lot since he'd gone away, surprised to realise just how much she missed him.

She had no urgent work to do, so scribbled a letter to him at her desk saying she would be home around six o'clock on Wednesday and would cook a meal for him.

That will give me a better chance of hearing all your news than going out. We can do that later in your leave.

Mum has been going out with Christopher Berry on Wednesday evenings, and it's a habit they rarely break. It isn't easy to get someone else to look after Rosie, as I can't ask Martha to do more than she already does. Please, please, don't refer to it as babysitting in Rosie's hearing, she'll be five in October and would never forgive you.

Susie posted her reply and told her mother what she planned to do that evening.

Louise had been awake pondering over Chris's proposal for half the night, and by morning she'd made up her mind and rehearsed the words to tell him. When she went to his office at mid-morning, he leapt out of his chair the moment he saw her, his dark eyes shining with hope.

She said briskly, 'I feel very honoured, Chris, that you've asked me to marry you, but I'm sorry, not at the moment. I can't walk out on Susie, she does still need me.'

She saw hope die on his face. 'Lou, forgive me, but I think the time for mothering Susie is over. She strikes me as very able. If you decided to marry again, she'd not want to stop you.'

Louise rushed on, eager to get this over. 'I feel I have to help her. She has no father you see. When Harold died I made a promise to myself that I'd bring up my daughters to have the best life possible. I feel that is my duty.'

'Duty? For heaven's sake! How old is Susie now?'

'Twenty-two, but I have Rosie to think of too.'

'No, you're wrong about that. I'd say Susie accepts Rosie as her own responsibility. She's her flesh and blood, her daughter, and she treats her in the same way you treat your daughters.'

That pulled her up; this wasn't going as she'd intended. 'I'd feel guilty if I abandoned them. Susie has no one else.'

'I don't understand what you can possibly feel guilty about. Your daughters are well-balanced girls and perfectly capable of getting on with their lives without you.'

Louise shuddered. She'd felt guilty for years, but not about her daughters, she wasn't being entirely honest about that. She'd hidden her guilt, deliberately pushed it into the background. Tried to forget it. She'd sensed over the years that Chris was doing the same, that there were things he just couldn't talk about. Things he wanted to keep hidden from her.

He put out both his hands and came to hold hers. 'Be honest with me,' he said, 'I can't sleep at night for thinking . . . I need to know how you think of marriage. Were you happy with Harold or was it a bad experience?'

'I was very happy, it isn't that.'

'What then?'

Louise took a deep breath. What they needed was to confess their sins, get everything out in the open. 'I told a lie to Harold and then couldn't bring myself to admit it. It lay between us.' Her voice wavered as she went on, 'He had a deep faith, thought a lot about religious matters and he was looking for a wife who thought the same way. Of course I wanted to have that too, and I hoped it might come with time. But I was in love with him and more than anything else I wanted to marry him and have his babies. So I pretended I had deep religious faith.'

She thought he was trying not to smile. 'Lou, he wanted a wife who could help him with his work and you did that.'

'I tried.'

'You succeeded. You gave me help when I needed it. You work hard for St Biddolphe's, isn't that what we all do? How old did you say you were when you married?'

'Seventeen.'

He was smiling openly. 'I'd say that was pretty normal behaviour for a seventeen year old.'

'Would you?'

He nodded. 'Can't I persuade you to forget motherhood and marry me?'

Louise felt she was no longer able to think straight. Did he think she was still in the mind-set of a silly seventeen year old? 'I'm sorry,' she managed.

'I'm sorry too,' he said. 'If you'd been willing, I'm sure we could have made it work. You will still be friends, come out with me? Invite me to your home for Sunday lunch?'

'Of course,' she said, 'nothing need change.'

But somehow it did cast a blight on their relationship. The ease that had developed between them seemed to fade after that.

CHAPTER TWENTY-THREE

SUSIE WAS REALLY LOOKING forward to Jamie's leave. She'd thought of asking Bert to bring her some of his best rump steak, but it was not something she was used to cooking and she'd have to do it when Jamie was with her. Also, Rosie had never eaten it and might decide she didn't like it and make a fuss.

She decided she'd stick to what she knew and make a stew the night before. She asked Bert to bring her braising steak – that would ensure the meat would be tender – and she'd buy a few mushrooms on the way home to lift it out of the ordinary. She'd make a trifle too for afters, so she'd just have to cook mashed potatoes and sprouts when she came home. No, not sprouts, Rosie could make a scene about those. It would have to be cabbage.

She pressed her best dress and put everything ready so she could have a quick wash and change as soon as she got home. Then she discovered that Mum had told Christopher that Jamie was coming on leave, and he told her to go home an hour earlier so she needn't rush too much. She felt very lucky to be working for him.

Even better, when she got home, Martha had peeled the potatoes, chopped the cabbage and even tidied up for her.

Rosie looked a grubby mess after a day at school, but she had plenty of time to wash her face and change her dress. All was ready by the time Mum was leaving. When Jamie rang the doorbell, Rosie ran to let him in. He swung her up in the air by way of greeting and she squealed with delight. When he'd put her down, Susie was behind her.

'Hello, Susie,' his broad smile was familiar but his brown eyes were searching her face. She hadn't seen him in his uniform before. He stood ramrod straight, just on six feet tall and looked smarter, fitter and more confident.

'I've brought a bottle of wine to have with this meal you're cooking,' he said. 'It smells delicious. I hope red is all right and that your mother allows wine in her house?'

'Yes, for special occasions.'

'To me, this is a very special occasion.' He put it on the table. 'Where d'you keep the bottle opener, Rosie?'

'I don't know,' she said. Susie had to find it and she brought out two wine glasses at the same time. 'But I want a glass of that pop too,' Rosie said.

'It isn't pop and I don't think you'll like it,' Jamie told her.

'It looks like raspberry flavour.'

'Here, try a sip of mine and see what you think.'

She took an eager mouthful but pulled a face and rushed to the sink to spit it out. 'Ugh! It's horrible, really awful.'

Jamie nodded. 'You have to be grown up to like it.'

Susie was pleased he was getting on well with Rosie and that everything in the kitchen was going according to plan. She dished up the dinner and Jamie praised her cooking, but inevitably, Rosie was taking most of their attention. They cleared away and washed up together, and later Jamie helped Susie put the child to bed.

'Shall I read you a story?' he asked her.

'I don't need to be read to any more,' she told him, 'I can read for myself. Nana takes me to the library and lets me choose my own books.' Susie found the current one, *Sinbad the Sailor*, for her, kissed her goodnight and led Jamie downstairs, leaving her light on.

Once back in the living room she threw herself down on the sofa. 'I'll go back in fifteen minutes or so and hopefully she'll be asleep, usually she is.' She smiled. 'Rosie's a bit of a distraction, isn't she?'

He joined her at the other corner of the sofa. 'She's lovely.' He had found the child a distraction, but so were Susie's long legs. They were encased in silk stockings, crossed at the knee now with one swinging slightly and dangling its sandal. He mustn't look at that.

'Now she's gone, what's been happening to you? I want to hear all about it.'

'I'm training to be a navigator,' he said, 'there's a lot to learn.'

'But you're enjoying it?' She looked up and smiled. Her hair was shining like spun gold in the lamplight.

'Yes, the flying part anyway. I was sent out at dusk with a trainee pilot and a course to set him on. We had to fly until we saw a beacon, then change to a different course and look for a flare path to guide us down.'

'It sounds nerve wracking to me.'

'We couldn't find the flare path, so I had to get him to return to the beacon and take new readings but we got it at the second attempt. The rest is like being back at school. Most of the navigation tutors are ex-school teachers and they're reacquainting us with logarithms.'

Jamie knew he wasn't doing this right, but then he'd rarely managed to do anything the right way. He wanted to tell her he'd been thinking about her and find out how she felt about him.

'They've sent you a long way from home.'

'Manston is a long way but it's all right. At least I'm still in England; there's talk of setting up RAF training schools in Canada and Australia. If the war starts they'll have to.'

'But you've had to leave your family and friends behind, you must find it lonely?'

'No, I'm living with a lot of men of my own age who've had to do the same. I'm enjoying that – there's no lack of interesting company.'

Jamie was instantly annoyed with himself; he'd said the wrong thing again. Why hadn't he said he was lonely and that he'd missed her? That would have put things on a more personal level.

'You'll be staying there?'

'Only until the course ends. After that I don't know. It depends on whether I'm considered competent at the end of it.'

She smiled, 'Don't you mean pass the exam?'

He wanted to touch her, hold her, kiss her, not blather on like this. Do it, he told himself. For heaven's sake, do it now.

'Susie,' he said, 'I'm a fool to put everything off as I do.' He leaned suddenly across and kissed her full on the lips. 'Now

Danny isn't here to claim you, there's no reason why I can't, is there?'

Her big golden brown eyes were staring at him, shining with pleasure. She shook her head.

'I mean, you haven't found another boyfriend, have you? I know nothing about your present life.'

'No, Danny has always seemed to be here beside me. I was never able to let go.'

'I guessed that,' he said. 'Will you try, for me?'

She smiled. 'I don't think I'll have to try very hard. And I know it's what he would've wanted. '

Susie went to bed that night feeling on top of the world. She'd spent the rest of the evening in Jamie's arms and his kisses had put back the clock and made her feel young and full of life. For years she'd thought of Jamie as a friend, only half aware that her feelings were deepening to love. She didn't sleep all that well – she was too excited.

She hadn't expected him to be so frank about his feelings. He'd said, 'Going right away from everything and everybody I knew made me realise how much you mean to me. I've thought about you ever since I left and I want you to know I love you. No, that's not putting it strongly enough. Susie, I'm madly in love with you.'

She'd laughed out loud. 'It's come as a lovely surprise, and a very welcome one. I think I feel the same way about you.'

He'd hugged her to him. 'That makes me wonderfully happy, and I've got the rest of my leave to enjoy you and to think of the future.'

Jamie had stayed with her until Mum came home, but they'd agreed to say nothing about being in love. It was too new and too soon, and they wanted to hug that to themselves, not tell everybody, but Mum volunteered to look after Rosie tomorrow evening and Jamie had said he'd meet her straight from the office.

Susie wore her best coat to work the next day and was walking on air. She'd never anticipated so keenly the sound of the five o'clock buzzer and was swept outside in the torrent of newly released workers. She saw Jamie waiting for her at the gates looking wonderfully handsome in his uniform and struggling through the crowd to kiss her cheek and take her arm. She knew she'd face comments and questions about him from her colleagues the next morning.

It was a fine evening and he took her on the New Brighton ferry to stroll along the promenade amongst the crowds. They had a meal in one of the many cafés along the front and they talked. Jamie wanted to know every last detail about her life with Rosie. They walked for miles and when at last he took her back to Milner Street, Susie felt full of fresh air and had never been happier.

On Friday, he brought a sandwich and met her at lunchtime to spend the hour with her and then met her again at five o'clock. 'We've got to make the most of what little time I have here,' Jamie said. He took her to Cooper's Café as he'd done several times before, but now it was more of a thrill and she couldn't drag her gaze from his. They had a light meal and went to the first house at the Empire to see music hall. They held hands and laughed a lot.

When they came out they walked down to the Pier Head. It should have been a fine late-summer evening, but it had been raining most of the day and the wind off the river was sharp. It was quite stormy and apart from passengers hurrying to change from the ferries to the buses there were not many people about. Dusk was early tonight and they stood by the rail watching the lights twinkling along the bank on the other side of the river, while a brightly lit ferry tossed in the heavy swell as it edged to the landing stage to tie up.

'It looks pretty at night, doesn't it?' Susie looked downriver to see a small tanker coming up.

'Quite romantic.' Jamie put his arm round her waist and pulled her closer. 'I want to ask you . . . Will you marry me?'

That took her breath away, making her gasp out loud. She had to search for words to answer.

'I'm sorry if you think I'm rushing you. I probably am, but I have only two more days here.'

'I don't need time, Jamie,' Susie reached up to kiss him. 'Nothing would give me more pleasure. Yes, I'd love to marry you.'

He held her even tighter. 'I'm afraid it's all very much in the future. With things the way they are, I don't know when I can be a real husband to you and a father to Rosie. Or when we can set up home together.'

She rubbed her forehead against his cheek. 'That we want to will have to be enough for the moment, won't it?'

'I suppose so. Consider yourself engaged. Tomorrow is Saturday, so I'll be able to spend all afternoon with you. We'll choose a ring.'

'Martha has said she'll take care of Rosie, and Mum says you must come to have Sunday lunch with us.'

'My train leaves just after two. Will there be time?'

'Yes, I told Martha that. She's says she'll have it on the table as early as possible.'

'Thank them for me. I'll book a taxi to collect me from your house then, Susie. Oh, I really do miss not having my car. We could have done so much more.'

'All I want is to be with you. These last few days have been marvellous.'

'I know, but if my car was here it would be very useful. I've got Jack's old one, a hand-me-down you might say. He chose to have a two-seater MG Midget, but when Kathleen had their first baby, Dad treated him to a new family car and I got his MG.'

'More suitable for a bachelor, and very sporty.'

'I like it, but the trouble is he's driven it hard for six years and now it isn't terribly reliable. I drove a friend, a fellow navigation student, up to London. We were going to have a big night out but it broke down halfway there. We found a garage to tow it in and repair it, but it caused me a load of trouble and I didn't want the same thing to happen on the way up here. I decided it would be better to come by train.'

'Well, you can't risk being late back.'

'No. I've been wondering if you'd like to babysit for Jack and Kathleen tomorrow evening? They have a comfy sofa and we'd be alone. The thing is, I could take you to the pictures, but it isn't entertainment we really want, is it? I just want to be with you and talk, well, and to kiss you too. Though Rory says there's a good play on at the Playhouse. What would you like to do?'

'Babysitting sounds a good option.'

'There's dancing at Reeces, but I'm not much of a dancer,

and the only other possibility is a pub or a café.'

'Jamie, babysitting sounds excellent. It'll give us warmth and privacy. That's what we want isn't it?'

'Exactly, well there's a café I know up that street that used to do good fish and chips. Let's go now. I think it's starting to rain.'

When Louise got home from work on Friday afternoon, she rattled Martha's letterbox as usual and then went to her window to indicate that she had something to say.

'It's about Susie,' she whispered when Martha opened the door. 'Come in, Mum.' Rosie was playing tiddlywinks with Jonjo on the dining table in the living room. Martha led the way through to the kitchen and half closed the door.

Louise said, 'I was wondering if Susie has said anything to you?'

'No, what about?'

'Jamie, he's invited her out again tonight. Suddenly she seems to be dancing on air, both in the office and at home. She's so much more energy, so much happier.'

'I had noticed,' Martha said. 'I think she and Jamie have found they're in love.'

'So do I, but it's amazing after all this time.'

'They'll tell us when they're ready. I don't think we should ask, at least not yet.'

'No, I'm very happy for her. She deserves more from life than she's having. I'll take Rosie home and start the dinner.'

At mid-morning the next day, Louise was having her coffee in Christopher's office when he mentioned that he'd heard Susie laughing and that suddenly she seemed much brighter.

Louise said, 'I think she's fallen in love,' and told him all she knew.

'Jamie Curtis?' Christopher knew Susie's story. 'Well, I think they'll suit each other very well. Jamie seems to have settled down, and nobody could say they don't know each other. Another of the Curtis boys, eh? Well, Susie could do a lot worse.'

Louise smiled. 'Don't say anything to her yet, they're keeping it to themselves at the moment.'

Christopher said, 'I'm very pleased for Susie, this will give her an independent life. She'll not need her mother so much.'

'No.' For the first time Louise thought of the effect that would have on her own life. Eventually she'd be living alone in that house.

'Lou,' Chris caught both her hands in his, 'I want you to think again about me and you. If Susie teams up with Jamie Curtis she won't be on her own any more, so why not? I'm sure we'd get on well together.'

Louise hesitated, biting on her lip. She wanted to, of course she did. But why didn't he say, 'I love you,' or kiss her properly instead of dropping chaste pecks on her cheek?

'I know we would,' she said slowly, taking the same line. 'But even if Susie and Jamie get married, they won't be able to set up home for a while, will they? Not with Jamie in the Air Force, and if there is a war coming, who knows what that'll bring? In the short term I can't see that it could make much difference to the way Susie lives now.'

'Perhaps not, but I want you to know that I haven't given up hope of you and I getting together. '

Louise sighed; they'd gone round in the same circle. 'I wish

Jamie hadn't joined up,' she said, 'he didn't have to. Working in the food industry, he'd have been in a reserved occupation. He'd have been safer at home making cakes.'

'But Jamie can't change his mind now even if he wanted to.'

CHAPTER TWENTY-FOUR

O N SATURDAY, JAMIE TOOK Susie out to lunch and then to a jeweller's shop in Dale Street. 'I came here this morning on my own to set up this visit,' he told her as he pushed the door open. 'Have you decided what sort of ring you'd like? Diamonds or sapphires, or what?'

She shook her head. 'I'd very much like to have a ring because of what it means, but I don't want to bankrupt you.' Her feet were sinking into deep carpet, and around her a wonderful array of jewellery was glittering in glass cases.

'You won't, that's why I came this morning. You are free to choose any of the rings you're shown, they'll all be within my budget. What sort did Danny give you?'

'None, he couldn't afford an engagement ring. We were going to be married with no hanging about. We did choose a wedding ring together, and Fee gave it to me with some of his other things, but I've never worn it.' She grimaced. 'Wasn't entitled to.'

'If I have my way, you soon will be. We can use Danny's ring or choose another, whichever you prefer.'

A bentwood chair was brought forward for Susie and a black velvet cloth was spread across the counter in front of her. An elderly shop assistant in striped trousers and black jacket brought a pad of diamond rings to show her.

'They're all absolutely beautiful,' she breathed.

'I like this one,' Jamie picked out a ring with three matching diamonds.

'I like it too.'

'Try it on,' the shop assistant pushed it on her finger. 'A little large for you,' he said, 'you have very slender fingers. Probably most of our rings will be too large, but we can make them fit you. Try on this solitaire, yes, that's a little large too. Would you like to see some coloured stones? We have some very nice sapphires.'

Susie tried on several of the rings but returned to the three matched diamonds. 'I think I like this one best.'

'We have a similar ring with a larger centre stone.' It was slipped on her finger, but she turned back to her original choice.

'They're quite big stones anyway.' Susie twisted it on her finger. They were bigger than the stones in Martha's ring. She smiled at Jamie. 'It'll impress them in the office.'

'It will need to be made smaller,' the shop assistant said. 'You'd be at risk of losing it as it is. About two sizes smaller, I think.' He brought out a string of base metal rings to try on her finger to check the size. 'Yes, so I'm afraid you won't be able to wear it straight away.'

'How long will it take to make it smaller?' Jamie asked.

'We can have it ready by Tuesday, sir.'

'I'm sorry I won't be able to put it on your finger,' Jamie said as he took out his cheque book. 'You'll have to come to collect it by yourself.'

Susie felt exhilarated as they went outside. The sun was

shining which matched her mood. 'I'm so happy,' she told him.

'So am I. Up on cloud nine.'

'What are we going to do now?'

'Let's go to Sefton Park. When we were kids, Dad used to take us there to sail our model boats on the lake. We can have a walk round, it's a huge place, do you know it?'

'Not really. Danny took me there once to see the Palmhouse, but I'd like to see it again.'

'Did he take you to the tea shop just outside the gates? If it's still there, we could get something to eat before we go to Jack's house to babysit. He and Kathleen have a house nearby.'

They didn't do much walking; instead they sat down in the sun on a bench overlooking the lake. Jamie took her hand in his. 'Once you start wearing my ring, you'll have to tell everybody we're engaged.'

'Yes,' Susie smiled, 'and goodness knows what the good ladies of St Biddolphe's are going to say when they hear of it. Probably that you're taking over Danny's girl, a woman of loose morals, and that you'd be better choosing a bride elsewhere.'

'They'll have forgotten all about Danny by now.'

'Your mother won't have. She'll say I'm determined to marry a Curtis come what may.'

He laughed. 'I've told Jack and I'll break the news to the parents before I leave. Do you want to come with me to do it?'

Susie remembered the time she'd been to his home, when Mum had insisted they go to talk to Victoria Curtis. 'Not really,' she said, 'just tell them. I can flash my engagement ring round at my family.'

'Perhaps it could be a little embarrassing. I'm sorry I won't be here to help with that. Heavens, what does it matter?'

'But it does, it embarrasses me because of the money your father gave me, and now it looks as though I'm roping in another member of his family to give more. And not just money for Rosie this time, you'll be giving her the right to use the Curtis name.'

Jamie laughed. 'Susie, I love you and want to look after you and Rosie. I want to help you bring her up. She's Danny's child, and already my niece.' He kissed her. 'My mother wouldn't approve of me doing that either. Not in public. It's time we got going, Jack asked me not to be late.'

'We haven't been to the Palmhouse yet.'

'I could bring you back tomorrow morning if you're free to come? Rosie too.'

'Yes, Martha says she'll see to lunch if I peel the vegetables tonight.' Susie was trying not to think that by tomorrow afternoon Jamie would be gone.

'This is Jack's place.'

Susie studied the almost new house, smart, detached but not overly large. She liked the look of it and wondered if she and Jamie would end up with something similar.

Kathleen came to the door holding her baby. 'Hello, Jamie, it's very good of you to do this,' she said, 'we haven't had a night out for ages. Congratulations are in order, so we've heard.'

'Yes,' Jamie said.

'How are you, Susie, you haven't changed a bit. How's Rosie?' She looked more mature, a contented wife and mother, and was dressed ready to go out with an apron on top of her dress. 'This is Colin, he's six months old and he's just finished his last bottle. He's started sleeping through the night, so with any luck once he's down you shouldn't hear any more of him, but I've left a drink ready for him if he does wake.'

'What about Denis? How old is he now?'

'Three, and a bit of a handful. Jack is reading his bedtime story, come on up.'

The house was bright and warm and smelled faintly of fresh paint. Denis was sleepy eyed and curled up in his bed. Jack ushered them back downstairs while Kathleen tucked the baby into his cot.

'You two are almost strangers,' Jack told them, and asked after Rosie. They were soon in a comfortable sitting room with a bright fire burning in the grate.

Kathleen joined them. 'If you want a bit of supper I've made a bowl of salad and there's cold sausages in the fridge. You know where everything is, don't you, Jamie? Help yourselves to drinks and anything else you fancy. Oh, and Jack has brought a few cakes from work.' There was a flurry of instructions and a last-minute check on the babies and they were alone at last.

'I'm going to start with a beer,' Jamie said, 'what would you like?' He threw open the doors of a cocktail cabinet and Susie saw a display of drinks, many of which she'd never heard of, let alone tasted.

'I'd like a glass of that sherry, please.' At least she recognised that. She crept upstairs. The door to the children's bedroom was open and in the glow from the night light, it seemed that both children had gone to sleep. She went back to the sitting room.

When he'd got their drinks Jamie threw himself down on the sofa. 'Rory is very grateful to us,' he said, 'he was booked to do this and reckons it's a favour he does too often.'

Susie had wanted to come as she knew they'd have privacy to kiss and cuddle, and privacy was difficult to find when they had nowhere of their own. 'Where have they gone?' she sat down beside him.

'To have dinner at a friend's house.' He put his arms round her and pulled her closer, his kisses thrilling her. 'This is more like it,' he whispered.

He was stroking her hair, planting butterfly kisses up her neck. It felt marvellous, and Susie was enchanted, returning his kisses, enjoying the moment. She felt his hands go underneath her jumper to stroke her bare skin, producing an exquisite thrill. He undid her bra and fondled her breast, and she could hardly breathe. She felt aroused and knew he did too, but when he tried to unzip her skirt and push it down, she put her hand over his. 'Jamie, please stop.'

He pulled away from her and jerked upright. He looked affronted.

'I'm sorry,' she whispered, 'I can't go on with this.'

'What's the matter?' He sounded indignant.

Susie was blinking back her tears. 'It's not that I don't want to carry on. I do, very much. I love you very much, but having gone down this route with Danny . . . Well, I bitterly regretted it when he was killed and I found myself pregnant and alone. I told myself then it was never worth it, that I'd never be such a fool to risk it again.' Susie was afraid she'd made him feel rejected, that the love she'd felt building between them had been jolted to a standstill, had suddenly stopped. She wanted to kick herself, she should have explained it more gently. Perhaps she should have told him that she couldn't face sex before marriage, that she couldn't allow him to get near it, or even appear to be heading towards it, and that to her, a show of passion on his part seemed a danger signal. That's how she saw it, as a very dangerous thing to do. She couldn't risk that again.

He was tight lipped. 'Let's have something to eat,' he said, and strode into the kitchen taking his glass. The first thing he did was to open another bottle of beer. 'Get yourself another glass of sherry,' he said coldly.

'I'd better take another look at the children.'

'They'll be flat out, they aren't making any noise.' Nevertheless, she crept upstairs to make sure. She'd certainly put him off. All the affection, the lovely feeling of warmth, the magic between them seemed to have gone. She returned to watch him laying out the food on the kitchen table, cutting some bread. 'Can I help?' she asked faintly.

'You could put the coffee percolator on.'

This was awful. 'I don't know how to,' she admitted, 'we don't drink coffee at home, we don't have a percolator.'

For the first time since she'd pushed him away, his dark eyes came up to meet hers. 'Would you rather have tea?'

'No, I like coffee, and it's more of a treat.'

He looked ashamed. 'Oh, Susie! I was going too far.' He dropped the bread knife and threw his arms round her. 'You must think I'm a real pig. I buy you a ring and immediately expect marriage privileges.' He pulled her closer, held her against his own body, gently patting her back. 'I should have known what having Rosie would do to you. Please forgive me.'

Susie couldn't answer, and when he lifted her away to see

why, he saw the tears streaming down her face. 'Don't cry, love,' he whispered, 'please don't cry,' but within moments she knew he was crying too. 'I'm a fool to hurt you like this. I didn't mean to.'

'Jamie, they're tears of joy! I was afraid I'd turned you right off.' She was smiling but laughing at the same time.

'It would take more than that now.' The food forgotten, they drifted back to the sitting room sofa. 'I promise I'll not let any love-making get out of hand until we're married, even though I can hardly keep my hands off you. But I'd like to get married as soon as possible.'

'So would I,' she smiled up at him, her eyes still wet.

'Why not? We've wasted years already, no point in wasting more.'

'Another thing that having a fatherless child has done to me is to make me long for a husband. You know, some of the men at work look at me as though I'm a real pushover, happy to have sex with anyone. I sank to the stage where I felt nobody half decent would look at me.'

'Susie, I'll be delighted to be your husband and very proud to have you as my wife. Rosie's a lovely little girl and I'll be glad to have her as my daughter, and the sooner the better. Thrilled in fact. I have to return to Manston tomorrow, but next time I come on leave . . .' He thought for a moment. 'When we finish this navigation course in January, we all get seven days' leave before being sent to a Bomber Command base on active service. Well, we do if we pass, otherwise it's eyes down and back to the classroom to sit the exam again.' He laughed. 'What d'you say to us getting married in January?'

'I'd love to,' she said eagerly.

'This will keep me up half the night studying; I'll have to pass that exam at the first attempt. Right, it'll be about the end of the month, but I'll let you know the dates later. We'll get married and have a few days' honeymoon. That's if your family is happy to take care of Rosie?'

'I'll have to ask, but for something as important as a honeymoon, I think it more than likely.'

'I'm hungry,' he said, 'let's have those sausages. We could do with a bottle of champagne to go with them – our Jack has most things here, but he won't have that.'

'He brought some cream cakes especially for us,' Susie reminded him, and he got up to take the box from the kitchen cabinet. 'I think they're absolutely delicious.'

There were four assorted fresh creams and between them they finished them off. 'I thought you didn't like them,' Susie said, 'you were quite disparaging about them in Cooper's Café.'

'I was,' he agreed, 'but that day I didn't like anything my father made or did. Now I've moved further away, everything looks different and I have to say I think his cakes are jolly good.'

Kathleen let herself in at about half ten and Susie said, 'We haven't heard a peep out of the babies, they've slept like logs.'

'Good, thanks very much for coming. Jack is waiting in the car outside to give you a lift home.'

Jamie sat on the back seat with Susie, holding her hand. She felt at peace again, all was well between her and Jamie, he loved her and they were going to be married. Jack stopped outside Susie's house and Jamie got out with her. He dropped a quick kiss on her cheek and whispered, 'Is nine o'clock too early to come round in the morning?'

CHAPTER TWENTY-FIVE

THE NEXT MORNING, BOTH Susie and Rosie were ready and waiting for Jamie, and were surprised to see him pull up outside their house in a smart red Morgan sports car. Rosie rushed out. 'Can we go for a ride in it?' she squealed, half dancing with excitement.

'Yes. Susie, I've brought my suitcase down and I'd like to leave it in your hall until I go.'

'Of course.' To Susie that was a painful reminder that it was the last day of his leave. Soon he'd be gone. 'You need to, to make room for us. It's a very smart car.'

'Yes, Rory wanted to go one better than Jack's MG. He took pity on me,' Jamie said, smiling at Susie, 'and lent me his car for a few hours this morning, but I've had to promise to have it back home before I have dinner at your house.'

'Where are you going to take us?' Rosie wanted to know.

'I told your Mum I'd take you both to see the Palmhouse in the park, so we'll go there first. I'm afraid you'll have to sit on your Mum's knee because there are only two seats.'

He drove them to Sefton Park where he'd taken Susie yesterday. On a mound of slightly higher ground in the centre was the glass Palmhouse, sparkling in the sun.

'It's beautiful,' Rosie breathed. It was circular, constructed entirely of panes of glass and stood seventy feet high. 'It's like a fairy's palace. Who lives in it?'

'Nobody, it's just a nice place for people to look round.'

'Anybody can go inside?'

'Yes, it's part of the park.'

Rosie couldn't wait to see inside. 'It's hot and it's full of plants and statues. I'd like to live in it.'

They had a cup of coffee in the little tea shop near the gate and Rosie had ice cream. Then Jamie took them for a spin along the East Lancashire Road. 'Rory says it'll do seventy-five miles an hour.' The top was down and they both loved the rush of wind through their hair.

Jamie turned it round. 'Time's getting on. I'd better take it back to Rory.'

When they reached Hillbark, he put the car in the garage. 'Come in with me, I have to say goodbye.'

Clutching Rosie by the hand, and fighting back her feelings of trepidation, Susie followed him inside to the drawing room. His family had just returned from church and were having a glass of sherry before their lunch. Rory had a glass of beer.

'I've come to say goodbye, Mother,' Jamie went to kiss her cheek. His father got to his feet and said, 'Susie, how are you? And this is Rosanna? Goodness, how you've grown. What a glorious mop of red hair you have.' It was wind-tossed and untidy. He patted it.

'What a grand house you have,' Rosie said, 'it's like a palace.'

Susie tried not to think of the occasion five years ago when she was last in this room. His mother's cold gaze was no less forbidding. 'We understand we are to congratulate you,' she said distantly.

Susie hardly recognised Julia without her pigtails; she'd grown up since she'd last seen her and was now a sophisticated young lady, but she was smiling and friendly. Rory said, 'Stay and have a drink with us.'

'I wish I could but I have to catch the two-twenty down to London. We must go.'

Susie was relieved to be outside again and they half jogged, half strode downhill to Milner Street, swinging the child between them. 'There, I've done my bit,' Jamie said, 'they can't say I haven't told them our news. Shall we tell yours before I go?'

'Higher,' Rosie shouted. 'Swing me higher. I want my feet to go right up.'

When Susie let them in, Martha said, 'You've timed that well. Everything is ready to dish up.' She brought the leg of lamb to the table for Bert to carve. Susie sent the children to wash their hands and suggested the adults sit at the table. It had been extended to its full size and set for six adults and two children, and Bert was sending plates of meat round. Christopher was refilling the sherry glasses from the bottle he'd brought.

Jonjo was settled in his seat before Rosie came downstairs. 'Do hurry, Rosie,' Louise said, and Jamie lifted her into the chair next to him.

'Uncle Jamie, you gave us a lovely time this morning,' she said, 'you were more like a daddy than an uncle. I've never had a real daddy to take me out. Will you do it again and be my pretend daddy?'

The chatter round the table stopped. Susie could see Jamie was caught on the back foot, but he recovered quickly and seized the opportunity. 'Well, young lady,' he smiled round at the expectant faces, 'I'm hoping to be your real daddy before much longer. Your mother and I have just agreed it shall be so.'

She clapped her hands. 'Honest? You'll come and live here with us?'

'Well, that's not so easy at the moment, but I promise, Rosie, we'll be seeing more of each other.'

The adults all spoke at once: 'Susie, you're going to get married?' 'Marvellous.'

Jamie looked round the table, his cheeks flushed, 'Yes, I'd like to say to the rest of your family that it is official, Susie has agreed to marry me and we want it to be as soon as possible.'

'Congratulations, Jamie.'

Susie smiled delightedly round at them all. They were pleased and excited but she couldn't eat much dinner, knowing only too well that these were the last hours of Jamie's visit. The family were still at the table and hadn't calmed down when the taxi appeared outside. Jamie stood up and thanked Louise for her hospitality and asked them all to look after Susie until he came back.

Susie rushed for her coat feeling tears prickling her eyes. She would have liked to have had the last moments alone with Jamie, but Rosie was reaching for her own coat and shouting, 'I want to come too. I want to see Uncle Jamie off.'

Jamie sat between them on the back seat of the taxi, and put an arm round each of them and pulled them close. At the station there were more people about in uniform and the train seemed full. He lifted Rosie up to kiss her goodbye, and then threw his arms round Susie. Rosie pushed her way in so he hugged them both. As the train prepared to leave, Jamie climbed in, opened the window and hung out to wave as it chugged out of the station. Susie felt desolate as she watched the last coach disappear from view. Rosie was still chirpy as they waited for a bus to take them home.

For Susie, the following weeks seemed empty; she was missing Jamie and could think of little else. She knew she wouldn't see him again until Christmas, and that was still months off. He wrote notes and letters to her every day and posted them in batches about twice a week. She was doing the same and encouraging Rosie to write to him too.

If we are to get married, Jamie wrote, *it will have to be at St Biddolphe's. If we did it anywhere else, my mother would be so upset she'd probably never speak to me again, and the good ladies of St Biddolphe's wouldn't believe we were properly married.*

It's what my mother would want too, Susie wrote back. *I think she's half afraid we'll opt for the register office.*

Another fortnight went by and Jamie wrote: *You know I've been in touch with Mr Coyne at the vicarage to arrange for our wedding, telling him that we want it to take place on 30th January. I've explained why it is dependent on my being given leave on that date and if things don't go my way, it is just possible we may have to delay it until later in the year. He wrote back to say he'd booked the ceremony for eleven in the morning and asks that you call in to see him.*

Susie went, but it was just to fill out the necessary forms. Apart from the wedding arrangements, Jamie complained he had little to write about. *It's all day in the classroom, and one beer in the mess with the lads before bed. It's what we all do. I think of you all the time. I love you and always will.*

Two weeks later he wrote: *Please don't worry too much about the wedding arrangements, and don't let your mum feel put out. I understand Mother wants to take full charge of all that, but she will do it well, I'm sure, and it will make her happy. I'm glad you're pleased with my suggestion of four nights in Windermere for our honeymoon; I've booked the Waterside Hotel. Mother wants us to spend our last night at Hillbark and it fits in quite well as I won't be returning here once I've finished the course and will have to bring all my belongings up.* On another occasion, Jamie enclosed a letter from Fee that was all excited anticipation as she told him she was expecting a baby. She'd written, *Mum sent me her congratulations and Dad sent me a cheque.*

When Louise was coming out of church the next Sunday morning, Mrs Curtis stopped her. 'I'm sure you're very busy, Mrs Ingram. The vicar and I will be happy to make all the arrangements for Jamie's wedding, and propose holding a buffet reception at Hillbark. All your family and friends will be welcome; you needn't worry about a thing.'

Louise had already asked Mr Coyne if the church hall would be free, and Bert was organised to supply ham, tongue and sausages, but Susie had warned her Mrs Curtis would take control. 'I'd be happy to help in any way,' she stammered. She almost went on to suggest she provide the wedding cake. She and Martha had baked two rich fruit cakes in readiness, one larger than the other. Although perhaps it would be more diplomatic to leave the cake to the management of Curtis Cakes.

'No need for you to do anything at all, Mrs Ingram. I'm sure going out to work leaves you little time to plan a wedding. Please leave all the arrangements to me.'

'Don't you want to know how many guests Susie and I want to invite?'

'Er, yes, that would be helpful.'

At home later, when Louise was eating her Sunday lunch with Chris and the family, he smiled round the table and said, 'Mrs Curtis has asked me to arrange the music for the wedding, and I told her I'd ask the bride what pieces she'd like. "No need," she said, "stick to what you played at Jack's wedding and keep to traditional pieces, I don't care for modern stuff at a wedding."'

Chris was treating Mrs Curtis's wishes in the matter as mildly funny. 'You make a list of what you want, Susie, or come round to my place and I'll play suitable pieces from which to make your choice.'

'I'd like Mendelsohn's "Wedding March", but otherwise I'll leave all that to you.'

Louise decided there was nothing she could do but let Mrs Curtis get on with it. She would think about a new outfit for the occasion, and help Martha with her sewing. She was going to make Susie a calf-length wedding dress in eau-de-nil-coloured chiffon over taffeta.

Rosie was taking a huge interest in the preparations. 'What colour is that?' she wanted to know.

'Palest delicate green,' Martha said, showing her a clipping of the material.

Louise protested, 'Susie, you'll need something warmer than that in January. You'll catch a chill in chiffon.'

'I knew you'd say that,' Martha laughed. 'Susie must have a bit of glamour on her wedding day, though. Becky has offered to lend her a fur coat to wear on the ride to church, she'll be fine.'

Rosie piped up, 'I want you to wear a white gown like a

proper bride. And I want to be your bridesmaid.'

'No, Rosie, I can't do that. We'll ask Martha to make you a dress of the same material as mine, but you can be my bridesmaid and walk up the aisle with me.'

Susie felt alternately full of anticipation and fear as her wedding day drew nearer. Jamie was safe enough all the time he was in training, but if he passed his navigation exam, he'd be in Bomber Command and on active service by next February. That filled her with dread. Jamie wrote: *We'll have Christmas together before all that. I can't wait to see you again, hold you again.*

Christmas was drawing closer, and this year Christmas Day would fall on a Monday, so with the benefit of the weekend, many people would have a four-day holiday. Jamie wrote that he planned to get up at five o'clock on the Saturday morning and catch an early train up from London. Susie went to meet him at Lime Street station.

He seemed almost a stranger as he strode up the platform towards her, but once his arms went round her in a great bear hug she knew it would be a blissful Christmas.

Susie took him home and Martha offered him her spare bedroom so he could spend as much time as possible with the family. On Christmas Eve, Bert was taking Louise, Martha and Jonjo to his family to share their European-style Christmas Eve festivities. Jamie's parents had invited Susie and Jamie to have dinner with them. 'We'll take Rosie with us,' Jamie decided.

Fiona and her husband were there but were planning to spend most of the holiday with Len's parents. Susie was delighted to see her again, though she was not at ease. She was afraid of how Rosie would manage a more formal meal than she was used to, and half expected her to be up and down from her chair and refusing unfamiliar foods, but she behaved beautifully, answering freely whenever she was spoken to, and they made a great fuss of her.

Susie helped her mother lay on a fine Christmas Day lunch for all the family and they had the usual cold supper at Martha's house in the evening. She and Jamie had little privacy, but they talked and talked, and made final plans for their wedding.

Susie felt she'd looked forward to Christmas for months, but it was over in a flash, and Jamie had gone again. She comforted herself with the thought that with luck he would be back for their wedding next month. His letters became more hurried; he apologised and said he had to give more time to studying.

Chris kept asking Susie how Jamie was getting on, and she asked him if she could take her annual holiday over his leave so they could get married and take their honeymoon. He said, 'You'll need a holiday in the summer too. You take the time off and enjoy yourself while you can. You worked overtime the week Miss Williams was off sick, and she'll do the same for you if it's needed. Marriage is a big step in life, Susie. Things will never seem quite the same afterwards.'

It seemed to Susie that the days she'd spent with Jamie during his last leave had been golden, and what she wanted most of all was for her and Rosie to be with him after they were married. Jamie had already mentioned this in his letters.

I only wish we could be together once we are married, but I'll be starting a new job and will have to concentrate hard to start with. I've heard I shall be posted to a Bomber Command unit based at Mildenhall if I get through. It's nearer than Manston and if I get weekends free I might be able to get home.

Dad has bought a new car for himself, and he's said he'll give me his old one. It's an SS Jaguar saloon, very nice, speedy and reliable. He says I can sell my old MG. He's afraid that we'll soon be at war and no new cars will be built for the duration. We sat our written examination today and I'm glad that's over, but we are now being taken up in turn on assessment flights. It's nerve wracking but I'm having my turn tomorrow if the weather allows it.

I thought I'd wait to post this until I could let you know how I got on. I was told that I'd done all right, that my calculations were correct and the pilot managed on the strength of them to end up on the right airfield. I have another assessment tomorrow on a circuitous flight back to Manston and then it will all be over. All my love and I'm keeping my fingers crossed that I manage to pass.

CHAPTER TWENTY-SIX

T HE NEXT DAY SUSIE received the letter she'd anticipated for so long.

Darling Susie,

Hurray, I'm considered to be a competent navigator and all our plans can go ahead. I can't wait to see you again. I'll have to drive home as I'll be bringing everything with me. I'll telephone you at the office if I can, to let you know what time I'm likely to arrive.

Susie was relieved and delighted to hear that their wedding could go ahead. Jamie was driving back the next day, but Susie went to work as usual. All morning she worked hard to get as much done as possible. Once lunchtime was over she was on tenterhooks waiting for his phone call. It came at last. To hear his voice sent her spirits soaring. 'Where are you now?' she sang out. 'How much longer will it take you to—'

'It's not good news, Susie,' he said, 'it's my car and the same old story. It was losing power for miles and about eleven this morning it refused to go any further. I'm in Northampton, but thank goodness I wasn't alone.

'I was giving a lift to George, who's been on the same course, and I was within two miles of dropping him off so he knew his way about. He rang a garage and they came quickly to tow us in. Then we took a bus to his home and his wife ran me to the station to catch a train. I'll be coming into Lime Street at five-twenty this afternoon.

'Will you phone Dad at his office to tell him what has happened? I'm in a public phone box and running out of change . . .' Susie heard the pips warning them they were running out of time, and managed to shout: 'I'll be at the station, Jamie,' before the line went dead.

When she'd calmed down, Susie lifted her phone again. 'It's Susie, Mr Curtis,' she said, and explained why she was ringing. 'Jamie will be coming into Lime Street on the London train at five-twenty this afternoon.'

He said, 'He'll have a lot of baggage, I'll meet him with the car.'

'I told him I'd meet him at the station, Mr Curtis,' she said.

'Then I'll pick you up and run you down, shall I?'

'No, it's out of your way to come here, and anyway, I want to go home to collect Rosie. I can't trouble you to pick me up.'

'It's no trouble. If you're going to be my daughter-in-law, I want to be kind and friendly.'

'You've always been kind and friendly towards me, Mr Curtis,' she said. 'I'll see you at the station.'

Rosie was fizzing with excitement, and having arrived in plenty of time, they found the right platform and waited behind the ticket collector, but the train was in five minutes early too. There were many men in uniform, but Jamie was out of the carriage the moment the train stopped and striding up the platform ahead of the crowd with the biggest smile on his face she'd ever seen.

Susie was conscious of his many bags being dropped at her feet and being swept into his arms. Then Rosie was pulling at them and clamouring for attention so Jamie swung her up in his arms and kissed her. She was still there when his father caught them up. 'Hello, son,' he said, 'welcome back.'

Jamie deposited Rosie in Susie's arms. She couldn't mistake the affection he showed to his father as he gave him a hug. After that Mr Curtis turned to Rosie and shook her hand, 'How are you, young lady?'

William Curtis told himself he must not feel resentment as he drove them to Hillbark. He'd sensed Susie would prefer to meet Jamie on her own, but what young woman in love would not? He loved Jamie too. If they were to stay close he must forgive his refusal to stay in the business. Jamie probably regretted that now, especially as it meant he'd be separated from the girl he was about to marry, and he'd have to fight in the thick of any coming war. But what father wouldn't be proud to see his son in uniform?

William had had a bad day. He'd paid a few visits to Raymond Grant's surgery recently, and today he'd heard the tests he'd undergone showed the problem was diabetes.

'You've been eating too many of those cakes you make,' Dr Grant had told him, 'you must stop that.' He'd arranged a long session with the district nurse who'd gone on and on about the diet he must follow in future. That had depressed him, but he mustn't blame Curtis Cakes. He was proud of growing it into a strong business.

He'd wanted to save his children from working as hard as he'd had to; he saw it as giving them a gift. He'd wanted to provide them with a comfortable living, and at the same time ensure that Curtis Cakes carried on trading profitably into the next century. They didn't seem to realise they'd need to work in the trade to gain experience if they were to do that. As a result he'd spent years fighting to overcome his feelings of being rejected by them.

Now, seated at the supper table, he could see Victoria bristling with dislike for Susie. He didn't want to end up like her, soured by her own feelings, but he knew that bringing Rosie here, with her red hair and strong resemblance to his family, would make his wife feel ten times worse. Her trouble was she couldn't ever admit she'd made a mistake.

'It sounds a bit like getting your come-uppance,' Victoria was telling him, 'diagnosed with diabetes and forbidden to eat your own cakes.'

'I think it's sad, Grandpa, that you can't eat them any more,' Rosie piped up.

'I was greedy when I was young, ate too many.'

'Grandpa, you're like Beethoven. We've been learning about him at school. Beethoven was deaf and couldn't hear the lovely music he wrote. You make lovely cakes but can't eat them.'

He laughed. 'That's rather a grandiose comparison for me, isn't it?' He'd always had a soft spot for Rosie. She was lovely, his oldest grandchild and the daughter of his dead son.

Jamie was lifting her down from the chair. 'Come on, let's get you home,' he said. William didn't miss the look of gratitude Susie shot in his direction.

'Lovely to be home again, Mother,' Jamie said. 'Thanks for a lovely meal. Susie needs to get Rosie to bed and I want to say hello to my in-laws. Don't wait up for me.'

*

Susie was full of happy anticipation and knew Jamie was thrilled and excited too. It was all about to happen for them. He was driving her and Rosie home in the Jaguar car that was his father's wedding present to them; it seemed the last word in luxury.

'This is a huge improvement on my old MG,' he said, 'a lovely car to drive.'

'I like it better than Auntie Becky's,' Rosie told them from the back seat. 'Will it go faster?'

What Susie wanted was time alone with Jamie. They hadn't seen each other for ages, and here they were on the eve of their big day and she was aching to kiss him properly. He lifted Rosie out of the car and carried her over his shoulder into Louise's house to drop her gently onto the sofa.

'You're looking very well, Jamie,' Louise said as she kissed his cheek.

'So are you,' he said, giving her a hug. 'Please forgive me for rushing Susie out again. We haven't had a moment to ourselves yet, and we need to catch up.'

'Don't keep her out late,' Louise said. 'You'll have plenty of time alone after tomorrow.'

'Not plenty,' he said, and Susie found herself being led back to the car. He drove to Pier Head, where he parked so they were facing the river.

'At last,' he pulled her into his arms, where it was marvellous to be held tight and feel his lips come down on hers and thrilling tingles dart up and down her spine.

Eventually they had to tear themselves apart. He drove her back to Milner Street but he wouldn't go in with her. They had one last hug. 'See you in church,' he said. 'Go, I'll wait until you're safely inside.'

Susie let herself in. 'Hello, Mum.'

Louise looked up from setting the table for breakfast. 'Not long to wait now, I'm glad you're not too late coming home.'

'We don't have to get up all that early,' Susie said.

'No, but we'll have plenty to do. Martha came round earlier to say Mrs Curtis had rung her with a message. She said, "I've ordered a car to be at your house at a quarter to eleven, to collect a wedding party of four adults and two children. I've instructed the chauffeur to drop some of you at the church and drive round for another five minutes with the bride." '

Susie laughed, 'You have to admit she's efficient.'

Martha said, 'I was delighted to tell her that Becky and her husband were coming and were planning to take us all to the church. Mrs Curtis was quite hoity-toity and said, "In that case, I'll tell the chauffeur to collect the bride and whoever is to give her away at ten to eleven." '

They laughed together. 'Did Rosie go off to sleep all right?' Susie asked.

'No, she's all excited about tomorrow, but she's asleep now. Do you want some cocoa?'

'No thanks. Come to bed, Mum, it'll be a busy day tomorrow for you.'

'I'll just make up the fire, we'll all want baths in the morning.'

Susie peeped into Rosie's room on the way; the dress she would wear was on a hanger hooked over the picture rail where she couldn't reach it. Clean petticoats and underwear were laid out in readiness, along with her patent leather ankle straps.

Only her mop of red curls showed against her pillow. She was fast asleep.

Susie went to her own bed and slept like a top. She didn't wake up until Rosie was pushing under her blankets and putting her cold feet against her. 'Mummy, I want to get dressed and put my party frock on.'

'No, not until we say so. You mustn't get it dirty.'

It was earlier than usual, and Susie tried to doze on but it wasn't possible. Her mother, wearing her dressing gown, came in with a cup of tea and drew back her curtains. 'I'm afraid it's a cold dank morning,' she said, 'not good wedding day weather. Would you like breakfast in bed this morning? It is traditional for brides on their wedding morning.'

'Not for this bride, I'm afraid. I'm already a mother and it'll be easier if we all go down.'

Susie heaved Rosie out of her bed and said, 'Put on your dressing gown and slippers,' and she did the same.

When she went down, she found Louise had organised a special breakfast of grapefruit with boiled eggs and soldiers to follow. She'd prepared half an orange for Rosie who thought grapefruit too sour. The fire blazed up and the room was warm, which was very different to a normal morning. 'It all feels a little unreal,' she said.

'It's your wedding day, it's bound to feel different and special, but it's real enough.'

Susie felt in a daze as she put on the wedding dress of eau de nil chiffon that Martha had made for her; it fitted beautifully. She strapped on the silver sandals she'd bought for her wedding to Danny and never worn, and they complemented her dress. When she was ready, she stood in front of her wardrobe mirror with Rosie by her side wearing her dress of the same material.

Becky and Max arrived bringing a bottle of champagne which they opened immediately. Martha and her family joined them; it was a jolly family party and they were all drinking to her health and happiness. Then suddenly it all went quiet, and she and Rosie were alone with Bert who was to give her away. Then the wedding car arrived and he was helping her into Becky's fur coat.

Susie shivered and snuggled into it. 'It feels lovely. Isn't she kind to lend it to me? She says it's chinchilla.'

'I bet she's hankering for mink,' he said, buttoning Rosie into her Sunday coat.

It seemed only seconds before the car had edged through the church gates and pulled up in front of the door.

'Come on,' Bert said, 'we're here, there's no backing out now.' He was trying to be jovial, but it didn't suit him, and neither did the stiff collar and new striped suit. Rosie shot out first and into the porch. Nurse O'Brien was taking charge of their coats. Susie shivered again and a thrill ran down her spine. Was this really the moment she'd been longing for for all these years?

The music changed. 'Come on,' Bert pulled Susie's arm through his. 'Not you, Rosie.' Nurse O'Brien held her back. 'You walk behind your mother, that's what bridesmaids do.'

'As I explained yesterday,' Susie murmured as Bert was leading her forward. Faces were turning to look at her, some she loved and respected, some she did not. But she knew them all well; they had always been part of her life.

Jamie was waiting for her at the front of the church in his

uniform. He turned to smile at her and she felt her cares falling away.

Rosie was feeling for her hand; she'd pushed forward and was walking up the aisle alongside her so they were three abreast. Susie moved her posy of flowers to her other hand and took Rosie's fist in hers. She squeezed it gently and exchanged fond glances with her daughter. What did it matter that this wasn't the traditional way? She was living the dream.

She reached Jamie and stood beside him and could see the love in his eyes. The service began. Mr Coyne's voice was loud and had a nasal tone. 'Dearly beloved . . .'

The ring Jamie slipped on her finger was not the one she'd chosen with Danny. Only two weeks ago, Jamie had written: *I think I'd like you to wear a wedding ring that I've chosen. You could wear Danny's ring as well if you like. After all, it's a memento of him. He loved you and was very much part of your life, he was Rosie's father and the brother I felt closest to.* So they had gone out and bought a new ring.

Jamie's voice was firm and steady as he made his responses, and he didn't take his eyes from her.

Susie remembered little of the reception at Hillbark, except she and Jamie holding onto each other. He drew her into the party atmosphere, raising his glass to her and eating heartily of the good things his family had provided, but he was equally keen to get away and start their honeymoon. She knew the more organised bride would be leaving in a new suit and smart hat, but she had not brought any of her things to Hillbark. Before Jamie led her out to his car, he helped her into Becky's fur coat. The guests trailed after them calling their good wishes and goodbyes, and throwing confetti.

Jamie lifted Rosie up to kiss her and Susie threw her arms round her to do the same. Her little hands clung on to her and she knew from Rosie's face that she was upset at being left behind, and Susie felt guilty. Louise peeled her away and she and Martha swung her between them, and as they drove away Rosie was waving.

'Don't worry about her,' Jamie murmured. 'They are part of her normal life and she'll be back at school tomorrow.'

He drove her to Milner Street, where Susie changed out of her wedding finery and into her best dress of cream wool. She pulled on her comfortable camel coat and picked up the suitcase she'd packed in readiness.

It wasn't quite three o'clock, but already the mist and rain were closing in and the daylight was going. It was dark long before they got to their hotel but Jamie had booked the best room, and it was large and comfortable with a bright log fire burning in the hearth. 'This is our honeymoon and we're going to enjoy it,' he said, taking her into his arms.

'At last,' Susie murmured, 'I can show you how much I love you.'

With one arm round her, Jamie started to unbutton her dress.

Later, they enjoyed a fine dinner in the dining room but soon returned to their room to get into bed. For the first time, they were able to talk about what the future would hold for them, and interspersed with love-making they talked long into the night.

'I wish we could live together from now on,' he said, 'that's what marriage is for, isn't it? But I don't know anything about Mildenhall or what it will be like working in Bomber Command.'

'I know you're starting a new job and that's never easy. You'll have to give it all your attention to get on top of it, so I know I mustn't distract you.'

'You wouldn't do that. It would be a comfort to have you with me. If there's any possibility of renting somewhere for you, you can be sure I will, but until I've seen the lay of the land, I'm afraid that the best thing for you is to stay with your family.'

'I'll hate being parted from you, but it won't be for ever.'

'Realistically, it could be until this war's over.'

Susie shivered; there was also the possibility that Jamie would never come back.

'We have Rosie,' he said carefully, 'and I intend to adopt her legally as soon as I can, although I know she is my niece, but I'd like us to have more children, a proper family.'

'So would I.'

'But not yet. The point is I don't want to leave you to have another baby on your own. Things will be difficult enough for you without that. When you do have another baby I want to be with you and share in everything.

'I know it happened that way for you and Danny and you've survived, but we are older and wiser now. I've brought a supply of French letters and I'll use them from now on.'

'But we're married now,' Susie said, 'there wouldn't be the same hurt, the same disgrace and the feeling I was letting Mum down. It would be more bearable.'

'No,' he said quietly. 'Looking at things realistically, it's not impossible that I could be killed. I don't want you to be faced with bringing up another child on your own. It's not a risk I want you to take.'

She tried to protest but knew he was right. For Danny it had been far less likely, but the worst had happened. If war came, Jamie would be in real danger. Even so . . .

She tried to explain, 'If I didn't have you . . . I think I'd like to have your child. Rosie has been a consolation to me.'

'Oh Susie, love! There's a war coming, nobody doubts that now. So until it's over we've no idea what's going to happen. It won't last forever.'

CHAPTER TWENTY-SEVEN

WHEN THE TIME CAME for Jamie to report for duty in Mildenhall, Susie missed him more than she'd thought possible. There were rumours and counter rumours about a coming war, but routine took over and the weeks began to pass.

Susie's mind had been on love not war, but she knew her mother felt sick with the fear of it. When she began to think seriously about it, she could see that by joining the Air Force when he had, now, in 1939, Jamie was trained and ready to fight in a coming war. He was likely to be in the thick of it. The thought terrified her.

Spring came, and Jamie was managing to come home for a weekend about once a month. Susie was looking forward to the warmer weather, but war began to look more likely and soon many were saying it was inevitable.

Midsummer came and went. Gas masks were being distributed to the population, and schools sent their pupils home with letters about impending evacuation plans. Susie was in two minds about letting Rosie go; her mother was all for it, saying her safety must come first, but Martha was vehement. 'I'm not letting Jonjo go anywhere. I couldn't bear to let him go to strangers. He's staying here with me.'

'In that case Rosie stays too,' Susie decided, 'we'll stay together.'

By the last days of August, all England was waiting in dread. Her mother didn't go to church on the Sunday morning war was declared because they all knew an announcement was due to be made at eleven o'clock. Louise wanted to stay with her family. 'We need to know what will happen now, and what to expect,' she said.

The official announcement only confirmed their worst fears without making anything clearer. It left Susie in a state of near panic about how Jamie would fare. Louise was worried about him too. To see Susie robbed of her happiness all over again would be unbearable; it would be too cruel.

Until now, Louise had been telling herself she must look on the bright side, that in this war there were no young men in the family who would be called up to fight. Bert was thirty-seven and his butcher's shop would be needed to help feed the civilian population, and the same applied to Christopher Berry. Max, Rebecca's husband, was fifty and managing a company making parts for the car industry. Becky told them production of new cars was to stop, and Max's factory would be making parts for armoured cars and tanks, so his was a vital contribution to the war effort. At work, Louise heard the women talking of stacking up bags of sugar and tins of fruit in their cupboards, and like everybody else she was making blackout curtains to cover her windows. The men spoke of the lawns they were digging up to build Anderson shelters and plant vegetables. Louise regretted the fact she only had a back-yard and could do neither of those things. She and her family would have to rely on public air raid shelters, and though these were being built throughout the city, there wasn't one near to where they lived.

Louise heard a good deal from Christopher about how the war was affecting the jam factory. There were skylights in the roof and these had to be painted black and covered with strips of sticky paper to prevent splintering should they be broken. The sewing room had had to run up hundreds of yards of blackout curtaining. Sugar was in short supply and the amount Peverill's would be allowed was strictly limited, which restricted the amount of jam they could make. In order to increase production, their laboratory was exploring artificial sweeteners, setting agents and preservatives with some urgency.

Now that war had been declared, everybody expected there to be air raids and gas attacks, but the days and weeks continued to pass quietly. Jamie seemed to have even less to write about in his letters: *I'm not in any danger, don't worry about me. The flights over enemy-occupied countries and into Germany are becoming routine, but we drop only leaflets, not bombs, and we all wonder when this phoney war will be over.*

Later he wrote, *I'm forbidden to tell you what I'm doing and exactly where we fly to, and my letters are to be censored in future.* But he was able to write that the Curtis family had bought a cottage in Cumbria so that if there were any air raids or gas attacks, Victoria and Julia could get away from Liverpool. *I'd like to take you and Rosie there on my next leave.*

On Merseyside the days and weeks continued to pass quietly and Martha and Susie were glad they'd kept the children with them, especially when those that had gone to the country began drifting back. They had a settled and orderly life, though war was shaking things up. Rationing was beginning to bite, but

Louise had registered with Bert for their meat ration of one shilling and twopence worth each a week, and he whispered that he would see she didn't go short.

There was also the blackout, the general shortages and bad news from the troops fighting in France to contend with. Apart from that, life went on as near to normal as people could make it.

Susie wrote to Jamie on Grand National Day in 1940: *I'm growing tired of all this horse racing fuss, though there seems less of it this year. None of the Liverpool firms gave their workers a half day off. So many of the staff are in the forces, there's quite a labour shortage here now. The good news is that I drew MacMoffat in the sweep and it came in second. But Bert and Martha went to Aintree as usual and picked Bogskar as the winner, so they are cock-a-hoop. Apparently his jockey, Mervyn Jones, is a Flight Sergeant in the RAF, who like you is a navigator and been given leave to race. Martha said a lot of the crowd were in uniform. It wasn't like the old days.*

Dear Jamie, I wish we could be together, I do miss you.

News bulletins on the wireless had been compulsory listening for Louise and her family since the start of the war, but when the news from France took a turn for the worse, most of the population were riveted to their sets. The Axis troops were advancing across France and driving the British Army back to the coast at Dunkirk. Everybody held their breath for days while the small boats ferried what was left of the British Army across the Channel. But now the German Army was only twenty-two miles away and reported to be gathering strength and making preparations to advance further. The threat of imminent invasion hung over them all.

Later in the summer, the news bulletins were filled with

stories of dog fights in the skies over Kent and the terrible toll on the lives of young Spitfire pilots. Susie understood that Jamie was now flying bombing missions over enemy territory and sometimes into the heart of Germany itself, and knew that he too was in grave danger.

CHAPTER TWENTY-EIGHT

FOR LOUISE AND HER family the last vestiges of the phoney war were blasted aside when in the autumn of 1940 the Luftwaffe started bombing the port of Liverpool. The raids were light and sporadic to start with, but once the darker nights came, they became heavier. Everybody was terrified.

Immediately, there was a new scheme to evacuate children to safer areas, and again Susie was tempted to allow Rosie to go, but Martha said she wouldn't be happy if she was separated from Jonjo and didn't think he would be either, so the children stayed.

The bombers did not come every night, and not knowing if or when they would come was very trying. Sometimes it was early in the night, sometimes very late. There was nothing worse than being woken from sleep by the wailing siren and getting out of a warm bed to run to the shelter on a cold wet night.

One Sunday evening early in December, Susie was bathing Rosie and washing her hair ready for another week at school, when the air raid siren suddenly blared out, making her squeal in panic. Susie's heart raced as she hurriedly rinsed the soap suds out of Rosie's hair and lifted her out of the bath. Never had the child been dried so hurriedly. Her clean nightdress was tugged over her head followed by some of her daytime clothing, the lot being topped off with the warm one-piece siren suit Martha had made for her.

Downstairs, Louise had washed up after their light Sunday supper and was re-setting the table for breakfast. She had the kettle on the stove to make a bedtime drink for Rosie with the cocoa powder already mixed in her cup. The Thermos flask always stood ready, she trebled the amount of cocoa in the cup, tipped it into the flask and filled it up. Then she pulled the two bags from under the stairs packed ready with blankets and biscuits, and threw in her handbag. These days everybody carried their birth certificates, money and insurance documents with them at all times.

She rushed upstairs to pull on warmer clothing, but already Bert was shouting, wanting to know if they were ready. 'Bring your umbrellas,' he said, 'it's raining.'

The siren continued to wail out, rising and falling across the city, sending shivers down Louise's spine. They were all struggling up the street laden with comforts when it finally stopped. She knew all adults were frightened in bombing raids, but she could see that Jonjo, who was now seven years of age, was not. The ear-splitting pounding of ackack guns from a nearby battery, the search lights sweeping across the sky and the general feeling of being under attack, thrilled him. Rosie took her cue from him.

They had to be dragged to the shelter staring up at the sky, screaming to each other if they heard the distinctive throb of German planes or saw what they thought were incendiary bombs falling out of the sky. Once inside, they were intoxicated with excitement and miles away from sleep, even on the nights they'd been lifted out of their beds.

The shelter soon filled up; it felt cold and dank when they first went in but could become hot after a few hours. The seats were of wooden slats laid over a concrete base and they counted themselves lucky if there was space for the children to lie down. Louise unpacked her blankets and pillows and tried to get comfortable, while Susie pushed Rosie's hood off her head and used the towel she'd brought to dry off her hair.

Some of their fellow shelterers had rushed straight from the bar of the Red Lion which was on the corner of the street. Sometimes they could be a little tipsy but tonight the raid had come early in the evening and they were grumbling loudly at having their drinking interrupted. Very soon they had more to worry about.

The noise outside was growing in volume; not only were the big guns firing, but ambulance and fire engine sirens were screeching. Then came explosions, one after the other, thankfully some distance away. 'Six,' Jonjo shouted, his dark eyes alight with the thrill of it.

Suddenly, an almighty bang half deafened them as a much nearer explosion shook the ground under their shelter. They all felt it, and there were a few hastily subdued screams, but it started the babies and toddlers crying in fright. Even Jonjo put his head on Martha's shoulder. It was after midnight when the all-clear sounded and they struggled stiffly to their feet to get away from the shelter as quickly as they could.

The children were sleepy and grumpy at being lifted to their feet and told to walk. Bert hurried them past six houses that had collapsed in the middle of a row, their feet crunching on glass and slate. Wardens were digging in the rubble while an ambulance stood by. Louise couldn't bear to look, but she knew fires were burning down on the docks and the air was heavy with the smell of smoke. Never before had bombs dropped so terrifyingly close to them, and it was a relief to get home and find both their houses undamaged.

They all fell into bed wanting sleep above all else. Yet it seemed only minutes before the air raid warning was blaring out again and Louise had to drag herself out of bed and pull on her clothes.

'This is awful,' she said as Martha and her family joined them on the pavement, 'twice in one night.'

'Hellish,' Bert yawned. It was four o'clock in the morning and the adults all felt dog tired as they trudged back to the shelter, but Jonjo and Rosie had their second wind. They were groping around on the pavement for shrapnel, fragments of bomb and shell casings.

'Come along, you two,' Bert urged, 'we don't want the bombers to come back and catch us out in the street, do we?'

'Look Dad, I've got a lovely big piece. I want to find more,' Jonjo was excited. 'I want to have the biggest collection in the class.'

'Don't be silly. Do you want to get us all killed?'

'It's too dark to see anything now,' Martha said mildly, taking Jonjo's hand, 'it'll be easier to see when we're going home.' But he pulled his hand free and stopped to crow with delight as a fire engine sped past them.

Bert lost his temper. 'Come along, you little fiend! Do as you're told. We all need more sleep.' He took a swipe at him and they all heard the crack of his palm against Jonjo's head.

The child screamed and threw himself into Martha's arms, yelling, 'I hate you, I hate you,' in a voice full of venom.

It upset Louise to see the cracks in Martha's happiness, and it delayed them yet again as she tried to comfort Jonjo. Clearly Bert worshipped the ground she walked on, but Martha had told her he thought she and Susie were not firm enough with the children. He believed in a much stricter regime. Jonjo in particular needed a tight rein.

Louise knew Bert could also be dogmatic about how Martha should run his house. He controlled the money and decided what they would eat, where they would go and what they would do. Susie thought he was full of self-importance; he wanted to be the head of the household and nobody must challenge that, but Martha said he was very kind to her when she wasn't well and always helped with the heavy work about the house. She could see Martha was devoted to him, but all the same, he was over-strict and heavy-handed with Jonjo.

Later in the shelter Martha had muttered excuses for Bert. 'He's very tense. His roots are in Germany and he can't help feeling sympathy for his blood relatives there.'

'Shush,' Bert hissed.

'Bert's sympathies have to be a deep secret now,' Martha whispered softly, 'this crowd would lynch him if they heard us saying this. His family feared internment in the last war.' Even now it seemed they didn't consider themselves to be truly English.

The shelter was not as crowded as it had been earlier in the night; some people had decided to risk it and stay in their beds. All were more subdued and there was room for them all to lie down on the slatted seats. Louise was folding her blanket in an effort to make it more comfortable when she heard a couple nearby talking about the raid earlier in the night. 'The wardens were still digging when we came back, but they were only bringing bodies out by then.'

'Where was this?' Louise asked.

'Branton Street, haven't you heard? The public air raid shelter received a direct hit, killing everybody in it. It was crowded.'

'That's less than half a mile away,' Susie was aghast. 'We saw terrible damage in Fullerton Road too.'

They were all shocked. 'Branton Street has a specially built shelter of bricks and reinforced concrete like this one. '

'We were told it would keep us safe.'

'Nothing is safe if it gets a direct hit,' Bert said.

Susie shuddered. This was death from the skies for anyone unlucky enough to be underneath. 'I'll never feel safe in here again,' she breathed.

CHAPTER TWENTY-NINE

BERT HAD TO GET up to open the shop the next morning, and as usual, Martha got up with him to cook his breakfast.

'I think we'll give that public shelter a miss in future,' he yawned. 'We'd do just as well under the stairs here, and it would be quicker and easier than rushing up there in the wet.'

'The government says the shelters are safer,' Martha said, 'but there's no comfort there.'

'We'd get more sleep if we stayed at home,' Bert said. 'It was a false alarm the second time, but the all-clear didn't sound for an hour after we got there.'

'We did hear bombs exploding, but they were further away. Probably Bootle got those.'

'I'll put a mattress under the stairs tonight, and we can all snuggle down together with plenty of pillows and blankets. It'll be warmer too.'

'What about Mum and Susie?'

'They won't want to go up there on their own. If you can get them to clear out the cupboard under their stairs, I'll carry down the mattress from Becky's old bed.'

'Bert! Rosie is sleeping in her room.'

'Of course. Then I'll see if there's a spare mattress at the shop.'

'Your mother and aunt will be using them. The shop cellar is their shelter.'

'Well, I'll see if there's anything else at the shop. What happened to the cot mattresses? Those or a pile of pillows would be more comfortable than being squashed amongst strangers on the seats in the shelter. We'll be cramped but at least it will cut out the frantic rush through the cold streets.'

Miraculously, during the recent frightening months while Louise and Susie were sagging under the burden of wakeful nights, Martha was brimming with health and energy.

She went up to Jonjo's bedroom when it was time to get him up for school, but found him deeply asleep. It seemed a shame to wake him when he'd had such a disturbed night. A little later, Susie brought Rosie round already dressed for school. 'She's only half awake,' she said, 'but that goes for all of us this morning. What a night!'

Martha put her to lie on the sofa in her living room and covered her with a rug. 'I think I'll let them sleep on for an hour or so,' she said, 'before I give them breakfast.'

'Why not?' Susie agreed. 'They can't learn if they're tired out.'

Schools had to remain open whatever their difficulties because mothers with school-age children were drafted into war work. Martha was exempt on account of ill health. She tried to ring the school because Nurse O'Brien had told her they were always anxious when their pupils failed to turn up after a bad night, but the operator told her the lines were down and nobody could be connected.

It was getting on for eleven by the time the children had eaten breakfast. Martha usually walked them to school and went on to the baths for a swim. As it was so much later she was in two minds about swimming this morning, but at the last moment decided to take her bathing suit and towel.

Fires were still burning down on the docks. Smoke was hanging over the city in black clouds, and the acrid smell of burning was everywhere. Rosie pulled her to a halt with a squeal as they turned the corner to go up Fullerton Road. 'Connie and Clovis lived in this house,' she shrieked, 'they are our friends.'

Martha was horrified to see the damage; she remembered the second house in the road well. It had been a large Victorian stone-faced house of four stories with a turret at one end. The name Fullerton House was engraved into one of the sandstone gateposts, which was slightly askew. Once it had belonged to a rich merchant, but the city had expanded and small houses had surrounded it; the merchant had moved out and the house had been turned into four flats. Now only three walls remained, reaching only to first floor height. Broken bricks, tiles and glass had been tossed into the road and broken furniture, banisters and doors, together with battered personal effects and general rubble, were strewn across the garden.

Jonjo wrinkled his nose. 'What a stink.' Always hanging over recently bombed buildings was a foul smell of old plaster and dust. A policeman stopped them going closer and directed them up a parallel street. Martha tried to hurry them away.

'Have Clovis and Connie been killed?' Jonjo pulled at her skirt. 'They lived in the ground floor flat.'

'Connie told us they used the cellar as their shelter,' Rosie said, 'that everybody in the house did. Do you think they would have been safe there?'

'Yes,' Martha told them firmly. 'Quite likely they are safe. They could be in school when you get there.'

'That policeman wouldn't let us see if the cellar was damaged, would he? But they won't be able to live there any longer.'

'They'll find somewhere else to live. Come along, you're going to be very late this morning.'

Rosie wailed, 'I loaned Connie my Christopher Robin book. Will I ever get it back?'

For the children, the quiet orderliness of school had gone. Workmen were sweeping up glass in the playground. Some of the windows in their classroom had been broken and other men were hammering sheets of plywood over the window frames. That shut out most of the daylight and the electric lights weren't working. Only half the children had turned up, but they were restless and making twice the usual noise. Miss Osborne, their teacher, was agitated and not at all her usual self.

Martha had told Jonjo he must apologise. 'Sorry we're late, Miss. Are the Gibson twins here, Clovis and Connie?'

'Have you seen them this morning?' she asked. Jonjo was shaking his head.

'No,' Rosie was scared and trying not to cry, 'their house has been bombed. It's in ruins.'

'Yes, we all saw it on the way into school. They may be safe; a lot of the class isn't here yet. We must be patient until we have definite news. Sit down, Jonjo. We'll go on saying our times tables together. Start again with times four. One four is four . . .'

A few more children came to school as the day wore on, but

not Clovis and Connie. At four o'clock, Rosie and Jonjo were trusted to walk home on their own, and they ran down to the bottom of Fullerton Road and were shocked again by the devastation, though the debris in the road had been cleared and the Civil Defence workers and the policeman had gone.

They saw then that there was a notice tied to the gatepost which Jonjo tried to read. 'It starts with a hard word but then it says "keep out". But that doesn't mean us, Mrs Gibson knows us. We've been here to play lots of times, haven't we? Let's have a proper look round, she won't mind.'

Rosie pulled on his arm. 'I've seen that word before on bombed buildings and I asked Auntie Martha. She said it says danger and we mustn't go near.'

'Come on, just a peep, we'll be careful. Perhaps their cellar is all right, perhaps the twins weren't hurt at all.' Jonjo had to tread carefully round the large lumps of masonry on the garden path. Rosie followed behind, scared, but she didn't want to be left on her own. Once she could see inside the house she gasped in horror at the shambles of bricks and broken furniture.

Jonjo was looking round with interest. 'This was their living room. See the lino here?' He used his foot to scrape the thick grey dust aside so Rosie could see more of it. 'It was fawn, wasn't it?'

'Look at their sofa, it's upside down!' Rosie remembered sitting on brown-patterned velvet; now like everything else it was covered in grey dust. 'Look at their wireless, and the sideboard. What a mess!'

'This was their parlour. The wall has gone in between, and gosh, look at their piano! Mrs Gibson wouldn't let me play it, she was afraid I'd damage it.' He pressed a few notes and sound came from some of them. 'It still works,' he laughed, 'but not very well.'

'I think this is where their kitchen was,' Rosie picked up a frying pan, 'there's nothing much wrong with this. Poor Connie, this was her home.'

'I can see their cellar through this hole in the floor.' Jonjo was excited now. 'See the steps going down against that wall?' He started to climb across to them.

'Be careful,' Rosie warned, 'the floor is shaking.'

'I am being careful. I'm going down into the cellar,' Jonjo said, growing more daring by the minute. 'It's dark down there but I think I can see all sorts of things, camp beds and deck chairs and toys and books.'

'Don't go,' Rosie protested, 'those steps might give way under you.' She was frightened, her heart beating furiously, 'We shouldn't be here at all.'

'They're solid stone steps all the way down. It's too dark to see much, I need my torch, and there's all this white stuff that's come down from the ceiling. Come on, it's safe enough. I don't think Clovis and Connie would have been killed.'

Rosie was peering down into the darkness. 'The banister has broken right off. I can see some of it at the bottom.'

'Kick the rubbish off the steps and stay close to the wall and you'll be perfectly safe. Come on, it's great down here.' Rosie felt her way down slowly, pressing her body against the wall as she went.

'Gosh,' Jonjo chortled, 'here's a tin of fruit, it's a bit dented but it's all right. I'm going to take it home. We could have it for our tea.'

Rosie picked up a book and slapped it against her thigh to

shake the dust off. 'Can you see what this is? I think it's my Christopher Robin book! What luck to find it.'

'There's lots of stuff worth having,' Jonjo said, 'here's part of Clovis's train set. Look round and see if you can find any more. We could take that too.'

'We aren't supposed to take anything from bombed buildings,' Rosie objected, 'it's stealing, isn't it?'

'I'll keep it and give it back to Clovis when we find out where he is. It's better if we take their things and do that. Somebody else could steal them if we don't. Anybody can come in.'

'Look at all these sheets of paper blown everywhere. There's writing on one side but we could draw on the other. It's nice thick paper. I asked Nana if I could have some drawing paper, but she said it's scarce now and she couldn't get any.'

'It's all been covered in this horrible dust and some sheets have dirty marks on them.' Jonjo picked up a large envelope file. 'Rosie, look what I've found. Inside is the same sort of paper and it's all clean, there's only writing on one side.'

'I'll take it, and I'm having this doll of Connie's. Its name is Matilda, I've always liked it,' Rosie said.

'It's filthy.'

'I can wash it. Gosh, Jonjo, it's getting dark, we'd better go. Auntie Martha will be cross with us for not going straight home.' She looked up and saw the first star was already out.

'There's lots more valuable stuff here but it's getting too dark to see it.'

'I'm going,' Rosie was making for the stone stairs.

They took their loot up to the first floor. 'Hang on, I can't carry all this, I want that blanket thing over there. If I put all this stuff onto it I'll carry it like a swagman.'

'We could come back tomorrow afternoon and get more,' Rosie said. 'Unless somebody else finds it before then and takes it away.'

'We could pull that lino over the hole so that nobody else can see it. This place would make a smashing den to play in at the weekend,' Jonjo said. But when they tried to move the lino they found it wouldn't budge. 'It's hopeless, there's too much stuff standing on it.'

'There's a bit of carpet over there and that looks loose,' Rosie said.

'It's a rug.' Jonjo moved some bricks and a broken chair off it. 'Come on, give us a hand, this will do. It won't quite cover the hole and it won't keep the rain out as well as the lino would, but it will do for now.'

The bus was crowded and Susie had to stand throughout the journey, but her mother had managed to find a seat near the front. They were on their way home from work and though it was barely half past five, it was already dark. As they neared their bus stop she saw her mother pull herself wearily to her feet in the unlit bus, and start to edge her way through the standing passengers. Once they were off and the bus gone, the blackout seemed to cut them off from life itself.

Susie felt for Louise's arm and shivered, very much afraid that the bombers might come again tonight. The moon would be full and would fill the night with silvery light; just the sort of night the Germans needed for their bombing raids. The River Mersey would shine like a mirror so the bomb aimers could pinpoint the docks and the ships, and the factories.

Not a glimmer of light showed from the houses as they

walked up Milner Street, but they knew every inch of the way. Susie rattled the knocker on Martha's door as they passed, to let her know they were home. Louise let them into their own house; it was a relief to hear the door click shut behind them and know work was over for the day.

Louise flicked at the electric light switch, but nothing happened. 'They haven't been able to restore power yet,' she said. Susie had to feel her way through the kitchen to unlock the back door for Rosie, who stayed with Jonjo when she returned from school. Now Martha knew they were home she would send her running up the backyard.

In the living room, the flickering fire provided a half light. Martha always came in half an hour before they were due home to put a match to it and draw their blackout curtains. The candles stood ready, as they always must. Susie lit two as her mother added coal sparingly to the fire. Martha was a marvellous help, they wouldn't be able to manage without her.

Susie took one candle into the kitchen so she could start cooking. They needed a hot meal on the table as soon as possible as an air raid could come at any time and they'd had nothing but a sandwich since breakfast. It would be a mistake to go to the shelter until they'd eaten. Bert had done them proud tonight: five small lamb chops were set out between two plates and Martha had peeled potatoes and washed some cabbage to go with them. Susie lit the gas and added salt to the pans. Where was Rosie? She was taking her time tonight. Then their back gate banged and she heard footsteps running up the yard.

But it was a distraught Martha who pushed the back door

open. 'The children haven't come home from school,' she said, 'I'm worried stiff.'

That took Susie's breath away. 'What? They should have been home an hour ago.'

'I know. I keep telling them they must run home, that it's dangerous to be out in the dark these days.'

Louise, looking anxious now, came to the kitchen, her weariness forgotten. 'Could they have been kept in? Bad behaviour or something, you know what Jonjo can be like.'

'They wouldn't do that now we're getting these raids,' Martha said, 'they know how anxious we are.'

'I'd better run up to the school to see if they're still there,' Susie said.

'I'll come with you. I've been once, but there was nobody about. I ran back in case they'd come home and found nobody here.'

'Little monkeys,' Louise said, 'why can't they do as they're told? You go, I'll see to the dinner.'

Susie hadn't yet taken her coat off. 'Are you ready, Martha?' She ushered her through the house, slammed the front door, and pushed her arm through her sister's. They set off at a brisk pace. 'Where can they have gone?'

'I've told them they mustn't stop to play with the other children; that they must come straight home.'

Above them the sky was filled with bobbing barrage balloons. 'They can't have gone far, and at least there's no air raid warning yet,' Susie said. They'd just reached the top of Milner Road when she pulled Martha to a standstill. Two pairs of footsteps were pounding towards them and she thought she'd heard a laugh that sounded like Rosie's. The next moment they were pulling up in front of them.

Martha was gasping with relief. 'Where have you been till now? I've been worried stiff.'

'To the twins' house.'

'They've been bombed out,' Rosie said, 'they didn't come to school today, so we went to see why. It's a ruin, everything's smashed to bits.'

'What's all that stuff you've got?' Martha asked. 'You haven't taken some of their things? That's against the law. There are police notices everywhere saying it is strictly forbidden to take anything from bombed premises.'

'The kids are OK, Martha,' Susie said, 'they've come to no harm. I've had enough, let's get back.'

They found Bert's van parked outside his house as they walked down the road. 'If he's found you're not at home, he'll be in our house,' Susie said, unlocking her front door. Bert was warming his back against the fire and talking to Louise.

'Thank goodness you're all safe,' she said. Then the children had to tell the whole story over again.

Bert was cross and turned on Jonjo. 'How many times do you have to be told to come straight home from school? I don't like you worrying your mother like this. And you know it's looting if you take things from a bomb site. The police can prosecute you for that, and if they find you guilty the punishment is death.'

The colour had drained from Jonjo's cheeks. 'You must have seen the notices they're posted everywhere. You can read, can't you?'

'This book about Christopher Robin is mine, isn't it, Mum?' Rosie said. 'I only loaned it to Connie, so I can take it back.'

'What about that doll you've got, young lady? Is that yours too?'

'Come on, Bert,' Martha said, 'let's go home, I want to start cooking dinner.'

CHAPTER THIRTY

BEFORE HE'D COME HOME, Bert had been feeling very much on edge about a business relationship he'd kept hidden from Martha. It had made him gasp to hear Jonjo mention Fullerton House. He gripped his shoulder none too gently and steered him home. Once inside, he stopped him heading for the stairs and said, 'I want to talk to you,' and marched him into the living room. 'Tell me more about these bombed premises you've been looting.'

Jonjo struggled to describe how little was left standing while Martha lit the gas in the kitchen. She left the door open. 'Don't be hard on him, Bert,' she said softly, 'he's only seven.'

'Do you know Mr O'Malley? Mickey O'Malley?' Bert went on. Jonjo shook his head. 'I think he might live in the top flat in that bombed house.'

'It had a turret on top.'

'Yes it had,' Bert said, making up his mind to look at the place in daylight. 'Right then, let's see the loot you've brought.' Jonjo obediently opened up the blanket on the floor. 'That's mostly broken toys.'

'They're not all broken. This is part of Clovis's train set. It isn't loot. I'll give it back to him when I see him.'

'Everything's very dirty.' Martha was watching from the kitchen door.

'It's junk.'

'I brought this tin of fruit salad.'

Bert studied the torn label. 'It's a big one; we haven't seen tins of fruit that size since the war started. We'll eat that.'

'Shouldn't we take it to the police?' Martha asked. 'It could go towards feeding those who are bombed out. We don't want to get into trouble.'

'No, this tin has been damaged by bomb blast,' he lied, to ease Martha's conscience. 'It's dented and I think there's a small hole in it, the fruit must be eaten up right away or it will go bad. We'll have it tonight, Martha. Get yourself washed, Jonjo, you're covered with grey dust.'

Bert flung himself down on the sofa to wait for his dinner and wondered if Mickey O'Malley had survived the bombing. It must be his place that had copped it; it was the only building with a turret on top. Tomorrow morning, he'd go and take a look at the place on his way to work. He hoped very much that Mickey was all right. It would be a disaster all round if he'd been killed just when meat rationing had put Bert in a privileged position and he'd begun to make real money at last. Mickey had set up a group to trade in the black market and was acting as the middle man.

Since meat rationing had started, all livestock ready for slaughter had to be sold direct to the Ministry of Food at a controlled price based on quality and weight of carcass. But stock for breeding, rearing or bringing on to a heavier weight had traditionally gone to auction at a stores market and was sold to the highest bidder. Now black market traders were stepping in to buy them.

The Ministry of Food employed officers to enforce this law, but in wartime many were elderly and town bred and could not tell the difference between a lamb ready for slaughter and one that could be legally sold through the stores market, though the difference was instantly recognisable to farmers and butchers. Mickey O'Malley had had the advantage of being brought up on a farm in Kerry.

Butchers were limited in the amount of meat they could obtain legally from wholesalers, having to hand in ration coupons collected from their customers. Mickey O'Malley had set himself up as an agent bringing together the farmers who wanted more money for their stock than the Ministry was prepared to pay, and the Liverpool butchers who had a ready sale for it through their shops. Bert had participated in Mickey O'Malley's scheme and found it worked perfectly.

Other things were going right for him too. He hadn't been able to believe his luck when only the other night Martha had told him that she thought she must be pregnant again and would go to see Dr Grant. This was a small miracle because he'd been trying to prevent it since Wendy had died; they'd decided that repeated pregnancies were damaging her health and were not resulting in the family they wanted. Martha was happy, or she had been before Jonjo had worried her by not coming home as he should, and she was healthier than she'd been for a long time, another miracle.

Next morning, Bert kissed Martha goodbye and drove off in his van. He didn't tell her that he planned to visit Fullerton House on the way to the shop as Martha knew nothing about his arrangements with O'Malley. She came from a God-fearing family and wouldn't approve.

Bert needed to know if what Jonjo had told him was true, and whether Mickey O'Malley had survived. Mickey had promised him a delivery of black market meat that week and he had to know whether or not that was on track. Mickey usually phoned the day before to tell him the cost and he was expected to pay cash on delivery. He no longer promptly banked his daily takings, so he hoped to have the cash ready, but it occasionally meant he had to draw money from the bank.

Bert was shocked to see that Fullerton House had been almost destroyed. Only the bleak ruins of three half-height walls were left standing against the grey sky. Could Mickey have survived this? He wanted to take a closer look, and if he came across another tin of fruit salad such as they'd had last night, he meant to pick it up. They'd all had second helpings and there was still enough left for Martha to have some for her lunch. He drove on a little further before parking, as his van had his name and address painted on each side and he didn't want to advertise what he was doing.

Once he was standing between those blackened walls, the devastation was even worse. He had to watch where he put his feet as once or twice he felt things moving under his weight, and there were bits of domestic bric-a-brac half buried in the dust. He was in what had once been a kitchen and took a few steps to look at what he thought might be tins of food, but no, it was just twisted metal of some sort.

He heard something small drop onto the rubble near him, which was scary. It had to be plaster or cement or something off the walls, which looked as though they might collapse at any moment. He was glad he'd told the kids they were forbidden to come here again as the place looked anything but safe.

His attention was caught by a handsome clock still fixed to one of the walls; it was still showing the right time and would look well in his house. He took a few steps towards it and suddenly the floor beneath him gave way. He knew he screamed in terror as he felt himself falling, and the crash when he landed on his back brought a searing pain in his leg. His head was spinning, he felt disorientated, and he couldn't see anything in the near dark.

That morning, Martha intended to go swimming again and walked the children to school using the route the policeman had directed them to the day before.

'Can't we go up Fullerton Road?' Jonjo asked. 'We could show you the ruins of Clovis's flat.'

'No,' she said, 'we all see more bomb sites than is good for our peace of mind, and I want you to stay well away from that place in future.'

When she kissed them goodbye at the school gates, Jonjo said to Rosie, 'We couldn't go now anyway, there was no air raid last night so we'd have no excuse if we were late. We'll go this afternoon on the way home.'

After morning prayers in the school hall, their head teacher told them that she'd heard of several pupils who had been caught in recent air raids. Some had been hurt and taken to hospital but would be returning to school in due course. Rosie listened carefully to the names she read out from a list.

'Others,' their head mistress went on, 'have had their homes damaged so badly they can't live in them any more. The

Gibson twins, Clovis and Connie, and their parents suffered only minor injuries but have had to go and stay with relatives in Southport until they can find alternative living accommodation nearer here.' She went on to deliver another warning about the danger of playing on bomb sites, of which there were several in the neighbourhood.

'We're still going,' Jonjo said at four o'clock, 'I've brought my torch and I want to look for more of Clovis's train set, especially more track. He'll want me to because I'll give it all back to him, but we'll be able to play with it while he's away.'

'I'm glad they weren't badly hurt,' Rosie said, falling into step beside him. 'It must be awful to lose your home and have all your toys and things mangled up and broken.'

'Gosh!' Jonjo grabbed at her arm and pulled her to a sudden halt. 'Look, there's Dad's van.'

Rosie shivered. 'He must be delivering meat round here.'

'No, he can't get petrol to do that now. He's hired a boy to deliver orders on his bike. I'm going to do that when I'm a bit older.'

'Could he be looking round the bomb site? But why would he?'

'Perhaps he's waiting to catch us?'

'They'll all say we're naughty to go again.'

'Dad would beat the living daylights out of me if he caught me there,' Jonjo said with bated breath. 'He might have come to look for more of that fruit salad. It went down a treat last night.'

'Let's run straight home,' Rosie said, 'I'm scared.'

'I'm not. I was looking forward to playing in our den, and with my torch we'll be able to see everything.'

'No, let's go home.'

'We could just peep to see if he is there. If not, we'll stay and play. Come on, Rosie, let's be quiet as mice and creep in.' He took her hand and helped her over the piles of rubble. Once inside the three walls, Jonjo straightened up. 'There's nobody here,' he said.

'Ssh,' Rosie put a finger over her lips and pointed. 'That rug we used to cover the hole in the floor,' she whispered, 'it's gone. And isn't the hole bigger than it was?' She craned forward. 'It's fallen in. Don't go near, you could fall in too.'

Jonjo edged round the other way towards the stairs going down to the cellar. Rosie was scared, she could feel herself shaking, but she clutched on to his coat and went along with him to peer down into the dark depths. She could see nothing until Jonjo took his torch from his pocket and shone it downwards.

Rosie's terrified scream broke the silence, making Jonjo click off his torch. She'd glimpsed the body of a man lying flat on his back. 'It's Uncle Bert,' she gasped, hanging on to Jonjo's arm with both hands.

'Is it?' Jonjo switched the torch on again and gingerly moved the beam to shine down into the cellar. 'It is!'

Rosie's voice was stiff with horror. 'He looks dead, his eyes are closed.'

'No, didn't you see him open them? He's moving!' The torch beam was jerking all over the place.

'Keep it still,' she urged, 'is he hurt?'

The voice from the depths was hoarse and breathless but unmistakable. 'Hello? Is that . . . Is that you Jonjo?' Jonjo dropped the torch and was backing away in horror and trying to drag Rosie with him. She shook herself free and picked the torch up to shine it down into the cellar again. She could see Uncle Bert trying to drag himself to the bottom of the steps. 'Help me,' he called, 'I'm hurt.'

'No, come away,' Jonjo whispered, 'we can't, let's go home.'

Rosie was aghast. 'We can't do that! He'll die if we leave him there.'

'We can,' Jonjo was dragging her further away, but Bert's voice followed them. 'Come back, Jonjo, I need you.'

'No, he'll kill me. Can't you see he's fallen into our den because he walked on that rug we pulled over the hole in the floor? He'll blame me.'

'You must, he's your father. Don't you love him?'

'I hate him. He's nasty to me.'

He was towing Rosie out into the garden, through the gate posts.

'I want him to die.'

'No you don't. We've got to tell somebody, a warden or a policeman. They'll be able to get him out.'

'No, he can stay there,' Jonjo said, 'he spoils everything.'

'What will your mother say?'

'If we run we'll not be late home.' Jonjo's feet began to pound along the pavement. 'Nobody will know we've been back there.'

Rosie could hardly keep up. 'We've got to tell Auntie Martha.'

'No, she'll be cross with us too. She forbade us to go there again.'

'But she won't want Uncle Bert to die!'

'She doesn't need him. We don't need him. You mustn't say

anything to anybody. It'll be our secret, yours and mine, that we went back and saw him there.'

'But we did go back and we saw him. What if she asks?'

'She won't. Promise, Rosie, that you won't say anything to anybody, not ever. Not when they find him dead because that would be even worse than telling them now.'

'But . . .'

'Come on, promise you'll keep your mouth shut and I'll be your best friend for ever.'

They were going up Jonjo's back yard and Rosie had no time to do anything but nod her agreement. It was a comfort to reach the familiar warmth and light of Auntie Martha's kitchen.

CHAPTER THIRTY-ONE

MARTHA USUALLY GREETED THEM with a smile and a kiss and had the living room fire burning up and a slice of bread and jam ready on the table for them. Today she was lying on the sofa, looking ill and white.

'Are you sick again, Auntie Martha?' Rosie asked.

'No, I'm all right, but something's happened to Bert. He's not been in the shop all day. He went off to work this morning but didn't get there.' She got up and began to pace up and down the room. 'His mother's almost out of her mind. Nobody knows where he's gone.'

Jonjo's face had gone even whiter than his mother's. Rosie pulled at his arm; surely this meant he'd tell her? He was pulling her towards the sofa. 'You promised,' he hissed as they climbed up. They sat very close together, holding on to each other.

'It's not as though there's been an air raid and he could have been hurt in that,' Martha said. 'I wish I knew where he was.'

Rosie sat stiff and silent, clutching onto Jonjo's hand, while Martha paced up and down looking agitated. She felt terrible, they were both going to get into awful trouble when Martha found out they knew where Uncle Bert was and hadn't told her. She closed her eyes and wished her mother and Nana would come home, they would know what to do.

She felt dazed and sick by the time she heard her mother rattle the letterbox on the front door and leapt up to run towards it. 'Mum!' she called. Louise already had the key in their own door and stepped inside, but Susie turned back to her. Rosie threw herself into her arms and buried her face in her coat. She half carried her back into Martha's living room.

'Has something happened?' Susie took in her sister's distress at a glance.

'It's Bert,' she sobbed, 'he's disappeared.'

Rosie had to listen to the whole story over again. She couldn't bring herself to say anything while Jonjo's dark eyes were watching her intently from the sofa. She wanted to get away from him and Auntie Martha, she wanted to go home. They were still talking on and on about it when Louise came round to say, 'Didn't Bert bring any meat for our dinner tonight?'

Martha was in tears by now and it all had to be explained yet again. Jonjo tugged at her, 'Mum, I'm hungry,' he said.

'Oh, I'm sorry, love. I'm not paying much attention to you tonight.' Martha got to her feet and seemed to pull herself together. 'Perhaps we'll feel better if we have something to eat. We've got eggs and bacon. That will do us for tonight.'

'We'll go home and get something to eat too,' Louise said, 'but it'll have to be beans on toast for us.'

Rosie held firmly onto both her mother and grandmother and walked between them. They were talking about Bert, wondering where he'd got to, and saying how sorry they felt for Martha. Rosie was on tenterhooks and once the darkness swallowed them up, she couldn't keep the words to herself any longer. They came bursting out in a storm of tears. 'It's all my fault,' she sobbed, 'I've done something terrible to Uncle Bert.'

'No, no, it isn't your fault,' Louise was comforting, 'it can't be.'

'It is, I know where he is,' she said. 'Jonjo and I found him.'

She felt herself being swung over the doorstep into her own home and stood up against the living-room door. They were both hurling questions at her and she couldn't get the answers out to make them understand. She couldn't stop crying and they were still firing questions at her when Martha came running up the yard, dragging Jonjo behind her.

'Bert's been found, he's been taken to Mill Road Infirmary,' she sang out, her relief plain to see. 'His mother's just rung to let me know. A man called Micky O'Malley drove Bert's van to the shop and put it in their garage. He said his flat in Fullerton Road was bombed the other night and he was taken to hospital with minor injuries.'

Rosie was staring at Martha feeling confused. Jonjo came over to clutch at her hand. He twisted it. 'Say nothing,' he hissed in her ear. She knew he was very frightened.

'When this man was released from hospital,' Auntie Martha went on, 'he went home and found Bert in the ruins, though he has no idea what he was doing there.'

'Was Bert hurt?' Susie asked.

'Yes, he was barely conscious. Mr O'Malley walked round to the Civil Defence Post in Alfred Road and they phoned for an ambulance for him.'

'At least you know where he is and that he's getting looked after,' Louise told her.

'But why didn't he say he knew somebody who lived there? Why didn't he tell me where he was going this morning? Will you look after Jonjo while I go to the hospital to find out how he is?'

'Martha, first go home and fry those eggs and bacon,' Louise said. 'You can't go without having a meal, especially not now you're having another baby, you might be kept waiting for ages. Anyway, it'll take time for them to find out what's wrong with Bert.'

Susie said, 'I'll come with you, Martha, but we all need to eat first. You've probably had a terrible day worrying about Bert. Mum can stay here to look after the children.'

When they'd eaten and her mother had gone next door, Rosie felt herself being lifted onto her grandmother's knee as she sat on the sofa. 'Now,' she said, 'I want you to tell me the full story. Why did you and Jonjo go to Fullerton House a second time, and what exactly did you see?'

Rosie cried, but she had to tell her how scared she'd been to see Uncle Bert lying on the cellar floor, and how Jonjo hated him and wanted to leave him there to die.

'You did the right thing by telling us,' Louise said, 'you must always tell a grown up if you know somebody has fallen and is in need of help.'

'But now Jonjo will hate me too, because I promised not to. I didn't want to promise, honest I didn't.'

'Shush, Rosie, Jonjo is coming now. I want you to leave this to me.' The key turned in the front door lock and Martha called, 'We're going now, Mum, I've brought Jonjo round. If we're late coming back, can you get him ready for bed?'

Jonjo came in slowly with his pyjamas under his arm looking

scared. 'Come in, Jonjo, and sit down.' Louise stood up and put Rosie to sit in the opposite corner of the sofa. 'You've been a naughty boy, haven't you?'

He wouldn't look at her. 'First of all, you disobeyed both your parents by returning to the ruins of your friends' house. Your father was hurt there and you could have been too. Worse, you took Rosie with you and put her in danger.'

He sniffled, 'I'm sorry. Nana.'

'It could have been too late to be sorry. You must think before you do things like that. But you did something much worse, didn't you, Jonjo? You saw your father had fallen into the cellar. You knew he was hurt and you did nothing to help him, and you made Rosie promise not to tell anybody. That was a terrible thing to do.'

Jonjo was crying noisily.

'Be quiet and listen to what I'm saying.'

'I am, Nana, I am.'

'If that man hadn't found your father, what do you think could have happened?'

'Uncle Bert would have died,' Rosie said in a loud voice.

'Yes, and after that?'

Jonjo mumbled, 'He'd have been buried.'

It took Louise a moment to curb her smile. 'I'm thinking of the effect that would have had, Jonjo. Your mother would have been very upset, wouldn't she?'

He gave another sniffle and a reluctant nod of agreement.

'If she'd known what you'd done, she would have been very angry with you. And how do you think you would feel?'

He let out a howl of anguish. Tears were coursing down his cheeks.

'Even if nobody knew but Rosie, you would feel it was your fault, and if your father had been left to die you'd feel guilty for the rest of your life, wouldn't you? You would regret what you'd done but it would be too late to help him. It would be on your conscience for ever.'

Jonjo was having a crescendo of tears. 'Please don't tell my dad, he'll kill me.'

'Well, I don't think for one moment he'd do that. Your dad loves you very much, we all do, but it would upset him, so I don't think we should tell him that you said you hated him.'

'I didn't!' he screamed. 'I mean I don't.'

'All right then, we'll say no more about this. Your father needn't know unless you tell him. In this case you were lucky, because somebody else called an ambulance to take him to hospital. So now I want you to make some promises. Are you ready?'

He nodded, the picture of misery.

'You must promise never to walk away from anybody in need of help. If you can't help them yourself, you must tell an adult as soon as you can. And you must also promise never again to make Rosie do something that you know is wrong.'

'I do, Nana, and I promise to be a good boy for everybody.'

Louise sat down beside him and pulled him into her arms. 'Come on then, give me a hug and a kiss and we won't say any more about that.' Rosie pushed into her arms too.

Louise knew that wasn't something she could have ignored. She breathed a sigh of relief now, feeling she'd done the right thing. It wasn't until she had the children ready for bed that she had time to think more about it, and at that point the air raid siren wailed its warning. Hastily, she pushed both children into the bed she'd arranged under the stairs and made all haste to get ready to join them. It scared her to think of her girls being out in a raid.

She filled the flask and set the table for breakfast, but all remained quiet. After an hour, she was relieved to hear the all-clear sounding. She put a little more coal on the fire, made herself a cup of tea and settled down on the sofa with her library book.

At five to ten the air raid warning sounded again, and this time the ackack guns opened up soon afterwards. Both the children were asleep when she looked under the stairs. In order to give herself room to lie down, she had to lift Rosie and set her to lie on cushions at Jonjo's feet. The space under the stairs was limited, but it was better than running out in the cold to a public shelter. She was really worried about Martha and Susie now. Being caught out in an air raid could be dangerous.

CHAPTER THIRTY-TWO

B Y THE TIME THEY reached the hospital, Susie could see Martha was calmer. They all worried about her, especially Mum, because she'd had so much ill health and was now pregnant again, but anyone would get het up if their husband disappeared as Bert had done. Susie had always thought him a bit strange.

When they reached the hospital and asked for Bert, they were directed to a ward and the sister told them, 'The doctors are examining him now, would you please take a seat over there until they've finished? There's already a man waiting to see Mr Dolland, and I'm afraid only two people are allowed at the bed at one time.'

The man heard her and said, 'I'm Mickey O'Malley, Bert buys some of his meat through my business and is something of a friend.'

Martha brightened up and introduced herself and Susie. 'I'm told you called an ambulance for him. Thank you for doing that.'

'I was surprised to find him in the ruins of my home. I live in the top flat in Fullerton House, that's the one with the turret. Well, I did live there. A bomb fell very close the night before last and we had to be dug out of the ruins. All the tenants of the flats used the cellar as an air raid shelter, but none of us was seriously hurt. We were taken to hospital and I was kept in for twenty-four hours.' He felt the plaster on his forehead. 'Just badly grazed but it was a bit of a shock.'

'We know the place,' Martha said, 'our children are friendly with the Gibson twins who lived in the ground floor flat. They went to see the damage yesterday. You were lucky to escape so lightly.'

'We were, very lucky, most of the house fell on our heads, but being in the cellar saved us. I've lost something though, something important. I was working on my business accounts during that raid, but in the panic after we were hit, I forgot about them and left them there. I'm worried about losing them, very worried. I went back to look for my file and account books, but I couldn't find them. I knew exactly where I was at the time, and I moved all the plaster and rubbish from that side of the cellar, but there was no sign of them. Do you mind my asking: did your children take anything away? It won't be easy to carry on my business without them.'

'Yes, they brought home some toys that belonged to the Gibson children.'

He was instantly alert. 'What exactly did they bring? I'm missing a notebook that I use to record my business transactions, and an envelope file with letters and documents in it.'

'Jonjo brought a blanket and some pieces of a train set. I don't remember a notebook. What did Rosie bring home?' she asked Susie, 'was it just toys?'

'I think so. The only thing I can bring to mind is a doll called Matilda. She spent a lot of time washing its clothes in the kitchen sink.'

Martha cut in, 'I've been worried because Bert didn't mention that he meant to go to your place.'

'I was surprised to find him there. I've come to ask him if he knows what happened to my things. I'm worried about losing them, very worried. It won't be easy to carry on my business without them. If you find my notebook, it's dark blue with hard covers, would you let me know? You can reach me on this number, or leave a message for me.' He was scribbling it down on a corner torn from his newspaper when a nurse came to say he could go in to see Bert.

A harassed house surgeon was coming to talk to them. 'Mrs Dolland?' he said. 'I understand your husband fell into a cellar in a bombed building.'

'Yes,' Martha said, 'is he badly hurt?'

'He suffered a head injury and I think he has some concussion, so he isn't able to tell us very much yet, but we think with rest that will clear. His main injury is a fracture of his lower left leg. He's had it X-rayed and fortunately it's a simple fracture of the tibia just below the knee. He'll need to go down to theatre to have it plastered tomorrow. He also has a couple of broken ribs, and some small cuts and abrasions. His cuts have been dressed and he's had painkillers, we've made him as comfortable as we can. You may go in and see him, but please don't stay long. Rest is what he needs now.'

Mr O'Malley stood up to leave when he saw them walking down the ward. 'You won't forget to look for my notebook, will you?' he said to Susie.

'No, of course not.'

Bert's head was bandaged and he had a dressing on one

cheek. Martha bent to kiss his other one and said, 'Hello, Bert, how are you feeling?'

'Better,' he said, 'now I'm out of that dark hole.'

'You're in hospital.'

'I know, yes. I've broken my leg.'

'How did you come to fall into that cellar?'

He was shaking his head. 'I was looking for Mickey O'Malley but the floor gave way beneath me. I was there for ages, thought I'd never get out. It was like a nightmare. I even thought I saw Jonjo and Rosie looking down at me.'

'Mr O'Malley has lost the notebook in which he keeps his business accounts,' she told him. 'He's anxious to have it back, and wants me to look among the bits and pieces Rosie and Jonjo took from there to see if I can find it.'

'Be sure to do that,' he said, 'he won't want it to fall into the wrong hands. It might not be good for me either.'

Susie and Martha were getting off the bus at the bottom of Milner Road just as the second air raid warning was sounding. They ran up the hill and found Jonjo and Rosie tucked up on a cot mattress under the stairs, and their mother ready to join them.

'Much better than going to the public shelter,' she said. 'I'll push in with the children, why don't you two bed down together next door?'

The throb of enemy aircraft could be heard overhead and then came the boom of explosions, fortunately not too close. Louise held her breath to listen. Martha and Susie took to their heels and the front door slammed behind them.

Louise settled down to sleep. She was glad Martha had

Susie with her; this was not a good night for her to be alone. She hadn't explained why Bert had gone to Fullerton House in the first place. It seemed he'd given no indication that he knew anybody who lived there, and he'd not told Martha where he was going this morning. If he had, he'd have been rescued much sooner. It seemed Bert might have secrets he didn't share with Martha.

The following evening, Susie was putting Rosie to bed when an envelope file in her bedroom caught her eye. 'Where did that come from?' she demanded. 'Did you bring it from the bombed house you went to?' When the child nodded, she went on, 'Rosie, you must never take anything from bombed premises. That's looting and you could be sent to prison for it.'

'I thought it was Connie's store of drawing paper,' she wailed. 'We thought it would be all right to look after the twins' toys and things until we saw them again.'

'Well it might be, but all the same . . .' Susie looked inside the file and drew out a dark blue hardbacked notebook. 'This belongs to somebody else, the man who got an ambulance for Uncle Bert, and he's very anxious to have it back. He lived in one of the flats above the twins.'

The first piece of paper she drew out of the file had some heavy red and yellow crayoning on the back. 'What's this supposed to be?'

'It's a bommie. At school, that's what we call a house that's been bombed.'

After she'd kissed Rosie goodnight, Susie took the file and its contents downstairs to take a closer look at it. 'That man, Mr O'Malley, was very keen to have it back,' she said to her mother, 'and Bert was keen that he should too.'

'Do you think that's why he went to that bomb site?'

'Yes, but it doesn't mean a great deal to me. Figures are more your line, Mum.'

Louise took the notebook to the table and flipped over the pages. 'These are not professional business accounts,' she said, 'not double entry book keeping. For tax purposes all businesses have to keep proper accounts.'

'What are they then?'

'Just figures jotted down to record cash transactions.'

Susie said slowly, 'For personal use? Mum, I've been wondering if Bert is dabbling in black market meat.'

'Oh my goodness!' Louise slammed the book shut. 'I have too, for some time. Bert is very generous to us. He gives us all the meat we can eat.'

'Gives,' Susie said, 'not sells. The ration is one shilling and twopence a week per person, but since we aren't charged, we don't know how much we are getting.'

'I've offered to pay several times but he waves my money away. "You do so much for Martha and me," he says.' Louise opened the notebook again and studied it. 'What was the name of the man this file belongs to?'

'Mickey O'Malley. He found Bert and called an ambulance for him, he did his best for him.'

'You said he was anxious to have these things back? If we're right, and he's involved in the black market, he'd be worried stiff. This notebook could tie him to criminal activity.'

'Yes, tie Bert to it too.'

Susie was spreading the documents in the file across the dining table. 'Here's a list of butchers' shops, with addresses and phone numbers and . . . Yes, Bert's shop is here.'

'What are we going to do?' Louise asked. 'We should let the police know.'

'No,' Susie said firmly, 'we do nothing.' She was putting the documents together. 'I don't want to hear about your conscience. We can't land Bert in trouble, can we?'

Louise was frowning. 'Isn't it our duty?'

'Martha would never forgive us. To hell with duty!'

'We ought to tell her what Bert is doing, shouldn't we?'

'Perhaps she knows?'

'No she doesn't, or he'd have told her he was going to that bomb site.'

'Well, it would upset her to know now, wouldn't it? She thinks the sun shines out of Bert. We are just surmising that's what he's doing, putting two and two together. We have no proof.'

Louise drummed her fingers on the file. 'This is the proof, Susie.'

'Well, I vote we keep our mouths shut.'

'And keep on eating his meat?'

'Yes, we have to, or you'll have to tell him the reason. There are times, Mum, when it's better to do nothing. Forget it.' Susie held up two more of Mickey O'Malley's letters. 'Good lord, look at the mess Rosie's made of these. More examples of her artwork, but he won't care about that, he'll be so glad to have them back. I'll ring the number he gave me.'

CHAPTER THIRTY-THREE

MARTHA SEEMED LOST WITHOUT Bert. Louise and Susie rallied round to help, concerned about her because she was pregnant, but she remained well. Susie continued to keep her company during bombing raids while Jonjo was put to bed under Louise's stairs. It didn't give any of them very much room, but they all preferred it to the public shelter.

Fortunately, Bert's younger brother Edward was able to run the butcher's shop while he couldn't work, and Derek, the shop boy, came on his bicycle two or three times a week to deliver their meat. Louise soon noticed that they were getting very much less, and had to ask Edward if he could send unrationed offal and sausages when he had them. She wondered if Bert was keeping him in ignorance of his black market activities, or whether he was being ultra-careful to hide them.

On Sundays while Bert was in hospital, Louise told Martha that she and Jonjo must come to her house for their Sunday lunch. 'I'm leaving you girls in charge of the cooking,' she said, 'and I'm going to church. I'll bring Chris back with me as usual.'

After they'd eaten an excellent lunch, Martha started clearing the table and went to the kitchen to start the washing up, lamenting that visiting was allowed at the hospital only on

Sunday and Wednesday afternoons. 'It starts at two o'clock so I need to get a move on.'

'I can give you and Jonjo a lift to the hospital,' Chris offered, but by then she had the taps on full and didn't hear.

'No,' Jonjo said, 'I don't want to go,' and he buried his face in a cushion.

Louise tried to lift him to his feet saying, 'Come on, Jonjo, you want to see your daddy, don't you?'

'No, I don't,' he was fighting to escape. 'I don't want him to come home ever. It's lovely when it's just me and Mum on our own.'

Martha had come back and looked absolutely horrified. 'What's the matter, Jonjo?' She tried to put her arms round him, but Jonjo was sobbing. 'Dad'll kill me when he comes home. He knows I saw him in that cellar, he saw me looking down at him.'

'No, how could he? Dad went the following day, not when you were there.'

'Me and Rosie went again. Dad said, "Is that you, Jonjo? Help me, I'm hurt." But we ran home instead and left him there.'

Martha straightened up with shock.

Rosie piped up, 'Jonjo, you didn't answer, so he won't know for sure it was us. And somebody else helped him.'

'But he had to lie there for a lot longer and he was hurt. He'll be mad with me over that.'

'You went a second time to that bomb site?'

'Yes,' Rosie said.

'I told you not to. It's dangerous.'

'I wish I hadn't,' Jonjo burst out. 'I wish I'd never been near the place.'

'It won't matter any more,' Rosie said. 'They've knocked the walls down and made the ground level.'

'They must have made it safe,' Martha said, 'that's a blessing.'

Louise said, 'You go alone, love. Bert would prefer that, I'm sure.'

'I was going alone. I can't take you with me, Jonjo. Children aren't allowed to visit. They don't let children in.' They could all see that Martha was upset, she was hugging Jonjo.

'Get your coat,' Christopher told her. 'No point in you being late. I'll take you there.'

'We'll look after Jonjo,' Louise said.

When they'd gone, she and Susie sat down on the sofa with the children and tried to soothe them, but Jonjo sobbed out, 'Dad is never nice to me, he doesn't like me. He hits me.'

'No, Jonjo, he loves you very much. Before you were born he used to tell us how much he wanted a son.'

Later that evening, when the children had gone down for the night, Susie said, 'I've thought for some time that Bert can be a bit heavy-handed with Jonjo. Is it just his way of disciplining him? Considering how Bert went on about wanting a son to carry on his business, you'd think he'd be a more indulgent father.'

Louise said nothing, but she too was worried about Jonjo. Who were his parents? Years ago, she remembered wondering if Becky was his mother. How could frail Martha have produced such a large, strong and healthy baby? True, she'd always treated him in a loving motherly fashion, but didn't she treat Rosie in exactly the same way?

*

Martha visited Bert whenever she could. He praised the treatment and the kindness he was receiving, but he was not recovering as quickly as he'd expected. 'I thought your broken leg was considered a simple fracture?'

'It is, but I've got a bit of infection in the grazes on my hands, so I won't be able to work in the shop until that's better, and it's everything else too.'

Martha flinched. She could see he had a large plaster on his leg. 'But you are getting better and you will be able to walk again?'

'Yes, I'm told my bones are knitting together, both my ribs and my tibia. It's just a question of time.'

Martha was unhappy when she was told Bert would be kept in hospital over Christmas. 'I hope to be home by mid-January,' he said, 'but I'll still have the plaster on.'

'At least you'll be home well before the new baby comes,' she said. Martha continued to visit, but found the buildings bleak and forbidding. It was common knowledge that it had once been the workhouse, and a plaque told her it had been opened in that capacity in 1841. A lot of rebuilding work had been done in 1893 and now there was a central building surrounded by many other large blocks of wards. It had reopened as Mill Road Infirmary with almost a thousand beds and served the city well.

The bombing raids were continuing and bomb sites could now be seen everywhere. The enemy planes came over under cover of darkness and at this time of the year it was getting dark by four o'clock. Restaurants and bars were closing early because people were scared to be out after dark. Only the children had any enthusiasm for this second wartime Christmas, their excitement fired up with Christmas stories and carols at school, and they were busy making their own Christmas cards and gifts. What everybody really wanted was a break from the bombing.

Becky rang Martha and told her Max was working overtime and was tired out. He was looking forward to having a few days off so he could catch up with his sleep. She invited them to have lunch at the Adelphi Hotel on the Saturday before Christmas, so they could all be home before dark. Louise watched her across the table and was fascinated by the confidence she was showing. She put them at ease and encouraged them to order expensive food, but then Becky had always been different to the rest of the family. She didn't even look like them.

Martha and Susie had her fair colouring, but Becky's dark brown hair had a gloss on it and was smartly styled, and she looked as though she'd come straight from the hairdresser. She was the only one in the family with really dark eyes, dimples and a light olive skin, and the family traits of work, duty and helping others had missed her. Becky had always gone out to enjoy life. Her rosy cheeks shone with health, and she had that look that said she spent time and money on herself.

Louise thoroughly enjoyed her Christmas lunch. Becky always wanted to be generous with presents for the children but very few toys were available in the shops. She gave them gifts of money instead.

Martha's in-laws invited Louise and her family to their celebrations on Christmas Eve and they gave her a larger than average joint of pork for Christmas dinner. Louise still had a few of the luxuries she'd stocked up on at the beginning of the war – tinned fruit, tinned cream and icing sugar – and she and

Susie did their best to put on a spread. She invited Chris to join them and he brought along a bottle of sherry. It was a quieter Christmas than usual, but as Martha was pregnant she didn't want to gad about. She continued to feel and look well.

At the end of January, with three inches of snow settled on the streets, Bert came home by ambulance. At eleven o'clock that night the air raid siren wailed its warning and soon the guns were firing and the bombs exploding around them.

With his leg in plaster, Bert managed to squeeze himself into the cupboard under the stairs but found it cramped and uncomfortable. With Martha being five months pregnant, what had been reasonable for her and Susie was a much tighter squeeze with Bert and Jonjo. When the all-clear went at two in the morning, both were glad to crawl out but had difficulty getting to their feet. At four there was another warning and they had to get back in the cupboard.

'This is impossible,' Bert said, dragging himself out at five o'clock to spend the rest of the night on the living room sofa.

'It's better than going out to a public shelter,' Martha told him, 'though I don't feel very safe under the stairs.'

'I've read that there's a new sort of shelter being developed, and it'll soon be available,' Bert said. 'It's for people like us who have no back garden to put up an Anderson.'

'The Morrison Shelter,' Martha said. 'I've read about it too, it's to be made of very heavy steel and will be large enough for two or three people to sit up in, or sleep in. It'll be like a big table and go in the living room.'

'Soon we'll be four, and we haven't enough space under the stairs now. It's got to be better than this. I think I'll put our name down for one.'

Bert was frustrated by his enforced idleness. He couldn't drive and found moving and standing difficult, and he knew they were struggling in the shop without him. He asked his brother Edward to collect him and drive him home so that he could work for a few hours a day.

Dr Grant had arranged for Martha to have her baby in Mill Road Infirmary, and also go there for antenatal check-ups. These days, it was considered safer for women to give birth in hospital rather than in their own homes, but Martha was not sure she liked the idea. With her husband at home and her mother and sister next door, she felt she'd be more at ease there.

She knew Mill Road Infirmary well because Bert was still attending clinics there. She had no clear idea where the maternity block was, and had to walk round in the rain looking for it. The place was vast, but once inside it was warm and the midwives were welcoming and friendly. They confirmed that her expected date of delivery would be 1 May, and she began to think that going in there wouldn't be too bad after all.

Bert hated having to wait for his brother to drive him about and felt he couldn't ask to be brought home for lunch. 'I'll need to drive you to the hospital when the time comes,' he told Martha, 'I don't want you waiting around for an ambulance.' So he climbed into the driving seat of his van, and though it was a little awkward, he didn't find it impossible to drive. Within days he was driving around just as he always had.

Their new air raid shelter was delivered and set up in their living room. Louise went to see it. 'It takes up a great deal of space,' she said.

'It's now our dining table,' Martha laughed. 'It seems funny eating meals off this. Bert has taken our table to the shop. He says they have plenty of room in their cellars to store it.'

After spending two nights in the new shelter, Louise asked them what they thought of it. Martha said, 'I feel much safer and it's a lot more comfortable, just like an ordinary bed.'

Bert said, 'I still have to crawl out on my hands and knees, but it is more comfortable. I think I should order one for you, Louise. You and Susie will get more sleep.'

She agreed. 'It's very cramped, and it's difficult to keep a clear head at work when we go short of sleep.'

They had to get on with their lives as best they could, and Louise was glad to find Bert in good spirits. He'd finally had his plaster off and said he was taking great care of Martha. 'I'm getting extra milk for her and making sure she takes her vitamins.' Martha did indeed seem in excellent health.

CHAPTER THIRTY-FOUR

LOUISE HAD HARDLY SAT down at her desk on Saturday morning when the phone rang. 'Hello, Lou.' She recognised Chris's voice immediately. 'I'm not feeling too good, I'm not coming in this morning. I'm going to stay in bed in the hope I'll be better by Monday. So I won't be coming for Sunday lunch tomorrow.'

'It's not this virulent flu bug that's going round is it?'

'Yes, I'm afraid it is. Several staff from the office and factory were off last week with temperatures, aching joints and sore throats.' Louise had already heard that Dr Grant was of the opinion that half the population was over-worked and tired out, and had no resistance to the infection because they were run down and stressed by the bombing.

'Shall I let everybody here know?'

'I'll ring Miss Rawlings. She can do it officially.'

'Will you be all right?' Louise knew he no longer had any help in the house. His housekeeper had left to work in a factory making parachutes. 'Do you have food in the house?'

'I don't think I'll want much to eat,' he said.

'I'll come round to see you this afternoon and make sure you have. About four.'

'Thank you.'

Louise felt guilty that she'd not paid more attention to Chris's needs. She'd accepted his devotion and kindness but given little in return except Sunday lunch, and Susie did the work to put that on the table.

Later that day when she went round, he came down to answer her knock in his pyjamas and dressing gown and looked really ill. He was shivering but his face was flushed. 'You look as though you've got a temperature,' she said.

'I shouldn't let you come near me,' he said, 'I think this affliction is quite infectious.'

'Have you rung Dr Grant?'

'I'm not really ill enough to call him out.'

Louise shook her head. 'I think you should, you're here on your own and he is a friend.'

'No, he's busy. I'll be fine in the morning.'

'You go back to bed, I'll go and buy your weekly rations, you've nothing much here.'

Louise bought back a few essentials to last him over the weekend, and then made him a pan of soup with some vegetables she found in his cupboard that were getting past their best.

He came downstairs again to see her and she ladled out a bowl of soup for him and sat him at the kitchen table to eat it, but despite the blanket he'd put round his shoulders, she could see he was shivering again. 'I should have brought the soup up to you,' she said, 'you go back to bed.'

'I've had enough, Lou, thank you,' he said, getting up.

'I see you've got two thermos flasks in your cupboard,' she said. 'I'll put the remains of the soup in one, and fill the other with tea, so you don't have to come down again tonight.'

'You're very thoughtful,' he said.

A few moments later, she heard him cry out followed by a crash. She called, 'Chris, are you all right?' With her heart in her mouth she ran out to see him spread-eagled on the stairs. 'What's happened?'

'I tripped.' He twisted round so he was sitting halfway up the staircase. He was holding his right wrist. 'I'll be all right in a minute.'

When she turned his hand over to see if he'd grazed it, she heard his sharp intake of breath. 'It hurts, doesn't it?'

'A little,' he sighed.

'That settles it. I am going to ring Dr Grant.'

It was his wife who answered. Louise told her that Chris had the flu and had just fallen on the stairs, that he'd put out his hand to break his fall and had hurt his right wrist.

Alice Grant said, 'Raymond's out on a visit at the moment. I'll tell him when he gets back. I expect he'll look in on him tonight.'

'I need to go home,' Louise said. 'Will you tell him Chris is on his own, and I'll leave his front door key under the plant pot on his front doorstep?'

The next morning, Louise decided she'd go to church and pop round to see Chris after she'd had lunch. Dr Grant caught up with her just as she arrived. 'Thank you for letting me know about Christopher,' he said. 'I took him to the hospital to have his wrist X-rayed, and as I suspected he has a Colles' fracture. As he can now do little for himself, I took him home for the night.'

'Oh my goodness! And that's on top of this flu that's going round?'

'Yes, I'm afraid so. Is your brood keeping well?'

'Yes, thank you. So Chris will be home by this afternoon?'

'No, I've persuaded him to stay with us. I think he needs a day or two off work, and he said he'd be glad of a bit of company.'

Chris wanted company? Louise took a deep breath and said curtly, 'I'll let them know in the office tomorrow.' She was searching for words to ask when she could expect him to be home again.

The doctor smiled. 'I'm sure he'll be in touch when he's feeling better.'

Louise turned away feeling she'd let Chris down. She was very fond of him and had spent a miserable day or two thinking about him. When he'd asked her to marry him she'd refused, and she was beginning to think now that had been a mistake. What a fool she was!

On Wednesday morning, Louise looked up from her ledgers to see Chris coming slowly towards her desk. He had his right arm in a sling.

'Hello,' he said. 'I have to thank you for asking Raymond Grant to call on me. I was in need of his help when he arrived.'

'So he told me. How are you?'

'I've broken my wrist.' He took it out of his sling to show her the plaster. 'I'm feeling better, but I've been told not to drive.' He was pale and drawn.

'It must hurt?'

'Raymond gave me plenty of painkillers.'

'But should you be at work? You won't be able to do a lot, certainly not write.'

314

'I can get others to write for me. There'll be decisions I need to make and things I have to organise.'

'But how are you going to look after yourself?'

'I'll be all right.'

He didn't look at all well. 'Shall I come home with you to cook a meal?'

He sighed. 'I don't think there's much at home to cook. When Raymond insisted on taking me to his place, I scooped up the food you brought and took it with me. Rationing makes it difficult to do anything else. Don't worry about me, Louise, I'll manage.'

She watched him go slowly on to his own office, stopping to talk to people on the way. He could of course go to a restaurant, though being unable to drive would make that difficult. She could take him home with her, but if he didn't feel well he'd probably prefer to stay in his own place. Then she thought of phoning Bert; he sometimes had unrationed sausages or offal.

On the spur of the moment, she spoke to Bert and told him of Chris's accident.

'I can find something for his dinner,' he said easily, 'but you'll have to come and pick it up.'

'I'll come this afternoon,' she told him.

Louise followed Chris into his office and found him sitting stiffly at his desk staring into space. She said, 'If you let me take an hour off I can do some shopping for you. I'll restock your larder and come and cook it for you tonight. You really must have food in your house or you'll never be able to cope.'

'You're right, of course,' he looked sad. 'I'd be glad if you'd come home with me this afternoon. Thank you, you're very kind.'

'You're not proposing to work all day?'

'I need to, if I'm to stay ahead,' he sighed. 'Would you ask Gordon Wilson to come and have a word with me?'

CHAPTER THIRTY-FIVE

LOUISE WOULD HAVE LIKED to go shopping in her lunch hour, but she knew Bert would be home with Martha then. It was mid-afternoon before she set off.

'What about lambs' liver?' Bert suggested.

'That would be excellent.'

He offered her a generous amount for two servings, a pound of sausages and a few slices of corned beef for a sandwich. As she had no idea what Chris had in his house, she went further along the parade of shops to buy potatoes, onions and a spring cabbage, and then a loaf of bread from the baker.

It was almost five o'clock when she returned and the typists were covering their typewriters and preparing to leave. Louise just had time to tell Susie she'd be late home as she intended to cook a meal for Chris. When she went to find him, he was still dictating letters to his secretary. 'Sorry, Louise,' he said, 'I'm coming now.'

She sat down in his secretary's chair for a few moments to give him time to finish. Miss Rawlings, a smart young brunette, came out, threw her pad and pencil in her desk drawer and locked it. 'Goodnight, Mrs Ingram,' she said.

A company driver came into the office. 'I've been told to

drive Mr Berry home and collect him again for work in the morning,' he said.

'He'll probably need you to do it for a few days,' Louise was saying when Chris came out. He looked exhausted and she could see he was a little unsteady on his feet. She took hold of his arm; the driver took most of her shopping and followed them down to the car park.

'It's this damned flu,' he said, looking defeated, 'it's made me as weak as a kitten. But Raymond Grant says we're only infectious when we first feel ill, and nobody can catch it from me now.' He stumbled and the driver came to support him on the other side.

He seemed almost too tired to talk on the ride home, and when the car drew up outside his house, the driver helped him indoors. Louise lit the gas fire in his sitting room. 'You sit back and have a rest,' she said, 'you've probably pushed yourself too hard today. I'm going to start cooking.' She was afraid a full day in the office had been too much for him.

Twenty minutes later, when she'd got the pans bubbling on the stove, he came to the kitchen with a bottle of sherry and produced two glasses from a cupboard.

'What am I thinking of? Not much of a host tonight, am I?'

'Chris, you're ill, I don't expect you to be. You'll feel better when you've eaten.'

'I feel better after that little rest. The dinner smells good.'

'It's best lambs' liver. When did you last eat?'

'Miss Rawlings ran out to get a pie for me from that café on the corner. It's good of you to come and cook a meal for me.'

Louise shook her head. 'No, don't say things like that,' she felt tears start to her eyes. 'I haven't done enough for you.'

He took her hand. 'Come and sit down. I expect you're tired too. Whatever makes you think you haven't done enough?'

She swallowed. 'You asked me to marry you and share your life. You offered me everything while I neglected you. I'm sorry. I've been fixated on mothering my girls. You were right, they no longer need me.'

'Lou,' he put out his arms and pulled her close, his plaster heavy across her shoulders, 'don't feel like that. You've been my prop for years, I don't know what I'd have done without you.'

She felt him push his handkerchief into her hand and knew tears were rolling down her face. 'The liver and onions are done,' she pushed him away. 'I just need to make the gravy so we can eat. We can't let food go to waste, not these days.'

'It won't go to waste. Lou, you're such a busy bee, always keeping your next job in mind.' Chris was getting out knives and forks and making room for them to sit at the kitchen table. 'I expect you're hungry?' He was half smiling at her.

'I am.' She knew she'd pushed him away yet again and wished she hadn't. 'I hope you are too.' She was dishing up furiously.

'Sort of empty, but you must forgive me if I can't finish all that. I haven't much appetite at the moment.' He pulled out a chair for her.

Louise started to eat but noticed immediately that he was clumsily trying to cut his liver with his left hand. 'Here,' she said, 'let me cut it up for you.'

'Just as you did for your children when they were small,' he had a broad smile on his face. 'Right now you're mothering me.' She laughed. 'You don't laugh often enough,' he told her.

'Do any of us these days?'

They had barely finished eating when the air raid warning blared out. 'My goodness, they're round early tonight,' he said. 'My shelter is in the cellar, we'd better go down. Alice Grant made me a sponge cake to bring home so we'll take that with us. Sorry, I have no coffee, but we can make a pot of tea down there as long as we take some milk.'

Louise had seen that the staircase in the hall went down as well as up. She followed him and looked round in surprise. 'Gosh, this is a luxury air raid shelter.'

'When this house was built, it was usual to have live-in help. The staff lived down here, so there is a bathroom of sorts, running water and electricity. It's come in very handy.'

'They lived down here in the cellar without daylight?'

'They did have some. The house is built into the ground because it falls away steeply to the river just here, and the ground was thought to be unstable. From the front there's little sign of the cellar, but there were windows at the back, quite high up. I had to have them bricked up to make it safer and to hide the light.'

'There's lots of space, palatial for a shelter.'

'Yes, I'm very lucky to have it. I brought down just enough furniture for my needs and put it against that wall, which is considered the safest part.' He had a single bed made up with bedclothes and an eiderdown, just as it would be upstairs. There was a rug on the floor, an armchair, a small table, a dining chair and a standard light.

Louise put the cake on the table. 'You've made yourself very comfortable down here.'

'Not so comfortable for two, but easy enough to bring more

furniture down.' He put the kettle on for tea. 'Can you cut the cake for us?'

'You're much better now you've eaten a good meal,' she said, 'you looked really down when we were leaving the office.'

He sighed. 'I was exhausted, my first day back. Flu takes it out of you.'

'You also seem a bit depressed.' He was standing very close. 'Are you depressed about me?'

'No, not about you exactly. Perhaps depressed that I haven't persuaded you to marry me.'

The ackack guns suddenly opened up nearby and the ear-splitting noise made her jump. She clutched at him for comfort and they both waited, expecting more, but the silence outside lengthened. His breath was warm against her forehead; it seemed thrillingly intimate. She felt his lips brush her cheek and couldn't breathe.

The next moment his arm was out of its sling and he was pulling her closer. His lips came down on hers; it was their first real lover's kiss. 'I've wanted to do that for a long time,' he breathed.

'You should have . . .' She was putting up her lips up for more when they heard an almighty crash outside. It made Louise jerk away and stand listening for a moment. She could feel her heart pounding.

He pulled her back into a hug. 'Trust the Luftwaffe to shatter that moment.'

'It was the Luftwaffe that set it up,' she stifled a giggle, 'the big guns firing at them.'

'You take the easy chair.' He pulled the other closer and sat down still holding her hand.

'We've got to talk Chris.' She was afraid she'd find it embarrassing. She'd done things she wasn't proud of, but she felt he was also holding something back from her. He never spoke of his feelings or his background. She knew he wasn't a Liverpudlian, but she'd no idea where he'd lived before he came here. They'd have to have it all out in the open if they were to make any progress.

She freed her hand to pour the tea; they might need it. 'It's me that's bothering you, isn't it?' she asked. 'What is it?'

He shook his head. 'You're always good humoured and friendly – lovely, really. You can't do enough for me. You show affection and concern for me, but you keep me at arm's length and tell me very forcefully that your girls have to come before me.'

The teapot shook and she spilt some, put it down hurriedly. 'I did, didn't I?'

He put up his hands to cradle her face, one soft and warm, one hard and heavy. She couldn't mistake the tenderness in his eyes. 'Lou, I love you.'

She stared at him in disbelief. 'You love me?' Like a fool, she pulled away from him yet again.

'Of course I do. I've been in love with you for years. I've asked you to marry me. I've asked you more than once and you promise to think about it but you don't give me an answer. You never mention it again. I feel bewildered and frustrated, and very much afraid you don't want to.'

Louise was shocked. 'I do, Chris. I wanted to marry you the first time you asked, but I want a proper marriage.'

'There's only one sort of marriage.'

'No,' she was indignant, 'you spoke about platonic marriage

and said we needn't sleep together.' His dark eyes were searching warily into hers. 'You made it sound like a business proposition. You could have been discussing a contract for jam.' She took a deep breath before going on, 'And you said you were prepared to wait indefinitely for an answer, as though you didn't care much one way or the other. That was off-putting.'

He looked contrite. 'What a mess I made. Not much of a proposal, was it? I didn't know whether you knew about my lapse. I didn't know how you felt about me, whether you'd want to marry a man who had done that.'

'Chris, what have you done? I don't know what you're talking about.'

'I was afraid you didn't love me, but I wanted to marry you even if you didn't. We get on so well together, I was sure we'd be fine.'

'You should have said straight off that you loved me,' Louise couldn't stop the words spilling out. 'I can't stop thinking about you. I'm in love with you and I want all of you. If we are to be married, I want it to be a real marriage. I want you to throw your arms round me, be romantic.'

He took hold of both her hands again. 'I'm sorry I'm so stiff. Set in my ways too, but you're right, there are things I must tell you first.'

Louise waited long enough to fear he wasn't going to go on.

His voice was scarcely above a whisper now. 'When I was young, I did something very wrong. I've lived a lie for most of my life.' He paused again.

Louise said, 'So have I. I told you I led Harold to believe I had a deep religious faith like him, when I hadn't. He said grace before every meal, and when he was killed I vowed I'd bring his children up as he would have wanted, but I stopped saying grace. It was difficult to find the time before breakfast, when I had to get the children to school and myself to work, but I feel guilty about that.'

'Lou, with three young children, a house to look after, giving unstinting help to St Biddolphe's and a full-time job, how could you ever find time for anything else? What I did was much worse than that.'

She looked at him, finding that hard to believe, but she could see he was finding it difficult to put into words.

'It was wrong in the eyes of the law as well as the eyes of the church. It has made me hide half of what was going on in my life. I couldn't talk about it. It's been on my conscience for years and it has altered me, made me a different person.'

He sounded so serious, she knew it must be something awful. 'Chris, everybody counts you a very kind person, full of empathy for—'

He held up his good hand. 'To start with, I thought I could marry you and tell you nothing, push it further away from me, but I can't. I'm sorry, but I feel it could lie between us if I don't tell you. And if I do, I'm afraid you might change your mind about marrying me.'

She was right, it must be something dreadful, something he was ashamed of. 'It can't be that bad,' she said uneasily.

'It can.'

'No, nothing would make me change my mind. I'll want to marry you whatever it is.'

He couldn't look at her. 'I'm not the cold person you think I am, and I'm definitely the last to want a platonic marriage. I was sixteen when I took a lover and she was only fifteen. Of course, we kept it hidden from our parents, hidden from everybody.'

Louise gasped. 'I'd have said that was out of character for you.' She'd seen him as staid, and compliant to conservative moral teaching. 'But there's nothing wrong with young love,' she said slowly.

'I told you it changed me. Mabel and I lived in the same road and I never wanted anybody else.'

'Mabel? It's rather nice to think you made up your minds at a young age and stayed together.'

'In our case it wasn't quite that simple.' He took a deep breath. 'I've always thought of myself as a passionate man, Lou, perhaps too passionate. I've grown to love you over recent years. If I gave you the impression that ours would be a platonic marriage, it was because I was aiming to keep my previous way of life hidden from you, but that would be wrong. You've a right to know the truth before we're married.'

Louise had a cold feeling in the pit of her stomach. 'Are you sure you really want to? I know you'd never hurt me in any way.'

'I couldn't, but let me finish. I want you to know. Mabel's parents didn't approve of me as a suitor. They wanted her to marry a family friend, a widower who could provide her with the standard of living she was used to. She'd known him almost all her life and said she really liked him.

'When she turned seventeen, they told her Alfred could give her everything she wanted and persuaded her to marry him. He was more than twice her age. Forty to be exact.

'Mabel knew almost immediately that she'd made a big

mistake. She found him old-fashioned and set in his ways. "Alfred has more in common with my father than he has with me," she confided. "I should have told Dad that I loved you and nobody else would do."

'We'd grown up in Oxford, but Alfred took her to live in a big house just outside the city. He spent long hours at work and she was alone for much of the time. I cycled to see her at lunchtime almost every day and could see she was getting quite depressed.'

Louise saw his fists tighten with tension. He was thinking of this as a confession. 'I'm ashamed to say that in no time at all I was making love to another man's wife. I was cuckolding her husband.'

Louise smiled; this wasn't as dire as Chris was trying to make out. 'At least you married Mabel in the end.'

He was shaking his head. 'She tried to persuade me to run away with her, but I told her we'd have to have a survival plan and do it properly. I knew we had to get away from those who knew us but it took me a long time. When I could, I took a job here in Liverpool, and when I'd made a home I was able to send for her. She found a job teaching music in a school and we settled down happily together. I promised her we'd be married just as soon as we could.

'We were brought up within a church in Oxford with a similar ideology to St Biddolphe's. I knew they counted themselves as non-judgemental. We isolated ourselves more than we should have done, except that we joined St Biddolphe's. I knew it would be safe and would provide all the social life we needed.'

'Did Mabel's husband never find you?'

'Yes, my parents had my address. Mabel's father found out

and brought Alfred and my father up to see us. They were furious, particularly with me. Alfred wanted to take Mabel home but she refused point blank. They cut us off, refused to have any more to do with us.'

'Oh dear!'

'It's what we both expected. While Mabel was alive, there was nobody else in the whole wide world I needed. We lived for each other but we had this secret that we never dare mention to others.'

Louise caught her breath. 'You never did marry?'

'No. Alfred refused to divorce her. Mabel had an aunt who was sympathetic and she let us know when Alfred died and she was free. But everybody already assumed we were an old married couple so we couldn't marry here, not when I was the church organist. We talked about a Gretna Green wedding but by then Mabel was ill, too ill to travel. It never did happen. Ours was an illicit union.'

Louise understood now why he blamed himself.

'If I'd been more patient as a teenager, done things differently, I might have been allowed to marry Mabel and our lives would have been very different. We'd have felt able to have children.'

Louise looked at him with wonder. 'And I thought you hadn't an ounce of romance in you! You must have spent years looking after her.'

'Nearly twenty.'

'That must have been hard.'

'Harder for her; I wanted to look after her. When she died it was as though I'd lost all reason to go on. Without you, I don't know what I'd have done.'

'It's taken years but that part of your life is over. I want you to forget about illicit love – you truly loved her.'

He took out his handkerchief to mop at his brow and there was relief on his face. He kissed her cheek. 'Can you forgive me?'

'There's nothing to forgive. I trust you. You've always behaved like a complete gentleman to me. I want us to be married as soon as possible without any fuss.'

'You're sure?'

'Absolutely sure.'

'Thank you.' His voice shook. 'I won't let you down, I promise.' He pulled her close and she felt his butterfly kisses flutter all over her face.

CHAPTER THIRTY-SIX

CHRISTOPHER WAS THRILLED THAT at last all was settled between himself and Louise. He'd felt he had to tell her, but she'd been wonderful and said that she loved and trusted him and that was enough. Now he could hardly drag his eyes away from her; her face had the other-worldly, gentle expression of one who has spent her life caring for others and expecting no reward.

He knew exactly how old she was, forty-nine now. Since she'd caught his eye several years ago, he'd tried to glean every fact he could about her. She looked younger than her years; her hair had been pale fawn and hardly showed the silvery threads in it. She'd kept her figure, still slim and svelte, and he put that down to the fact that she was always on her feet busy with some chore. Despite having an office job, her hands showed the hard work they'd done.

While the bombs continued to be heard overhead, Christopher and Louise started to plan their wedding. 'We've wasted too much time already,' he said, 'but we're agreed we'll be married as soon as possible? How soon can you be ready?'

'A month or six weeks, to give the family time to get used to the idea. Martha's baby is due at the beginning of May, but what about the end of May or early in June?'

'Excellent.' He'd brought a calendar down with him. 'Then what about Friday the thirtieth of May? I can't take much time off for a honeymoon but the second of June is the Whitsun Bank Holiday so that would give us a long weekend. Will you be happy to move in here with me afterwards? Do you mind?'

'Of course not.'

'It's said that a second marriage is better started in a new house, but housing is so scarce after all these air raids that it isn't possible, and neither will we be able to do this place up until this war is over.'

Louise was smiling happily. 'I didn't expect anything else. You know very well that your house is better than the one I'll leave, and this shelter must equal the one at Buckingham Palace.'

'I don't know about that,' he laughed, 'but I can offer you my bed for the night.'

'No, you're the invalid, I came here to look after you.'

'I insist, and—' Another explosion outside made him break off. The lights flickered but came back on. 'Further away than the last.'

For once he was not displeased about the raid. 'You'll have to stay here with me,' he said with satisfaction. 'It wouldn't be safe to let you walk home in this, not until the all-clear sounds. The buses will stop running and I can't drive you.'

He could see Louise had a broad smile and, half teasing him, she said, 'I expected you to worry about me spending even half the night with you. That it would ruin my reputation.'

He pulled a wry face. 'Better that than the physical danger outside. Do you mind?'

She laughed. 'Of course not. Only Susie need know I wasn't at home.'

'I'm going upstairs to get some more bedding,' Chris said. 'We might as well make ourselves as comfortable as possible.' She went with him to help him carry it and they moved the armchair against the bed and turned it round the other way, 'so I'll be able to see you,' he said, positioning the upright chair where he could put his feet on it.

'Come on then, up on the bed, we might as well get settled.' He took off his shoes and Louise did the same. 'So where shall we spend our weekend honeymoon?'

Her feet were small and shapely, encased in stockings that showed a neatly mended ladder and darning at one heel, and they made her seem vulnerable. He put out his hand and fondled one; it brought such a rush of love that he wanted to move closer. He eased himself up on the bed beside her and was taking her into his arms to kiss her when the all-clear blasted out. For once he didn't welcome it. What could he say but, 'Do you want to go home now?'

Her blue eyes looked up into his. 'What time is it?'

'Five minutes past midnight. Stay with me,' he brushed the hair off her forehead, 'let's make a night of it.'

Louise was up early to make breakfast for herself and Chris, and to cut sandwiches for their lunch. 'I need to go home to change my clothes and ask Susie not to tell anyone that we've spent the night together.'

She didn't doubt now that Chris was a passionate man; it had been her first experience of love since Harold had died. 'Do we announce our forthcoming marriage in the office?'

He smiled. 'I've found that if I tell one or two people, the news gets round. That's saved me making many official announcements.'

It was a fine bright morning; Louise walked home briskly, feeling she could jump up and touch the sky. There had been more damage in the streets that surrounded them, but all she could think of was Chris. She'd spent a wonderful night with him and he'd made her feel young again.

When Louise reached home, Rosie was playing up and Susie was eating cornflakes, but they forgot about breakfast when she told them her news. Susie's mouth opened in surprise, but she was laughing with delight too. Rosie squealed with excitement, 'I want to be your bridesmaid and have a party dress just like yours.'

'I wasn't planning on having bridesmaids, Rosie,' she said gently.

'But you must. Don't all brides have them?'

Susie said, 'I never thought you and Chris would get round to it, you're both so staid and old-fashioned in your ways. When is this to be?'

'As soon as we can make the arrangements.'

'In just a few weeks then?'

Susie dragged her next door to tell Martha, who offered to make her wedding outfit. 'I'll look out my pattern books and you must choose something you'd like. Don't think of what you need or what you might find useful.'

'That's sweet of you, Martha, but will you have time? Your baby's due soon. Will you feel up to it?'

'Of course I will. I'll love doing it, but I'll need to get started so it's finished before the baby comes.'

'Thank you, love, I'm very lucky to have you making my clothes.' Only utility clothing was being made now, which meant the same styles were made in every size and colour. A dressmaker was essential if you wanted anything different.

'Oh, Mum, I hope you'll be as happy as me and Bert.'

'And me and Jamie,' Susie said. 'Bound to be. Chris is kind to everybody. He's very popular in the office.'

Louise smiled fondly. 'He says he treats the staff in the way he'd like to be treated.'

'It pays off,' Susie said, 'most can't do enough for him. But they say he's a bit strange in one way; he takes a big interest in everyone's families, but he never says much about his own affairs.'

'He's a bit shy,' Louise came to his defence.

'No, he stands up at work and lays down the law about what we must all do,' Susie said.

'He keeps himself very much to himself,' Martha said thoughtfully. 'He doesn't say much about his own affairs, but he knows how to get others to talk about theirs.'

'It's almost as though there are things he doesn't want others to know about him.'

'What nonsense you two talk,' Louise said. 'He discusses everything under the sun with me.'

When Chris and Louise went to see the vicar to arrange for their wedding, Louise told him they wanted a short service with no frills, but Mr Coyne said, 'Mr Berry, you must have music. You've provided it for so many of our services it wouldn't feel right for you not to have it. I'll ask Mrs Pollard to play. What about an anthem from the choir?'

'No, thank you. We want a simple service as soon as you can

fit us in. After all, we're no longer young and it is the second time for both of us.'

'You must allow time for the banns to be read, let me see . . .'

Louise was pleased when he agreed that he could marry them at three o'clock on Friday afternoon, 30 May.

Martha and Bert offered to put on the wedding reception in their house once they heard Louise wanted little fuss, and just the family and a handful of friends were to be invited.

'It's not a good time to get married, Mum,' Susie said, 'the shops are empty and there are no luxuries of any sort to be had.'

But Martha managed to buy a length of peach delaine, a luxury light wool fabric, from the end of a damaged roll following a warehouse fire. Within days she'd made her mother a skirt and a little matching jacket, which she brought round one evening for her to try on.

'I'm very pleased with this,' Louise said, preening in front of her wardrobe mirror, 'it fits beautifully.'

'Deliciously smart and spring-like,' Susie told her.

'I'll be able to wear my camel coat over it, and my brown hat will go well with it.'

'Mum,' Martha was aghast, 'your old camel coat will spoil the whole effect. You won't need a coat, it'll be warm by then.'

'What about me?' Rosie wailed. 'I wanted an outfit like Nana's. You said you'd make it.'

'Not enough material to make you a matching outfit, love,' Martha said, 'but there was just enough to make you a pinafore dress, which you can wear over your frilly white blouse.'

'That's not what I wanted!' Rosie was ready to stamp her foot.

'Come on,' Susie said, 'there's a war on, you know. We none of us can have exactly what we want. Thank Auntie Martha now and try it on.'

'If you don't like it,' Martha said, 'you could wear that kilt I made for you last autumn.'

'No,' Rosie admitted, 'I like this better. Thank you, I'll wear it for Nana's wedding.'

'Mum, if there wasn't a war on,' Susie said, 'I'd bin your brown hat. I'll take you round the shops next Saturday to look for something suitable and more spring-like.'

Susie wanted Becky's opinion and rang her, so she decided to come too and treat them to lunch in town first. But though they trailed round all the big shops, they found nothing halfway suitable. 'I have two that might do,' Becky said, 'a cap of tan-coloured feathers, or a large, dressier hat in burnt orange. I'll bring them both so you can choose.'

When Chris came to lunch the following Sunday, Martha and Susie tried to persuade him to buy a new suit for the occasion, but he said, 'No, the only suits available are utility standard, and I've no clothing coupons anyway, so I'll wear the best suit I already have.' Nothing they said could make him change his mind. 'All your mother and I want is to be married. We don't want a big fuss.'

'But you'll be moving in with Chris?' Susie asked.

'Of course, you didn't expect otherwise?'

'No,' Susie said, 'but it means Jamie and I can take over the tenancy of this house and have an easy start to married life when he comes home. Where will you go for your honeymoon?'

'I'm going to book us into a hotel in Southport for the weekend,' Chris said. 'It'll be far enough to get away from the

Luftwaffe and we can take the train. I'm told the plaster should be off my wrist within six weeks, but after that I'll need a splint. I might be able to drive, but I don't have petrol coupons to spare so it makes no difference.'

'Only for a weekend?' Susie asked. 'Even Jamie and I had a week.'

'Yes,' Chris said, 'but we'll have the Monday as well because it's the Whitsun Bank Holiday. I can't afford to spend much time away from the factory now, but we'll have a good long holiday when this war is over,' he said.

CHAPTER THIRTY-SEVEN

T WO DAYS LATER, AS the trolley with their elevenses was pushed into the office, Susie was trying to finish an urgent letter the sales manager had dictated to her when the phone on her desk rang. She picked it up and recognised Martha's voice, and immediately felt her muscles tighten. Martha wouldn't ring her unless something awful had happened to Rosie.

'I'm so sorry,' her sister's voice was full of concern. 'A telegram has just come for you.'

Susie felt the strength ebb from her. Everybody knew what a telegram meant.

'Susie, are you still there?'

'Yes, yes.' Her mouth had gone dry, her tongue felt too big and she could hardly get the words out. 'Open it and tell me what it says.'

Martha's voice shook. '*It is with deep regret we have to inform you that Flying Officer James Alexander Curtis did not return from a bombing mission over enemy territory. He is listed as missing, believed to have been killed.*'

Susie couldn't get her breath, she was unable to move. This was what she'd been dreading for months.

'Susie, say something.'

337

The tears were running down her face. 'Read it again. I couldn't take it all in.'

'I'm so sorry, Susie. But it doesn't say definitely that he's been killed. Jamie may still be all right.'

'Thank you, Martha.' There was misery in her voice. She put the phone down quietly, rested her head on her typewriter in despair.

Hilda Jones at a neighbouring desk understood, and ran to the accounts department to tell Susie's mother. Louise rushed to throw her arms round Susie, though she knew there was little she could do that would comfort her.

Work in the office stopped and Louise felt the support of Susie's colleagues, but there was nothing they could do either.

Somebody must have told Chris because he came to usher them both into the privacy of his office. 'Susie,' he said, 'Jamie may have been able to bail out. Many of them do. Don't give up hope.' The next thing they knew, a company driver was running them home in Chris's car.

Martha made tea and lit their fire for them, but nothing could stem Susie's grief. Louise wept with her; hadn't she been through this in the last war? But Susie had also been through this with Danny, and it had taken her seven years to recover and have a second chance with Jamie. It seemed too cruel that her happiness should be dashed from her again.

That night, after putting a tearful Rosie to bed, Susie said, 'This will be my life in future, living here, looking after Rosie and working for Chris. I thank God for you and Martha.' She looked absolutely drained and desolate. 'What would I have done without you?'

It put all thoughts of her wedding out of Louise's mind.

She returned to work the next morning, but decided Susie was in need of a quiet day with Martha. She needed time to get her tears under control and come to terms with her loss.

Susie felt in a languid stupor and decided that if she'd lost Jamie she'd lost the reason for doing anything. Martha kept reminding her that he could still be alive, but she was only trying to give her hope.

To watch Martha whisking round her housework made Susie feel lazy and unable to summon an ounce of energy, and she made the mistake of saying so.

'Here's something for you to do.' Martha gave her one of Bert's Aunt Gertrude's jackets to unpick. 'It's good-quality cloth and will cut down to make warm trousers for Jonjo.' But Susie found even that too much.

'What would you like for lunch? I have some Cumberland sausages, or I could make a sandwich with Bratwurst.'

Susie opened her mouth to say she wasn't hungry when the phone rang in the hall. Martha answered it and came to the door. 'It's for you. Come and talk to him.'

'Who is it?'

'He says his name is George Barlow and he's a friend of Jamie's.'

She went reluctantly. 'Hello?' Susie's voice quivered; she was expecting more of the condolences she'd been receiving from neighbours and colleagues at work.

'Hello, is that Susie Curtis, Jamie's wife?'

'Yes, I had a telegram yesterday to say his plane hadn't returned and that he's posted as missing.'

'That's why I'm phoning. We've just heard that Jamie's

plane was damaged by flak over the target and he was injured. The pilot managed to limp back as far as the Channel and came down somewhere off Dover. The rest of the crew were unhurt and got the inflatable dinghy out and managed to move Jamie into it. Air Sea Rescue picked them up a few hours later and he's been taken to a Military Hospital near Folkestone. They say he'll be all right.'

Susie could feel happiness and relief surging through her. 'Oh how marvellous! Thank you for letting me know.' She wanted to laugh out loud. 'That's wonderful news!'

'I've got the hospital phone number here. They can tell you more about his injuries and how he's doing.'

'I need something to write it down,' she said, but Martha was pushing pencil and paper in front of her. 'I can't thank you enough.' Tears of joy were streaming down her face.

'You'll get an official letter telling you all this, but Jamie would want me to tell you as soon as possible. I understand that shortly he'll be sent by ambulance to a hospital near you.'

'He's alive and safe, that's the main thing. Such good news. Thank you so much. Goodbye.' Susie swept Martha into a hug of delight. 'Marvellous news!'

'Aren't you going to ring the hospital to find out how he is?'

'Yes, yes. Oh, I need to calm down, I'm so excited. Jamie is safe and in hospital.'

When she finally got through to the hospital, the ward sister said, 'Flying Officer James Alexander Curtis has been in theatre this morning and only returned to the ward a few minutes ago. He isn't fully round from the anaesthetic yet, but his condition is satisfactory and everything went according to plan.'

'I didn't know he needed an operation,' Susie faltered.

'Yes, hold on a sec while I open his file. He's had a bullet and three bits of shrapnel removed from his left leg. Also, he has multiple fractures of his tibia and fibula – the two bones below his knee – and had metal plates inserted to support them. In addition, yes, minor burns on his hands and wrists which have been dressed. If you ring again this evening, he'll have come round and we'll be able to give you an update.'

All the family were delighted with the news, Louise especially, knowing that Susie could now relax. Susie wrote to Jamie and a few days later had a letter in return, though at first she didn't recognise his handwriting and it wasn't easy to read.

Darling Susie,

Sorry about the writing but my hand is bandaged because of slight burns. Sorry to have given you such a fright but I'm going to be perfectly all right in the long run, so there is no need for you to worry. The lower bones in my left leg have been badly fractured and I've been operated on to remove bullets and have steel plates inserted, but I'm feeling better and they tell me that though it will take time, it shouldn't stop me walking normally.

Here is the really good news. Next Monday, two of us are being sent up to Liverpool by ambulance. We are being transferred to Mill Road Infirmary, and you'll be able to come and visit. I can't wait to see you again.

Susie caught her breath, she was thrilled. To have Jamie in Mill Road Infirmary and know he was safe in a hospital bed instead of flying over enemy occupied territory was absolutely marvellous. She was counting the hours until she could see him again. Even better, she'd now be able to visit him regularly.

Before she left work on Monday afternoon, she rang the hospital and her call was transferred to the ward sister. 'Yes,' she told her, 'Flying Officer Jamie Curtis arrived about an hour ago. He's tired but in high spirits. For Military Personnel, visitors are welcome most of the time, but please avoid meal times and be gone by nine in the evening.'

Susie went home feeling on top of the world. 'I don't like the idea of you going out after dark in case you're caught in a raid,' Louise said, 'but I suppose nothing will stop you going tonight?'

'Absolutely nothing,' Susie breathed. It frustrated her to have to wait for a bus. She thought she'd have no trouble finding him in the hospital because she'd gone with Martha to visit Bert when he'd had his accident, but it took her a long time to find the right ward. She spoke to a nurse in the corridor. 'Yes, you'll find Flying Officer Curtis down at the far end on the right.'

Susie pushed open the ward door and let her gaze travel slowly down the line of beds. The patients were all young men wearing hospital blues, and at first she didn't realise the figure clumsily using wooden crutches to hurry towards her was Jamie. She ran to meet him and he threw his arms round her in a huge hug. One of his crutches clattered noisily to the floor and Susie found she had to support him.

'Flying Officer Curtis!' The formidable ward sister came to pick up his crutch. 'Back to your bed this moment,' she ordered. 'You are only allowed up to visit the bathroom, and on no account must you put any weight on that leg.'

He was herded back to his bed, his crutches were parked behind the bedhead, and a chair pulled out for Susie. Nothing could wipe the broad smile from his face.

'Thank God you're safe,' she whispered. They held hands decorously, knowing many eyes were on them.

Louise was spending more time with Chris. He encouraged her to treat his house as her home and she took over some of the housekeeping and cooking. Martha had been as good as her word and had finished making her wedding outfit in plenty of time. She'd tried it on and both daughters said they were pleased with it. Louise was delighted with it and it now hung ready in her wardrobe together with Rosie's pinafore dress.

Chris was feeling better and said waiting around for a company driver was frustrating. He started driving again before Dr Grant thought he should. 'It's my right wrist,' he said, 'all I have to do is keep it on the steering wheel. The plaster ensures that the bones are kept in place.' With such a petrol shortage, he couldn't go far.

As Martha's time drew near, Louise was on tenterhooks and thinking more about the coming baby than her wedding. She was glad Bert was on hand and keeping a watchful eye on her daughter.

Nothing happened when the date Martha had been given for the birth came. Louise and Susie went off to work and the children went to school as usual.

Back at home that evening, Martha shook her head. 'Not a twinge of any sort of pain. I feel perfectly fine, but I wish it would start. I've had enough of being pregnant. I want to hold this baby in my arms.'

'You will before much longer,' Louise told her, 'just be patient.'

Susie put Rosie down to sleep in the shelter, while Louise

turned the wireless down low and they sat by the dying fire listening to it. They'd had two or three quiet nights recently and Louise said, 'I think I'll go upstairs to my own bed for a change, I always have a better night's rest there.'

'I'll have to stay here now,' Susie said.

Louise was woken out of a deep sleep at half eleven by the wailing air raid siren, and after a moment to collect her wits she felt for her dressing gown and ran downstairs. Rosie hardly stirred as Susie lifted her and put her to sleep at their feet to give them more room.

Louise was about to put the kettle on to make a hot drink for their thermos in case they had a wakeful night, when an ear-splitting blast from a nearby explosion sent her running to join the others in the shelter. She felt Susie's arms come round her and pull her close and they clung together in terrified silence. Rosie whimpered and turned over but settled down again. Louise could feel Susie's heart pounding away.

Soon there was bedlam outside, explosion after explosion, ackack guns banging away, fire engine bells ringing and sirens from ambulances and police cars screaming through the streets.

'Thank goodness we've got a proper shelter,' Susie whispered. 'The instruction sheet that came with it said it was bomb-proof and would keep us safe even if the house collapsed on top of it.'

'Yes, and I'm glad Bert is with Martha. At least he hasn't started fire watching again, though he says he feels guilty that he isn't doing more to help the war effort.'

The bombers kept coming over, wave after wave. Louise dozed only fitfully during one of the worst nights they'd had. The all-clear sounded at half five, and she and Susie then slept soundly for another couple of hours until the alarm went off. They struggled out of the shelter feeling sleep sodden, but life had to go on. A job in a jam-making factory was considered important war work; the population had to be fed.

Louise was ready to set out before Susie, so taking Rosie by the hand, she rang Martha's bell.

'What a terrible night,' she said, 'how are you? All that disturbance hasn't started you off?'

'No, worse luck. Come in, Rosie.'

'It can't be long now. Bye bye.'

Susie caught up with her mother as she went down Milner Street to catch the bus. All morning, Louise couldn't stop thinking about Martha. She'd had lunch and was back at her desk when Bert rang her. She heard the note of excitement in his voice as he said, 'I went home for lunch and Martha was starting in labour so I took her to the hospital.'

'Are you there now?'

'No, I'm at home. They sent me away and told me to ring up at five o'clock to see how she is. Martha had lunch ready but I didn't stop to eat it then. I'll eat now and I think I might go back to the shop after that. Everything is ready for the baby, the cot is made up and all that. There's nothing more to do and I feel on pins here on my own.'

'What about the children coming home from school? Will you be back by then?'

'Oh dear, I'd forgotten about them, it's getting on for three now. I'd better stay, hadn't I?'

'It would help, Bert. Why don't you start getting your evening meal ready? Or pack a suitcase for when Martha and the baby come home?'

'They said she'd be in for two weeks.'

Louise smiled, 'The time will pass, Bert.'

She could feel a ball of delighted anticipation building in her stomach, and it was difficult to settle down to work again. She went to tell Susie, and then she rang Becky. 'Bert's in a flat spin,' she told them, then went to Christopher's office.

'Go home early,' he said, 'then you can be there for the children.'

'I'd rather do that tomorrow, so Bert can stay at work – if that's all right with you?'

Louise and Susie went home at their usual time in a fever of excitement and knocked at Martha's house. Jonjo came to the door.

'Is there any news?' Susie asked.

'We're playing Snakes and Ladders,' he said, 'and I'm winning.'

'Come in, Louise.' Bert came up behind the boy. 'There's no news yet. I rang at five and they said Martha was in second stage labour and it was all going normally.'

'Well that's good news.'

'They told me to ring again at seven. I wish they'd let me stay there. Poor Martha, she's probably having a terrible time now.'

Louise took Bert and the children to her house and she and Susie cooked a meal for them. He was like a cat on hot bricks watching the hands of the clock crawl round. At five to seven he went home to telephone and Louise waited with bated breath, her heart going out to Martha.

He came running back in moments, his face scarlet with joy and unable to keep still. 'It's a baby boy,' he shouted, 'weighing

346

six pounds two ounces. Isn't that marvellous? We so wanted a son. Martha had him at quarter past six. I could have rung earlier instead of waiting.'

'How are they?'

'Both are well and I can go in to see them. I'm going now, straight away.'

'Give Martha our love,' Louise said.

'Gosh, he's over the moon,' Susie was all smiles, 'and Martha will be too. She'll be glad it's over, glad it's a boy.'

CHAPTER THIRTY-EIGHT

'**D**ID YOU HEAR THAT, Jonjo?' Louise asked. 'Your father says you have a new baby brother.'

He looked serious. 'Will my mum be his mum too?' He didn't seem all that pleased.

They could talk of nothing else all evening. When the siren sounded just after eight, Bert had not returned, but they had the children in their pyjamas ready for bed. Susie pushed them into their Morrison shelter while Louise finished making cocoa for them all.

The bombs started falling almost immediately and it took the children a long time to get to sleep. Louise found it impossible; she was both excited and frightened. The bombardment was just as bad as the night before, and she and Susie hugged each other for comfort.

There was a lull in the early hours of the morning. Louise was just nodding off when she heard a knock on their door. She got up and found a rather dishevelled Bert on the step. 'Are you all right?' she asked.

'I got caught out in the raid and was herded into a public shelter. The baby's lovely and Martha's made up with him. So am I, of course. We're going to call him Adam Edward. Is Jonjo with you?'

'Yes, he's slept through most of it. Leave him here, there's no point in waking him now. It's Saturday tomorrow, and Lena Smith has offered to look after the children while Martha is in hospital and we're at work.' Lena lived almost opposite them and was Martha's friend. 'We'll give them breakfast and take them over.'

'There's terrible damage everywhere, big fires burning down on the docks, and almost as light as day with the full moon and the glow in the sky from the fires. I've walked home, it's total chaos out there.'

'Get to bed, Bert, and try and get some rest.'

'I'll bed down in our shelter. The all-clear hasn't gone yet so there's no guarantee there won't be more.'

Louise put the kettle on to make some tea. There was no electricity but the gas still worked. She didn't want to think about what would happen if the gas works were hit. 'I do hope Martha and the baby are all right,' she said to Susie, 'she'll be scared.'

'She's not alone, Mum, there'll be nurses looking after them.'

The Luftwaffe returned within the hour and gave Merseyside another two-hour blasting. 'It's a bit further away, thank goodness,' Susie said. 'I reckon somewhere else is getting it now.'

Louise was bleary eyed when it was time to get up. Susie took the children across to Lena and they set off to work at their usual time. They waited for a bus but none came, and as other would-be passengers were giving up and starting to walk, they did the same. They'd already walked some distance when they were surprised by a car tooting its horn at them, and they found Mr Curtis, Jamie's father, was offering them a lift. His cake factory was on the Dock Road too.

He passed his own premises to pull up outside the jam factory. 'It looks as though it took a bit of a battering last night,' he said. Slates had come off the roof and glass from the windows had been blown all over the yard.

'Hope your place has had better luck,' Susie said.

Louise was shocked when she went into the office. There was broken glass, dirt and dust all over the desks, file cabinets and floor. The girls were laughing because they were leaving footprints in it, chatting about the difficulties they'd had getting to work. Buses had had to make detours because of the potholes and the rubble littering the roads, and many had had to walk.

'I saw fire crews still battling to put out fires,' one said. 'So did I,' others chorused, and all were horrified by the scenes of utter destruction.

Louise was saddened by it and went to Chris's office. 'What a mess the place is in this morning,' he said. 'The factory is no better than the office. I've managed to make arrangements to have the damage repaired, as food factories are being given priority. I'm expecting a gang of glaziers to turn up in the next couple of hours, but I'm afraid some of the windows will have to be boarded up, as they haven't much glass left.'

'You've seen some of the slates have come off the roof?'

'And all the guttering along the back has come down. I don't know when we can expect the roofers; they can't give me a date. It will be at least next week before they come, but that needn't stop production. I'm worried, though,' he went on, 'because many of our workers have not turned up. Gordon Wilson for one.' Gordon was the accountant and Louise's immediate boss. 'I've asked one of the foremen to take a roll call.'

'Some will have their own problems,' Louise said, 'homes that have been damaged or family members hurt.'

'Brian Gilmore didn't feel well yesterday,' he said, 'and there are three others that we know about, off with flu. I'd better have a word with those that have come in.'

Chris got to his feet looking tired and concerned, and went to the main office to rap on a desk for attention. Dust flew up. 'I want to thank you all for coming in after such heavy raids last night,' he said. 'Especially on a Saturday morning, and I don't suppose the buses are running properly yet.'

Several chorused, 'We had to walk.'

'Our premises are in a terrible mess, and we can't make jam until all this glass has been swept up and everything has been washed down, so I must ask you all to help with that.'

'We've got to get rid of this dreadful dust,' someone called, 'it's catching in my throat.'

'We received a ship load of Seville oranges yesterday,' Christopher went on, 'enough to keep the factory making marmalade for a couple of weeks, but some of them will need to be washed before we can use them, so we won't be boiling up until Monday.'

'There's no electricity on anyway.'

'We can manage without that. I've switched over to the standby generators. Once the place is clean, I'm going to send you all home. We need to catch up with our sleep, I don't think anybody got much last night. It was one of the heaviest air raids we've had.'

'Who's to say there won't be another tonight,' somebody

called, 'and we'll come in on Monday to find the place in a worse mess?' Everybody laughed.

'We're due for a change of fortune,' Christopher said. 'We just have to hope it'll stay in the pristine state you're going to put it in.'

Everybody mucked in with a will, laughing and chattering and enjoying the novelty of it. When the office was clean, the girls from the typing pool went to help in the factory, where a high standard of hygiene had to be achieved. The atmosphere of gloom lifted and everybody began to feel better.

The older women turned their attention to the kitchen, and when the mid-morning break came they had urns of tea ready for all. Louise poured two cups and took them on a tray to Christopher's office.

'By the way,' he said, 'Gordon has popped in to see me. He and his wife are unhurt, thank goodness, but his house has been damaged beyond repair. I've offered them a room in my house until he can find somewhere of his own, so at least he'll be in to work on Monday.'

'Goodness! Poor Gordon. But there's been so much bad news this morning that I haven't got round to telling you my good news. Martha has had her baby, a boy, and everything went well.' Just to think about it made her bubble over with the joy of it. 'I'm dying to see him. Becky has promised to come over for lunch on Sunday afternoon so that she can see him.'

'I'm glad we've got some good news to think about in all this,' he smiled in his gentle manner. 'Why don't you go straight down to the hospital from here and ask if you can see him?'

'But will they let me in?'

'I'm told hospitals are less rigid about visiting times than they used to be. I'm afraid I won't be able to take you out to lunch today, I've got too much to do here.'

'Aren't you taking a half day?'

'No, this has given me more to do and I'd rather stay on now.'

'I have plenty of work to do, too.'

'If it isn't urgent, leave it,' he said. 'You're very kind and I know I have a standing invite to Sunday lunch at your house, but will you want me tomorrow? You'll have all your family round.'

'Of course I will.'

'I don't know, Lou. Gordon and his wife will have to look after themselves if I do.'

'Will I see you at morning service?'

'Mrs Pollard will be playing the organ, but yes, definitely.'

When the time came to leave work, Louise decided she'd do what Chris had suggested, go straight to the hospital and ask to be allowed to see Martha and her new baby.

Susie said, 'You're more likely to get in if you're on your own. I'll go straight home, get some lunch on the table and see to the children. When you come home I'll go to Mill Road. I can pop in to see the new baby before visiting Jamie.'

When Louise reached the hospital it was desperately busy with ambulances queuing outside some of the blocks because of last night's heavy raid. By comparison, the maternity block seemed relatively calm, and the sister said, 'Go on then, but please don't stay long. Is it your first grandchild?'

Louise felt she had to say, 'Actually, it's my third.'

Martha was sitting up smiling at her as she walked up the

ward, and her baby was sleeping in a cot at the foot of her bed. 'What an awful night we had,' she said, 'I was worried about you, Mum.'

'We're all fine, how are you?'

'Thrilled to bits with my new son, and so is Bert. Adam is exactly what we wanted, we couldn't be happier.'

The infant stirred at that moment and Martha slid out of bed. 'I know I ought to leave him alone, but I can't resist picking him up. Isn't he gorgeous?' Even in his hospital gown he looked idyllic; his face was not crumpled and red like the average newborn.

'Why, he's just like you when you were born, very pretty with lovely soft down on his head. Can I hold him?'

Martha put the child in her arms and he opened his eyes for a moment. 'Quite a small baby,' Louise said, 'not at all like Jonjo.'

'They're all different,' Martha smiled. 'How is Jonjo?'

'He's fine, taking everything in his stride. Making screeching sounds to frighten us, and telling us it's a bomb falling on our house.'

Martha laughed. 'Bert's aunt is going to lend him her camera and he's going to take some photos of the baby when he comes in tonight.'

Louise was delighted that all had gone well for her daughter, and that she still had healthy pink cheeks.

She needed to buy vegetables and bread for the weekend and stopped at the neighbourhood parade of shops on the way home. In the window of a ladies' outfitters she saw a white cotton nightdress. It wasn't anything special as they were all utility standard, but it was new and fresh and better than anything she had, so she bought it for her honeymoon. Once home, she slept on the sofa for the rest of the afternoon.

Bert was feeling on top of the world. He was thrilled with his newborn son and relieved that Martha had come through the birth so well. He'd had a smile on his face since last night after he'd seen them; his mother had remarked on it. He'd recovered from his fall and was able to walk about with ease, and had taken over the running of the shop again. Best of all, it had cemented his relationship with Mickey O'Malley.

Most shops were making less profit because rationing and shortages meant they had limited stock to sell, but Mickey trusted Bert because Susie had returned his accounts book to him and they'd all kept their mouths shut. Being on good terms with Mickey meant he had an excellent supply of black market meat and the business was making more profit than it had ever done.

He really missed not having Martha with him at home. The place seemed soulless without her, but husbands were allowed in to see their wives and new babies every evening and he was really looking forward to seeing them again tonight. The shop was busy, it always was on Saturdays, and he told his customers about his new son, and everybody was congratulating him.

When he closed the shop and cashed up the day's takings, he found it was one of the best day's trading he'd ever had. Aunt Gertrude fried large steaks for them all before Bert set out for the hospital. He arrived at the maternity block at five minutes to seven and had to wait for the ward doors to be opened to visitors.

Tonight, Martha had made herself pretty with powder and

lipstick and looked so happy. She had to wake their son so Bert could hold him. He kissed them both and could feel tears stinging his eyes; becoming a father again brought emotional moments. He'd brought his aunt's camera with enough film in it to take four pictures, but he fiddled about taking them for so long that the visiting time seemed gone in an instant. The sister came in ringing a bell and telling them it was time to leave. He could hardly believe they'd been allowed to stay longer than the official time and that the best part of an hour had gone. He almost forgot to give Martha the chocolate his mother had bought for her.

Everybody was hoping for a quiet night and a good sleep. They'd had two nights of heavy raids and felt it was time the Luftwaffe went elsewhere and gave them a rest, but the siren was blaring out its warning before he reached home.

CHAPTER THIRTY-NINE

SUSIE AND LOUISE HAD cleared up after their evening meal and were about to play Snakes and Ladders with the children when Bert knocked on their door. Rosie let him in.

'Hello, Jonjo, you all right? I've been to see your new baby brother. Your mother sends her love. Thank you for looking after him,' he said to Susie. 'I've brought you a leg of lamb for your Sunday dinner,' he went on. It had been in the back of his van since he'd left the shop. 'Would you mind looking after Jonjo again tomorrow? The shop will be closed but I need to go in to make sausages and do some cutting up, and my mother has asked me to stay and have Sunday dinner there.'

'Don't worry about Jonjo,' Susie said, 'he's fine with us and no trouble.'

'Thanks, I want to see Martha and the baby again in the afternoon.'

'So do we. Becky's coming over to see them so we may have to take turns. They usually say only two to a bed.'

'We'll manage, do you want me to come and give you a lift?'

'No thanks, Bert. Becky will come by car.'

'I'll see you there then.'

They were only halfway through their first game of Snakes and Ladders when the siren wailed its warning. Susie said, 'Oh

Lord! Here they are again and they're awfully early tonight.'

'I wish they'd leave us alone,' Rosie said, 'they're horrible, I hate them. Shouldn't we get in our shelter now?'

'It may not be much,' Louise said, taking her turn to shake the dice, 'and you aren't ready for bed yet. Let's see what happens.'

There was a burst of gunfire which made them all stop and listen, but then all went quiet again. Rosie said, 'It's your turn, Nana.'

'Can you hear the drone of German engines?' Louise found that the most fearful thing.

'Don't listen.'

They all had another turn. Susie was just sliding her counter down a snake when the light flickered and went out. 'Bother!' she said. 'Power was only restored this afternoon.'

'My torch is on the sideboard.' Louise was standing up to get it when there was an almighty crash followed by the sound of falling debris. She felt the floor move beneath her feet.

'Get in the shelter,' Susie screamed, pushing first the children and then her mother inside. The debris continued to rain down on top of the Morrison, the noise magnified by the metal.

'What's happening?' Rosie screamed.

'The house has been hit,' Jonjo told her, 'we've been bombed. That's the ceiling coming down on top of us.'

'No, I don't think so.' Susie was terrified but making an effort not to show it and frighten Rosie more. She found the torch and switched it on. Her mother was sitting with an arm round each child and they all looked scared stiff.

Susie crawled out of the Morrison and shone the beam

round the room. 'The grate is full of soot and it's put the fire out. Ugh, it stinks.' There were other noises outside now, ambulance and police sirens.

'Are the windows all right?' Louise asked. 'I heard the tinkle of glass.'

'Yes,' Susie said, 'they're intact here, thank goodness. That bomb came down very close but not in Milner Street. It looks all right outside. Oh no! Gosh, I think it's Gorton Street that got it.' That ran parallel with Milner Street. 'There's an ambulance there. It must have fallen almost opposite our house.'

'Here's Bert coming round,' Susie said, and went to the front door.

'Are you all right, Susie? Nobody's hurt? That was a near one. It's blown our bedroom windows out. There's a terrible mess, glass all over the bed, it's a good job we stuck that sticky paper on it, at least it's in big pieces and not splinters.'

Louise crawled out. 'I'm going upstairs to make sure all is well here. Give me that torch for a moment.'

'I've left my handbag on my bedside table,' Susie said, 'would you bring it down for me?'

Louise's spirits sank when she looked in her bedroom: her window had been blown in too. Mostly the glass had been held together by the paper strips she'd stuck on it, but there were plenty of splinters and shards crunching under her feet and lying on her eiderdown.

Soot had blown out of the chimney and filled the small Victorian iron grate, though she couldn't remember how long it was since she'd lit a fire there. Rosie's little bedroom was also at the back, but the window was open and the glass unbroken. The bathroom and Susie's room faced the front and the windows were intact there too, for which she was grateful.

She went downstairs and said, 'There's an awful mess in my bedroom, but I expected worse. I really thought the whole place was coming down on us.'

The guns opened up again. 'I've kept a circular that gives a number to ring if we suffer bomb damage,' Bert said. 'I'll report your broken window when I do mine tomorrow. They'll come round and board up the windows for us, and put glass in later when they've got some.'

'We'll have a bit of clearing up to do as well,' Louise pulled a face.

'I'd better go home,' Bert said, 'though I doubt we're going to get much sleep. Do you want to come home with me, Jonjo?'

They shone their torches into the shelter to see Jonjo cringing back against Rosie. 'Leave him here,' Louise advised, 'but we'll need his pyjamas and toothbrush.'

Before settling down for the night, Susie set her alarm clock for a very early start. 'It'll take at least a couple of hours to clean up this mess before we can think of cooking that lamb,' she whispered, 'no Sunday lie-in this week. When I see Rosie frightened out of her wits on nights like this, I wish I'd agreed to her being evacuated.'

'We're all frightened,' Louise said, 'but we'll survive if fear is all we have to contend with. This is the first night we haven't set the table ready for breakfast, but if we had it would have been covered with soot too, so it's just as well.'

On Sunday morning, Bert woke up early, his mind still happily on Martha and the new baby. He crawled out of his Morrison shelter, keen to make a start on cleaning up his house so that it would be fit for his family to return to. He collected a bucket and brush, and with the coal shovel emptied the living room grate of soot and swept up the worst of it.

Then he went upstairs, lifted the counterpane off the double bed and carried it out to the bin in his backyard to get rid of the glass. There was more to sweep up but thank goodness no soot there as he'd had the grate bricked up years ago.

He went out to his van and saw Susie shaking dust and soot off a rug at her front door. 'Good morning,' he called.

She waved. 'Don't know how good it's going to be. There's an awful mess everywhere.'

He drove to the shop and in the kitchen upstairs he made tea and toast for his mother and his aunt, and took breakfast trays up to them just as they were waking up in their beds. They found it difficult to sleep in the cellar, and as they both worked in the shop, Sunday was the only morning they could enjoy an hour's extra rest.

Bert fried eggs and bacon for his breakfast and listened to the BBC news on the wireless. Then, feeling full of energy, he ran downstairs to start work. Behind the shop he had a preparation room equipped with a chopping table, a refrigerator, scales, and space where he could hang a couple of carcasses until he used them.

Since he'd been on better terms with Mickey O'Malley he'd had to spend more time behind the counter, because he needed to serve those customers buying black market meat personally. He preferred to work in the shop, but it meant that the rest of the family couldn't keep up with the preparation work. They could really use another full-time assistant, but they didn't stand much chance as workers were being directed into the munitions factories.

On the stroke of nine the bell on the top of the shop door frame rang loud and long. Bert went to unlock the door. He'd asked their delivery boy and general dogsbody to do a couple of hours overtime this morning. He was yawning on the step. 'Good morning, Derek,' he said.

'Is it good, Boss? I'm half asleep, we had a terrible night.'

'You've survived, haven't you? We're all here to live another day. Get your coat off and you can start by bringing up two tins of corned beef from the cellar.'

The trade was provided with forty-pound tins of corned beef to solve a problem. As meat was rationed by price, when a customer bought a joint or several chops for the family, the ration entitlement frequently had to be made up with a couple of slices of corned beef. Bert ruminated that once his family had roasted large joints of beef and pork and sold it sliced up ready for the plate, but with rationing that was no longer practical.

They'd almost run out of mince yesterday, and he started by making up a few trays of stewing steak. He took from his fridge large pieces of shin, flank and skirt and sliced them up as stewing beef, tossing the trimmings of flesh and fat into two separate containers, the best of it was for mincing, the less savoury pieces would be turned into sausages.

Derek knew it was his job to turn the heavy hand-operated mincing machine, and he set about it. Soon the trays that would be set out in the shop tomorrow were being filled. Derek was getting better at arranging mince to look as appetising as possible before he stacked the trays in the fridge.

They were making good progress when the shop doorbell rang through the building again. 'Go and see who that is,' Bert said, 'tell them we're closed.'

Derek came back. 'He says his name's Eric Downs and he wants to talk to you, Boss, if you can spare a minute.'

'Eric? OK,' Bert wiped his hands on a cloth. Eric arranged fire watching rotas. To help the war effort, Bert had enrolled as an unpaid part-timer with the Auxiliary Fire Service, and before he'd had his fall he'd regularly done fire watching duties.

An elderly and tired figure supported himself against the door. 'Bert,' he said, 'I hoped I'd catch you here. How are you?'

'Better, near enough back to normal. I was thinking about coming round to see you.'

'Thank goodness for that,' Eric said, 'we're all exhausted, just about on our knees. Can I put you on the rota again? What about tonight?'

Bert felt guilty. 'I didn't want to leave Martha alone, but she's in hospital now and we have a new baby son. All right,' he said, 'I'll do it tonight.'

'Thanks,' Eric said. 'Merseyside has really copped it the last few nights, but last night was the worst ever. Half the berths on the docks are still burning and a ferry boat has been sunk at its moorings at Seacomb pier.'

'I don't know how much more of this we can put up with.'

'And there's worse. I hear there's been a major incident at one of the big Liverpool hospitals and there's likely to be lots of casualties.'

Bert said uneasily, 'I listened to the BBC news but there was no mention of a hospital being hit.'

'There never is, they talk about damage to churches and the fires on the docks,' Eric yawned.

Bert was struggling to get his breath. 'Which hospital was it?'

Eric yawned again. 'I'm not sure, it might have been Mill Road. I'll see you tonight then at nine o'clock, but earlier if there's an alert.'

Bert had to hold onto the door, there was a sinking feeling in his stomach. 'Oh my God!' What if Martha had been hurt? He staggered back into the cutting room and said to Derek, 'I've got to go out. Get my mother to come down and take over.'

He didn't stop to take off his apron or put on his coat, but went straight out to his van and drove towards Mill Road Infirmary.

CHAPTER FORTY

Susie woke up at five o'clock the next morning. She listened: there was the distant sound of an ambulance but the almighty raid they'd had earlier in the night seemed to be over. She switched off her alarm clock and decided the sooner she got up and started cleaning up the mess, the better. The children slept on but she'd disturbed her mother.

'Stay where you are and snooze,' she told her as she crawled out of the Morrison, 'it's Sunday, you could do with a lie-in.'

'I can't leave all the work to you.' Louise crawled out too and began dressing. Together they swept up the broken glass; that was comparatively easy compared to getting rid of the soot, which stuck to the fabric of the sofa and the rugs and took a lot of brushing out. They went upstairs and made Louise's bedroom useable again.

That done, they started peeling potatoes for Sunday dinner, and by the time the children were getting up, the fire had been lit and they were ready to sit down for breakfast.

'I feel I've done a full day's work already,' Louise said as she poured herself a second cup of tea.

'You need a rest instead of going to church,' Susie told her.

'I meant to go to find out if Chris was able to come for dinner this week.'

'There's no need. If he comes we'll have enough to feed him.'

'You're right, Susie, I don't think I will go. I'll have half an hour on the sofa and then Rosie can help me make an apple pie for dinner.'

'There's a lot of noise outside this morning.' Susie opened the front door and realised there was quite a crowd outside shouting to each other. She was shocked to see the houses opposite had broken windows and there was shattered glass, slates and debris all over the road. She returned to get the yard brush to sweep in front of their house. The air was heavy with the smell of smoke and burning.

'What a terrible night,' Mrs Pugh called. 'The docks are still blazing; they can't put the fires out. I can see them from upstairs. I've never known anything like it.'

Someone shouted, 'We can all see Merseyside took a beating last night.'

'And the night before, and the night before that. On the news it said there's terrible damage.'

Susie had listened to the news on the wireless over breakfast. 'I heard that a ferry boat had been sunk on its moorings at Seacomb,' she said.

Mr Mathews from number thirty was coming up the street with his Sunday newspaper under his arm. 'Did you hear that terrible bang, it shook the foundations of our house.'

'I reckon it was that that broke our windows.'

'It says in the paper that an ammunition ship blew up in the docks.'

Susie took her broom inside. Her mother was lying on the sofa and the children were squabbling over a game of Ludo on top of their shelter. 'I'm going to run down the street and buy a newspaper, Mum. We all know Liverpool got a pounding last night and they're saying there are details of the damage in the papers.'

'I hope Peverill's didn't get it again,' she sighed.

Susie pulled on her coat and picked up her purse. As she ran down the street she could see the fires still blazing on the docks, with huge plumes of smoke and dust drifting over the city. There was a crowd outside the newsagent's saying much the same things as they had outside her house. Horror and disbelief was on every face. 'We can't stand much more of this,' one man said, 'it'll finish us.'

Susie had to push her way inside the shop. She and Mum didn't buy many newspapers, but on most nights of the week she picked up a *Liverpool Echo* for Bert as she got off the bus.

Mr Halligan knew her. 'There's only the *News of the World* or the *Sunday Mirror* left, love, which do you want?'

'Can I have both please?' The paper shortage had reduced all newspapers to three pages, and they needed paper to light their fires. Like everything else, toilet paper was in short supply too, and occasionally they had to fall back on newspaper. Rosie and Jonjo cut it into neat squares for them.

'Course you can, love,' he pushed them across the counter to her. 'They're going like hot cakes this morning.'

'It's all the bad news,' a woman shouted from the doorway, 'we all want to know the worst.'

'There's a lot worse than what they print in newspapers,' a man said beside Susie.

She scanned the front pages. 'Gosh, Lewis's department store badly damaged by fire. The cathedral slightly damaged and an historic suburban church burned out. Two railway stations out of action and the lines blocked. Heavy casualties feared. It looks pretty bad.'

'This is worse,' another customer read from a different paper. '"An ammunition ship, the *Malakand*, was being loaded with one thousand tons of high explosives when fire in nearby dock warehouses set it alight. Desperate attempts were made to control the blaze but the ship blew up hours after the all-clear sounded, killing four firefighters and causing widespread devastation. The fire continues to burn."'

'There's still worse that they don't dare print,' the man beside her said quietly. 'A big Liverpool hospital caught it last night. A bomb fell in the courtyard behind it and destroyed the ambulance station. It set fire to ambulances and killed some of the drivers.'

Susie had seen the ambulances behind the maternity block at Mill Road and suddenly felt sick with fear. 'Which hospital was it?' She followed the man out of the shop. Silently she implored the powers that be, please, please, don't let it be Mill Road Infirmary. Both Jamie and Martha were in there.

She asked again, 'Which hospital was it? Why won't they tell us?'

He turned to her on the pavement outside and she saw he was wearing the uniform of an ARP warden. 'Direct hits on hospitals are bad for civilian moral, so they keep news like that to themselves. It seems we civilians cope better if the damage we hear about is to docks and churches.'

Susie caught at his arm and said urgently, 'I've got to know, was it Mill Road Infirmary? Please tell me, my husband and sister are in there.'

She saw sympathy in his eyes and his formal manner relaxed. 'I think it was. The news came to our ARP post.'

'Oh my God!' She clutched at his arm. 'I've got to go. I want to see . . .' She was only a few yards from a bus stop, 'But it's Sunday and not many buses run.'

'You'd be better going home and waiting for news there.'

'No,' her cry was agonised, 'I must see for myself. I must.'

'All right, I can give you a lift to Breck Road, it's not far to walk from there.'

'Thank you.' He ushered her into the front seat of a van advertising a fruit and vegetable shop. Susie could feel her heart racing. 'You've been on duty all night?'

'Yes, I'm shattered. I've got to have a sleep.'

As they drew near the hospital there was more traffic and they found the roads had been cordoned off. 'I'm not allowed to go any closer,' he said. 'It's definitely Mill Road Infirmary that's been bombed.'

'I'll walk from here, thank you.' Susie's mouth had gone dry; she was afraid she was going to lose two people she loved very much. 'It's this way?'

'Yes, you can't miss it.'

She ran until the crowd became too thick and she had to push her way through it. The devastation she saw was horrific. Three big buildings had been totally destroyed and many of the others badly damaged. Fires on the site were not yet under control. Civil Defence workers were everywhere and a low barrier had been erected to hold people back.

Many in the crowd were growing frustrated at being unable to get news of their loved ones. Some were anxious and others angry at being held back. Susie tried to push forward to speak to the police, but others were doing the same. A police officer finally lifted a loudhailer to his lips.

'Please go home,' he said, 'you are getting in the way of the rescue workers. Patients are being transferred by ambulance to both Walton and Broad Green Hospitals, anywhere it's safe so their treatment can continue. It's a question of getting as many people out as quickly as possible.'

People in the crowd were shouting, 'Have you news of John Ackers? Thomas Eldridge? Mary Oakes?'

'It is no good asking for news of individuals, we just don't know until the lists are prepared. Please go home and allow our Civil Defence workers to get the job done.'

Tears were rolling down Susie's face. Surely no one could have survived in this disaster area? She walked blindly to what had once been a six-foot-high wall, but which was now reduced to seat height for most of its length. She sat down for a few moments but couldn't remain still. The crowd hung around with grim, tear-stained faces, waiting for news.

She could hear voices and the shovels of the rescue workers scraping against bricks. As far as she could make out it was coming from the rubble where the maternity block had once stood. It had been razed to the ground, annihilated. Martha and her new baby wouldn't have stood a chance. Susie knew she'd have to accept that they couldn't have got out alive.

But what of Jamie? Across the barrier the police were erecting to hold back the crowd, she could see the ruins of the building she thought Jamie had been in. Doors and windows had been blown off and part of the roof was missing. Patients in pyjamas were being lined up, some wrapped in blankets, some in dressing gowns, but all gripping personal possessions close to them. Were they being loaded into vehicles? There were police cars and a bus. She saw an ambulance leave and another take its place, but the vehicles hid most of what was going on. She prayed that Jamie was amongst the patients she'd glimpsed, but they were too far away, too covered with dust for her to recognise him.

She returned to the wall she'd sat on earlier, but there were people sitting all along it now. Feeling totally drained, Susie sank down next to another young woman, who mopped her eyes. 'I think my husband might be trapped under all that rubble,' she said.

'I think mine could be too,' Susie admitted and shivered.

'They say they started digging before the raid was over. They say they've been ferrying patients out for hours, but they still can't tell us who is alive and who isn't.'

'Soon,' Susie tried to comfort her. 'Perhaps they'll be able to soon.'

'I thought Paul was safe,' she wept, 'he's just been shipped home after being injured in the Libyan desert.'

Susie sighed. 'I'm in the same position, except Jamie was in the Air Force.' She looked at her watch and was surprised to find how much time had passed. 'I ought to go home, Mum will wonder where I am.' But how could she tell her the awful news? It would break her heart.

'I'm going to wait,' the girl was no older than she was, and seemed desperate. 'If I knew they'd moved him to another hospital, it would settle my mind.'

Susie closed her eyes; that would settle her mind too. Please let Jamie be spared, she prayed. She'd been rejoicing since he'd been picked up in the Channel, believing all would be well, but now this. 'They're still moving patients,' she said, 'and I expect they're working flat out to draw up a list.'

Susie stayed where she was, hoping she'd have news of Jamie soon. She told her companion about Martha and her baby, but she was horribly afraid there was no hope for them. She felt sick at the thought.

Bert had been sitting in his van for hours. He'd been unable to drive as close to the hospital as he had on previous visits, but he'd walked the rest of the way and joined the crowd. It had taken him quite a while to work out where the maternity block had stood, and when he did, he was appalled. Was it possible that Martha and the baby had survived?

Ambulances were ferrying patients away, and that gave him hope. Why oh why had Dr Grant sent her here? She would have been safe at home with him. Poor, poor Martha. He couldn't accept it.

The woman standing next to him said, 'They're trying to dig our Emily out.'

Bert couldn't stand it. He felt exhausted and totally depressed. He went home, but without Martha in the house, and with the knowledge that she might never be there again, it was cold and cheerless and the silence heavy. He threw himself down on the living room sofa and wept. The devastation he'd seen was horrendous, and he was so afraid that his darling Martha had been killed.

CHAPTER FORTY-ONE

LOUISE WAS GROWING ANXIOUS; Susie had been gone for a very long time. She went out to the door and looked down the street but there was no sign of her. Thank goodness there wasn't a raid on. There were fewer people about now; they'd all calmed down and were cooking the most important meal of the week, their Sunday dinner.

Her leg of lamb was sizzling in the oven with all its accompaniments, and she'd just popped the apple pie in too, when the children who had been watching at the window shouted that Auntie Becky had arrived.

'She's got a very posh car,' Jonjo shouted, both children jumping up and down with excitement. Louise opened the door and they all rushed out to greet her. They'd been looking forward to this visit because they hadn't seen her since Christmas. The children launched themselves at her. 'Auntie, what a lovely big car you have!' Jonjo screamed.

'It's Uncle Max's car,' she told him, 'he let me borrow it because he's exhausted and needs to stay at home and have a rest day.'

'Where is yours?'

'It's had to go up on blocks for the duration because there's no petrol. I wish this war would finish.'

Louise flung her arms round her. 'Becky, you have an easy time compared with many. You live far enough away to miss these air raids.'

She laughed. 'Well, most of them, but the war *has* changed my life. Did Martha tell you I had to get a job?'

'Yes, it's the law now. All women without young children have to work.'

'I was directed into a munitions factory, but Max found me a better job in his office in the nick of time.'

'What as?'

'Receptionist and general office help. I have plenty to keep me busy.'

'You have a good life with Max,' Louise smiled, 'you look marvellous, as though you've stepped off the cover of a magazine!'

'Thank you, Mother. I've brought you those two hats that might do for your wedding. You must show me your outfit so I can help you decide which would be better, but I fear you still won't look like the bride of the year.'

She turned and took two other bags from the car. 'What else have you brought?' Rosie asked.

The children followed her indoors and hovered close as she opened one of the bags. 'I've managed to find a present for the new baby,' she said, bringing out a gift-wrapped box. 'A silver rattle,' she whispered to her mother, 'I bought it at an antiques fair, and I've got some chocolates for Martha.'

'What about me and Rosie?' Jonjo craned his head into the bag.

Becky laughed. 'Well, yes, I do have some toys.' She gave them each a parcel to unwrap and they screamed with excitement and delight as they tore off the paper. There was a clockwork bus for Jonjo and a doll for Rosie. 'Second hand,' she mouthed, 'but hardly used at all. I bought them at auction. It's the only way to get anything these days. I've brought some of my old things for Susie, because she says that's what she likes.' She paused. 'Where is Susie?'

'I wish I knew. She ran down the road hours ago to get a newspaper.' Louise went to the kitchen to check on the dinner and came back with the knives and forks.

'Come on,' she said to the children, 'pick up all this paper and fold it carefully, we can use it again. Then I want you to set the table, dinner is nearly ready. Susie will be home soon and if Chris doesn't come there's just us for dinner today.'

'Then I'll run us down to the hospital to see Martha and the baby. How are they?'

'Martha came through it very well and the baby's lovely. Bert is over the moon.'

'I want to see my mum,' Jonjo said.

'I'm afraid they won't let children in,' Becky said, 'you and Rosie will have to stay in the car.'

'But I want to see my mum,' he protested.

'I've just told you, Jonjo, that won't be possible, not until she comes home. Mum, is there anything I can do to help with the dinner?'

'Yes, you can make some mint sauce. Martha's friend Lena grows mint in a window box and is always happy to give us a bit. I'll just go across the road to get some.'

Louise opened the front door and they streamed out after her. She pulled up in surprise to see Bert's van parked outside his house.

'Dad's at home,' Jonjo said.

Louise was irritated. Bert had told her he'd be staying at his mother's to have his dinner, so why had he come home? With Martha in hospital she felt she had to feed him, and he had a big appetite. She wouldn't have enough roast potatoes to go round now. She banged on his front door. It took him some time to open it, and when he did his face shocked her. It was ravaged with tears. 'What's happened, Bert?'

He sighed. 'You'd better come in.'

'No, I'm cooking, come to our house.' With red and swollen eyes that refused to look at her, he came.

'Has Martha taken ill again?' Becky asked. He shook his head.

'What's happened?' Louise demanded. 'Is it Martha?'

'Yes.' He took a damp handkerchief from his pocket and blew his nose. 'The hospital was bombed last night. Flattened, there's nothing left but a pile of rubble. I'm frightened that . . . Well, I think Martha might have been killed.'

'What?' Louise was filled with horror. 'Oh my God! How awful!' She collapsed back on the sofa.

Becky's mouth had opened with shock. 'Don't you know? For sure, I mean?'

'No, I went to look. The maternity block has gone, it's just a heap of rubble.'

'Oh my lord,' Becky exclaimed, 'when did this happen?'

'In the middle of the night. They're still digging for people.'

'Perhaps they've got Martha and the baby out by now?'

'I do hope so, but it was chaotic there.'

Louise let out a cry of agony and collapsed back against the cushions. Her face mirrored shock, horror and utter grief. A moment later she jerked upright, her cheeks red with anger, to burst out, 'These bombing raids are wicked, totally evil. What are they hoping to achieve?' Then she collapsed again in a tumult of tears. Her poor, sweet Martha, who had suffered all her life with ill health, to die like that? Just when she was well and happy and had a healthy baby to take little Wendy's place? 'How cruel! Poor Martha.'

Rosie climbed onto her knee to comfort her and Becky tiptoed to the kitchen where she could hear the cabbage pan boiling over.

Jonjo let out a wail of anguish. 'Is Mummy dead?' he demanded. 'Tell me. Is she?'

'We don't know, Jonjo. The hospital has been bombed, but she might be perfectly all right.'

He continued to sob noisily. Louise had one arm round Rosie and put the other round his shoulders. 'You must be brave, Jonjo, and not cry until we know definitely. Your mum would want you to be brave, wouldn't she?'

Jonjo's cries became louder and Rosie began to weep in sympathy.

'I think I'll go back to the hospital to see if there's any news yet,' Bert said.

'Stay and have something to eat first.'

'I feel sick, I don't want—'

'You must eat, Bert. You'll feel better if you do. It's all ready. I was waiting for Susie, but I'll start dishing up. You didn't see her at the hospital?'

'No, there's a huge crowd down there.'

'I'm worried about her, look out for her when you go again.'

'All right, I'll just pop next door to see if the phone is on yet.

They were transferring patients to other hospitals. I'll ring round and see if Martha and Adam have been taken somewhere else.'

Becky's face was stricken. When he'd gone, she said, 'Mum, this is awful, what are we going to do?'

Moments later, Bert was banging on the door again. 'The phone lines are still down,' he said, 'no news.'

Louise felt sick; somebody must know what was happening to Martha. She said, 'Bert, come and carve this leg of lamb. Becky, get the children up to the table.'

They ate in silence in an atmosphere of gloom and despair. Louise was surprised how good everything tasted, even without mint sauce. Neither complimented her on the apple tart. For once they didn't care what it tasted like. Afterwards Bert said, 'I'm going back to the hospital because they said they'd make a list of all those evacuated to other hospitals.'

'I want to go with you,' Louise said, 'I need to see the place for myself.'

'Better if you stay here with the children,' Bert told her, 'the devastation is frightening.'

'No, I must see it.'

Becky was fighting to control her tears. 'I'll stay here with the children.'

'No,' Jonjo protested. 'I want to go, she's my mummy.'

Becky hugged him to her, afraid the sight would give him nightmares. 'No, Jonjo, you and Rosie can help me wash up, and then I'll see if your mum's friend Lena Smith across the road will let you play with her children.'

'No, I don't like them, they're just babies,' he wailed. 'I don't want to go there.'

'I'm going,' Bert moved towards the door.

'Look out for Susie,' Louise reminded him, 'don't forget her.'

'I won't,' he said, as the front door slammed behind him.

'Please God let Martha be safe,' Louise moaned, 'but they must dig them out soon. It's a long time for a new baby . . . How long is it since it happened? Do you know?'

Becky was weeping openly. 'Mum, we'll go to the hospital on our own. That was the plan, wasn't it, that I'd take you? Martha was always such a good friend to me.'

Susie felt she'd been waiting for hours. To start with she'd hardly dared look at the huge stretch of rubble in front of her. Broken beams, shattered floorboards, slates and bricks were being tirelessly worked over by teams of Civil Defence workers, using spades and even their bare hands. Mentally, she urged them on because surely Martha and her baby must be underneath, struggling to breathe through the dust and dirt.

She caught her breath – a woman was being dug out and she seemed to have a baby in her arms. She knew the victim was alive by the way the rescuers wiped her face and cleared her nose and mouth. She was being carried to a waiting ambulance. Sometimes they just covered the face and put the body to one side under a piece of tarpaulin. It was impossible to know if any one of them might be Martha as they were all coated with thick grey dust.

Susie had removed her coat and was using it to cushion the hard and uneven seat upon which she'd been sitting for so long. The sun was hot on her face and she was beginning to feel comatosed. Her companion had dozed off and was now slumped against her. She'd told Susie she'd been married for four years and that her name was Rita.

Their spirits had been buoyed up by the snippets of explanation and news that had been passed by word of mouth through the waiting crowd. They didn't need to be told that they were sitting on what was left of the wall that had enclosed the courtyard behind the hospital.

This was where the original explosion had taken place, setting fire to the ambulance station and flattening the maternity hospital next to it. She knew Jamie had been in the block alongside which had been full of serving soldiers, sailors and airmen. She could see it was badly damaged, but word had gone round that, amazingly, no military personnel had received further injuries from the blast.

Susie and Rita had hugged each other at that news, but looking at the doomed building with some of its roof gone as well as its windows and doors, Susie had asked, 'But how do we know that is true?'

'We don't,' Rita said, but it gave them reason to hope.

Through the hours she'd waited to hear where Jamie had been sent, Susie had felt alternately euphoric with joy and in the depths of total grief. All sorts of rumours and stories circulated. She heard there had been an operation in progress in a basement theatre when the building above them collapsed. It brought debris down on top of them and trapped them in the theatre. A nurse climbed out through a window and gave the alarm, saving the lives of several nurses and doctors because there was another fall of rubble shortly afterwards. The woman next to Rita completed the story. 'The surgeons who were operating were killed but the patient survived and has been transferred to Broad Green Hospital.'

'That sounds like a miracle,' Rita said, 'we've got to hope for another.'

'It would be a miracle if my sister has survived.' Poor Martha, she didn't deserve an end like this. She'd always been so willing to help everybody; nothing was too much trouble for her. She'd always made the most of what little she had.

They all thought their wait was over when in the mid-afternoon they saw the crowd getting to their feet and the police coming to speak to them. But they were moving them further back behind a temporary wire fence that had been erected. Most were reluctant to move; they could see very much less and had nowhere to sit but on the ground. Susie spread her coat down on the dust and they both sat on that.

Not long afterwards she saw a movement ripple through the waiting crowd, and those sitting down were getting to their feet.

She and Rita did the same and moved forward. 'The police are fixing notices to the fence,' Rita said. 'Are these the lists we've been waiting for?'

Soon they were struggling in a heaving, pushing scrum to read the names. She and Rita hung on to each other and pushed as one. Susie was able to see they were arranged in alphabetical order and find Jamie's name. 'He's been sent to Walton Hospital,' she shouted out loud. She was sweating with relief. 'Thank God for that, at least Jamie has been spared.'

'Here's my husband!' Rita's finger stabbed excitedly at the list.

Susie read: Warrant Officer Douglas Pugh, transferred to Walton Hospital. 'They're safe, we now know they're definitely safe.' She was laughing with relief. 'I need to see Jamie in the flesh after a shock like that.'

'Why don't we go? They'll surely let us in to see them.'

'D'you know how to get to Walton Hospital?'

'Yes, I think so, I grew up near there. It'll be difficult trying to cut across town, better if we get a bus to the Pier Head and another out to Walton.'

The buses were full, and few and far between that day, and it took time. Walton was another big hospital and Susie parted from Rita in the crowd round the gates, never to see her again. She was swept along endless corridors by the crowd before she found Jamie's ward. The atmosphere was very different to Mill Road; that had been a busy hospital, but Walton seemed almost overwhelmed by its increased intake of patients.

The staff had no time to direct visitors. A few patients were up and wearing dressing gowns, crowding the windows and watching the door. Others were lying on their beds asleep. She asked for Jamie by name, but they didn't know him. Susie went down the line of beds, looking at each face until she found him. She pulled a chair close, collapsed on it, put her head down on his bed and burst into tears.

She felt him stir, felt his arm pull out and go round her. 'Susie, my love,' he whispered.

'I'm here. Have you been hurt again?' She could see a fresh bandage on his arm, sticking plaster on his face.

'Minor grazes from falling debris. Nothing to worry about.'

'Thank God. When I saw you flat out on the bed, I was afraid.'

'I'm all right. Just had a bad night and catching up on my sleep.'

Susie made an effort to pull herself together. 'Such a relief to see you, touch you again and know . . .'

He kissed her, a real lover's kiss, but holding her close gave a little giggle. 'Not much privacy here for that. I had to wait to get a bed. They had to turf other patients out to make room for us. How are you? I bet you've been worried stiff.'

Susie mopped at her face.

'I hoped you'd be able to find me. It didn't take you long.'

'It took me all day.' She told him about Martha and the terrible time she'd had waiting for news. Then she thought of her mother doing the same and felt guilty. 'Mum doesn't know where I am, she doesn't know about Martha . . . Although, yes, she might by now, Becky was going to take us to visit her. Oh gosh! She'll be going spare. I left home this morning before nine o'clock to buy newspapers. She'll be worried stiff.'

Jamie gave her a little hug. 'I'm told there's a public phone box downstairs in the hall, and the phones are back on.'

'I saw it as I came in,' Susie said, 'there was a queue of people waiting to use it.'

'It might be better now. Go and ring Bert and leave a message, and while you're there, let my family know. They'll be worried too.' He gave her a small notebook with phone numbers written down.

'I know the number for Hillbark by heart.'

'I know you do, but you're more likely to get Dad at this number, he's more or less moved in with his lady friend. And in case they're out, this is Jack's number.' Jamie understood how she felt about his mother since Rosie had come along.

They both counted out their pennies and Susie said, 'I'll be right back.'

She rang Bert with a message for her mother. For a moment his voice was alert and expectant, and he said, 'Oh, it's you, Susie, have you got news of Martha?'

'No, sorry, I've heard nothing about her. I just want you to tell Mum that I've found Jamie in Walton Hospital and he's all right.' She knew that would send his spirits spiralling to rock bottom.

There was a pause, then, 'Good, I'll tell her.'

She knew Bert was in despair and searched for words to give him hope, but there weren't any. 'I'm so sorry.' Tears were stinging her eyes again.

When she'd recovered a little she rang the number Jamie had given her. She knew it was Lily Milman who picked up the phone, but she just asked for Mr Curtis. 'Tell him it's Susie, his daughter-in-law,' she said.

A few moments later, she heard him say, 'Hello, Susie, such good news about Jamie being picked up in the Channel. He was in good form when I saw him on Saturday and quite convinced he'll have no difficulty walk—'

'Mr Curtis,' Susie interrupted, 'Mill Road Infirmary got a direct hit on Saturday night, haven't you heard?'

'No, no – is Jamie all right?'

'Yes, no further injuries, but the hospital was badly destroyed.' She told him about the terrible day she'd had waiting for news and the utter destruction she'd seen. 'Martha, my sister, has just had another baby in Mill Road and there's no news of them. I'm afraid they haven't been as lucky as Jamie.' Susie was crying again. 'He asked me to ring you and let you know he's been evacuated to Walton. He thought you'd be worried. I'm there now and was so relieved to find him.'

'Susie! I didn't know Mill Road had been bombed. Thank you for letting me know, I'd have been out of my mind with worry. But Jamie has survived yet again, he must have nine lives.'

Susie heard what she'd been dreading. 'Oh goodness, there goes the siren again.'

William Curtis said, 'It surely must be time the Luftwaffe bombed somewhere else. Susie, how are you going to get home?'

'The bus . . . I don't know.'

'It's not safe for you to be out and about by yourself. You know all buses are instructed to stop near a street shelter when there's a raid. Jamie would never forgive me if anything happened to you now. Wait there, I'll come and get you and congratulate Jamie on another escape.'

CHAPTER FORTY-TWO

L OUISE FELT HER WORLD was collapsing around her. Bert was saying he thought Martha had been killed, and Susie seemed to have disappeared off the face of the earth. She must know they'd worry about her.

After lunch, Becky took her to see what remained of Mill Road Infirmary. Both wished they hadn't gone. To know that Martha and her baby, and countless others, were trapped beneath all that debris left her gasping.

'The rescue workers are still at work,' Becky pointed out, but she was in tears. 'Don't give up hope, Mum. You know Martha has a will of iron, she's a fighter. She won't have given up.'

'It's more than twelve hours now since it happened.' Louise was agonised. 'How long can Martha survive under that, let alone a newborn baby?' Becky led her back to her car through the despairing crowd.

'We'd better pull ourselves together before you collect the children,' Louise said when they reached home, 'no point in upsetting them more than we have to.' She went to wash her face. To have seen the total destruction of the maternity block wiped out any hope she still had. And where was Susie? She was counting this one of the worst days of her life.

It seemed hours later, they were playing Ludo with the children when Bert tapped on their window to let them know he had some news. Becky leapt to her feet to go to the door, hoping Martha had been found. But his woebegone tear-stained face made Louise concentrate harder on her dice.

Becky brought him in. 'Susie's just phoned,' he mumbled, 'she asked me to tell you that she's found Jamie alive and well in Walton Hospital.'

'Is that where she is?' Louise was sweating. She wiped her forehead on her sleeve. At that moment they heard the air raid siren blast out another warning. It seemed the last straw. 'To think of Susie out there alone in an air raid terrifies me. She'll have no way of getting home.'

Bert went on, 'Susie said you were not to worry, she's perfectly all right and don't expect her until you see her.'

'But that was before the siren went.'

'Can I use your phone before another bomb knocks it out again?' Becky asked. 'I told Max I'd be home before now and he'll be worried about me.' They went off together.

'My mummy's dead, isn't she?' Jonjo was pulling a face.

'I'm afraid we still don't know,' Louise told him. 'Your daddy's gone back to the hospital to see if he can find out.'

Becky came back alone. 'I'm afraid I'm going to have to go home,' she said, reaching for her coat. 'Max is insisting I should start straight away. It's still quiet here and they've had no warning there.'

'Let's hope it's a false alarm.' Becky kissed them all and left.

Louise busied herself with the children's evening routine, put them to sleep in the shelter and sat listening. All was quiet outside; there was no hum of German engines above, no ackack guns firing, no explosions. Hopefully Becky was right and it was a false alarm. She heard a car in the street, and that was a sufficiently rare sound to send her to the window, though she had to be careful to show no light. She could see nothing, but a car door slammed and there were running footsteps. It was Susie. Thank God! She went to the front door and the next moment Susie threw her arms round her.

'I'm so glad about Jamie,' Louise told her. But Martha was still missing.

Half an hour later the all-clear sounded so Louise decided she'd go upstairs to her own bed. She slept better there and she needed a decent night's sleep after a day like this.

'I'll stay down here with the children,' Susie said, though usually nothing woke them once they were asleep.

Though it remained quiet, Louise tossed and turned for most of the night. She couldn't stop thinking of Martha. After all the illness she'd suffered in her life, she'd suddenly bloomed with good health in this pregnancy. To have it end like this was a savage blow to them all.

Louise felt like a zombie when she got up the next morning, but Susie was full of energy. She got the breakfast, got the children ready and sent them on their way to school.

'Are you coming to work, Mum?'

'Of course,' Louise said, but it was an effort to put one foot in front of the other. Susie cut their sandwiches and hurried her down to the bus stop.

She sat at her desk and opened her ledgers but the figures were swimming before her eyes. She couldn't think of anything but Martha and her new baby buried beneath that huge stretch of rubble. Would it be possible for them to be still alive?

Gordon Wilson came and started to tell her something of his troubles. 'My wife and I have lost just about everything we own.' But all she could do was look at him blankly. He said, 'Louise, you're in a worst state than I am. What's the matter?'

She told him about Martha and her baby, and the next thing she knew Christopher was standing over her and urging her to her feet. 'Come to my office,' he said softly, 'it's more private.' He put an arm round her waist and led her there, and once inside closed the door firmly behind them.

Louise felt his arms go round her. 'Louise, I'm so sorry about Martha, you must have had a terrible weekend.'

Sympathy was the last thing she could cope with, and it brought her tears welling up. She put her head on his shoulder and wept. He hugged her close. 'Don't give up hope for Martha. It's too soon.'

'It's thirty hours now.'

'People have survived in earthquakes for longer.'

'I just don't think she could, and certainly not a newborn baby. Not now I've seen where it happened. Martha did so much for us,' she choked. 'She kept us going, made it possible for both Susie and me to work. Did half our housework and looked after Rosie.'

'Shall I run you home? You'll be able to rest . . .'

'No, it's worse there. Martha was always in and out of my place. We all fussed over her because she was often ill, but she gave us so much. At times I leaned on her, depended on her to help with the younger ones.' Louise straightened up and wiped her eyes with Christopher's handkerchief. 'I'm sorry. I need to pull myself together. I'm doing nothing and I'm stopping you working.'

He gave her another hug. 'Don't worry about that. We've got power and telephones and the factory's working hard. The machines are chopping up the oranges and we'll make marmalade this morning.'

'You're very kind and considerate.'

'Louise, you were a great comfort to me when Mabel died, and you have been ever since. I'll have to leave you, but I'm going to ask for a tray of tea for you, and I want you to sit here until you feel well enough to go back to work.'

'Thank you.'

'Do go home if you'd rather.'

'No, I'll be all right in a few minutes. I'll stay here.'

'Right, I'm going to have a word with Susie,' he said, and went to find her. She was typing hard. 'Your mother's told me about Martha and the baby,' he said. 'I'm so sorry. How are you?'

'Better than Mum, she's in shreds. I know Jamie has survived, thank goodness, and I'm trying to stay hopeful about Martha.'

'It must be terrible, the endless waiting for news.'

'Bert will ring us if there is any.'

'Thank you for coming in, and do feel free to go if it gets too much for you. Go early anyway. I know you've got Rosie to think of.'

'And Jonjo too, now.'

'Yes, poor child. If your mother stays till closing time, I'll run her home. Perhaps take her for a drink if she'll come. Take care of her Susie; she's going to need you now.'

Susie had no memories of her father and was more than pleased to have Christopher Berry as her stepfather. She fully approved of him and was sure her mother would be happy with him. He was unfailingly kind and understanding towards everybody.

She took him at his word and left early, but had to wait ages for a bus because they weren't able to run to the normal timetable as some had been damaged.

When she got home, Bert was lying on her sofa and the children were sitting at the table. Rosie had found the tin in which her mother kept an emergency reserve of biscuits.

'There's no milk,' Rosie complained.

'I wouldn't let them drink it,' Bert sat up, 'or there'd be none to make tea.'

'I'll put the kettle on,' Susie said, and went to do it.

'I forgot all about the kids,' Bert told her. 'They walked home on their own.'

'They've been doing it for some time,' Susie said.

Jonjo piped up, 'Mummy said we were old enough.'

'You are,' Susie agreed, 'and you walk to school on your own too.' Without Martha, they'd have to.

'Yes,' Rosie said, 'and I know about the back door key being under that big plant pot.'

Susie poured out tea for them all. 'Bert, have you brought any meat for tonight's dinner?'

He groaned, 'No, I'm sorry. Everything's gone out of my mind.'

'Don't worry, but we'll have to find something to eat.' She went into the kitchen to see what food they had. Usually there was meat left over from Sunday's joint for Monday's dinner, but not this week. What little had been left had gone into the sandwiches they'd taken to work.

'We have potatoes certainly, and last night Mum put dried butter beans to soak.' They'd swollen to twice their size so they had plenty of those. In the cupboard she found a tin of spam, but it wasn't enough for three adults and two children. She found a little dripping and a bit of lard. 'I could make spam fritters and fried potatoes,' she said. 'Bert, if you have another tin of spam I could feed you too.'

'I feel sick, I don't want—'

'Have you eaten anything today?'

He shook his head. 'Then you must. Come on, let's see what Martha has in her cupboard.'

Susie found an identical tin of spam, and while she was there she borrowed Martha's frying pan as she thought she'd need it.

She tried to concentrate on preparing the family dinner, but nothing was as it used to be. Bert looked terrible, he wasn't sleeping and he wasn't shaving, but who could blame him? She couldn't get the horror of what might have happened to Martha out of her mind.

Susie switched on the wireless, thinking she might hear news of what had happened. A direct hit on Mill Road Infirmary and such a large death toll was a big tragedy for Liverpool, but there was no mention of it. It had had a profound impact on their lives, but was not reported anywhere because of the effect it might have on public moral. Only the people in the immediate vicinity, and the patients and their families knew about it. It seemed that the rest of the world ignored it.

Chris brought Louise to the door and said, 'I'm not

stopping, Susie. I just wondered if you had any news.'

Bert shook his head. 'I've rung round all the city hospitals asking about Martha, but I couldn't find her. They're still digging where the maternity hospital was, but they're saying it's bodies they're bringing out now.'

'Oh God,' Louise moaned. 'It's nearly forty hours, and I don't suppose they'll be able to carry on once it gets dark. If Martha is alive, she'll think she's never going to get out.'

Susie went back to the kitchen. The scent of frying was soon making her mouth water. She called, 'Everything's ready, I'm going to dish up.'

They ate in silence in an atmosphere of growing despair, but Bert did try. 'A good dinner, Susie, from virtually nothing,' he said. 'Sorry, Louise, I forgot to bring you any meat today.'

'You won't forget tomorrow, will you?'

'I like this dinner better,' Jonjo said.

'But we wouldn't want it every day,' Susie told him. 'Anyway, I've used up our ration of fat.'

Louise became increasingly on edge as the days dragged on without any news of Martha or her baby. She could see Bert was losing hope, and that made hers drain away too. Three large hospital blocks had collapsed, trapping so many patients and staff below huge piles of debris that rescue workers were faced with an almost impossible task.

Chris tried to talk of their future to take her mind off Martha. 'I can't think of our wedding, or my own happiness now this has happened,' she said.

One evening, Bert came to knock on their door shortly after she and Susie reached home. Louise rushed to speak to him thinking he had news, but Bert's eyes were red and he looked very downcast. 'I've had the photographs I took of Martha and the baby developed and enlarged. I thought you'd like to have a copy of each one.' He handed her an envelope.

'Aren't you coming in?' she asked. She could see he was full up with tears that were barely under control. 'Come and eat with us, it's what Martha would want you to do.'

She shook the photographs out on the dining table already set for their evening meal. One was a portrait of Martha smiling up from her hospital bed, her swaddled infant in her arms. There was another with Bert sitting on the bed beside them. They seemed so happy, and so pleased. There was another of Adam in his hospital cot, showing his face. In the fourth, Martha had removed the swaddling sheets from the baby and was holding him up in his hospital nightdress. They were looking at each other and there was such love and joy on Martha's face.

Susie came out of the kitchen to look at them, and the children, always anxious not to miss anything, pushed close. 'I know my mummy has been killed,' Jonjo said. 'She won't ever come back, will she?'

'No,' Bert told him, 'I'm afraid she can't,' and the family wept together.

In the end Louise had to make herself think of Chris instead of Martha; it was the only way she could stay sane and continue to function. Chris was doing his best to support and comfort her, but they had less time alone now he had the Wilsons staying in his house. He came to her desk soon after she arrived at work to ask if she'd any news of Martha, and then said,

'Come to my office at lunchtime,' but it wasn't food he wanted to share.

As soon as she went in, he leapt to his feet and took her into his arms. 'Darling dearest love,' he said tenderly, raining kisses on her face. 'I can't tell you how much it means to know you love me and I'll not have to wait much longer until we're married.'

Louise felt that at last she had somebody who loved her and who she could turn to for help.

He'd always kept his office door open for the staff; now the two of them stood behind it so nobody could walk in and surprise them.

Last night she'd had dinner at his house cooked by Alice Wilson, but though the food was good, Chris's easy, relaxed manner had gone in company. Their love was too new to carry it off. Louise had been uncomfortable too.

At three o'clock that afternoon, he came bounding to her desk to take hold of her hand and whisper, 'Good news, darling. Very good news. Alice has been offered rooms with an elderly aunt of hers in Wallasey and they will be moving out of my house tomorrow.'

She was glad, really glad, but there was one thing she wanted even more. That same day, Louise and Susie went home from work to find Bert quite agitated. 'There's nobody working on the hospital site today,' he said. 'I can't believe they've given up.'

'Is there a crowd still waiting for news?' Susie asked.

'No, they've drifted away over the last few days, there's nobody waiting now. A few like me come and go, but I know there are lots of people still under that rubble.'

Very slowly, Louise said, 'They've given up hope of finding anybody else alive.' She winced. 'It's been four days since they did. I'm afraid we have to accept . . .'

Bert's face was wet with tears. 'If only she'd had this baby at home, she'd be with us now.'

'Dr Grant thought it would be safer for her,' Susie said. 'He says all babies will be born in hospital in future. It's the modern trend to make things safer.'

'But it wasn't safer, was it? She had Wendy at home and she was all right then.'

'You can't blame Dr Grant or the hospital for that. It was the fault of the Luftwaffe.'

'That's another thing,' Bert's face screwed in agony. 'I'm being torn in two by this war. I'm half German, my family feel like Germans, but they daren't say so in the shop or they'd be lynched.'

'Bert, that's always been the case.'

'Yes, but it's all getting on top of me.'

By the weekend, there was worse news. Bert said, 'I've heard the Army is being called in to spread lime over where the maternity block and the ambulance station used to be, and then cement them over.'

Louise hugged Bert to her. He felt stiff and inert and couldn't respond. 'It's beyond awful to have that as Martha's last resting place,' she said.

She had mourned the fact that in the carnage of the Great War, her husband had no known grave. She'd written to the War Graves Commission but they'd not been able to trace what had happened to Harold. Now the same thing had happened to Martha, and she had no real grave either.

Bert mopped at his eyes. 'A list has been drawn up of all those known to have lost their lives at the hospital. I've brought you a copy.'

She made herself read down it until she found their names: Martha Jane Dolland aged 32 and Baby Adam Dolland aged 2 days.

'There are seventy-eight names in all,' he said in a hard voice, 'but the true figure is believed to be much higher. When the bomb exploded the hospital had been treating patients and receiving casualties from all over the city. Many members of staff as well as patients lost their lives.'

CHAPTER FORTY-THREE

ON SUNDAY MORNINGS, AS Chris could no longer play the organ, he'd taken to sitting with Louise at church. Today she arrived before him, and he didn't appear until the last minute. He smiled and his dark eyes were full of love for her. 'Overslept,' he whispered as he slid past her in the pew so his good hand would be next to her. To have him sitting close was reassuring and comforting now that none of her girls would come.

After the first hymn his good hand crept along the seat to hold hers. 'The banns will be called for the first time this morning,' he reminded her, which made her realise how close their wedding was.

Outside afterwards, many in the congregation congratulated them, while others spoke with sadness of Martha's death.

'What terrible times these are,' she said to Chris as they walked to her house to have lunch. 'Happiness and grief don't sit well together,' she said, 'but I don't want to put off our wedding.'

'Martha wouldn't want that,' he said, 'and neither would I. Better for us all if we go ahead with it.'

Martha and Bert had been going to host the wedding breakfast, but of course that couldn't happen now. Louise had talked it over with Susie and they'd decided they'd have to put it on at home. 'A buffet wouldn't be too much trouble,' Susie said, 'we can set it up before we go to church. It's going to be mostly family anyway.'

Chris frowned when she told him. 'You and Susie have so much to cope with at the moment. Let me think about it.'

This morning he said, 'How would it be if we held the wedding breakfast at my house? Nurse O'Brien and Mrs Pollard have offered to help me.'

Louise knew Susie would be pleased. 'That would be a lot off my mind, but are you sure?'

'Of course I'm sure. The good ladies are well used to putting on a party spread. Have you been able to do anything about the food?'

'Not really. When Martha offered to do it, Bert said he'd provide meat of some kind. He was hoping to get a tongue and perhaps some ham to go with it, but of course, that was before . . . I'll remind him.'

In the midst of her own grief, Louise couldn't help but feel sympathy for Bert. She'd seen enough of him to know he'd truly loved Martha, and had been looking forward to the birth of baby Adam. To lose them both had affected him profoundly.

Over the following days he was very prickly with everyone, but particularly so with Jonjo, who was suddenly more difficult to handle. He was having tantrums and was more demanding of attention; even Susie was gritting her teeth and having to be patient with him, because poor Jonjo was grieving too. Rosie told them he was naughty at school, too ready to hit out at other children, and getting into trouble with his teacher.

Louise suggested to Bert that he go into the school and tell

Jonjo's teacher what had happened to his mother, so she'd understand. 'I can't,' he said, 'I can't talk about it.'

Susie understood that some things were too painful to talk about and did it on his behalf. Nobody wanted the child to be punished for what must look like plain bad behaviour.

For Jonjo, it had all happened too quickly. Louise was afraid that because they'd been so worried themselves, they hadn't made sure that Jonjo understood what had happened to Martha. There had been no funeral; there was no grave on which he could put flowers. To him it must seem that she'd vanished into fresh air.

Since Martha had gone into hospital, Jonjo had, of necessity, spent more time with her and Susie, and since Martha's death they'd more or less taken over responsibility for him. Bert too had been eating his evening meal with them almost every night and these arrangements looked like becoming permanent. Bert handed over their rations and provided cash as well as meat and other things in short supply, but it gave her and Susie a lot more work, while what Susie wanted to do was spend all the time she could with Jamie.

Louise was trying to encourage Bert to start fending for his own household, but she knew he was hardly coping with his work, and the effort to keep the shop running was taking its toll on his family. His mother called to see Louise. 'I'm worried about Bert,' she said, 'he's lost interest in everything, even the shop. He seems to have no energy and waits for us to make all the decisions.'

Louise thought Jonjo might be better if he went to his own home to sleep at night time. She found this very difficult to suggest, but finally felt she had to. 'Jonjo needs you, Bert,' she said, 'and his company will be a comfort to you.'

She sensed that Bert didn't want this, that he preferred his own company, and further, she found Jonjo didn't want to go. But Louise insisted. For one thing, there was hardly room for four of them in their shelter, although since the heavy raids of early May, they'd been having far fewer. The trouble was they were all grieving for Martha. They'd found her death very hard to accept. Louise tried to keep her mind on her wedding, and encouraged Susie to help with the preparations.

A week later, at half past eleven one night, Louise was woken by Jonjo crying noisily in the street outside, ringing their bell and hammering on their door. 'Nana, Nana!'

Susie leapt out of bed and ran down to open the door. 'Jonjo! What is it? What's the matter?'

'Dad hates me,' he screamed. 'He hit me, he's always hitting me. He's hurt me.'

'Shush, love. You'll wake half the street. Let's close the door so we can put the light on and have a look.' She pulled him inside and gave him a hug. He felt very cold, and was wearing nothing but his pyjamas. 'Where did he hit you?'

'He caned me, it hurts here.' He vaguely indicated his back. It was Louise who lifted his pyjama jacket and saw the welts and bruises there.

'When did this happen? It doesn't look recent.'

'Lower it's sore,' he cried, 'he's done it lots of times. Tonight it was lower.' Susie pulled his pyjama bottoms away from his body to see more bright red weals across his bottom and thighs.

She gasped. 'Oh my goodness! Your dad has done this tonight?'

'Yes, he hates me, everybody hates me. I want my mum.'

Susie backed onto the sofa and lifted him onto her knee. 'We'd like nothing better than to get your mum for you, but we can't. She's gone to heaven. I know she'd want to be here with you if she could.' His feet were bare and felt like blocks of ice, the soles black with road dirt and dust.

'You should have been asleep in bed ages ago. Were you naughty?'

He sniffed and nodded. 'But not very naughty. Don't send me back, please, he'll get me again. I want to stay here with you and Nana.'

Louise was shocked. 'Well, I think you should stay for the rest of tonight. I'm going to put the kettle on to make us all a hot drink, and while it boils I'm going to wash your dirty feet, Jonjo, and find you some socks. Luckily the bed in the Morrison shelter is always ready. You can sleep there tonight, and we'll lock our door so your dad won't be able to come anywhere near you.'

She looked up to find Susie staring at her in horror. 'I think you'll have to talk to Bert about this,' she whispered, 'this can't go on.'

It was the last thing Louise felt like doing, but she couldn't put it off. 'I'll go and see if he's still up.' She had on her dressing gown and slippers and reached for her outdoor coat to put on top. 'I'll need his key, and where's my torch?' Her fingers closed over it in her pocket and she let herself out into the street. There was a hard ball of dread in her throat.

She let herself in to the house and closed the door swiftly. They'd all learned to do that to stop any light showing outside. There was only one dim light on in the living room and she went towards it. Bert was lolling in an armchair wearing pyjamas she'd seen Martha making for him.

'I thought you might come,' he said. He looked thoroughly ashamed of himself.

Louise wanted to cry. 'You've been beating Jonjo! Why, for goodness sake?'

'He's a cheeky little devil, and he's got out of hand. He was asking for a clout.'

Bert was a strong man, dark skinned and bushy haired, and Louise had always been a little wary of him. 'But this isn't the first time you've laid into him; there are scars on his back.' Louise caught sight of a silver-headed walking stick and said, 'Did you use that?'

'No,' he denied.

'What did you use?' He shook his head.

Louise went on, 'I know you're in a state because you've lost Martha, we all are, but Jonjo has lost his mother. Don't you think he's suffering too? He's only seven, Bert.'

'Eight this year.'

'Yes, well, he's still just a child – your child and Martha's. You're so upset about losing baby Adam, but what about Jonjo? He's your son too.'

'No,' he said, 'he isn't.'

'What? Don't be silly, of course he is.' Louise stared at him in the prolonged silence. It felt as though she had a block of ice in her stomach as she remembered the time of Jonjo's birth.

Tears were streaming down Bert's face; he looked a broken man, totally defeated. 'No, he isn't mine or Martha's, though Becky tried to persuade me that he was.'

Louise gasped. 'Becky? What has she got to do with this?'

But hadn't she guessed when Martha had first brought him home? She was struggling for breath. Becky was his mother!

'Martha persuaded me. She'd had two miscarriages and was desperate for a baby, and Becky was desperate to get rid of one without any fuss. You were in a flat spin with Susie being pregnant. You couldn't have stood having two daughters with the same problem. At the time it seemed the answer, but now Martha's dead and Becky doesn't want anything to do with Jonjo.'

'You mean you've spoken to Becky about it. Recently?'

'Of course, several times on the telephone. The last thing she wants is for Max to find out now. So I'm left to bring him up by myself.'

'Bert, you'd better tell me how all this came about.'

He shrugged. 'You know.'

'But I don't. Who is Jonjo's father? You're saying you aren't and neither is Max? So who was he?'

'That was Becky's problem. She doesn't know.'

Louise was aghast. 'Bert, how can you say such a thing?'

'Just remember what Becky was like before she married her well-heeled husband. He adores her and gives her everything she wants, and once she got him she settled down as a respectable wife, but she wasn't always like that.'

Louise was struggling for breath. It was what she'd surmised, but to hear it spoken about like this was a shock.

'Becky was a go-getter, a real live wire.' She could hear the anger in his voice now. 'Becky took up with me, she made all the running. I was her boyfriend until she grew tired of me. I didn't spend freely enough to please her and she took up with some theatre manager. Her intention was to fob me off with

Martha, but actually it was the only favour she ever did me. Martha was worth ten of her. We were very happy. What Becky wanted was a career on the stage. She saw that as the stairway to fame and fortune.'

'Yes, I know, but—'

'Like many others she found it wasn't that easy, acting jobs were few and far between, and she barely earned enough to survive.'

Louise took a long shaky breath. 'She always seemed to have plenty of money. She brought lavish presents home to her sisters.'

'She borrowed money from anyone willing to lend it, from me for one. Then she figured out another way to get it. She was taken on by an escort agency.'

Louise's head reeled. 'What's that?'

'They find glamorous partners for men who want to go out on the town and have a good time.'

'In Liverpool?'

'No, she went down to London, didn't she? Becky had the looks and the personality for it. She loved being wined and dined by a never-ending list of men who knew the expensive nightspots in London. They paid for everything while she was paid to partner them. They gave her a marvellous time and it didn't bother her that they usually expected to take her to bed at the end of the evening.'

'Surely not!' Louise was horrified. 'That's . . . That's . . .'

'Nobody calls it prostitution, Louise, it's escort work, and the top end of the market. Becky said she made them all wear French letters and thought that would be all right. But somehow she got pregnant.'

Louise felt the strength drain from her legs and sank down on a chair. 'Oh my God!'

'Yes, it's not exactly on a par with how Susie managed it, is it?'

'But . . . But how does Max fit into this?'

'To him, Becky was the beautiful stage-struck girl he fell in love with. According to Becky, he was the first man she'd truly loved, and he knew nothing of her escort job. She was preparing to go to Australia with him for the trip of a lifetime when she found she was pregnant. To explain things to Max, she invented the offer of a job in the West End.'

Louise was horrified. 'I did suspect . . .'

'Becky was desperate and asked if she could come and stay with us for a few days.'

'In the spring. We were glad to see her, but she seemed relaxed.'

'She was an actress, Louise. She came to confide in Martha. When Martha miscarried for the third time they hatched this plan. "I'm never going to carry a baby of my own," Martha said to me, "this is the only way for us."'

'I didn't know she'd miscarried!'

'You weren't meant to. It seemed it jolted Max when Becky preferred to work rather than go to Australia with him because he proposed when he came back. She thought it had all worked out wonderfully.'

'So you and Martha took Jonjo?'

'I only did it to please Martha. I was against it at first, but she very much wanted the baby, and she wanted to help Becky.'

He opened his arms in an attitude of despair. 'What I

wanted has been taken from me and I'm left holding the baby I didn't want. It doesn't seem fair.'

Louise felt a shaft of anger; he was feeling sorry for himself. 'It doesn't seem fair to Jonjo either, and it's no excuse for beating the living daylights out of him.'

She couldn't stand any more and got up to leave. 'I brought my daughters up to be decent, clean-living girls, but between them they've made a right mess.' Louise could see no hope of happiness for either the child or Bert. He was full of resentment at what fate had done to him.

'I'll have a word with Becky,' she said. 'If he's her son, then ultimately he is her responsibility. Let me see what I can arrange.'

'Thank you,' Bert said stiffly, 'but I've asked her to take him back or make other arrangements for him. She refused.'

Louise sighed. 'Leave Becky to me, and for the time being say nothing to anybody. Better leave Jonjo with me too. He can stay with us until we get this sorted.'

She went home and saw it was gone one o'clock. She crept upstairs but Susie called out, 'I'm awake, Mum, what did Bert say?'

She went into her bedroom. 'Move over,' she said, 'I'm cold and it's a long and complicated story. It's far worse than I ever imagined.' She got into the narrow bed and snuggled up to Susie's comforting warmth to pour out the whole sad story.

Susie dozed off eventually, and Louise crept to her own cold bed and tried to decide what she should do. It was gone three o'clock that morning before she slept.

CHAPTER FORTY-FOUR

ONE OF THE AMBULANCE drivers killed at Mill Road was a fellow member of St Biddolphe's church, and Mr Coyne visited Louise one evening, catching them in the middle of their meal. 'Do please carry on eating,' he said, 'I'm so sorry to have come at an inconvenient moment.'

She could see Susie resented his presence. The children's attention was all on him now. Louise left the table to sit on the sofa, which fortunately faced the other way.

'It's about Mr Thompson, George Thompson, who was killed in the same raid as your daughter and grandchild.' The vicar seemed equally ill at ease. 'Erm, in lieu of a funeral, his family have requested a memorial service and . . . Er, they thought perhaps you would like Martha to be included.'

Louise swallowed hard. 'We've thought about a memorial service, of course, but with my wedding coming . . .' It was all happening too quickly for her. She felt the happiness generated by her forthcoming wedding reduced and belittled her feelings of loss for Martha. She would have liked to have put it off for six months or so, until she could give it her full attention.

Mr Coyne was wringing his hands. 'The Thompson family are keen to have it as soon as possible. Mr Thompson senior, George's father, is ill. Nearing his end, I fear, and they think a memorial service would be a comfort to him. They suggest the soonest possible date.'

'My wedding . . . it's so difficult . . .'

She was aware that Susie had come to lean on the back of the sofa. 'Mum's being torn apart,' she said, 'everything's on top of her at the moment.'

'It is,' Louise muttered.

'I think it would be a good idea to go ahead with this service,' Susie said firmly. 'Then it'll all be behind us and we can concentrate on your wedding.'

'Well, I'm not sure that . . .'

'Yes, Mother. Let's do what the Thompson family and Mr Coyne want, a joint memorial service.'

'Good,' the vicar was rubbing his palms together. 'The date they suggest is Wednesday, May twenty-first. I'll announce it next Sunday.' He couldn't get to the door quick enough, but he turned back on the step. 'I was hoping Martha's husband would be here with you.'

'Bert's eating with his mother tonight because he's been roped in for fire watching afterwards. We all have to do what we can towards the war effort, don't we?'

'Well, I'm sure he'll be pleased with this arrangement. Goodnight.'

'I'm not too happy about this,' Louise said, 'Martha will feel—'

'Martha won't feel anything, Mum, she's dead.'

That's not what St Biddolphe's had taught Louise. 'She might know we're talking about her. We don't really know.'

'If she does, she won't mind. She'll know how much you cared about her. I think we need to get over our troubles as soon as possible and snatch what pleasures we can.'

Louise was afraid that poor Susie had had a hard life; she couldn't blame her.

It was a quiet night without a raid, and when Bert came home later, Louise went to tell him about the memorial service. He was clearly grieving for Martha and it might help him accept what had happened. He'd lit his fire and seemed to have been reading his newspaper. 'I've never agreed with all your church stuff,' he told her, 'you can count me out of that.'

'Oh! But as Martha couldn't have a funeral, surely a memorial service would be a comfort to you? You'll feel you've laid her to rest.'

'I wouldn't. What difference will that sort of fuss make? It won't bring her back.'

'No, but you used to—'

'I only went to please Martha,' he said. 'She wanted to go, and I wanted to be with her. What a gathering of self-satisfied old women – I didn't like St Biddolphe's.'

'Well, we'll all be going,' Louise told him, 'and I'd like to take Jonjo, if you don't mind. I think it might help him.'

'You can do what you like with him,' Bert said.

'Right, can I use your phone to let Becky know? I think she might come, she and Martha were always the best of friends.'

'Help yourself.'

Louise rang her. 'I'll come, of course,' she said, 'but two o'clock on a week day will be difficult for Max.'

'Please do come,' she said, 'there is something we need to discuss and it might be better if you come alone.'

Becky was instantly alert and anxious. 'What do you mean? What do we need to discuss?'

'Well, Jonjo's future,' Louise said, knowing that would give her two weeks of worry. 'Think about it. Goodbye.'

She put the phone down but had hardly reached the front door when Becky rang back. 'Mother, tell me what's happened.'

'Bert has told me everything. He wants to be rid of Jonjo.'

'Rid of him?'

'Yes, you know well enough that Bert isn't his father and Martha wasn't his mother. How can he go to work and look after someone else's child? Why would he want to?'

'After nearly eight years I hoped he'd grown fond of him, that he'd want to keep him.'

'Well he doesn't, and as you're his mother and legally responsible for him, I want you to think over what is to be done.'

Straight away Louise could hear the fear in her daughter's voice. 'Max mustn't know, Mum, I can't tell him after all this time. Can't you and Susie keep him? He's always with Rosie in your house when I've come.'

'We must think of what would be best for Jonjo.'

'I think to stay with you and Susie. I do, I really do.'

'But Susie and I work full time. Without Martha, the children will have to do a lot more on their own. There won't be anybody to oversee them.'

'Surely it would be better for Rosie if Jonjo was with her?'

'He can lead her into mischief. He's naturally more of a risk taker than she is, and less obedient.'

'I'd be willing to contribute towards his keep, say a pound a week.'

'That's a generous amount, Becky, I reckon half that would cover what it costs, but that isn't the point. When you see Jonjo, don't you feel drawn to him?' She knew she did, she'd seen it on her face, in the way she hung onto every word he said, and in the gifts she went to such lengths to find for him.

There was a pause and her voice broke. 'Of course I do.'

'The best advice I can give you is to tell Max the truth. I'd strongly advise you to, and ask if—'

Becky cut in firmly, 'Thank you, Mother, but I couldn't.'

Louise sighed. 'Come to Martha's memorial service and afterwards we'll talk about it.'

She walked past Bert to let herself out. He looked smugly satisfied, and she knew he'd overheard every word; he could hardly have avoided it.

The next day, Louise was surprised to get a call from Becky at the office. 'I can't wait till the memorial service,' she said, 'I'm too churned up about this. Besides, I want to think of Martha at the service, not worry about Max finding out about Jonjo. Please, please, Mum, do this for me, I beg you. Max would never forgive me for keeping it from him for all these years. Promise you'll never tell him.'

'Becky, calm down, we haven't seen Max for ages. We'd have no opportunity to tell him.'

'Jonjo has spent a lot of time with you and Susie. He knows you, and living with you is what he'd expect and want, isn't it?'

'Becky, stop! When a young mother dies, it's not unusual for a sister to bring up her child. Couldn't you suggest that to Max? Would you have to explain that he is your child? Would it even occur to Max that you could be Jonjo's mother?' Becky didn't answer, but her ragged breathing was audible. 'Wouldn't Max think it natural for you to want to bring him up?'

Another pause, and then in quite a different tone, 'Mother,

I can't believe you of all people would suggest such a thing. It isn't honest.'

'Well, I'm surprised you haven't thought of it yourself. Wouldn't that be the best thing for both you and Jonjo?'

Two weeks later, on the day before Martha's memorial service, Becky rang her mother at work. 'I've arranged to come over early tomorrow and see Bert before the service,' she said. 'I'm going to put it to him that Max and I would like to bring Jonjo up.'

That put all thought of work out of Louise's mind. 'Becky, I'm so pleased, that's really good news. Max was not against the idea then?'

'No, he said he could see I was full of compassion for the child, and thought it would be a good thing for me. He said we should adopt him.'

'You've put my mind at rest,' Louise told her. 'I didn't want Susie to have to do it. Her marriage is new and she already has one child to bring into it. Two would be a lot for Jamie to accept.'

'I'll collect them from school and bring them to the church,' she said, 'and afterwards perhaps we could put it to Jonjo and see what he thinks of the idea.'

'You'll not take him straight back with you?'

'No, Max thinks that would be too quick for him. Better if he has time to think it over, stay at the school he's used to until the end of the summer term. That will give us time to enter him in a school here and fix up a bedroom for him.'

'You're being so sensible about this, Becky. It's what I would suggest, but I can't believe it. Not of you.'

'I've grown up, Mum. This has brought me to my senses.'

The next day, Louise was surprised to see that Becky had persuaded Bert to come to St Biddolphe's with her. He'd put on his Sunday clothes and looked a little better, though he was losing weight.

The old church and the familiar hymns soothed Louise and she was able to sit through the service with her family beside her and think of Martha's life. Of her three daughters, Martha had suffered most and been the most unfortunate, but she'd had some happy times too. Martha had had a look of diffidence, of childlike innocence that had made people feel protective of her. Everybody who knew her had loved her. Louise knew she must celebrate that.

Afterwards, Chris suggested he take them all to Fuller's Tea Rooms for afternoon tea. 'They sell Curtis cakes there,' he said, and smiled at Susie.

Bert declined. 'Sorry, I don't feel up to it.' He'd spent much of the service in tears. He kissed Becky's cheek as he left them and whispered, 'Thank you.'

In Fuller's, the children were disappointed to learn that all the cakes had been sold, and only tea cakes and scones were available. They sat round the table in the window and talked about Martha, about all she'd done for them, all the clothes she'd made for them, and how much they'd miss her. They all noticed that Jonjo couldn't sit still, that his cheeks were red and he was pulling faces.

Becky said, 'One thing your mother will regret, Jonjo, is that she's had to leave you. She really wanted you and loved you dearly, but now she's gone to Heaven, somebody else will have to look after you.' His eyes were glassy with tears. 'Uncle

Max and I would like to bring you up, and we've been wondering if you'd like to come and live with us?'

His big dark eyes fastened on her face but he couldn't get any words out.

'We have no children of our own, you see.'

'You mean, come and live in your big house? Stay there all the time?'

'Yes, it will mean big changes for you, but there have to be changes anyway with your mother not being here.'

'Yes,' he said, 'yes, I'd like that.'

Becky took hold of his hand. 'Then this is what we'll do. You'll stay with Nana and Susie for a bit longer while I fix up a bedroom for you in our house. You must come to visit and see it and help me choose some of the things.'

The tears were pouring down his face now, but he was nodding. 'But what about Dad?'

'He is willing to let you come to us. You see, he has to spend all day running his shop and wouldn't have time to look after you properly.'

The child's lips straightened into a hard line. 'He doesn't like me, he never has.'

'Oh, Jonjo, we think he loves you, but things are difficult for him too. He's very upset about losing your mum.'

'He doesn't want me.'

'But I do, and Uncle Max wants you too. If you agree to come, I'll need to look for a school for you near where we live.'

'Yes,' he nodded, 'yes, I'd like to come and live with you.'

'That's what I'll do then, and until I've got things organised you'll stay with Nana and Susie.'

'And me,' Rosie said, 'don't forget me.'

'But only for a few more weeks until the summer holidays start.'

The tears Jonjo had shed had left runnels down his cheeks; he nodded and gave Becky a wavering smile.

Louise wanted to ease things for him by turning the attention elsewhere. 'Susie,' she said, 'tell them your good news about Jamie.'

Susie's smile was bright. 'He's making such good progress that they're talking of discharging him early. I gather there's a shortage of beds and they need his. Jamie can't wait to get home to us.'

'Everything is working out,' Chris said, 'your mother and I will be married at the end of the month and she'll move in with me.'

'Mum,' Susie said, 'does that mean Jamie and I will be able to take over the rent book of your house?'

'You know it does.'

She smiled happily. 'We're very lucky to have a whole house when so much property has been lost in the blitz.'

Two days later and without warning, Jamie was shipped to Milner Street by ambulance just after Susie and Louise had left for work. Susie had already given Lena Smith a front door key and asked her to keep an eye out for the ambulance, because she'd heard it had happened to others out of the blue.

Lena, followed by her two young children, ran across to unlock the door for him. 'Susie's going to be thrilled,' she told him, 'over the moon to have you home.' She put a match to the fire, put the kettle on and showed him where the things for making tea were kept.

Jamie sat thinking about the stairs, knowing they could give him a problem. He'd been told firmly that it was too soon to put any weight on his left leg; he must not do that for three months. 'If you can't get up,' Susie had said, 'you can sleep in the shelter downstairs, so it won't matter.'

He'd grown used to swinging himself around the ward on the wooden crutches in his armpits, and was determined to get up to Susie's bedroom. That was where he wanted to sleep. He didn't want the children pushing in alongside them, not yet. While he was alone, he practised sitting on the stairs and pushing himself up with his hands and arms one at a time.

At lunchtime Lena brought him some sandwiches and said, 'I'd like to let Susie know you're here, but Bert doesn't come home for his lunch these days so I can't get to his phone. I'll walk my kids down to the Post Office this afternoon.'

'No, Lena, don't bother, let it come as a surprise. You've been very kind.' He felt tired. 'I shall have a little nap and then be quite happy reading until she comes.'

Rosie and Jonjo came home from school and were the first to discover Jamie was home. Rosie let out shrieks of pleasure when she saw him, and by the time Susie came home, they were playing Ludo together.

Liverpool had not had a serious air raid since the one in which Martha had been killed, but they were still taking place in other parts of the country. They had an occasional warning, but nothing much happened, so the city had time to make urgent repairs. Most people felt better, too, because they were able to catch up on their sleep.

Christopher had been told it would take many months to

recover fully from his Colles' fracture and was very pleased to receive a clinic appointment the week before his wedding, when if all was well with his wrist he'd have his plaster removed. Now that he had his house to himself again, he kept trying to persuade Louise to go home with him straight from work. 'It means we can be alone and Susie and Jamie can be alone, which is what we both want,' he said, 'so why not?'

As soon as the front door closed behind them, Louise would feel his arms go round her and her body tingle in response. 'I've been aching to do this for ages but held back,' he whispered, 'because I thought you didn't love me. Now I know you do, it gives me a marvellous feeling.'

'We shouldn't anticipate marriage in the way we do,' she murmured, 'and I shouldn't stay all night with you.'

Chris smiled and hugged her tighter. 'You look and sound prim and proper, a lady of St Biddolphe's through and through, but I know now you aren't. We've got a lot of time to make up.'

'But what would the congregation say if they knew?'

'Louise, I believe quite a few are not as pure as you are, but they all help each other when they can, and they're always friendly and supportive.'

'Only if lack of purity can be hidden from view.' Louise was thinking of Susie's experience. 'The ladies can back-bite and be quite nasty.'

One night when she did go home with Susie, she broke a plate before they got the meal on the table, and afterwards she upset Jonjo's tea which went over Jamie's trousers. 'I'm sorry,' she said, 'I'm not usually so clumsy.'

'Don't worry,' Jamie said as he mopped it up, 'we put it down to pre-wedding nerves.'

Louise laughed, she'd seen it happen to other brides. 'That won't happen to me. I'm older and I've seen more of the world. Besides, it's the second time round for both of us and I have no doubts.'

'You were quite shirty with Rosie the other day,' Susie pointed out.

'I'm sure marrying Chris is the right thing for me to do, and therefore—'

'Of course you are, but tension builds up for all brides, like night follows day.'

'Susie, if I'm tense it's because we've had a terrible time recently with the bombing and Martha and all that. We need to calm down. I want my wedding to be as plain as possible, and I've told everybody I want no fuss. We just want to make it legal.'

Louise felt the heat run up her cheeks; did that sound like an admission that they were anticipating marriage? Having sex?

Susie was chewing on her meat which was unusually tough, and she asked, 'Have you decided which of Becky's two hats you'll wear?'

'Well, you both advise the tan-coloured feathers, and as I own a pair of tan court shoes which would go well, I think it will be that one.'

'Try your whole outfit on now,' Susie said, 'so we can see.'

'I'll try mine on too, Nana, so we can see how I look,' said Rosie.

'No need,' Louise said, 'I'll be fine. The cap of feathers is plainer than the large burnt orange tulle confection.'

Their wedding day dawned; it was a warm, spring-like day

with blue skies and sunshine. Louise and Susie didn't go to work that day, but they knew Chris would for a few hours. Becky arrived early and brought a bottle of champagne. 'This is for us now,' she said. 'Max will go direct to the church. He's had to go to the office for a couple of hours.'

'How d'you manage to get this?' Susie wanted to know as she found the glasses.

'Not easy,' Becky smiled.

As her two daughters were insisting, Louise allowed them to help her dress. Susie took the peach-coloured suit from her wardrobe and laid it on her bed. 'Marvellous that Martha managed to finish it,' she said.

'She was always very organised.'

'We aren't going to weep,' Becky said, blinking hard, 'not today. Martha would want us to be happy.'

Louise had to swallow hard. She looked in her mirror and decided the cap of feathers suited her, and even gave her a touch of Becky's elegance. She felt very smart in her new outfit.

Chris collected her in his car; Becky was to bring Bert and the rest of the family. She knew Chris had gone to the vicarage to have another chat with Mr Coyne and told him they wanted no fuss. 'All that tradition is fine for a young bride, but there is nobody to give Louise away. It doesn't apply to us.'

They arrived in the church porch and paused for a moment, then when Mrs Pollard got the signal, the organ swelled and they walked down the aisle hand in hand. She hadn't expected the church to be decorated with flowers or to find almost all the St Biddolphe ladies had come to wish them well.

At the altar, Chris was able to use his right hand to hold hers as he said the familiar words, 'I Christopher, take thee,

Louise, to my wedded wife, to have and to hold from this day forward, for better for worse, for richer for poorer, in sickness and in health, to love and to cherish till death us do part.'

Louise could see the adoration in his eyes, and for her it turned out to be a very special day after all.

EPILOGUE

Grand National Day, Saturday 29 March, 1947

L OUISE HAD HAD A marvellous day. She'd been looking
forward to it since Jamie had told her that his father was
making up a party of family and friends to spend the day in
style at Aintree. During the last five years of war, the race had
had to be abandoned, but it had started up again last year, and
Liverpool had certainly been in the grip of Grand National
fever today.

The afternoon had been bright but blustery enough to make
the array of flags at the entrance to the Aintree course flap and
flutter so noisily that she'd occasionally been able to hear it
from her seat inside when the brass band stopped playing and
the crowd had not been cheering or screaming encouragement
to their favourite horse. William had been in good form,
herding them from paddock to weighing room, from restaurant
to bar, all the time issuing advice as to the best horse to back in
each race.

Not that Louise had won any money; in fact she was well
down on the day. Rosie had picked out Caughoo, the Grand
National winner, with a pin, and advised them all to back it at
100 to 1. Only Gramps had done it to please her and they were

both cockahoop as a result. Caughoo was an Irish outsider said to have been bought for £50.

Now, sitting in the car in the heavy traffic on the way home, Louise mused on the years since her marriage. They had been very happy and her whole family seemed to have prospered. Chris was still running Peverill's Preserves. They'd moved to a different house, though not a new one; it was the sort of house Louise had only dreamed of when she'd been on her own, a town house built by a Victorian merchant.

Susie had continued to work at Peverill's until her second daughter, Alice, was born in 1944, and at the beginning of this year she'd given birth to Danny, a son to carry on the Curtis name. She and Jamie had also moved, to a new, larger and more comfortable house, though Susie had been reluctant to leave her friends in Milner Street, especially as Bert had gone to live with his mother and Aunt Gertrude had moved in next door and was more than happy to babysit. Jonjo was happy with his Aunt Becky and Uncle Max.

Jamie had recovered from his injury, though he still walked with a slight limp. He'd returned to the RAF to fly another sixty missions over German territory and had survived without mishap. He'd spent the last year of the war in a training post and, when it ended, he felt he'd got flying out of his blood. He'd become more family orientated and had delighted his father by asking if he might work in the family business.

It gave William great satisfaction to know that Curtis Cakes Limited had thrived during the war and was expanding rapidly now, but he'd never quite overcome the loss of Danny on this fateful day, fourteen years ago. It eased the pain that he and Jamie were on good terms now.

And as for Rosie – she was the apple of his eye. His hair was completely white now, but hers was exactly the shade of dark red that his had once been. When she was old enough he'd encourage her to join the family business too.

He'd discovered one great truth in his dotage. After spending his youth believing that accumulating wealth was the most important thing in life, he'd come to realise now that it was family that mattered most to him.

A Liverpool Legacy

Anne Baker

Set in Liverpool at the end of the Second World War, Anne Baker's latest saga will move you to tears of sadness and joy.

On a spring day in 1947, Millie and Pete Maynard take their daughter Sylvie on a boat trip that is to end in tragedy. Poor Sylvie blames herself for the accident and Millie needs all her strength to comfort her children and overcome her grief. Then Pete's will is read and further heartache lies in store . . .

Meanwhile, Pete's younger brother and his good-for-nothing sons try to take control of the family business, but they've underestimated Millie's indomitable spirit. She's worked in Maynard's perfume laboratory for eighteen years and is determined to protect her husband's legacy no matter what obstacles are thrown in her way . . .

Praise for Anne Baker's gripping Merseyside sagas:

'A stirring tale of romance and passion, poverty and ambition' *Liverpool Echo*

'Baker's understanding and compassion for very human dilemmas makes her one of romantic fiction's most popular authors' *Lancashire Evening Post*

'With characters who are strong, warm and sincere, this is a joy to read' *Coventry Evening Telegraph*

978 0 7553 9960 4

headline

Now you can buy any of these other bestselling books by **Anne Baker** from your bookshop or *direct from her publisher*.

FREE P&P AND UK DELIVERY
(Overseas and Ireland £3.50 per book)

A Liverpool Legacy	£6.99
Daughters of the Mersey	£6.99
Love is Blind	£8.99
Liverpool Love Song	£6.99
Nancy's War	£7.99
Through Rose-Coloured Glasses	£8.99
All That Glistens	£8.99
The Best of Fathers	£8.99
A Labour of Love	£8.99
The Wild Child	£8.99
Liverpool Lies	£8.99
Carousel of Secrets	£8.99
Let The Bells Ring	£8.99

TO ORDER SIMPLY CALL THIS NUMBER

01235 400 414

or visit our website: www.headline.co.uk

Prices and availability subject to change without notice